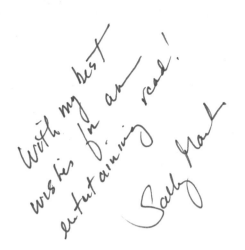

THE SHAPE OF DARK

by

Sally Martin

ISBN: 0-9726510-0-4

Library of Congress Control Number: 2002094613

This book is printed on acid free paper.

Printed in the United States of America

AUTHOR'S ACKNOWLEDGMENTS:

I can't begin to express my gratitude to the countless family and friends who read *The Shape of Dark* and offered valuable suggestions. My dear friend and mentor Victoria Poole was my support from the beginning of the project, and Janet Nichols, Phyllis Coggeshall, and Candace Karu all made specific observations that were instrumental in the development of the book. My three children were all involved offering feedback: Tommy and Katie responding to the content, and Bobby using his skills as a writer to help me with the final draft. And most of all, my husband's unfailing belief in *The Shape of Dark* and his willingness to read it tirelessly have been the most important ingredients in my ability to move forward.

THE SHAPE OF DARK-- Prologue

When Kate Hammond's car stalled at the end of the lane leading through the liveoaks to the cottage that she and Max were renting, she allowed herself to curse but quickly gathered up her packages and trudged toward the dark house. She was surprised there were no lights on, since it was nearly eight o'clock and time for Jessica to be getting ready for bed. The May evening was steamy and warm, its humidity unrelieved by the ocean breeze that often refreshed the sea islands along the coast of Georgia. Kate was uncomfortably aware of a cloud of mosquitoes whining around her sticky face, while crickets trilled furiously in the thick undergrowth lining the path to Max's studio.

Glad to be home hours early from a meeting that was supposed to have lasted until midnight, Kate wearily hauled herself and her belongings into the house and promised herself a glass of wine as a reward for driving all the way to Brunswick, only to discover that the chairman of the committee reporting to the Arts Commission had become ill, causing an abrupt adjournment.

"Max? Jessie?" Kate turned on the kitchen lights and saw the remains of dinner still on the counter. Grumbling to herself about welcome mats for cockroaches, Kate quickly rinsed off the dishes and loaded them into the dishwasher before continuing to search for her husband and daughter.

When the house proved to be empty, Kate went outside and looked toward the studio where Max worked daily on the luminous paintings for which he was receiving critical acclaim. It, too, was dark, but Kate could see a faint flickering, and she could imagine Max telling a mesmerized Jessica a ghost story by candlelight, surrounded by the dancing shapes and colors of the many canvases that lined the small room.

Tiptoeing up to the door, Kate heard music playing softly and the sound of Max's deep voice intermingled with four-year-old Jessica's insistent whimpering. Although his words were not intelligible from outside, Kate could tell that Max was becoming very angry, and she hurried to pull open the heavy wooden door before he lost his temper with the little girl.

Inside, several candles were burning, but the studio was so shadowy that at first Kate didn't see Max and Jessica on the threadbare flowered sofa in the corner of the room. When her eyes became accustomed to the dimness, Kate tasted bile in her throat as her stomach contracted sharply, sending waves of nausea throughout her body. Although she knew she had to help her daughter, Kate felt as if her feet were nailed to the rough floor, and she was momentarily immobilized.

"WHAT DO YOU THINK YOU'RE DOING?" Kate's voice exploded into the studio, causing Max to leap from where he had been kneeling beside the sofa, breathing hard as he frantically attempted to pull up his faded denim shorts. Rushing over to where her daughter lay sobbing, her small body curled into a tight ball, Kate pulled a dirty sheet from one of Max's paintings and covered Jessica's quivering nakedness.

"I thought you weren't coming home until later," Max slurred, wiping his mouth on the back of his hand. "Jessica was hot, so I let her go to sleep out here while I worked a little." Max didn't meet Kate's eyes, but his voice was coarse and defensive. "No matter what you thought you saw, nothing was going on."

"You make me sick," Kate hissed. "For weeks Jessie has been clinging to me, and now, God help me, I know why. Don't even *try* to deny it, although you're so wasted most of the time you probably don't remember half of what you've done."

Max lurched toward Kate. "If you weren't such a frigid cockteaser, I wouldn't need to drink. And if you're planning to tell anybody about what you think was happening tonight, you're sadly mistaken." Max brandished the bottle he held, but his knees buckled and he had to grab the edge of a table for support.

"You're disgusting! Jessie and I are leaving, something we should have done long ago."

His red-rimmed eyes glittering with rage, Max picked up a knife from the tray of his easel and stumbled toward Kate, who stepped aside, causing him to crash into a pile of canvases which was stacked in the corner. "So help me, I'll kill both of you bitches before I let you go!"

Kate's heart raced at the boiling venom in Max's voice, and she looked around frantically for some kind of protection. A can of paint thinner stood on the table next to her, and she grabbed it, hearing the liquid slosh inside.

Max lunged again, the point of his knife barely missing Kate's arm, and she threw the bulky metal container, managing to hit him on the shoulder, knocking the top off and drenching him with the powerful solvent. As the fumes rose in the room, Kate backed away from her husband, terrified by the rage in his eyes as he moved toward her, the rusty, paint-splattered knife pointed at her stomach.

"Don't, Max!" Kate screamed as he drew his arm back. She desperately twisted away, causing him to bump into a cluttered bookcase. One of the candles that had been sputtering on the top shelf toppled over, and within seconds Max was engulfed in flames, screaming as the fire ate through his clothing and seared his flesh.

Kate grabbed Jessica from the sofa and ran out of the studio and into the house, locking the door behind her. Through the window, she watched her husband's futile attempts to extinguish the fire, which continued to feed on his alcohol-soaked clothing, while tongues of yellow flame erupted on his charred body. Finally, Max staggered through the deep shadows behind the studio and disappeared into the oily darkness of the swampy woods while Kate clutched her daughter and stared in horror at the silent gloom.

THE SHAPE OF DARK-- Chapter One

From the annoying blue numbers on her alarm clock, Kate could see that it was nearly 5:00 am, but she had been awake since that dream around 3:30 had left her heart pounding and her stomach churning. Kate always knew when the opening day of school approached, because the first week in September regularly brought several nights where her sleep was tormented by images of classes out of control, lost lesson plans, feet glued to the ground as she struggled to get to a class on time. The worst nightmare usually featured thirty hostile teenagers grinning with evil satisfaction as she frantically tried to remember what she was going to say.

"Get a grip," she muttered to herself as she clicked off the alarm button and stumbled into the bathroom. While she groped for the light switch, Kate glanced out the window toward the ocean, where the sun was rising slowly, spreading pink ribbons across the quiet waves. A few gulls were circling over the two lobster boats tied up in Morning Cove, but otherwise the world was silent and peaceful, mocking the nervous agitation that filled Kate as she squinted at her reflection in the mirror.

The face that stared back certainly looked different from the exhausted, fragile woman who had come to Silvertree Farm only a month before. When Mildred Worthington had first suggested that Kate and Jessica move to the coast of Maine, Kate had declined her aunt's offer, insisting that she had to stay in Georgia and face whatever notoriety came her way. But, as the weeks following Max's death had crept by and people still pointed and whispered, Kate allowed herself to be convinced that Mildred's gracious oceanfront home might give her and Jessica the new start they needed to recover from the pain of the previous year.

After only a few weeks of sun, salt air, long walks on the beach, and tempting meals prepared by Mildred's ancient cook, Kate's vibrant, delicately featured face only occasionally darkened with the horrifying memories of the spring and early summer. Her red-gold hair was once again lustrous and curled smoothly around her shoulders, while clear aqua eyes framed with unusually dark eyelashes were set above a straight nose and soft generous lips. A determined regimen of swimming in Mildred's large pool had restored the firm muscle tone to her trim figure, and her skin had tanned to a healthy glow.

Standing naked in front of the full-length mirror on the door of her closet, Kate smiled at the tiny strips of white left by her bikini and wondered what any of those leering adolescents on Half Moon Beach would say if they had known that they had been gawking at their future English teacher. On several occasions during the past few weeks, some of the braver boys had attempted to make conversation with the striking stranger, but their clumsy retrievals of purposely misthrown Frisbees or footballs had been ignored behind Kate's oversized sunglasses as she dug in the sand with the silent child at her side.

"Well, now they'll know," she thought, as she carefully selected clothes for the first day of school which would minimize any connection between the new faculty member and the mysterious woman on the beach. A slim gray skirt, white silk blouse, crisp blue and gray linen blazer, and bold, hand-crafted silver earrings and bracelet were refined yet feminine, and Kate viewed herself with satisfaction as she hastily made her bed and headed though the connecting door to Jessica's bedroom.

"Wake up, ladybug!" Kate threw open the curtains to admit the warmth and light of the sun, which was now fully risen. "Big day for Mama, Jessie!"

Kate continued to chatter to the sleepy child while bustling around the cheerful little room gathering Jessica's outfit for the day. When her daughter plodded into the bathroom, Kate drew the pink- and-white coverlet over the bed, fluffed the pillows, and laid Jessica's favorite toy, a threadbare blue teddy bear named Cynthia in its accustomed place on the bed. Even now, Kate found it hard to handle Cynthia and marveled that Jessie refused to part with the stuffed animal, in spite of the painful experiences it evoked.

Looking out at the brilliant terrace gardens beneath her window, Kate realized that the last month in Maine had truly saved her sanity, and she felt strong enough to tackle the stomach-twisting challenges of the first day at Rocky Shore High School, where she had been hired at the last minute to replace an English teacher whose husband had been transferred to Iowa.

Kate bid goodbye to Jessica who was sitting mutely in front of a bowl of Cheerios and hurriedly thanked Mildred for taking the little girl to her first day of nursery school. The neighboring estate, Rocky Shore, had been donated to Cape Mariana in 1968 by its eccentric owner so that the town could have its own high school instead of sending students to a regional school ten miles away. As she maneuvered her car up the long, winding driveway, Kate had the sensation that she was approaching the castle of some feudal baron until she saw the groups of students lounging on the two stone lions which guarded the massive portico and heavy oak doors.

Stepping out of her car in the parking lot, Kate found herself surrounded by five boys dressed in ties and jackets bearing the insignia of the school on one sleeve and the words "Green Shield" on the other. Immediately, Kate recognized two of the Frisbee players from Half-Moon Beach, and from the admiration in their eyes, it was clear that they, too, recalled the occasion. The tallest member of the group, an imposing young man with curly dark hair and a confident expression on his face, stepped forward and took the bookbag from a startled Kate.

"Allow me, please, Mrs. Hammond. I'm Chickie George and I've been assigned to help you today. Each new teacher has a member of the Green Shield, and I'm yours." Chickie's last words were drawled with the kind of bold assurance that Kate would expect to find in a much older man, and she noticed that the other boys watched Chickie with barely concealed envy. As she and her escort walked toward the school, Kate could feel the eyes of the other Green Shield members boring into her back, and she was disgusted to find herself blushing, in spite of her best efforts to be unaffected by the adolescent attention. Furtively glancing up at Chickie to see if he had noticed her discomfort, Kate's eyes met his, and she quickly looked away, but not before she had seen his gaze move from her face down the length of her body. When Chickie reached in front of Kate to open the front door, his arm brushed across her, and she felt herself jump at the touch.

"Sorry, Mrs. Hammond." Chickie looked down at Kate with a slow, lazy smile. "Your room is on the second floor, isn't it? We can take the stairs over there." Chickie led the way to the back of the handsome lobby, where two broad sets of steps led to the classrooms above.

Just then, a loud bell rang and students began to stream into the building. Kate found herself jostled on all sides as the crowds of young people bounded up the stairs and pushed their way into the classrooms that lined the two long hallways projecting out from the center of the building. Chickie opened the door of Room 215 where several students had already found seats and were talking among themselves. No sooner had he laid Kate's bag on the oak desk at the front of the room than there was a deafening roar and the sound of breaking glass.

Smoke had almost completely filled the corridor outside of Kate's classroom by the time that she followed Chickie into the hall. In the haze, Kate could see that the polished dark wood floor was covered with tiny bits of broken glass, and several students peered curiously around a boy in a Green Shield jacket who was preventing anyone from entering the hallway.

Chickie pushed by Kate and pulled the fire alarm on the wall opposite her room. The insistent scream of the siren propelled most of the students toward the exit doors, but Chickie and the other Green Shield member waited with Kate, who seemed slightly dazed by the destruction. Almost immediately, a tall, powerfully built man bounded up the stairs two at a time, an angry expression clouding his face as he approached the small group standing in the middle of the shards of glass.

"O.K. Chickie, what the hell happened here?" In spite of Chickie's height and poise, he still seemed intimidated as Alex Stamos, the principal of Rocky Shore High School loomed over him.

Chickie looked around and pointed to the floor on the other side of the hall. A large fire extinguisher was on the ground and part of the case, which had held it on the wall, hung in its original place, while the rest of the glass was in thousands of pieces. Chickie bent and picked up a metal cylinder from the floor beside the extinguisher.

"Look at this, Mr. Stamos. It's one of those mini pipe bombs that was used to blow up the storage shed last spring." Chickie handed the object to the principal, who stuffed it into his pocket and looked around at the people assembled in the hall.

"Don't say anything about this until we find out what happened. I'd rather not have rumors flying around here. School hasn't even started yet, for God's sake." Alex looked over at Kate who was standing by the door to her classroom. "Did you see or hear anything, Mrs. Hammond?" Alex's tone was brusque.

"No, Mr. Stamos, nothing." Kate backed nervously into her room as Alex waved off the volunteer firemen who had appeared at the end of the hall.

"Just one of those stupid pranks, boys. We'll clean it up." Before he followed the firemen downstairs, Alex stuck his head in Kate's door. "Welcome to Rocky Shore High School." Motioning for Chickie to follow him, Alex strode away, nodding curtly to several other teachers who had gathered nearby.

By the time the glass was cleaned up and students were allowed to come back in the building, the carefully organized opening day of school was in chaos. After spending the first 45 minutes with her homeroom, helping juniors fill out schedules and information cards, Kate was relieved when a bell indicated the end of the orientation part of the day and the beginning of regular classes.

Watching her senior class file in, Kate remembered how she always enjoyed the first meeting of a new group, even when there was not a single familiar face in the room. It was always a challenge to see how fast she could match the various individuals with the names she had tried to memorize, and she even made life more difficult for herself by letting the students sit where they wanted to, rather than in the more traditional alphabetical order.

The bell rang again to signal the start of class, and Kate noticed that there were several empty seats in a group that should have filled the room. Most of the boys sat on one side, including four wearing jackets with the Green Shield insignia on the sleeve. Chickie George lounged easily in a desk that looked too small for his muscular body while carrying on a conversation with a tall, gangly boy with dark blond hair. In front of them was a small young man with oversized glasses and curly red hair, and Kate wondered if he were in the wrong class, since he looked years younger than the bigger boys behind him. On the other half of the room, most of the back seats filled up first, leaving the five front desks empty until a girl with long dark hair rushed in at the sound of the bell and took the seat in the front of the center row of arm desks.

"Good morning, everyone. I'm Mrs. Hammond, and we'll be studying English Literature together this year. Let's see who's here today."

Kate worked her way down the roster of students, discovering that the boy slouched next to Chickie was Eric Lundgren, while the person she had thought might be a freshman answered to the name of Kyle Monkton. "Jean-Pierro Rossoni?" Kate looked around curiously and was not surprised when a wiry young man with long black hair raised his hand.

"Si, senora." As Jean-Pierro spoke, the girl in the front seat turned around and gave him a thumbs-up gesture.

"Am I to assume that you are an exchange student? With whom are you living?" Kate walked back to where Jean-Pierro was sitting and smiled encouragingly, knowing how difficult it was for most foreign students to speak English in front of a group.

Jean-Pierro ducked his head but continued. "I come from Italy and I am with my cousin, Sophia, who sits there." The boy pointed toward the front.

"Then I know who you are, too." Kate decided that she liked Sophia and patted her shoulder as she walked back to her desk to continue taking attendance. Before she could read another name, however, the door burst open and two girls crossed in front of Kate and sat down.

"Where have you folks been?" Kate pointed to the clock, which indicated that class had been in session for nearly ten minutes. "Do you have a pass?"

The taller of the two girls, a statuesque brunette with her hair sculpted into an elaborate French braid, looked around at the rest of the group. "Oh, we don't need a pass. My father will excuse us." The other late arrival, a compact, buxom blond with smoldering blue eyes and a petulant expression, nodded her agreement and stared defiantly at Kate.

Feeling the hair rise on the back of her neck at the barely concealed rudeness of the girls, Kate resisted any comment. "And who might you be?" she asked.

9

"I'm Phaedra Stamos and this is Kelly Lundgren." Phaedra's dark eyes flashed a challenge at Kate as she slid into her seat.

Kate located the two names on her list and came to the immediate conclusion that the insolent brunette was the principal's daughter. Determined to ignore the intrusion, Kate finished calling the roll and was about to begin the class, when the door opened again, and a slender, pale young woman with downcast eyes looked around the room in confusion.

"Is this senior English?"

Kate could hardly hear the soft words, but she recognized a new student, caught in the grip of first day nervousness. "You must be Eve Calvert," she said, checking off the only remaining name on her list. "Come on in and take a seat, Eve. Welcome to Rocky Shore." Kate watched as Eve crossed tentatively over to the girls' side of the room and slid into a desk next to Sophia Rossoni, while all eyes in the room scrutinized the newcomer.

"Where did you move from?" Kate asked as she passed out paper to the class, eliciting automatic groans from several of the students.

"I've lived in Cape Mariana for several years, but I was being tutored at home." Kate noticed that Eve suffered from the same uncontrollable blushing that plagued her, and she felt a rush of sympathy for the girl's discomfort.

"Well, I'm sure everyone will make you feel at home. It's hard to enter a new school in your senior year." Kate glared at Phaedra and Kelly, who were whispering loudly, obviously commenting negatively on Eve's unbecoming clothing, which looked old-fashioned and ill- fitting.

Chickie followed Kate's eyes and leaned over to Eric, speaking clearly enough so that the whole room could hear. "Not bad." Eric seemed surprised but nodded his agreement, while Eve's face flamed and Phaedra threw Chickie a furious look.

Quickly, Kate called for the attention of the class. "Before we begin tackling English literature, I think that you need to understand what kind of a teacher I am. I'm not going to give you a bunch of facts and ask you to spew them back to me on a test. Nor am I going to tell you what the right answer is to questions that we are going to raise about a lot of things. The bottom line in this classroom is thoughtfulness—about the material we study, about the issues we discuss, and about the sensibilities and feelings of the people in the class."

Phaedra raised her hand languidly. "That sounds like you want us to do your job for you."

Kate was momentarily stunned by Phaedra's attack, but she drew a deep breath and answered. "Actually, just the opposite, at least as far as I'm concerned. I'll be a better, more effective teacher if you are invested in what's happening in the class. I want thought to be awakened by our time together, not put to sleep."

Eric spoke out. "Do you mean it about wanting the class to be interesting? I hear teachers say that all the time, but they bore you to death anyway."

"I absolutely do, Eric. I've found that the only way for literature to come alive is for the kids to determine what it is that the great writers are saying about issues that matter today. If you CARE about something Shakespeare wrote, for example, chances are that his words are touching some part of your own life. If we can find those connections, the class will be meaningful and important."

Most of the students looked receptive, and Kate pointed to the paper she had handed out. "I want you to go home and think about what I've said. Then brainstorm some ideas about what you'd like to discuss, some basic questions that might have been raised last year that intrigued you, any notions you have about projects that could be fun, and most important, what it is that you would like to get from and give to this course. We'll talk about your lists tomorrow and then you'll write a paper tomorrow night on a subject that we'll determine together."

"I knew there was a catch," Eric groaned under his breath. "Can't we just decide to talk about stuff like sex all year and guarantee that everybody will be turned on?" Eric looked around for the approval of his friends and squinted at Kate, waiting for her reaction.

"Not a bad idea, Eric. We'd all stay awake." Kate walked over to where Chickie and Eric were sitting. "Why, aside from the obvious reasons, do you think it's important to read and talk about sex in an English course?" As she looked intently at Eric, waiting for his response, she noticed that he seemed fascinated with the front of her jacket and couldn't seem to meet her eyes.

Eric shifted a bit in his seat, but he soon regained his composure. "Because sex is on everyone's mind, and it certainly wouldn't be as deadly as the stuff we usually read." Once again, the boys around Eric laughed appreciatively, and he stared at Kate, daring her to get angry.

"Fair enough," she replied, moving to the front of the room. "Does anyone else have any other reasons why sex would be a relevant issue for us to discuss? Kyle?"

"Because sexual fulfillment is one of man's basic needs and one of the prime motivating forces in various kinds of social relationships." Kyle's thin, squeaky voice traveled to the back of the room, and after a moment of silence, acted on the other boys like a match to a firecracker. Suddenly, the room was filled with loud, unrestrained hooting, and even the girls had difficulty controlling themselves.

"Right on, Einstein!" Eric chortled as he made an obscene gesture toward Kyle, while Chickie pulled at his arm to make him sit down. "That old sexual fulfillment stuff will get you every time, won't it, little man?"

By this time, the entire class was in an uproar, and Kate had the sinking feeling that one of her nightmares was coming true. "Hey, everybody, settle down." As she raised her voice above the level of the laughter, she could see the triumphant malice on Eric's face and the tears glittering in Kyle's stricken eyes. Clearly, something was going on here that she didn't understand, and she looked anxiously around the room, hoping that help would come from someone.

It did. Chickie glowered at Eric and raised his hand. "Sorry, Mrs. Hammond. Lundgren here doesn't know that there's nothing deader than old news. But I'll tell you what I like to read about—guys fighting dragons and all that bloody stuff. I remember that we read a book in sophomore year by some dead Greek, and it was terrific! Dr. Henry told us that it was the greatest war story ever written."

Kate sighed with relief. "You must mean the *Iliad,* by Homer, with Achilles and all those other heroes of the Trojan War."

"Yeah, that's the one. Can we read something like that this year?"

"It's funny that you should mention it, because one of my all-time favorites and something I thought we could start with is about a superhero who saves a country from two horrible monsters, one of them a woman. He does things like swim through lakes of fire, cut off arms and heads, and finally fights a huge dragon that's guarding a magnificent treasure. How does that sound?" Kate picked up a copy of *Beowulf* and showed it to the class. "This was written over a thousand years ago, but it still reads like *Star Wars*."

The whole class, with the exception of a pouting Eric, began to chatter enthusiastically, and Kate felt her pulse slow down to somewhere near normal as the bell rang. She was about to thank Chickie for his rescue when Phaedra pushed by her and grabbed his arm, snuggling against his green jacket. Kyle waited until Eric had left and then shuffled out, while Sophia went over to Eve and held out her hand.

"Come on, Eve, I'll show you where your next class meets." Trailed by Jean-Pierro, the two girls made their way into the crowded hallway and Kate collapsed in exhaustion at her desk.

"Don't die yet. It's only the third period!" The heavily accented voice of a bright-eyed, swarthy young man rang out from the doorway. "I'm your next-door neighbor, Carlo Brito." Kate had the fleeting thought that every girl in the school was probably in love with this attractive individual, and she stood to shake hands, surprised to find that Carlo was only slightly taller than she was.

"Hi, Carlo. I'm Kate Hammond, English." Kate saw Carlo's eyes sweep across her, and his smile gleamed in his tanned face.

"Spanish and soccer coach, at your service." Carlo bowed, holding Kate's hand long enough to brush his lips across it with elaborate chivalry.

"You're just what I need after that last class! The strangest thing happened, and I can't figure it out. Maybe you can help me." Kate described the incident between Eric and Kyle and was surprised to see Carlo look very embarrassed.

"You hit a gusher with that one, if you'll pardon the pun." Carlo grinned at his own bad joke and went on to explain. "Two years ago, when the boys were sophomores, Kyle was only twelve, being a real genius. Apparently, Eric caught Kyle, uh, masturbating in the boys' room. I'm not sure exactly how it happened, but it took Eric all of about three minutes to spread the word to the whole school. Poor Kyle was devastated, and he stayed home for a week. Finally, his mother, Sandra, our assistant principal, persuaded Chickie George to talk to Kyle, and somehow Chickie convinced the kid that it would all blow over as soon as Kyle bit the bullet and faced everyone. Chickie walked into school with Kyle the next morning and sat with him at lunch, and then everything seemed to die down. Until today, I guess."

"Poor Kyle. It's difficult enough being so much younger than everyone else without being persecuted."

Carlo nodded grimly. "I know. Most of the kids have been great to Kyle, but Eric seems to go out of his way to be mean. Just a word of warning, Kate. Both of those Lundgren kids are bad news, and their parents are impossible. Stay clear of them if you can."

"That's enough of that, Carlo. You'll scare the poor woman away before she's begun." Alex Stamos strode briskly into the room, seeming larger than ever beside the diminutive Spanish teacher. "Everything all right so far?" Alex's dark eyes were cool and businesslike as he quickly glanced around the room.

"Fine," Kate answered with equal efficiency. "I think that I met your daughter last period."

Alex's jaw hardened slightly. "Ah, yes, Phaedra."

Kate waited for further comment, but Alex simply turned on his heel and walked from the room, nodding curtly to the silver-haired man coming through the door.

Carlo laughed at the confused expression on Kate's face. "That's our Herr Stamos, as the kids call him. He's one of the toughest men I've ever met, but he runs a terrific school. Ask Alistair." Carlo gestured to the slim elegant older man wearing a bachelor button in his lapel.

"Mrs. Hammond. Welcome to Rocky Shore." Alistair Henry offered a firm handshake, his twinkling gray eyes approving of Kate's appearance. "Don't believe anything that this little devil tells you unless he's talking about soccer. By the way, Carlo, I understand that you have a ringer this year."

Carlo's face lit up in delight. "Have I ever! One of Italy's best junior players, no less. State championship, here we come!"

"You must mean Jean-Pierro Rossoni." Kate chimed in. "He was in my last class, and he seems like an awfully nice kid, as does his cousin, Sophia. I just wish I could say the same for our principal's daughter."

"Oh, yes, Queen Phaedra." Alistair looked disgusted. "She's the type that is best ignored, although she's famous for hating beautiful women teachers."

"I'll be careful," Kate promised. "Thanks for the advice."

Alistair beamed. "That's what I'm here for. I'm only sorry that I couldn't welcome you earlier, but Alex assured me that you had a strong background, and I'm sure he's right. As your Department Chairman, my job is to make things easier for you, so don't hesitate to call on me." Kate had already heard of Alistair Henry through Mildred, who served on the Board of Trustees at Rocky Shore, and she knew that he was a noted Shakespearean scholar who could have taught in any university that he wanted. Long ago, Mildred had explained, Alistair had decided that he liked the atmosphere in Cape Mariana, so he bought a small house and settled into a comfortable bachelor existence of writing and teaching.

"Thanks. I'll probably bother you often." Kate glanced at the clock above the door, amazed to see that it was almost time for the next class. "I have freshmen next, so I'd better get my armor on!"

"Just yell if you get attacked, and I'll come running." Carlo promised as he left for his own classroom.

Alistair lingered for a moment and looked at Kate. "Mildred has told me what a difficult time you have been through, my dear. Please depend on me as much as you can, especially at the beginning. Some of these kids can be hard to deal with." After patting Kate's hand, Alistair allowed himself to be swept into the swarm of students that had been released by the bell.

15

THE SHAPE OF DARK – Chapter Two

The rest of the morning passed very quickly, and before Kate realized it, she was following a stream of chattering students into the school dining hall, a surprisingly beautiful space which had been made by combining the mansion's former living and dining rooms. Completely paneled, with large French windows looking out onto the school's rolling lawns, the handsome, high-ceilinged chamber had a curtained stage at one end and twenty round tables, each seating eight people. Off the main dining room was a smaller faculty area, formerly the library of Rocky Shore. Here, amidst glass-fronted cabinets filled with the original owner's extensive collection of rare and valuable books, was a quiet sanctuary for the teachers to use for eating, studying, or an occasional cup of coffee.

It was in this room that Kate first met Alex Stamos in mid-August. Alerted by Mildred of an upcoming resignation in the English department, Kate requested an interview and was reluctantly granted an appointment with the principal by his fiercely protective secretary, Marta Stone.

"Don't mind her," Alex commented after Kate was ushered into the deserted teachers' lounge by a tight-lipped Marta. "She hates almost everyone. Coffee?"

Kate shook her head nervously, intimidated by the powerful aura of the man sitting across from her. In addition to his imposing physical size, his square, strong face communicated stern confidence, and Kate could not imagine that anyone would dispute his authority. Although he was dressed casually in chino pants and a short-sleeved polo shirt, Alex's deeply tanned face was completely serious as he leafed through Kate's credentials.

"You haven't had a lot of experience, Mrs. Hammond, but your recommendations are outstanding. Our students are very sophisticated, and they've been known to challenge teachers. Can you deal with that?"

Kate squirmed, pulling her navy linen skirt over her knees. "I've never had any trouble, aside from a few boys who developed crushes."

Alex glanced at her coolly. "And how did you handle them?" Although Kate was dressed conservatively in a crisp white linen blouse, she felt herself flushing under the principal's scrutiny.

"I simply ignored them, and they became discouraged." It was difficult to tell from Alex's expression whether he approved of her response, but after posing a few more questions about her educational philosophy, he closed her file.

"Now tell me something about yourself that isn't in your resume. What do you like to do in your spare time?"

Kate was taken by surprise and she struggled to form an intelligent answer. "Well, to tell you the truth, my daughter keeps me pretty busy, but I do have one passion, music."

"Oh?" Alex looked interested. "What instrument do you play?"

"The piano. I started taking classical lessons when I was six, but I've sort of metamorphosed into a barroom pianist. I pride myself on playing almost anything by ear, especially if it was written before 1950. When I was very young, my parents used to wake me up in the middle of the night to play for their parties."

Alex stood up and held out his hand, completely engulfing hers in a firm grasp. "By the way, I know about what happened to your husband, and I'm sorry."

Before Kate could reply, the principal led the way to the front door of the school. "See you in September," he said tersely, leaving Kate to wander down the broad front steps, confused by the abrupt manner of the man who had just dismissed her.

When she returned to Silvertree Farm and told Mildred about her meeting with Alex Stamos, the older woman chuckled. "Alex is one of the most fascinating men that I know, even if he is young enough to be my son. The kids are terrified of him, but underneath all that toughness, I swear there's a very nice human being."

"Yeah, right," Kate grumbled as she went upstairs to change for her daily swim.

****

There were certainly no signs of softness in Alex Stamos on the first day of school, and when he convened the faculty at 2:30, his face was grim. "Before I introduce our new colleagues, I want you all to know that somebody put a pipe bomb in the fire extinguisher case on the second floor. Luckily, nobody was hurt, this time. Keep your ears open and listen for any student scuttlebutt that might lead us to the person who did it."

Through the windows of the teacher's lounge, Kate could see the students walking toward their cars or to the locker rooms to change for soccer and field hockey practice. Around her, teachers were slumped in positions of varying degrees of exhaustion, as Alex continued.

"O.K. folks, let's make this quick. You'll all have a chance to get better acquainted as time goes on, so I'll just introduce a few new faces and we'll call it a day. Steve Barton—stand up Steve—is our physical education teacher and new swim coach. I know we all hated to see Gus retire, but Steve will do a great job, I'm sure."

Alex waited for the light, polite applause to stop. "Kate Hammond has joined our English Department, having just moved here from Georgia. Right next to Kate is Josh Temple, who will be a student intern in the English Department, working with Alistair and Kate. Josh has come to teaching from the very different world of a professional musician!" At this news, everyone turned and looked curiously at Josh, whose long blond hair curled over his collar.

"And last, Susan Moore is our part-time replacement in art. Susan has her own studio in Portland, but she's going to help us in the morning." All heads swung toward the door where Susan Moore had just come in, and it was clear from the audible gasps that few people had seen the art teacher before now.

Kate thought that she had never seen such a beautiful woman. In her late twenties, Susan had long blond hair that shimmered in the sun streaming in the west windows, and her sculpted cheekbones and delicate features made her look more like a model than a teacher. Dressed in tight, faded jeans and an oversized multi-colored wool poncho, Susan let a small smile cross her face as she took a seat next to a clearly dazzled Josh Temple. Although she knew that she had never met Susan, Kate had a strange feeling that she had seen her somewhere else.

Several people had announcements to make after Alex completed his brief introductions, and the meeting was dismissed shortly before 3:00, much to the relief of the tired faculty. People straggled back to their classrooms to lock up, while the coaches headed to the fields to join their teams.

When Kate finally came back down into the nearly deserted school lobby and pushed open the heavy front door, she saw Alex talking to a skinny, black-haired janitor who was lowering the school flag. "Make sure you check the locks carefully, Alf," Kate heard Alex instruct. "I don't want any more excitement around here."

"Sure, Mr. Stamos, no problem. You know you can count on me."

Alex nodded and turned to reenter the building, bumping into Kate who was carrying a bulging satchel of books. "Sorry. Can I help you with that?"

In spite of her uneasiness around the principal, Kate accepted his offer and tried to make conversation as they walked toward her car. "Can you tell me about this Green Shield organization? I was greeted this morning by my own private bodyguard."

Alex let his stern face relax. "That must have been Chickie George. He told me that he was the winner of the 'teacher grab'."

Kate laughed. "From what I saw this afternoon, he grabbed the wrong person! Susan Moore is quite a beauty."

"It's all a matter of taste, I guess." Alex slung Kate's bag into the back seat of the BMW that Mildred had insisted she use. "Actually, I'd have a much harder time running the school without the Green Shield. Each spring ten members of the incoming senior class are elected to be prefects of the school. They comprise the student government and generally do a lot to keep order. The selection usually turns out to be a popularity contest, but the faculty has the right of veto, which it seldom exercises. Most of the kids really rise to the occasion, since it's such an important position to have. There was some discussion on one boy, Eric Lundgren, but we lacked a majority vote for a veto, so we're keeping our fingers crossed."

"He's in my senior English class, and I kind of wondered about him." Kate slid into the driver's seat. "Thanks for the help and the information." Before her words were finished, Kate realized that Alex had turned away and was heading toward the school.

As she drove out of the school gates, Kate found herself thinking about Alex Stamos and his aloofness, but his face was soon driven from her mind by the long list of errands that she had to do before returning home.

Most of the stores in Cape Mariana were located in the Ocean Gate Shopping Center, including the boutique which Tikka Worthington was busily stocking with elegant clothing and jewelry from all over the world. As she parked in front of Dunham's, the immaculate market, Kate could see Tikka's sports car at the far end of the line of stores, and she decided to buy her friend a treat from the bakery.

Threading her way through the crowded store toward the bakery, Kate noticed that Bob Dunham's normally smiling face was knotted into an expression of distaste. As he stood at the head of an aisle in which the store's vast array of fresh pastas and sauces were located, Bob shook his head at the back of a stylishly dressed woman who had a tight grip on the upper arm of a little girl, dragging her roughly away from a now-toppled display of linguini.

"Honestly, you are so stupid! I told you not to touch anything!" The woman made no attempt to lower her voice as she yelled at the child, who appeared to be six or seven years old. "Every time I take you out in public, you do something dumb!" As her mother spit out her irritation, the child began to whimper and tried to pull away.

Bob Dunham moved quickly down the aisle and began to pick up the scattered boxes. "No problem, ma'am. This happens all the time. We'll just have to stack these displays more carefully." Bob looked sympathetically at the little girl, but his soothing words had no effect on the woman, who was now shaking her daughter so hard that the child's head snapped back and forth.

Kate, who was a short distance from the unpleasant exchange, caught Bob's eye as he straightened up and tried once more to distract the raging woman from her determined punishment of the clearly terrified child. "Why don't I take your daughter back to the bakery for a cookie while you finish your shopping? I think that the butcher has some of that rib-eye steak that you folks like, and you really need to try his latest batch of sausage."

The woman reluctantly loosened her grip and allowed Bob to lead away the sobbing child, as she turned her shopping cart toward the meat department. "What do you think you're looking at?" she fumed at Kate.

Kate lowered her eyes quickly and mumbled a few unintelligible words as she hurried past the woman's still visible fury. Then, annoyed with herself for her cowardice, Kate swung back and stared, holding her gaze until the woman stalked off.

At the bakery, Bob was still trying to comfort the little girl. "Thank heaven this doesn't happen often," he said over the child's head. "If she acts like that in public, imagine what she does in private!"

Shaken by the incident, Kate bought some poppyseed muffins and walked down the sidewalk toward *Avesta*, the shop that Tikka had named after the city in Sweden where she had been raised. Although it had not yet opened, Avesta had already received enthusiastic comments from the designers who were in the fall/winter collection, and women in the Greater Portland area who were looking forward to having access to sophisticated clothing and jewelry.

The heavy glass door of Avesta was propped open by boxes when Kate arrived, while Tikka wrestled with large bolts of fabric in one of the two display windows. Rippling lengths of watered silk in deep tones of purple, teal, and jade cascaded everywhere, escaping Tikka's attempts to drape them, and Kate had to smile at her friend's obvious frustration.

"Need a hand?" Kate grabbed one corner of a billowing swatch of purple silk and held it firmly while Tikka anchored it on one wall of the window area.

"I quit!" Tikka's silver-blond hair flew around her face and her startling green eyes were blazing. "Nothing is going right this afternoon, so I'm going to leave everything and begin again tomorrow." She collapsed on one of the satin-striped sofas in the shop and reached for the muffin Kate offered.

"Things look, ah, interesting." Trying hard to be diplomatic, Kate looked around at the piles of boxes and incomplete decoration, wondering how Tikka could ever pull it together by the shop's scheduled opening. "Where's that jewelry that you were raving about last night?"

Tikka jumped up and unlocked a closet, her fatigue dispelled by a burst of enthusiasm. "Here it is, and it's marvelous. You've probably met the designer already because she's teaching at the high school during the first semester."

Kate studied the exquisite pieces that Tikka had laid out on the top of her glass counter. "She's obviously talented as well as beautiful!

These things are incredible." The recessed lighting over the counter was captured in the colorful gemstones that were set in unusual sterling silver and solid gold designs, and tiny sparkles of light reflected on the soft peach walls of the boutique as Kate and Tikka examined the various pieces in the collection.

"Now if the rest of the shop can only live up to this jewelry," Tikka sighed. "I'll be so happy." Groaning, Tikka pulled herself to her feet and resumed her struggle with the window drapery.

When Tikka firmly refused her offer of help, Kate drove the short distance to Silvertree Farm, where she found Jessica sitting silently in a rocking chair in the kitchen where Julia was making cookies. Mildred was talking quietly to the little girl who stared out the window at the ocean. Everyone looked up as Kate plodded through the pantry door and collapsed into the nearest chair.

"How was your day, ladybug? Did you like your school?" Kate leaned toward Jessica encouragingly, hoping to draw her daughter into some interaction. "I'll tell you about Rocky Shore." When Jessica remained silent and dropped her eyes to her lap, Kate looked at Mildred, whose expression of concern was etched in the deep lines in her face.

"The teacher called in the middle of the morning because she was afraid that Jessie might be sick. I guess that she was so quiet they became worried. But I explained that Jessie might be a bit shy and to give her a bit longer to adjust. When I picked her up at noon, she was listening to a story with the rest of the group, so I'd say that she did fine. Right, Jessie?" Mildred knelt beside the rocking chair and tried to catch Jessica's eye. When the child kept her face averted, Mildred looked at Kate and shook her head.

Kate sighed and wrapped her hands around a steaming mug of tea that Julia passed to her. Determined to create a positive atmosphere for her daughter, she walked to the window and watched the seagulls circle around the lobster boat that was returning to Morning Cove after a day of fishing. In the middle of the cove, the twin points of Angel Rock momentarily hid the boat from view, but it eventually reappeared and tied up at the long pier that had been built on one end of the beach.

"Do you ever get tired of looking out at that, Millie?"

Mildred came over and stood next to Kate. "Never. No matter what has gone wrong in my life, the healing power of the ocean has made it bearable." Mildred lowered her voice and looked at Jessica who was slowly turning the pages of a picture book that Julia had put on her lap. "I only hope that this place can work its magic on that little muffin."

Kate nodded. "I know, Millie. It breaks my heart to see so much pain in such a small person. If things don't improve, I really think we need to get some help for her."

Mildred patted Kate's shoulder and started to leave the kitchen. "Wait, Millie, I've been meaning to ask you something." Kate followed her aunt into the dining room and pointed at the unusual moldings. "Did the same architect who designed this house also do Rocky Shore? I noticed today that there are some similarities, although Rocky Shore is much bigger."

"You have a good eye," Mildred replied. "Actually Paul Allen Mitchell worked on both houses during the same time period. Rocky Shore was built for a very wealthy shipbuilder in 1913. It cost over one hundred and fifty thousand dollars to construct, but it would take untold millions to duplicate it today. I think that it was the largest private house ever built in Maine. The estate was bought in 1935 by Cyrus Lombard, a highly eccentric man who had made his fortune by gambling on the repeal of Prohibition, and who continued to coin money during the Depression by speculating on real estate that nobody else could afford."

"One of the students told me today that the house is filled with secret rooms and hidden passages," Kate commented. "Is that just a figment of teenage imagination?"

"I'm not sure, but I wouldn't be surprised. My house has a couple of strange quirks to it, so it's entirely possible that Rocky Shore has some too."

"Why did Lombard give Rocky Shore to the town? Didn't his family object?"

"Cyrus was a bachelor, and when he died in 1969, he had no immediate family, so he divided his estate roughly into two parts. He gave his home and 160 acres to the town of Cape Mariana, providing that it would be used as a high school, and he included a sizable bequest for the improvement and maintenance of the property. He specified that a Board of Trustees oversee the management of the money, and I was one of the original members." Mildred was clearly involved in the history and success of the school, which Kate had learned was one of the finest in the state.

"Well, it certainly is a beautiful facility for a public high school," Kate commented. "I went down into the basement to the indoor swimming pool, and it was like being in a Roman bath. The swim team must love practicing surrounded by statues of gods and naked nymphs."

Mildred laughed. "I think it inspires them to great heights! Both our swimming and soccer teams have been state champions in recent years."

"You said that Lombard divided his estate in half. What happened to the rest of it?"

"Cyrus had a huge collection of American Impressionist paintings, which he gave to the Portland Museum of Art, with the exception of that portrait of him which hangs in the school lobby. There was some talk years ago that some of his most valuable pieces were missing at the time of his death, but nobody knows for sure. Cyrus could have sold them when he became ill."

Kate was about to ask Mildred another question when the kitchen telephone rang, interrupting their conversation. Alex Stamos' deep voice sounded angry on the other end of the line. "Mrs. Hammond, something very strange took place here at school late this afternoon. I need to talk to you about it before class tomorrow."

Puzzled, Kate agreed to come in early, and as she hung up, she turned worried eyes toward Mildred. "He sounded really upset. I wonder what could have happened…"

THE SHAPE OF DARK- Chapter Three

Early the next morning, Kate hurried through a chilly, driving rain to get to school well before the bell for the first class. Rocky Shore High School had a rotating schedule, so the order in which Kate would meet her various groups of students would be different each day, and the senior class in which Kyle Monkton had suffered would be in the middle of the day. As much as she hated to admit it, Kate had a fairly unpleasant sense of dread about facing Eric Lundgren again, and she recognized her tension as she walked toward Alex Stamos' office.

Marta was at her desk, guarding the principal's door with a tight-lipped expression, but she waved Kate by, obviously having been told to expect her. Marta looked disapprovingly at Kate's dripping raincoat and umbrella, reluctantly stifling any comment as Alex's door closed behind the new English teacher.

"Thank you for coming in so promptly, especially on a day like this." Alex gestured to a chair opposite his desk, and Kate sank into it slowly. "Something really odd happened yesterday afternoon, and I wanted you to know about it before you met your seniors today." Alex's grim expression caused Kate's anxiety to congeal into a knot in her stomach.

"Did you ask Sandra Monkton to give Eric Lundgren a note requesting that he meet you in your classroom after soccer practice?" When Kate shook her head, Alex continued. "Apparently, someone left such a message in the main office, and Sandy delivered it to the soccer field just before she left for the day. According to Carlo, Eric made some kind of comment about you having the hots for him, and he said that he needed to be excused a bit early so that he could keep his appointment with you. Carlo asked to see the note, and he was satisfied that it was legitimate. It appears that Eric went to your room, which was completely empty and pretty dark by that time in the afternoon. Eric said he looked around and then saw a light in the little storage closet at the end of the classroom."

Kate interrupted Alex. "I wondered where that door went. When I was given the keys to my room, desk, and filing cabinet, I found that none of them fit that lock, so I just figured that it was book storage or something." Kate saw Alex scowl slightly. "Please, excuse me. Go on."

Alex leaned forward and continued. "Eric must have thought that you were in that closet, but when he went back to look in, someone pushed him through the door and locked the door. The light switch is outside the closet, so Eric found himself in complete darkness." Alex sat back in his chair and looked seriously at Kate. "Unfortunately, it was almost 5:30, and there was no one near that part of the building. The soccer team was down in the locker room, Sandra and Marta had gone home, and I was down in the custodian's office talking to Alf Stanton about his schedule. Eric said he really panicked after he had shouted and pounded on the door for a while because it was so dark that he couldn't see to orient himself. Luckily for Eric, Kyle Monkton came back to the school about 5:45 to get a book from his locker, and when he got Lenny, the other custodian, to let him into the building, they heard Eric screaming upstairs. I guess he was in really bad shape, crying and about to pass out."

In spite of Eric's rudeness the day before, Kate felt a surge of sympathy for the scare he had received.

"It gets worse." Alex got up from behind his desk and moved to stand beside Kate. "Bill Lundgren called me last night, absolutely furious, and said that Eric had been really shaken up by the experience because the kid has had claustrophobia ever since he was little. Apparently, yesterday's brief imprisonment made him, in Bill's words, 'shit his pants,' and Eric was terribly embarrassed to have someone find him in that condition. The most unbelievable part is that Eric swears that it was you who pushed him into the closet. He told his parents that he smelled your perfume. Alex was conscious of the subtly sweet fragrance that surrounded Kate as he spoke. "Do you always wear the same scent?"

"Lots of people wear this kind of perfume, and I certainly can't imagine a teenage kid able to identify it." Kate's initial sympathy for Eric began to shift into anger.

Alex looked very uncomfortable and cleared his throat several times before he asked the next question. "This is ridiculous, of course, but I suppose I should know. Where were you yesterday between 4:30 and 5:30? The Lundgrens are out for blood."

Kate relaxed a bit. "I was at Dunham's Market, and then with my cousin at her boutique until 5:00, when I went home and was talking to Millie when you called."

"That's a help. Nobody is going to challenge the word of Mildred Worthington, except perhaps the Lundgrens, who don't trust anyone. Try to forget about this mess, and I'll keep you posted if anything new develops. At least you won't have to face Eric this morning because his mother called earlier and said he was coming in after lunch."

When he pulled his office door open, Alex noticed that Marta Stone was standing next to the coffee maker by the entrance to his office. Her triumphant expression led him to suspect that she had listened to his whole conversation with Kate, and he added the possibility to the long list of irritations that he was experiencing with his secretary.

Alex watched as the warning bell sounded and hundreds of arriving students swept Kate's slim body up the broad stairs toward the second floor. Before he could speculate any further as to possible explanations for Eric's experience, Marta handed Alex a sheaf of messages, and he returned to his office to tackle the morning's business.

To her great relief, Kate's early classes went remarkably well, in spite of the upsetting beginning of her day. The seniors began the period with a lively discussion of the lists that they had made the night before, and Kate noticed with gratitude that Chickie, one of the last students to arrive in class, took a seat next to Kyle. Once again, Phaedra and Kelly were missing, but Kate didn't concern herself with their empty seats beyond noting their absence in her attendance record.

After the chalkboard had been filled with essential questions that the students wanted to explore during the year, Kate gave the first assignment in *Beowulf.* She read the opening passage of the book, a description of the funeral of a Viking king, and she was pleased to see that several of the students were flipping the pages to see what lay ahead in the story.

"This looks easy to read, doesn't it?" Kate turned to one of the boys who had been especially appreciative of Eric's rudeness yesterday, anxious to see how he would behave in the absence of his leader.

"Well, it's poetry, and that's not good." The boy colored a bit when everyone in the class laughed, but he looked at Kate good-naturedly. "The words seem easy to understand, so I guess it will be O.K."

"Would it surprise you to know that this version is a translation of the original?" When everybody but Kyle looked confused, Kate continued. "You thought that this was a course in English Literature, right? Listen to a few lines of this as it was first written, and then you tell me what language you think it is."

Kate took a deep breath and recited the beginning of *Beowulf* in the deep guttural sounds of Old English. There was absolute silence in the room, and Kate mentally thanked the college professor who had insisted that his students learn some of the Anglo-Saxon poem in its original form.

"Cool." Chickie commented when Kate finished speaking. "That sounds like German."

Before Kate could respond, Kyle offered information about the development of Anglo-Saxon culture after the Romans abandoned England, and Kate was amazed at the amount of knowledge that the youngster had at his fingertips. She was also delighted by the courtesy of the other students and was about to ask Kyle a few questions, when the door opened and Phaedra and Kelly strolled in. The two girls walked in front of Kate without comment and settled into two vacant desks at the side of the room. Since the clock showed that there were only ten minutes left in the period, Kate moved up the aisle until she stood directly in front of Kelly.

"Well, ladies, this is getting to be a habit. What reason do you have for being late this time?" Kate struggled to be calm and polite as she spoke to the girls in a low voice, which was barely audible to the rest of the class. When neither Kelly nor Phaedra replied, Kate stared hard at Eric's sister. "Kelly, do you have a pass from the office?"

Without answering her teacher's question, Kelly turned around to Phaedra and spoke deliberately, clearly intending to be heard by everyone in the classroom. "Did you get that, Phaedra? This woman wants to know why we're not on time for her stupid class, after what she did to my brother. I suppose she thinks that the pain she has inflicted on my whole family is no excuse for the fact that it has taken me all this time to pull myself together so that I could even stand to look at her." Kelly kept her back to Kate as Phaedra giggled and then both girls stared coldly at their stunned teacher.

The rest of the class was absolutely silent. In spite of the reputation that both Kelly and Phaedra had for baiting teachers, no one had ever witnessed such blatant disrespect for a faculty member, and all eyes swung to Kate to see how she would react.

Of the few aspects of teaching that Kate detested, losing her temper in front of a group of students was one of the worst, forming the core of most of her school nightmares. With a sinking sensation in her stomach and color rising into her cheeks, Kate realized that this well might be one of those times in which control eluded her.

In desperation, Kate resorted to her last trick to remain composed in the face of obnoxious adolescent behavior. Stepping closer to Kelly's smirking face, Kate leaned forward and put both of her hands on the surface of the desk. "Kelly," Kate breathed, "I'm afraid that I didn't hear what you said. Could you repeat yourself a little more distinctly?"

Kelly looked back at Phaedra in confusion, but with her friend's encouragement,, she repeated her insolent remarks directly at Kate, enunciating each syllable as if she were speaking to someone who was either mentally deficient or hearing impaired. In the back of the room, someone tittered, but otherwise, the only sound was the loud ticking of the clock on the wall.

Kate felt her heart beating more calmly, and she moved forward again until she was standing directly over Kelly, who was now looking rather bewildered by her teacher's strange reaction. "Once more, Kelly, if you please. I want to be absolutely certain that I understand everything that you have just said."

This time, Kelly was really baffled, but with another glance back at Phaedra for moral support, she let the offending words flow clearly and distinctly at Kate, who was so concentrated on maintaining her equilibrium that neither she nor any of the students heard the classroom door open quietly.

"Quite a speech, Miss Lundgren. You certainly have a way with words." Alex Stamos' deep voice boomed out across the room, and everyone present, including Kate, jumped at the unexpected sound.

"If you will excuse this young lady, Mrs. Hammond, I think that we need to have a little chat." Alex beckoned to Kelly, who looked back at Phaedra for help, only to find her friend staring at the desk, refusing to raise her head. Angrily, Kelly grabbed her books and stormed from the room, pausing long enough to give Kate a murderous look.

As soon as her father and Kelly left, Phaedra put her head down on her desk and refused to exchange glances with any of the other students who were now loudly discussing Kelly's possible fate. Kate took a deep breath and walked toward the front of the room, stopping to wink at Sophia, who had a broad grin on her face.

Alex was waiting outside of Kate's classroom when the final bell rang at 2:30. It was clear from the stern expression on his face that his conversation with Kelly had been less than pleasant. "I've suspended Kelly for one day, so we'll have more good news for the Lundgrens, who are now on their way over to the school. Are you ready for this?"

When Kate reassured him that she was prepared to do battle with Eric's parents, Alex nodded and handed her the key to the storage closet which had briefly served as Eric's prison. Together, they inspected the space containing floor to ceiling shelves on which were stacked old textbooks, boxes of discarded papers, and a few pieces of dusty audio-visual equipment. It was clear from the disarray in the closet that Eric had probably felt his way across the shelves, trying to find something to use to free himself. A strong odor in the enclosed space indicated that Eric had indeed soiled himself in his panic, and Alex promised to have the custodian give the closet a thorough cleaning.

Just as Alex was turning to leave the closet and reenter the classroom, the door from the corridor was flung open and a stocky man with iron gray hair and a florid face burst in. To her dismay, Kate saw that directly behind the clearly angry visitor was the woman who had caused the scene in Dunham's the previous afternoon. Eric's parents had arrived.

"There you are, Stamos." Bill Lundgren closed in on Alex who had instinctively moved in front of Kate. "And this is Mrs. Hammond, I presume." Kate could see Mona Lundgren's eyes widen in surprise as she recognized Kate from the grocery store, but she said nothing as her fuming husband stood menacingly close to Kate. "I hope that you're satisfied with your little trick on my son, Mrs. Hammond, because I intend to have you fired."

"Now wait a minute, Mr. Lundgren." Alex kept his voice level and calm, but his eyes were steely as he watched the other man's threatening stance. "We have no clear knowledge of what happened yesterday, but I know that Mrs. Hammond had nothing to do with Eric's unfortunate experience."

Mona Lundgren watched Kate with narrowed eyes while her husband spluttered in frustration. "Listen, Stamos, I don't give a shit what kind of an alibi this so-called teacher has. I believe my son, and Eric is absolutely positive that it was Mrs. Hammond who pushed him, probably to get back at him for making a few funny remarks about that little pervert Kyle Monkton." Bill Lundgren wheeled on Kate who was looking surprised that he knew about Eric's cruel treatment of Kyle. "Don't worry, lady. My son told me everything that happened in that class yesterday, including the fact that you have no sense of humor or understanding about how teenagers operate. I also heard from my daughter that you embarrassed her and Phaedra because they were a few minutes late to class."

At the mention of his daughter's name, Alex's eyebrows raised slightly, but he remained silent as Bill Lundgren stormed on. "You new teachers think you have to lord it over all of the kids, and I'm sick and tired of my children being persecuted by power-hungry academic types who can't make a living doing anything else!" The volume of Bill Lundgren's voice rose, and it was clear from the curious faces that passed by the classroom door that he could be heard in the otherwise quiet hallway.

"That's enough!" Alex spoke firmly as he shut the classroom door, excluding the audience in the hall from the growing vehemence of Lundgren's accusations. "You're way out of line, and I won't have you badgering one of my teachers like this. I will talk to Eric tomorrow and tell him that someone other than Mrs. Hammond played a cruel joke on him. And let me assure you that there are plenty of students around here who have reasons for having done that to Eric. Meantime, I suggest that you get a grip on yourself before you say something you will regret."

Mona Lundgren glared at Alex as he was speaking to her husband, and she seemed about to say something, but she clamped her lips together and tossed her sleekly coifed head. Kate noticed that Mona's long fingernails were painted in exactly the same shade as her tight mouth, and a large emerald and diamond ring glinted under the buzzing fluorescent lights as she placed her hand on Bill's sleeve.

Somewhere, Kate found her voice and responded to Eric's furious parents. "I can't tell you how badly I feel about this whole situation, in spite of the fact that I had nothing to do with it. Eric must have been very frightened, and I hope that he's all right now." In the middle of Kate's statement, Bill Lundgren snorted in disgust and motioned his wife out of the room.

"You may have fooled Alex Stamos, but you haven't convinced me. Just watch your treatment of my children, lady, or you'll have more trouble than you can handle." The intensity of Bill's words was matched by a look of pure hatred on his wife's face, and the two left Kate and Alex standing in the doorway of the classroom.

"They're a fun couple, aren't they?" Alex commented at the stiff backs of the Lundgrens as they disappeared down the stairs toward the lobby. "Wait until they find out about Kelly's suspension. They'll be back, fully armed."

The strain of the interview showed on Kate's face as she sat down in one of the student desks. "What thoroughly unpleasant people! No wonder their children suffer from terminal rudeness."

Alex looked thoughtful as he slid into the desk next to Kate's. "There's something very strange about that whole family. I've been told that they moved here six years ago, when Eric and Kelly were going into the seventh grade. Right away Eric began causing trouble, bullying other kids and even doing mean things to the animals in their neighborhood. There was an old lady who lived a couple of houses away from the Lundgrens who finally complained to the police that Eric tied two of her cats together with a short piece of rope that had nooses at each end. The cats choked each other trying to get apart. Each time someone criticized Eric, his parents were so belligerent that people finally kept quiet and just kept their kids away from him."

"What about Kelly? She seems as unpleasant as her brother. More so, to me, at least."

"Kelly started out O.K., as far as I can remember. When we moved here, Phaedra was going into the eighth grade, and the Lundgrens had been in Cape Mariana for about a year. Kelly and

Phaedra became very good friends and spent a lot of time together. By that time, it was obvious that Eric was a terrific athlete, and his involvement in sports seemed to tone him down a bit. He was and is an awesome soccer player."

Kate thought about the little girl that Mona had been mistreating in the market. "How does their youngest child fit into the family profile?"

Alex rubbed the back of his neck as he shook his head. "When Molly came along, the Lundgrens hired an *au pair* from France to take care of the kids while they concentrated on their real estate company. Poor little Molly just sort of grew on her own, but she seems like a sweet child. Maybe influence other than her parents was a blessing for her." Alex paused when a student knocked on the door and handed him a message.

"You'll have to excuse me. There's yet another crisis in the office. But before I go, I hope you understand why I responded as I did to Kelly's insolence in your class. Disciplining students is the prerogative of the teacher, but I wanted to take advantage of actually having witnessed her rudeness to teach that young lady a lesson." Alex wheeled on his heel and disappeared into the corridor.

Alone in the echoing classroom, Kate glanced around at the bare walls and sparse furnishings, thinking how ironic it was to spend a great deal of time in such gloomy surroundings, when she took such pleasure in the gracious atmosphere at Silvertree Farm. Perhaps she could brighten up her own space at Rocky Shore High School and make a more pleasant environment for herself and her students. Hastily, Kate drew a sketch of the room and estimated its dimensions before she packed her bookbag and prepared to leave for the day.

As she moved to close the windows, Kate heard familiar voices coming from the courtyard below, and she looked out to see Carlo Brito talking earnestly to Chickie, whose face was twisted into the pained expression of a person who was trying not to cry. Both Carlo and Chickie were dressed for soccer practice, and Carlo kept fingering the whistle that was around his neck as he struggled to explain his recent and difficult decision to Chickie.

"Look, my friend, I really have no choice. You are a terrific player, one of the strongest on the team, but this Rossoni boy is in a class by himself. You know that Jean Pierro has been on the Italian

33

youth national teams since he was ten years old. His skills are the best that I have ever seen, and you as captain know how valuable he could be to us. We have a great shot at the state championship, and we might even go to the nationals with him in the front line. My problem is who to replace with Jean Pierro. In my judgment, you're the most adaptable player and can move back to sweeper more effectively than Eric or Ted."

"I'm sorry, coach. I don't mean to make this difficult for you. I agree with you about Jean Pierro—he's terrific. And I don't mind playing somewhere else, but when I told my father that you might switch me, he really hit the ceiling and told me to tell you that no wop was going to take my position. My father's afraid that the college scouts won't pay any attention to me unless I'm scoring goals, and he says that I absolutely have to get an athletic scholarship or I can't go to college." Chickie paused and wiped his eyes with the back of his hand. "My dad's not a bad guy, but he gets awfully mad when he thinks that he's being cheated out of something he deserves."

By this time, Kate was listening intently to the conversation, not in the least ashamed that she was eavesdropping. Looking down, she saw Carlo pat Chickie's back in sympathy. Chickie sat on the stone bench at the rim of the courtyard with his elbows on his knees and his head drooping forward.

"I understand all of that, Chickie, but I've made up my mind, and your father is going to have to try to accept it. I'll work all I can with you to get you comfortable at sweeper. You're the only one that I feel confident about moving from the front line. Go home and tell your dad that the captain of a state championship team will be noticed by college scouts, no matter where he plays." Carlo's heavy Spanish accent drifted up through Kate's window, and she recognized the determination in his voice. "I'm going to tell the team about my decision at practice today, but I wanted you to know first. Your attitude will really affect how the rest of the boys accept Jean Pierro."

Chickie nodded and looked away as Carlo got up and walked toward the soccer field. Kate could see that tears were running down Chickie's face, and she felt deep sympathy for the young man's distress. As silently as possible, Kate slid the window shut and watched Chickie rise slowly from the bench and follow Carlo.

When she left the building and moved toward her car, Kate saw the soccer team sitting on the grass facing Carlo, who was talking and gesturing toward Jean Pierro, sitting at the edge of the group. Even from a distance, Kate recognized the angry expressions on the faces of some of the players, and then Chickie stood up and joined the coach in front of the other boys. Kate couldn't hear what was being said, but from the way the tension seemed to leave the group, she imagined that Chickie had accepted Carlo's decision and was urging the others to do so also.

Somewhat distracted, Kate opened her car door and slid her bookbag and purse onto the passenger seat. Without warning, her nostrils were assaulted by a vile odor that seemed to fill the hot interior of the small vehicle. When she could see nothing unusual in the front part of the car, Kate stepped outside and opened the rear door, gagging as she recognized the contents of three plastic bags on the carpeted floor of the back seat. One of the bags had spilled what appeared to be human vomit, and the soured-milk smell mingled with the stench of feces and bloody tampons and sanitary napkins which were in the other two bags. On the seat of the car near the disgusting display was a sheet of paper on which was scrawled "Get out of town. We don't want a killer here."

THE SHAPE OF DARK—Chapter Four

Kate didn't want to touch anything, so she slammed the door shut and ran back to the school building. To her relief, Alex was standing in the main lobby talking to Sandra Monkton, so Kate didn't have to encounter Marta Stone and her disapproval. Both Alex and Sandra ran forward at the sight of Kate's white, stricken face, and as she described the contents of the bags and the accompanying message, Sandra phoned for the custodian, while Alex sprinted out to the parking lot to inspect the damage to Kate's car.

"What's up, Mr. Stamos?" The pockmarked face of Alfred Stanton, the school janitor, appeared around the far side of the BMW, and he wrinkled his nose in distaste as he realized what was on the floor of the car. "Phew! What a mess!" Alfred, better known as "Alf" to the students and faculty, gingerly transferred the offending small bags to the larger one that he had brought with him. "I've got to come back with a pail and disinfectant to get the rest of this." Alf held the green trash bag at arm's length and jogged back to the side of the building where his custodial supplies were stored.

While he waited for Alf's return, Alex lifted the note by one corner and looked at it carefully. There was something oddly familiar about the round, childish handwriting, but Alex wasn't sure what it was, so he folded the sheet of paper and put it in his pocket.

Within fifteen minutes, Alf had removed most of the malodorous material from the car, and a shaken Kate insisted that she was perfectly able to drive the short distance to Silvertree Farm. Later, when she described the day's events to Mildred, her aunt immediately placed a call to the principal.

"What in God's name is going on in that school, Alex?" Mildred bristled at the stress that had been placed on Kate, and she clearly expected some answers.

"Honestly, Mildred, I have no idea why all of this is happening, but I can promise you that I'm going to find out. Tomorrow's Friday. Why doesn't Kate take the day off and use the weekend to regroup? By that time, maybe I can get some answers as to why somebody seems determined to drive her away from here." Hearing steely resolve in Alex's voice, Mildred nodded her approval of the suggestion, but Kate shook her head when Mildred relayed the message.

"Absolutely not. If I don't show up tomorrow, whoever did this will think that he or she has won and that I'm running scared. Well, I'm not going to let them get away with it." The color began to come back to Kate's face, and her chin was set in a determined expression. "I swore when I left Georgia that I would never run away again."

****

The hardest thing for Kate to reconcile was that life with Max had once been so wonderful. From the first time she had seen the ruggedly handsome tennis player on the courts of the exclusive Cloister Hotel on Sea Island, Kate had admired his easy power and graceful energy as he defeated one opponent after another in a charity tournament. Kate had found herself drawn into the gallery day after day as Max Hammond edged himself toward the championship. Finally, at dinner in the Cloister dining room the night after the third day of play, Kate was introduced to Max by one of the tournament sponsors, and they began a rapidly escalating relationship that ultimately culminated in Max's proposal of marriage.

Since Kate's parents had been killed in an airplane accident, Kate and Max were married six months later, at her aunt's home, Silvertree Farm, on the coast of Maine. After a short honeymoon, they returned to Cape Mariana until the end of July in order for Max to figure out the direction that he wanted his life to take. Although he had won several tournaments in his two years on the tour, Max had begun to find himself more and more restless with the traveling and constant training, and just before their wedding, he had seriously resumed painting.

In her house in Atlanta, Marissa Hammond had built a studio for her son, clearly proud of his talent and achievement as an art major at Emory University, and when Max had shown Kate his early work, she had been astonished at its quality. During the years that the seduction of the tennis circuit had prevailed over Marissa's objections, she had simply closed the door on his unfinished paintings and waited for him to rediscover his real vocation.

"Max doesn't know how good he is," Marissa had confided to Kate when they first met. "The tennis thing was so glamorous that he got swept away, but I'm sure that one day he'll tire of it and begin to paint seriously." Max's mother opened the studio door, revealing partially completed canvasses of such beauty that Kate's breath was taken away, and she could only marvel at the magic that had flowed from her fiancé's brush.

By the time they left Cape Mariana in August, Max had decided to leave the tennis world and try to complete some of the work he had begun in Atlanta and in Maine. While Kate returned to the Sea Islands to find them a house, Max toiled in the studio in Atlanta, producing several paintings in a short period of time. He was staggered to discover that his mother's old friend, Appleton Kingston, owner of the largest art gallery in Atlanta, was eager to represent him, finding a ready market for his impressionistic landscapes and city scenes.

"I want to do your portrait," Max murmured after making slow and passionate love to her in their rented cottage on St. Simons Island, across the causeway from Brunswick. "You found such a wonderful place for us to live that I want my first work here to be a picture of my beautiful wife." Max had spent the afternoon arranging his art supplies in the studio behind the house, and now the blank canvas perched on his easel was an irresistible challenge.

Propelled by creative energy, Max leapt out of bed and stood looking down at Kate, stretched languorously on the rumpled sheets, her undulating curves partially hidden in the early evening shadows. "Come on, Madame, genius is being wasted."

Kate groaned but allowed herself to be moved from her comfortable position. "What shall I wear for this masterpiece?"

"What do you think about my doing a nude? I've always wanted to try one, and you've certainly got the body for it. Would you feel funny?" Max hurriedly shrugged into his own clothes while gazing at Kate, luminescent in her nakedness.

To her surprise, Kate agreed and pulled on her silk dressing gown before padding after Max through the heavy Georgia dusk to the studio. "I can't believe I'm doing this, you Svengali. It's only because you're such a good painter that I'm unveiling my self to the world."

Max busied himself arranging Kate on a decrepit sofa, on which he had flung a piece of bottle green velvet, with Kate's violet robe making a slash of color across the back of the couch. After a little more than an hour, Max put down his brush and draped his canvas with a sheet. "This is really going to work, Katie. Will you hang in there with me so that I can finish it this week? I'm afraid once your school starts, we'll be living in separate worlds."

Kate was only too happy to spend most of the following several days posing for her excited husband, who hummed as he worked, careful to take enough breaks so that his model could stretch and change positions. Finally, six evenings after the project had begun, Max proudly lifted back the drape and showed Kate his "Lady on Green."

"On my God, Max, it's incredible!" Kate could hardly believe that she was actually the exquisite woman who bloomed on the canvas in front of her. Max had introduced light and shadow into the composition so that Kate's sensuous curves gleamed against the rich dark green background, but her face was partially obscured by a drape of coppery curls across her cheek, leaving her features suggested rather than defined. A shimmering length of purple silk floated across the pubic area, elevating the dignity of the portrait, while the translucent breasts swelled with restrained passion, merely hinting of the model's smoldering sensuality.

"What are you going to do with it?" Kate spoke in a hushed voice, mesmerized by the sleek, fluid interplay of pearly flesh and vibrant jewel-toned fabrics.

"I really should give it to you," Max admitted, "But at least let me show it to Appleton. I told him I was working on something entirely different from my usual stuff, and he made me promise to let him see it. When you start back to school, I'll drive up to Atlanta. Meanwhile, we both deserve some time off."

The few days remaining in the summer were pure bliss for Kate. Max closed up his studio and they spent endless hours on the beach at Sea Island, riding gentle horses, splashing in the wild surf from an offshore hurricane, or simply lying on the warm sand. By the time that Glen Academy began in September, Kate was bronzed, rested, and pregnant.

"Lady on Green" was an instant success, and a wealthy collector from Europe made an offer that was so high that Kate didn't hesitate to agree to the sale of the painting. "After all," Max had mused, "this is an iffy business I'm in, and I'd better grab anything I can get, especially with a baby on the way!" To his delight, however, the subsequent nudes he painted using professional models were also received well, and before the end of that year, the name of Maximillian Hammond was becoming increasingly well known in the art world.

As Kate began to show the signs of her pregnancy, Max, at the urging of Appleton Kingsley, took a trip north to visit some of the galleries that had expressed appreciation for his work and were now competing for the canvases that he continued to produce with enviable speed. Max had granted exclusive rights to his "Lady On" series to Appleton, but when a new dealer in Boston showed keen interest in some of the landscapes Max had done in Maine, he took those paintings out of Kingsley's and boarded a plane in mid-November to negotiate with Adam Loring, whose gallery on Newbury Street was highly regarded by collectors.

"Are you going to be all right alone?" Max worried as he kissed Kate goodbye at the airport in Brunswick. Kate's stomach was gently rounding as she entered her fourth month, but she was over the bouts of morning sickness that had made teaching a daily challenge, and she had become radiant in recent weeks.

"No problem, darling. Millie will be down in a few days, and I'll go over and stay with her if something happens. You take your time and enjoy Boston and New York." Kate felt very content in spite of her reluctance to have her husband away.

After Max's return, the rest of the year was a blur for Kate, marked primarily by a swelling body and a growing impatience to finish the third quarter at school, after which she was taking maternity leave to await the birth of her child in April. When Max announced in the early part of the month that he had to rush up to Boston for a few days, Kate was temporarily upset at his leaving, fearing that the baby would come early. However, she smiled bravely and agreed after he explained that Adam Loring needed to discuss a very lucrative commission in Prides Crossing, on the North Shore of Boston.

"I promise I'll do this in record time," Max insisted, shoving clothes into a small bag. "Just sit in one place and don't sneeze!"

"Don't worry, Daddy. If Millie had gone back to Maine, I'd be in a panic, but she's determined to wait for the baby, so I'll go out to Sea Island until you get back." Kate's optimism lasted three hours after Max's departure when, while wheeling a grocery cart past the deli counter, she felt a vise grip her lower abdomen, sending a sharp pain through her body.

Thirteen hours later, Jessica Sinclair Hammond made her way into the world, screaming and red-faced as she was laid on Kate's sweat-drenched breast. Mildred, who had filled in as Kate's Lamaze coach, felt her mask grow damp as the tears of relief ran down her face. Kate closed her eyes as the nurse lifted Jessica to clean her and prepare her for the pediatrician's examination.

"She's gorgeous, Katie," Mildred whispered, in spite of the fact that she understood how disappointed her niece was that her husband hadn't been with her. "As soon as Max hears about Jessica, he'll be right on the next plane."

Instead, Kate and Jessica were driven home from the hospital by Mildred, who continued to fume that Max had not come directly back when he received the news of his daughter's birth. "This is a really big deal up here, Millie," he had said when she had phoned him about the baby's arrival. "This guy wants me to paint six different portraits of his family, and he's willing to pay megabucks. I just can't afford to turn it down. All I need to do is to make a few sketches now, and take some pictures, and then I can do the actual portraits over the summer. Just ask Kate to give me a day or two, and I'll be right back."

"Don't fret, Millie," Kate said as she kissed the velvety cheek of her soundly sleeping daughter. "Max promised that he'd be home late tonight, and we'll be fine until then. I understand about the big project up north, and I thought you did too, especially since you're going to let Jessie and me stay with you at Silvertree Farm while Max works in Prides Crossing."

Kate didn't know exactly when Max would arrive, and he finally came through the door in the rainy early morning while Jessica was nursing sleepily in her mother's arms. When he walked into the bedroom and caught his first sight of his beautiful wife and daughter, tough, hard-driving Max allowed tears to cascade down his unshaven cheeks as he knelt beside Kate's rocker.

"Hi little girl," Max whispered hoarsely to the baby. "I've brought you a friend to keep you company." Max reached into his carryon bag and drew out a fluffy, light-blue teddy bear. "This is Cynthia, and I've brought her all the way from Boston." Max settled the bear into Kate's lap and smoothed the silky top of his tiny daughter's head.

"Hey you. Say hello to the other woman in your life."

In less than a month, Max, Kate, and Jessica flew to Portland, where they all settled in at Silvertree Farm, surrounded by the glorious lilacs known to horticulturists as the Worthington Collection and long hedges of mountain laurel which bloomed pinkly in the warm June sun. Kate and her baby were swept into the capable arms of Julia Murray, who had been Mildred's cook for twenty years, while Max huddled in the paneled library making arrangements for his work in Prides Crossing, where he planned to paint during the week and return to Maine on weekends.

Soon everyone's life settled into a pleasant routine, and Jessica grew into a cherubic, smiling baby, who cried only to be fed or changed. Kate swam regularly and quickly regained her slim figure, while Max struggled to complete the first of the six portraits that he had agreed to paint. His subject, Mrs. Simon Wentworth, was a faded, elegant alcoholic, who showed up sporadically for sittings, always accompanied by a small silver flask of vodka. By the time that an hour passed, Mrs. Wentworth's posture became rubbery, and Max found himself reduced to working from a photograph much of the time.

Finally, at the end of August, Kate insisted on returning to Georgia with Jessica, in spite of Mildred's objections. "I'm sorry, Millie. I adore Maine, but I miss my little house, and I want to be on my own for a while. Julia is so wonderful about helping with Jessie that I'm getting awfully spoiled. Besides, Max has several months before he's due to start the next Wentworth masterpiece, and he's anxious to paint the Sea Islands in the fall."

As it turned out, Kate and Jessica were by themselves when they drove onto St. Simons Island. At the last minute, Simon Wentworth had demanded some changes in his wife's portrait, so Max had been unable to leave Prides Crossing as originally planned. Rather than wait any longer, Kate juggled baggage and her baby, stopping in Atlanta for a visit with Max's mother, who had only seen Jessica once since her birth.

Tears gathered in Marissa's dark brown eyes when she caught a glimpse of Kate and her granddaughter in the airport, in spite of her initial disappointment that Max was not with them. "Your poor son is much worse off than we are," Kate laughed as they drove toward Marissa's townhouse. "He's struggling with this drunken woman who wants to be twenty years younger than she is, and can't accept a portrait that looks like her. According to Max, her husband is having an affair with one of the chambermaids, so he wants to keep his wife happy at all cost. Needless to say, Max is anxious to get home and lose himself in the birds and marshes."

Marissa turned into her driveway and stopped the car. "That's been one of the hallmarks of Max's life—pleasing other people when he'd rather be doing something else. And in spite of everything, dear Max often gets treated very badly."

Kate looked at her mother-in-law. "What are you talking about, Marissa? I thought Max led a golden life with your friend Appleton Kingsley as his benefactor."

"Appleton was wonderful to us, that's true. He saw what a fine athlete Max was and insisted on paying for tennis lessons all through junior high and high school. Then, when Max showed a flair for painting, Appleton sent him to a program at Emory for teenagers. No, after Clinton was gone, things were much better for Max, but they were awful while his father was around."

Kate handed Jessica to Marissa and collected their luggage from the back seat. "Actually, Max refuses to talk about his father, so I suspected they didn't particularly get along. How did Max react when your husband left?"

Holding Jessica carefully, Marissa unlocked the front door and led Kate into the cool interior of the charming old house. "It was the best and the worst for both Max and me. When Clinton left twenty-seven years ago, he took my daughter with him."

Kate was stunned. "Max never told me he has a sister! Come to think of it, he's never said much about his childhood, except to talk about you and Appleton." Jessica began to cry, so Kate took her from Marissa and sat down in the darkened living room to nurse.

"I hate to think about a lot of it," Marissa sighed, "but I guess you have the right to know. It's so painful for Max to remember that he's probably blanked everything out. The kind of abuse that he suffered at Clinton's hands leaves most children horribly scarred, but I think Max had an inner strength that allowed him to cope, even then."

Kate looked down at her daughter. "I've never been able to understand how an adult could hurt a child. To me, it's the most horrible thing a person can do, especially to someone he's supposed to love and protect."

"I agree wholeheartedly, but I wasn't able to stop him." Marissa looked pained as she talked about her husband. "At first, Clinton was an absent but kind father, in spite of the fact that he was sort of forced to marry me. He traveled a lot of the time, but when Max was a baby, Clinton really seemed to enjoy him. Then Clinton met Brother Josiah and everything changed."

"Who was Brother Josiah?"

"He was this crackpot who had a small church out in the country called the House of the Holy Light. Clinton heard about him from one of his customers and he was curious to see why people found the man so intriguing. One Sunday, Clinton demanded that Max and I go with him to a service at a broken-down building miles from Atlanta, in spite of the fact that I told him very clearly I wanted nothing to do with evangelistic types. When we got there, it was like the people in the congregation were hypnotized by this man, who stood up in the front wearing a big black hat, ranting and raving about driving the demons off of the earth."

"Brother Josiah sounds really weird!" Kate propped Jessica on her shoulder and rubbed her back gently, eliciting a loud burp from the drowsy baby. "Let me put this child to bed before you go on."

When Kate came back downstairs, Marissa had poured a glass of wine for herself and a cup of tea for her daughter-in-law. "O.K.," Kate urged, settling in a corner of the sofa. "Continue."

"The scariest thing happened shortly after we got there, and I'm sure that it had something to do with the way that Clinton treated Max afterwards. Brother Josiah was screaming about sin and evil, when he suddenly wheeled and pointed to Max, who was only five years old.

'How do you know,' he bellowed, 'that this child is not the anti-Christ? If his father fails to teach him right from wrong, he may destroy us all.' Max was absolutely terrified and so was I. I told Clinton that I would never go back again, but he insisted on taking Max Sunday after Sunday for more of that fanatic's verbal abuse."

Kate was confused. "Why did you allow Clinton to subject your son to that kind of treatment?"

"Because I was weak and afraid of my husband. He had hit me a couple of times, and I didn't want to make him angry. Now I know that emotional abuse is as harmful as physical punishment to a child, but I honestly didn't think that the words of a crazy old man would hurt Max." Marissa was clearly uncomfortable admitting her inability to protect her son.

"The real trouble began when Clinton started to beat Max for the smallest infraction of his many rules. Apparently, Brother Josiah had told Clinton that it was his duty to 'scar the back of the devil", and poor Max had to endure years of vicious whippings, in spite of my feeble efforts to intervene. On two occasions, I thought that Max needed medical attention, but Clinton ignored me and locked Max in his room for the night."

"That must have been awful for you to watch." Kate looked over sympathetically at her mother-in-law, whose voice was quivering. "But why did you stay?"

"For some reason, which is hard for me to understand now, I was afraid to leave Clinton because I had no skills or education. When Max was six and a half, I got pregnant and Samantha was born. Then, I was really trapped, although Clinton absolutely adored the baby and actually began to be nicer to Max. Samantha was a golden child and she seemed to soften Clinton somehow."

"But you said that he left. What happened?"

Marissa shook her had sadly. "I'll never forget that day as long as I live. There was some money missing from Clinton's bureau, and he blamed Max for taking it. When Max denied having even seen the money, Clinton beat him so unmercifully that the child passed out, making Clinton angry enough that he stormed out of the house. I took Samantha next door and left her with a neighbor, while I carried Max to the hospital, in spite of the fact that I knew Clinton would be furious. The doctors at the hospital insisted on keeping Max overnight, and I knew they would report the abuse, so I hurried home to get Samantha and leave. When I got to my neighbor's house, she told me that Clinton had come about an hour earlier and had taken Samantha home. Of course, she had no reason to refuse to give Clinton his daughter."

"Is that when he disappeared?" Kate asked quietly.

"Yes, I never saw either one of them again, in spite of all kinds of help from the police, the FBI, and even private detectives that Appleton hired after I went to work for him. They simply vanished, and so did Brother Josiah."

"What became of you and Max after that?"

"Poor Max. It took him quite awhile to be able to sleep without nightmares, and I really wondered how we would live, since Clinton left us with nothing, except the few dollars that had fallen down behind his bureau. Luckily, I saw an ad for an assistant in an art gallery, and in spite of the fact that I had no experience, Appleton Kingsley decided to give me a chance. The rest you know."

Kate stretched her legs out in front of her, suddenly feeling stiff and tired. "I know it was hard for you to relive all of that, but I'm grateful to know what happened to Max. Sometimes he cries out at night and wakes up in a cold sweat, but he says he doesn't remember his dream. That's a heavy load to carry around, even for someone as strong as Max."

Several weeks later when Max finally finished Mrs. Wentworth's portrait to her satisfaction and returned to Georgia, Kate mentioned the fact that Marissa had told her the story of his childhood. Expecting Max to be relieved that the details were out in the open, Kate was amazed when he tersely informed her that she was never to speak of the situation again. "It's something I want to forget," he said angrily, "and I don't appreciate being reminded of it."

Kate immediately changed the subject and although the names of Clinton and Samantha were never raised again, Kate felt vaguely guilty at having mentioned them in the first place, since Max seemed to suffer increasingly from the nightmares which had only occasionally plagued him earlier. In fact, after each trip north to the Wentworths, Max seemed to grow more irritable, often snapping at Kate over some insignificant matter.

At the end of the next summer, shortly after they had returned from their visit to Maine, Kate asked Max how he would feel about her accepting a part-time teaching job at a small private school on St. Simons Island. "I'm really ready to get back into the classroom, and Jessie's old enough to be in a preschool for part of the day. I think it would be good for all of us and would let you have more privacy to work when you're home."

Max took a long gulp of Jack Daniels and stared at Kate. "Are you sure this is what you want?" It was six o'clock at night, and Max's words were slightly slurred from the effects of drinking steadily since he had finished in the studio around four. Kate was increasingly aware that alcohol was playing an important role in Max's life, but she pushed her anxiety aside by telling herself that the strain of finishing the Wentworth portraits was responsible.

"Only if it's all right with you." Kate looked up from the floor where she was building blocks with Jessica. "Millie's coming down early this year, so when you go back to do the last of those damned pictures, I'll have some help if Jessie should get sick."

"Do whatever you want." Max snapped as he got up to replenish his drink. "Just don't expect me to be a baby-sitter when I'm home."

Kate wasn't surprised to hear Max say that because he had grown extremely impatient with his daughter, even slapping her on a couple of occasions when she wouldn't stop crying. Horrified, Kate had told him that she wouldn't stand for that kind of treatment, and he had seemed genuinely sorry, apologizing to both of them and rocking Jessica in his arms. He always seemed more short-tempered after his return from the north, so Kate tried hard to keep Jessica occupied and quiet during the first few days following his arrival home.

As it turned out, Max spent most of the fall in New England, while both Kate and Jessica adjusted happily to their new lives. Kate taught ninth and tenth grade English, and Jessica was enrolled in Little Tots, a private preschool across the street from Golden Isles Prep. Sadly, the only difficult moments came when Max was home and was forced to take care of Jessica on those few occasions when Kate could not take the child with her. Each time that Jessica stayed with her father, she'd be sobbing on Kate's return and would cling to her mother, while Max shook his head in bewilderment at the little girl's reaction.

"I don't think she likes me anymore," Max complained. "You're no sooner out the door than she starts howling and won't stop. I've finally decided to put her in her room and let her yell, because when I do that, she generally quiets down after a while and goes to sleep."

"She's probably just tired from school," Kate suggested. "Of course she likes you, you're her father." But in spite of her reassuring words, a growing doubt began to build in Kate's mind, reinforced by the terror that she thought she saw in Jessica's eyes at the sight of Max.

Of equal concern to Kate was the fact that her own relationship with her husband was more strained every day. Sexually, life had become a nightmare. On the first night that he was home from Massachusetts, Max usually claimed his wife's body with a cruel passion that left Kate shivering and weeping long after Max had fallen into a deep but restless sleep. This pattern of lovemaking characterized their deteriorating marriage and continued through the early spring when Max began to signal his desire by drinking too much and making salacious comments until after Jessica's bedtime, after which he would lock their bedroom door and force Kate to participate in sexual activities that either hurt or disgusted her. In spite of her efforts to discuss the situation in the sober calm of the next day, Max persisted in his behavior and ignored Kate's growing distaste until matters came to a head in the middle of April.

It was unusually hot in Georgia, and even St. Simons Island, which was ordinarily cooled by a sea breeze, sat baking in the late afternoon sun. Kate had stopped by the grocery store on her way home from school, and Jessica was so tired and cranky that she fussed and whined in her car seat when Kate parked in front of the cottage and began to wrestle with the bulky brown bags.

"Can't you keep that kid quiet, Kate?" Max's exasperated face appeared on the passenger side of the car, where he retrieved the mail and newspaper from the front seat, leaving Kate to manage the groceries on her own.

As he stalked toward the house, Kate could smell whisky and she caught a glimpse of his slightly glassy expression, which signaled that Max had probably been drinking for most of the afternoon. Sighing, Kate struggled into the kitchen with her bundles and then returned to the car to unbuckle Jessica, who by this time was yelling at the top of her lungs.

"Shhh, ladybug," Kate whispered to the little girl as they moved inside. "Daddy's tired and grumpy, so don't let's annoy him." For some reason, Jessica responded to Kate's soothing tone by crying even more loudly, and in less than a minute, Max had thrown his newspaper on the living room floor and was standing glowering in the kitchen door.

"Goddamn it, Jessie, SHUT UP, or I'll give you something to really cry about." Max's tone was so vicious that Kate winced and Jessica, startled, ducked her head into Kate's shoulder and sniffled fearfully. "You spoil that kid, Kate, and I'm sick of it!" Max strode over to his wife and daughter and yanked Jessica from Kate's arms, setting the child roughly down on her feet.

Max snarled once more at his daughter to be quiet and marched back into the living room, where he peevishly snapped open his paper, and took a long drink of the tall glass of dark brown liquid beside his chair. Kate hurriedly put Jessica into her room to play and began to fix Max's favorite dinner, which she hoped would sweeten his disposition.

To her surprise, Kate heard Max leave the house about fifteen minutes later, in spite of the tantalizing aroma of fried chicken that was floating through the house. When the car started and the tires squealed down the driveway, Kate knew immediately that Max had probably gone to a local bar where he spent many hours, and she feared that she was in for a difficult evening.

Kate fed Jessica her supper at the usual hour and put the tired child to bed, cooling her hot cheeks with a wet washcloth while she sang the same lullaby that Jessica required every night while she snuggled with Cynthia and positioned her thumb effectively in her mouth. The final part of the ritual came when Kate draped Jessica's threadbare blanket across her daughter and whispered "Later, alligator."

Just as she was finishing the dishes and wrapping a plate that she could heat later for Max, she heard her husband's heavy footsteps in the living room. Before she could turn around, Max was behind her as she stood at the sink, wrapping his arms around her and squeezing her breasts painfully, while whispering lewd suggestions in a hot, whiskey-redolent voice. Kate shrugged away from him and wiped her hands on her apron, only to have him grab her roughly and aim a scratchy kiss at her unwilling lips.

"Come on, Max, take it easy." Kate slid along the counter to where his dinner was neatly wrapped in plastic, ready to be heated in the microwave. "Let me get you some dinner. Then we'll talk."

The sound of shattering china grated on Kate's ears as Max hurled the plate of food on the floor, scattering chicken, mashed potatoes, and peas in all directions. "I don't want to eat, goddamn it, I want to FUCK! NOW!" Max grabbed Kate's wrist and twisted it painfully, dragging her across the slippery kitchen floor toward their bedroom. Jessica, who had barely gone to sleep, was awakened by the commotion and began to cry, calling for Kate.

Max snapped. He threw Kate against the wall opposite Jessica's door and stormed into the child's bedroom, ripping the covers off of her bed and throwing her to the floor. While Kate watched in frozen horror, Max snatched off his belt and began to whip Jessica's back as she cowered beside her bed. When her daughter's screams jolted her into action, Kate rushed over to Max and grabbed his arm as it rose to hit his daughter once again. Furious, he whirled on Kate and began to hit her, catching her cheek, where a bright red welt rose almost immediately.

As she was attempting to evade his blows, Kate caught sight of the expression on Max's face, and she knew that he had completely lost control. There were bubbles of spit at the corners of his mouth, and his eyes were glittering with a kind of frenzied hatred that led Kate to believe he would kill both her and Jessica if he could.

"RUN, Jessie!" Kate screamed to her daughter who was huddled in the corner. "Go hide." Afterwards, Kate reflected that it had been unreasonable to expect a three-year-old to follow such instructions, but fortunately, Jessica did what she was told. In spite of Max's attempts to stop her, the little girl slipped out of his grasp and ran shrieking out the front door, while Kate dodged the searing pain of the heavy belt.

Suddenly, Max dropped his weapon and grabbed Kate by the throat. With his bulging eyes close to hers, he tightened his grip as he forced Kate onto Jessica's bed. "Listen to me, BITCH. You've never really understood who runs this show, but I'm going to show you."

There was blank fury in Max's voice as he spoke hoarsely to Kate. "You think that you're so perfect, but you don't know how to be a real woman." Max's hand was like a steel band on Kate's neck, and she felt herself barely able to breathe.

With one hand holding Kate motionless, Max viciously ripped open the front of her light cotton shirt and bra, exposing her breasts to his sweaty hand. As he bent over her, Kate raised her leg quickly and jammed her knee into this crotch, causing him to clutch himself in pain. Seizing the moment, she ran down the hall and into the kitchen where she had barely enough time to grab a butcher knife, which she held in front of her before Max staggered out of the bedroom door, groaning in agony.

"So help me, Max, if you come one step closer, I'll use this." Kate's teeth were chattering as she faced her dazed husband, and she watched in shock as he crumpled on the ground, sobbing loudly.

"Oh my God, Katie, what have I done?" Max's big body shook convulsively while tears streamed down his face.

Kate looked down at Max, encased in icy revulsion. "I need to look for Jessica," she muttered and walked out the door, leaving her husband whimpering on the floor. When she came back, having discovered the little girl under the couch in Max's studio, Kate was relieved to find a note from Max saying that he was going to Atlanta to stay with his mother.

"I don't know, Millie," Kate said the next day as she helped her aunt pack for her return to Maine. "It seems like the Max that I married has been replaced with a stranger. Each time he comes back from up north, he has a harder edge, but when I ask him what has happened to make him like that, he just changes the subject. The trouble is that I still love him, or at least I love the memory of the man he used to be."

Mildred looked carefully at her niece, whose eyes were ringed with dark circles. "Something is not right, Kate. I'm very fond of Max, but for almost a year there has been an expression on his face that frightens me. I really wish that you would come to Maine with me right now and give him some time to fight whatever demons are chasing him."

"If only I could but there are still six weeks left of school. We'll be all right until summer, and then Jessica and I will definitely come up to Cape Mariana." Kate tried to keep her voice light, but she hated to see Mildred leave Sea Island.

When Max called from Atlanta that evening, his voice was quiet and serious. "I've done a lot of thinking, Kate, and I know I've been very difficult to live with recently. I'd like to blame it all on the stress of work, but that's a cop out. I'm going to check myself into the Holt Institute for a couple of weeks and see if they can help me."

Kate felt a profound sense of relief at Max's decision and she forced herself to be pleasant and supportive. "I'm really glad, Max, because there seems to be something preying on your mind that I can't understand. And Jessie was so frightened the other night that we can never let anything like that happen again."

"Trust me, Katie. Neither one of you will every have cause to be afraid, even if I have to stay at Holt for a year!" Max sounded strong and more confident than Kate had heard him for a long time, so when they hung up, she felt faintly optimistic about putting the ugly incidents behind her.

Max came back to St. Simons Island in the beginning of May looking fit, calm, and relaxed. During his stay at Holt, Kate had visited once, surprised to find him on the tennis court giving a master lesson to four other patients. The doctor in charge of his case had told Kate that Max's progress had been spectacular, and that exhaustion and stress had probably caused much of the bizarre behavior. As they walked under the lacy trees on the Institute grounds, Max had held Kate's hand and apologized again for his abusive treatment of her and Jessica.

"Whenever I think of myself hitting you and Jessie, I feel sick. The combination of booze and fatigue must have reduced me to some kind of animal. Believe me, there's no way that could happen again."

Later, when the District Attorney questioned her about the two weeks following Max's return home, Kate mostly remembered the good things that had happened. Although Jessica had continued to be wary of her father, she had occasionally responded to his warmth and good humor, allowing him to carry her on his shoulders as they walked the beach on Sea Island. The old Max had also returned to their bedroom, a sweet considerate lover who was patient with Kate's initial aversion to his touch. There had been no clues that he could turn into the monster that he became that night in the studio.

In hindsight, Kate realized that she could have saved herself a lot of pain had she not been so honest about the circumstances of Max's death. When the fire department and police were unable to find Max's body in the murky swamp, Kate explained exactly what had happened, including her discovery of Max's abuse of their daughter. Questioned separately, Jessica corroborated her story detail for detail. In spite of his immediate certainty of Kate's honesty, the detective conducting the investigation had to turn in a report to the District Attorney of Glynn County, who decided independently that Kate was telling the truth.

Marissa Hammond was beside herself with fury when she heard that Kate had been acquitted of all responsibility in Max's death. When she learned of the gruesome circumstances in which her son had perished, an irrational hatred for the woman she had accepted as a daughter filled Marissa's soul to the point that she was unable to accept Kate's description of Max's mental collapse. "Impossible!" Marissa fumed to Appleton Kingsley. "You know Max. Do you think that he could molest his own daughter? I think that Kate is making the whole thing up to cover herself." A fanatic gleam came into Marissa's eyes. "What if Kate killed Max for another reason?"

By the time that she reached St. Simons Island on the day of Max's funeral, Marissa was convinced that Kate was guilty and should be punished. Holding her temper through the short memorial service, Marissa stalked over to Kate and sobbed out her hatred and grief while Appleton tried futilely to calm her down.

"My son belongs to me now! His murderess has no right to any part of his memory!" Marissa's face was contorted as she ranted, oblivious to the horrified reactions of the few other people attending the service. "No matter what the authorities say, you and I both know that you're guilty."

Standing behind Marissa, Appleton shook his head sadly at Kate, but she was too stunned by her mother-in-law's reaction to recognize his sympathy. "You're wrong, Marissa." Kate turned away, brushing angry tears from her eyes, as she prepared to face the reporters who had been following her since the night of Max's death.

"Kate, may I speak with you a moment?" Appleton's kind, deeply lined face loomed above her. "Max had a number of canvasses in his studio. Were they damaged by the fire?"

"No, I don't think so. Why?" It seemed odd to discuss Max's paintings at this moment, but Kate trusted Appleton and stopped her movement toward the door.

"Because galleries all over the country will be after you for anything that's finished, and I wanted you to know that I'd be happy to help you to make arrangements to dispose of the paintings so that you're treated fairly."

Kate felt a rush of gratitude for Appleton's interest, especially given Marissa's obvious hostility, and she invited him to come by that afternoon to make an inventory of the work in the studio. "See if Marissa would like any of Max's things, Appleton. I'll leave while you're there so that it won't be awkward."

Both Marissa and Appleton were gone by the time that Kate and Jessica arrived home after spending the rest of the day on Sea Island with Mildred, who had flown down from Maine as soon as she heard about Max's death. During the course of the afternoon, Mildred was able to convince Kate that it was pointless to stay in Georgia any longer, and Kate agreed to sublet her cottage and move to Cape Mariana, at least for the summer.

"Who knows, Millie, we might like it so much in Maine that we'll stay." Kate watched Jessica who was propped up in a chair turning the pages of a brightly colored picture book. "I'm so worried about Jessie. She hardly speaks and seems completely withdrawn."

Mildred nodded. "That child needs a whole lot of healing, and Silvertree Farm may help erase some of the memory of these awful days. However, things have gotten a little livelier recently. Do you remember the Swedish girl that Tom married just before he died?" One of the great tragedies in Mildred Worthington's life was the loss of her son in a skiing accident in Europe several years before. Kate recalled a stunning blond woman appearing at his funeral in Cape Mariana and then disappearing shortly afterwards.

"Yes, I do. Wasn't her name Tikka?"

"That's she. Well, she's come to America after having spent the last few years in Paris, working in one of the fashion houses. Now she wants to open her own boutique over here and she's living with me until she decides where she wants to settle down. Although I didn't know her very well when she and Tom were married, I'm finding her to be delightful, if a bit, ah, unpredictable."

During the next several weeks while she was packing and making arrangements for the distribution of Max's paintings according to the suggestions that Appleton had made, Kate found herself increasingly grateful to be leaving Georgia. Every room in the cottage seemed to have painful reminders of her life with Max. Finally, after receiving several anonymous telephone calls in which she was accused of murdering her husband, Kate abruptly closed her house and took the next available plane to Maine, where she hoped the world would leave her alone.

Silvertree Farm was as close to a sanctuary as Kate could hope to find. Located on twenty acres of woods and fields overlooking the rocky Maine coast, the enormous frame and stucco "cottage" was a landmark in Cape Mariana. Mildred's father-in-law had commissioned the house in 1912, working with one of Maine's most famous architects to incorporate nine bedrooms and seven bathrooms into a graceful, rambling structure that was both imposing and informal. In 1915, a stunning roman-arch pool was added along with a poolhouse containing dressing rooms and a central recreation area. Finally, Albert Worthington, an amateur horticulturist of some note, had planned formal gardens and ornamental bushes and trees that after nearly ninety years filled the property with lush flowers from May to October.

Looking out at the brilliant terrace gardens beneath her window, Kate realized that the last two months in Maine had truly saved her sanity, and she felt strong enough to tackle the stomach-twisting challenges of another day at Rocky Shore High School. -

THE SHAPE OF DARK- Chapter Five

Kate's alarm rang early the next morning, and she found herself regretting that she hadn't accepted Alex's suggestion that she stay home for the day. Climbing out of her warm bed, Kate discovered that the relatively mild September weather yesterday had suddenly changed into a bone-chilling autumn frost, causing her to hurry into a peach cashmere turtleneck sweater and tailored merino wool slacks. In spite of the coolness of the day, Kate noticed that a bright, clear sun was pushing out of the ocean, and her spirits rose considerably as she gulped a cup of coffee and kissed Jessica goodbye.

Driving toward school, Kate saw that the sugar maples lining the entrance to Silvertree Farm had begun to display their brilliant crimson foliage, and the sky above the canopy of trees was a deep, purpled blue that Kate had seldom experienced in Georgia. Even the chattering students milling around the front of the school had a brisk air about them. Kate decided as she pulled open the heavy front door, that she had made the right decision about the day.

Inside, the vaulted central lobby was almost deserted, making Kate's footsteps echo on the black-and-white marble tiles as she headed for the second floor. When she worked her way up the crowded stairs, Kate realized that the nagging headache that had been with her since yesterday afternoon had vanished, and as she exchanged greetings with various teachers along the corridor, Kate felt none of the misgivings that had bothered her all night.

The morning progressed very smoothly as the day warmed up and the students buzzed about the evening's bonfire preceding Saturday's opening soccer game with neighboring Lake Richmond. After a first period study hall, Kate was happy to see most of the seniors bound in with considerable enthusiasm, in spite of the sullen silence of Phaedra Stamos, who arrived in class exactly as the bell rang. The seating dynamic of the group had changed slightly as Jean Pierro, Eve, and Sophia all chose seats in the middle of the boys. Several minutes after the bell, Chickie came hurtling through the door and whispered to Kate that he had been delayed because of a fight in the parking lot which he and another Green Shield member had broken up.

"O.K. everybody," Kate wondered if this class would ever start on time. "Let's get down to work." Most of the students grumbled slightly but were opening their books when Sophia raised her hand. "Mrs. Hammond, you promised to tell us about the novels that we're going to write for senior projects. I can't imagine filling up this many pages about anything, so I'd like to get started." The rest of the class broke into a variety of comments, some supportive of Sophia's enthusiasm, some mildly negative, and a few clearly insulting references to Sophia's motives. Undaunted, Sophia ignored her critics, and then looked up at Kate.

"You're absolutely right, Sophia. It is time for us to get going on this. In spite of the fact that few of you have ever done writing of this magnitude, I think you'll enjoy it, because you'll be writing about the subject you know and love best—YOU. Now, I know that several of you have probably kept journals of one sort or another, maybe even for a class. But this is going to be different. This time you're going to use all of the techniques and principles that we'll be studying in English Literature to write a 'novel'." Kate paused and indicated quotation marks with her fingers. "This will be about a past you, a present you, or a future you. By the time that you're finished, you will have 150-200 pages of unified, creative expression that will count for one quarter of your grade each marking period."

Eve Calvert spoke above the murmuring of the class as they digested Kate's description. "What do you mean about the past, present, and future? Is the story supposed to be true?"

"Not necessarily. If you decide to write about you in the past, I want you to select a time in history that interests you. The Middle Ages, for example. Then write about Eve Calvert as she might have lived during that era. You'll need to do research and construct a plot and other characters, just as any writer of historical fiction would do. The difference is that the protagonist, the main character, will be as much like you as you can make her, including her physical, emotional, and psychological qualities. You can alter yourself slightly, but only in ways that would be possible and you can include real or fictional people as your other characters. You can fantasize all you want, and even end up in a romantic entanglement with, for example, an innkeeper who looks like Brad Pitt!" Everyone in the class laughed at the thought of shy Eve Calvert with a torrid romance, and Eve's cheeks turned crimson.

"O.K., Mrs. Hammond, that sounds like fun. What about the PRESENT YOU?" One of the boys in the back of the room spoke up, and Kate noticed that even Phaedra was beginning to look interested.

"Well, that's a little trickier in some ways and easier in others. You wouldn't have to do the kind of research that you would for historical fiction, but sometimes its harder to construct a strong plot from familiar surroundings. Again, the only character who has to be real is the protagonist, and the same rules apply about using real or imaginary supporting characters."

As the class digested Kate's explanation, Jean Pierro shyly raised his hand. "I would please like to know about FUTURE. Is this to be a science fiction?"

"Not necessarily, Jean Pierro. I've seen the FUTURE YOU done in many different ways. You can think ahead to what your own life could be like in, say, ten or fifteen years. Or, you could place yourself in a far-distant time and create a fantastic society, still keeping yourself as realistic as possible. The idea here is to decide whether you would probably be basically the same person, no matter when you lived. It's an important question to which there is no right answer. It's just a chance for you to do some serious thinking about human nature versus human nurture."Kate paused and looked around the room. Without exception, each student was involved in thinking about the possibilities, and Kate was relieved to see that both Eric and Phaedra had the same expressions on their faces that the other students displayed.

"I think it's going to be great!" Sophia's dark eyes sparkled with enthusiasm, and she rifled the pages of the notebook that Kate had passed out on the first day. "When can we start?"

"Anytime you want to. Before you actually begin to write, come and talk to me about your basic idea, because sometimes I can offer some suggestions that will make your work easier. I'll show you how to make character and story boards and how to keep track of your research. But for now, just do some brainstorming on some possibilities." Kate sat on the corner of her desk and looked around the class. "Right now, this sounds like a lot of fun to most of you. But I promise that there will be moments when you'll want to burn this notebook and hang me from the flagpole for the assignment. Just remember that the ups and downs that you'll be experiencing are the same that professional writers go through. Since we'll be studying some of the best writers in the world, it seems reasonable for you to walk in their shoes."

As Kate finished her few words of caution, the bell rang, and the students streamed out, talking among themselves. Jean Pierro hung back a bit and looked at Kate with a worried expression. "Do you think I can do this, Mrs. Hammond? My English is so little."

Kate chuckled. "Don't worry Jean Pierro, I'll help you. Luckily for both of us, I read and write Italian, so if you get stuck, you can work first in Italian and we'll translate into English. Gradually, you'll become as comfortable with English skills as you are with a soccer ball!" Kate grinned at Jean Pierro's obvious surprise that she knew about his athletic ability. "Your first assignment is to score plenty of goals tomorrow. Then you'll have lots to write about because you'll be a genuine hero around here."

Jean Pierro looked relieved and ran down the hall to his next class, while Kate grabbed her purse and headed for lunch. In the teacher's lounge, a few faculty members were seated at the round tables, and Kate almost collided with Susan Moore as she balanced a bowl of clam chowder while struggling to pour a cup of coffee. "Grab the cream, will you Kate?" Susan headed off across the room to a small table in the corner. Kate obligingly followed and realized that Julia's insistence on packing a lunch for her had saved a time-consuming trip through the cafeteria line.

Susan eyed Kate's roasted chicken salad with envy, but she dove into her own soup and sighed. "I never enjoy lunch as much as I do while I'm at school. Everything just seems in sharper focus when you're surrounded by flying hormones."

"I know, it's the strangest thing. Dealing with teenagers is kind of like being addicted to a drug. It nearly kills you while you're doing it, but you miss it like crazy when you're not around the little darlings. However, I am finding out that the older they are, the better I like them. Freshman girls and sophomore boys should be bottled and sold as chemical warfare, capable of destroying entire populations."

Susan's gray eyes twinkled as she endorsed Kate's assessment. "Do you believe in the myth of the 'junior summer?' Mr. Stamos told me that something miraculous happens, especially to boys, in the summer between their sophomore and junior years, and they come back to school as real human beings. Now that I think about it, he's got a point. I'm finding the upperclassmen in Studio Art to be terrific."

Before either Kate or Susan had a chance to finish their lunches, the bell rang, and they hastily gathered up their belongings and followed the rush of students from the cafeteria. "So much for getting acquainted, Kate. Let's try again tomorrow, shall we? I've got to run into the library to get some prints for my Art History class," Susan called as she disappeared through the broad double doors of what had formerly been the ballroom of Cyrus Lombard's mansion.

About five minutes before the end of school, Alex's voice came over the loudspeaker for the announcements that traditionally closed the day. The click of the intercom being turned on was the signal for students to begin to organize their departure, with the result that Sandra Monkton, who usually read the notices, was often drowned out in the loud shuffling of papers and banging of books.

Today, however, Alex's deep bass resonated throughout the building. "Don't forget, everybody, that the bonfire will begin promptly at 7:30 in the lower parking lot. The Boosters Club will be serving cider and doughnuts after the rally, and there will be a dance in the dining hall from 8:30 to 10:00 so that the soccer team can get home in time for 10:30 curfew. The game tomorrow starts at 1:00, so be there, wearing the green!" Alex's enthusiasm was contagious, and the freshmen in Kate's class grinned at each other in anticipation of their first high school social event.

****

The evening was very cool, but clear and brightly moonlit when Kate, Jessica, and Mildred arrived for the bonfire. From the crowds of people who were streaming down the hill toward the lower parking lot, it appeared that most of Cape Mariana had turned out to circle the large pile of wood that had been constructed during the afternoon. Two fire trucks stood by, and one of the local jazz bands, the Lazy River Boys, played lively music as students, teachers, parents, and other townspeople gathered together.

A few minutes after 7:30, Alex scrambled onto the back of a flatbed truck and spoke into a bullhorn. "Here they come, folks!

Show them your support." The town's third fire engine rolled down the hill toward the bonfire, which had now been touched off, and members of the soccer team, dressed in their varsity jackets, hung all over the vehicle, yelling loudly. As soon as the crowd caught sight of the team, it burst into applause and then broke into a lusty singing of the school song, led by the Lazy River Boys.

When the fire engine rolled to a stop, Alex introduced Carlo Brito, who grabbed the bullhorn and called off the names of his team, each one of whom ran around the fire and joined a line in front of the flatbed truck. At the mention of Jean Pierro Rossoni's name, there was polite applause from most of the gathering, and a stocky gentleman standing next to Kate stamped and whistled his approval of the young Italian. The final player to be presented was the captain, Chickie George. As the crowd roared its approval, the beaming young man, his eyes sparkling in the firelight, thanked all of the people for their support.

Jessica, riding on Kate's shoulders, seemed overcome with the excitement of the moment. Her eyes widened and she clutched her mother's head as she watched the boys circle the fire, whooping loudly and slapping each other on their rear-ends. When the crowd began to disperse and move toward the school for refreshments and the dance, Chickie stopped in front of Kate and Jessica and held up his arms to the little girl. Both Kate and Mildred were amazed when the child wrapped herself around Chickie's neck and giggled as the handsome athlete who was so obviously a hero whirled her around.

"Look out, Chickie," Kate yelled over the continuing noise of the rally, "you've got yourself a new girlfriend." The abject adoration in Jessica's normally expressionless face made even Mildred misty-eyed at Chickie's gallant kindness to the little girl.

"Well, Mrs. Hammond, it's not every day that a guy gets to meet such a beautiful young lady." Chickie smiled broadly at Jessica and set her gently on her feet. "Are you coming to the game tomorrow?" At Jessica's wordless nod, Chickie knelt down and gave her a high five. "Great! Wish us luck!" With Jessica looking dazed but delighted, Chickie bounded up the hill.

"What a nice kid." Kate smiled over Jessica's head at Mildred as they trudged after the crowd moving toward the school building.

Walking silently between the two women, Jessica suddenly yawned loudly and Mildred looked down in concern.

"Why don't I take this ladybug home and let Julia put her to bed? If you'd like to stay here for a while, I'll come back and pick you up later." By this time, Jessica was stumbling in fatigue, and Kate lifted her into her arms.

"No need, Mildred. I'll give Kate a ride home." Alex came up behind the women and smiled slightly at the sight of Jessica dozing against her mother. "I'd certainly appreciate some moral support at the dance, Kate. Not too many faculty members stayed, and the kids are all stirred up."

Watching Alex's powerful arms lay a soundly sleeping Jessica on the back seat of Mildred's car, Kate thought that he could probably handle any disturbance single-handedly, but she said goodbye to Mildred and hurried to keep up with his long strides as they walked back to the school. Sounds of loud rock music could be heard pounding over the excited voices and laughter of the several hundred students who were jammed into the dining hall. The floor of the building literally shook as the teenage bodies moved in obedience to the bandleader's command to "Twist and Shout." Although it was really difficult to determine which students were partners on the fast dances, as soon as the music slowed, the crowd sorted itself out into swaying couples, and Kate began to get a sense of the romantic configuration of the Rocky Shore High School population.

Chickie George and Phaedra Stamos were a tall, closely-entwined pair in the center of the floor, while in a dark corner, Kelly Lundgren was glued up against another soccer player. Kate noticed that Eve Calvert shook her head in response to Eric Lundgren's invitation to dance, as did Sophia Rossoni, eliciting an angry frown from Eric before he turned his attention to one of the starry-eyed freshmen standing clumped together near the door. During the lengthy song Phaedra kept caressing the back of Chickie's neck, and Kate was amused by his periodic attempts to disengage himself.

Alex followed Kate's eyes and watched his daughter's behavior with a frown. "Last spring, Phaedra and Chickie went together steadily for about four months, and it actually got pretty serious. Then, for some reason, Chickie broke it off. It looks like Phaedra is trying to recapture his attention."

As the last few notes of the slow ballad faded, some of the students began to drift out of the stifling heat of the dining hall into the cool night air outside the building. A few of the boys surreptitiously drank from cans and bottles they had in their pockets, but most of the crowd simply waited for the beginning of the next song.

"Usually we make them stay inside to cut down on the drinking, but it's so hot in there that I've changed the rules a bit and will hope for the best." Alex strode across the dance floor to speak to the other teachers who had agreed to chaperone, and Kate decided that she would retrieve a book that she had left in her classroom and needed for a lesson she was planning for Monday.

On her way up the stairs to the second floor, Kate said hello to Bob Wallace, better known as "Chief", who was responsible for keeping students from going up to the classrooms above. Chief Wallace was the Athletic Director and a highly respected and feared history teacher, famous for demanding that students rise immediately when called upon or suffer the consequences of standing in the back of the room for the rest of the period. In spite of the Chief's idiosyncrasies, including a legendary appreciation for the bodies of his female students, his classes were greatly sought after and produced top-quality history students who invariably received high scores on the Advanced Placement Examination.

As Kate passed him, the Chief was engaged in deep conversation with Susan Moore, and from the expression on his face, Kate doubted whether he had noticed anything or anyone else during the evening. The upstairs hall was dark and quiet, however, so Kate revised her opinion of the Chief's attention to duty, until she heard low voices coming from Carlo Brito's classroom next to hers.

"I told you, Jean, it's a tradition. Every new member of the team has to pass the initiation, or he can't play in the first game. Now choose, goddamn it. Pound, piss, or pussy." Kate recognized Eric's voice in the darkness, and she could hear several other deep murmurs and chuckles.

"But Eric, is hard for me, unless you explain what is each." Jean Pierro's voice quavered, and it was easy to tell from his tone that he was in this situation against his will.

"Listen, you little twerp. I'm tired of fooling around, but since we need you tomorrow, I'll spell them out for you. But then you had better choose fast. If you take 'pound,' you have to drink six beers in ten minutes. 'Piss' means that you have to take a leak in front of at least six people, including one girl, and 'pussy', which is my personal favorite, is that you dance with a girl of our choice and grab her pussy, or as they say in Italian, 'el cunto.'" Eric snickered at his own joke and Kate could hear Jean Pierro breathing hard as he wrestled with the problem.

Just then, the music started up down below, and Kate retraced her steps to the top of the staircase, where she found the light switch and illuminated the second floor. She walked purposefully past Carlo's classroom and into her own, making plenty of noise as she unlocked the door and turned on the lights. Next door, Kate could hear whispering and stealthy footsteps, but she ignored them until they faded away. When she looked out of her doorway, she saw that the entire floor was deserted.

Wondering how the boys had gotten past Chief Wallace, Kate found her book and returned to the lower floor, which was now vibrating. She looked for Alex to tell him what had happened upstairs, but she was interrupted by a loud scream from the center of the dance floor. As the crowd peeled away, it was soon evident that the shrieking was coming from Eve Calvert, who was surrounded by a circle of leering boys, led in laughter by Eric Lundgren. Standing miserably in the midst of the group was Jean Pierro, and it was very clear from Eve's hand spread protectively across her crotch which initiation had been chosen.

Before any of the teachers could react, the dancers on the floor closed ranks, and Eve and Jean Pierro disappeared from sight, only to reemerge almost immediately, Eve sniffling tearfully, and Jean Pierro stumbling behind, his face a bright red. Although Kate couldn't hear what he was saying, he was frantically attempting to apologize, while Eric and the other conspirators were doubled over in their enjoyment of his discomfort.

"Oh, shit!" Alex snorted in disgust. "I told those kids that there would be no more hazing or else. Goddamn that Eric. I'll bet he was behind this. And poor Eve, just getting used to public high school."

Kate's eyebrows rose in surprise that Alex knew so much about the initiation rites, but she decided to be quiet about having overheard the conversation upstairs, anxious instead to see what would happen next. Alex stalked over to where Eric and his friends were standing and motioned for them to follow him with an angry jerk of his head. When they all reached the nearly empty lobby outside the dining hall, Kate heard Alex growl at Eric.

"What did I tell you last spring Mr. Lundgren? I promised you that any more hazing would mean serious trouble. Who's responsible for this one?" By this time, Chickie had joined the group, along with Chief Wallace and Carlo Brito.

"Hey, Mr. Stamos, what's going on?" Chickie was clearly confused by Alex's anger, until he caught sight of the triumphant expression on Eric's face. As he looked around at the varying degrees of satisfaction and guilt present in the other boys' eyes, Chickie knew without being told what had just happened.

"You asshole!" he exploded at Eric. "I specifically told you to leave Jean Pierro alone. And I could break your neck for using someone like Eve for your lame stunt." Chickie turned to Alex. "I'm really sorry, Mr. Stamos. This was a shitty thing for them to do, but most of the team wasn't involved."

"Involved in what?" Eric's question was presented in such a sweetly innocent tone, that even Kate had to stifle a smile. Alex, however, was not in the least amused, especially when Susan Moore led a still weeping Eve out of the dining hall and into the principal's office. Jean Pierro shuffled out next, and Alex grabbed him by the arm before he could go anywhere.

"O.K. Jean Pierro, what was that all about?" Alex tightened his grip. "As if I didn't know."

Eric broke in before Jean Pierro could answer. "I'm telling you, Mr. Stamos, it was nothing at all. The kid probably stepped on Eve's foot or something. Maybe he's a rotten dancer." Eric looked steadily at Jean Pierro who was squirming in Alex's grasp. "That's right, isn't it, amigo?"

Jean Pierro nodded reluctantly and refused to meet Chickie's troubled gaze. "Yes, I am a very bad dancer, it is true. May I offer my apologies?"

"You'll be saying you're sorry from the sidelines!" Alex raged. "I don't really hold you completely responsible, Jean Pierro, but you should have known better."

Chief Wallace stepped forward and put his arm around Alex's shoulders. "Hey, take it easy, Alex. Let's give the kids the benefit of the doubt. You know how sheltered Eve Calvert is, with those crazy parents of hers, born again whatever-they-are. They think it's a sin for people to hold hands before marriage, let along do anything else. She probably overreacted. Now, how about we let Jean Pierro make amends with Eve and overlook the whole thing? These guys have a big game tomorrow and need to get home to bed."

Eric and his cronies nodded at Chief Wallace and then looked to Alex for his reaction. Only Chickie and Jean Pierro seemed upset by the incident, but they, too, looked relieved when Alex deferred to the Athletic Director's suggestion.

"All right, Chief. This is really your department, so I'll play it your way. But Eric," Alex suppressed an almost overwhelming urge to slap the victorious look from the boy's face. "If you ever pull anything like this again, I'll personally nail you to the wall. Do you understand?"

"Yes, Mr. Stamos, SIR." Eric spoke meekly, while his eyes gleamed with insolence. "Come on guys, let's blow this stupid dance." Trailed by his five henchmen, Eric swaggered out the front door and burst into loud laughter as soon as he was out of the building.

Chickie cleared his throat, while Jean Pierro stared at the ground. "Thanks, Mr. Stamos. Maybe Jean can apologize to Eve."

"I think that's a good idea," Alex agreed. He led the two boys into his office and beckoned for Susan Moore to leave the teenagers alone. "If anyone can straighten this out, Chickie can. Let's give him a shot. Meanwhile, I've got to think about what will happen if the Calverts find out about this."

Alex's concern about facing Eve's parents proved to be premature, since whatever Chickie and Jean Pierro said to the girl seemed to mollify her. After about fifteen minutes, the office door opened and Eve, pale but composed, came into the lobby, followed by the two boys, both of whom looked relieved. Sophia, waiting to drive

Eve home, glared at Jean Pierro but said nothing to her cousin as all four students walked toward the parking lot.

"Thank God that's over and so's this endless dance." Alex glanced at the towering grandfather clock behind Sandra Monkton's desk. When the gong struck ten, the music stopped, and flushed, tired students streamed out into the chilly night. Alex looked around the building quickly to make sure there were no stragglers and then signaled to Alf so that he could begin cleaning up.

After they had said goodnight to the other chaperones, Kate and Alex strolled toward his car, an old dark-green Jaguar, which was his pride and joy. As she settled into the smooth, tan leather seat, Kate felt the tensions of the day and evening evaporate while the motor hummed to life.

"Can I persuade you to join me for a bite to eat? My wife is in Boston for the weekend, and I'm starving." Alex paused at the end of the school driveway and waited for Kate's reply. "Have you ever been to Rossoni's? I know they'll be open because they have music on Friday and Saturday nights."

When Kate nodded, Alex swung his car toward Half-Moon Beach. Kate had been so well fed by Julia that she had eaten out only once since her arrival in Maine. Several times, Mildred had suggested that they go to Rossoni's, located about a mile down the road from Silvertree Farm, but each time something else had interfered, and Kate was delighted for the opportunity to visit the popular local spot and to meet Sophia's parents.

As he steered along the winding road that hugged the Cape Mariana shoreline, Alex fiddled with the car radio until lacy jazz filled the air. Kate glanced over at her companion, the planes of his strong face clearly visible in the moonlight, and in spite of his stern demeanor, she experienced a sense of ease, which had eluded her since Max's death. Feeling Kate's gaze, Alex stared hard at the road but was keenly aware of the fragrant presence of the graceful woman by his side.

Within minutes, the twinkling white lights which covered the trees in front of Rossoni's came into view, and Alex swung into a parking lot which was crowded with every kind of vehicle, including two trucks with "George Construction Company" emblazoned on the doors. "Looks like Big Ed and the boys are here." Alex commented. "That means that things could get very interesting."

Kate wondered what Alex meant, but her attention was diverted by the delicious aromas that greeted them as they entered the bustling, noisy restaurant. Large enough to hold about seventy customers at a time, Rossoni's was a beamed, low-ceilinged room with a fireplace at one end and a small stage at the other. Round tables covered with red-checked cloths and lighted with winking candles were filled with people dressed in everything from business suits to flannel shirts and heavy boots from nearby LL Bean.

"That's Big Ed George, Chickie's father." Alex whispered, indicating a large man with a flushed face who was sitting with a group of five other men at a round table near the bar. "He's quite a character and a really nice guy, unless he gets drinking, which it looks like he's been doing tonight!" The table at which Big Ed and his friends were sitting was covered with shot glasses and beer bottles, causing Alex to nudge Kate and say under his breath, "beware the boilermaker."

"Mr. Stamos! Welcome!" A short, plump woman with salt-and-pepper hair piled on her head bustled up and beamed as she surveyed the room for a desirable table. Kate recognized the same soft brown eyes that were so appealing in Sophia and decided that this must be her mother. Mrs. Rossoni clucked in disappointment that the only vacant table was next to Big Ed's party, but Alex said the table was fine, and soon he and Kate were studying the menu and ordering a bottle of chardonnay.

When Mrs. Rossoni returned with their wine, Alex introduced Sophia's mother, who enthusiastically clasped Kate's hand. "Oh, Mrs. Hammond, my daughter loves your class. She says she is going to write a novel about herself and she's thrilled. I told her that she'd better describe me thirty pounds lighter and a child bride, or I would make her sorry!" Mrs. Rossoni babbled on, but changed her expression quickly when a bottle shattered at the table behind her.

Both Kate and Alex jumped as brown glass flew everywhere. The men at the next table roared with laughter, but no one else in the restaurant found the situation amusing. Almost immediately, the stocky man who had applauded Jean Pierro so vigorously at the bonfire emerged from the kitchen, swathed in a voluminous white apron. He hurried over to the large table where Big Ed George and his employees sat making fun of the slight, unshaven man whose head had fallen into the large plate of spaghetti in front of him.

Arthur Rossoni beckoned to a busboy to clear the rest of the beer bottles and shot glasses from the cluttered table. "That's it, Ed," the proprietor wheezed. "You boys are shut off. Time to go home." A waitress materialized with a broom, quickly sweeping up the splintered glass, and Mrs. Rossoni hurried to remove the empty plates before there was any further breakage.

"Oh, come on Art. Me and the boys are just celebrating finishing up a big job. Grady there can't hold his liquor too well, but the rest of us are fine. We're sorry about the broken glass." Ed George smiled ingratiatingly at Arthur Rossoni, but it was his wife who answered, her hands planted firmly on her broad hips.

"Ed George, everyone else in here wants to have a quiet dinner and listen to some nice music. That young guitarist had to quit before because you people were being so loud, and it's time for him to play again. So you men are out of here, NOW." Maria Rossoni peered up at Ed George who had risen from his seat and was looming at least a foot above the furious little woman. Ed opened his mouth to speak, but changed his mind and yanked several bills from his wallet and threw them on the table. He jammed his Caterpillar Tractor cap on his thick, graying hair and stomped away, followed by his men, two of whom dragged the unfortunate Grady between them.

When the door closed behind Big Ed and his men, Arthur Rossoni spread his hands and shrugged his shoulders in a helpless gesture. "Sorry about that, folks. Now let's have a little peace and quiet in here and bring back a wonderful young musician for your listening pleasure. Here's Josh Temple!"

Kate and Alex looked around in surprise as Rocky Shore's student teacher walked to the small stage and began to tune his guitar. In the small spotlight that shone down from above, Josh looked relaxed and confident as he began to play softly. The conversation in the restaurant lowered in volume, but people continued to talk quietly as the delicate notes flowed from Josh's fingers. Any tension that had been in the room during the incident with Big Ed evaporated, and Rossoni's resumed the gracious ambiance for which it was so popular.

"Now this is more like it." Alex smiled at Kate over his drink. "To you and your success and happiness in Maine." Kate touched his glass with hers and felt her stomach warm slightly as she sipped the delicious wine. They ordered small salads and Arthur Rossoni's specialty, "Pollo Maria," a delectable baked breast of chicken rolled with proscuitto and asparagus and topped with a rich sauce of cream and boursin cheese.

By the time they finished fluted dishes of champagne sorbet and coffee, Alex pushed back his chair and groaned happily. Most of the other tables had emptied, and Josh was playing his last set of the evening, Alex signalled to Maria for the check, and when she came to the table, she was carrying a dusty bottle and two exquisite Waterford brandy snifters. "Before you go, Mr. Stamos, Arthur insists that you and Mrs. Hammond sample this special cognac. After all, no school tomorrow!" Maria bustled away with Alex's credit card and at Kate's nod, he poured two glasses of the liqueur.

"Do you mind staying a minute more? We were so busy eating that we scarcely had a chance to talk." Alex moved his chair around the table so that he was sitting next to Kate where they could chat while still enjoying Josh's music.

"Not at all, Alex!" Kate found that she felt somewhat awkward calling the principal by his first name, but she reminded herself that they were both adults and away from the school setting. "Since you know everything in the world about me, it's your turn to talk." Kate's aqua eyes were luminous in the candlelight, and Alex found that he had to concentrate hard to keep from staring at her full, soft lips. As she leaned toward him, the scent of Kate's perfume wafted by, increasing a growing attraction that Alex was experiencing in spite of himself, and he was nearly undone when their hands touched briefly as he handed her the cognac.

Alex frowned, trying to gather his thoughts. "Actually, it's not a very interesting story. I was born and brought up in Newton, Massachusetts, where my father had a fruit and vegetable business. I went to Newton North High School and played football and baseball. Did the same at Dartmouth. Then, would you believe that I was recruited by the Dallas Cowboys and played professional football for about a minute. My knee blew, and I spent the next year bumming around trying to figure what I wanted to be when I grew up."

"Finally, I took a job teaching history in a small boarding school and discovered that I loved working with kids. So, I went to Harvard and got my Masters in Education, met Claire, and got married."

"That was quick," Kate laughed. "Was your wife in one of your classes?"

"No, Claire was a second-year student at Harvard Law the year when I started. We hit it off right away, and before we knew it, she was pregnant and we were married. Phaedra, who's named after my mother, was born while Claire was in her third year, but we made it because we had moved out to Newton to live with my parents. My mother really raised Phaedra for the first few years."

Kate kept her face carefully expressionless when Alex mentioned his daughter, but she noticed that his features hardened slightly at the mention of both of the women in his life.

"Claire graduated and became associated with a firm in Portland, and I got a job teaching in Gorham. We lived in the city for a while, moved out to a farm in the country for several years when I became the principal of a regional high school near Lake Sebago, and then we relocated to Cape Mariana. At that point, I decided to go for my PhD., and because Claire's practice was so successful and I had inherited some money from my parents, I was able to afford to go to the University of New Hampshire. Just after I finished my dissertation, the man who had been principal of Rocky Shore died suddenly, and Mildred Worthington asked me to apply for the job. I've been there for eight years."

"Does Claire still practice law?"

"Yes. She's the number one choice among women in Portland who want to get a good divorce settlement. She's really tough." Alex's eyes were cold as he spoke, making Kate glad for the appearance of Josh Temple at their table.

"Hope you folks enjoyed yourself." Josh had packed up his guitar and stood ready to leave. "This is a great gig for me, since I'm far more at home on a stage than in a classroom. God, what a humbling experience. See you at the game."

"Almost forgot!" Alex stood up and shook hands with Arthur Rossoni after thanking him for the cognac. "Be sure to feed Jean Pierro well, Arthur. We're expecting great things from that kid." Alex winked at Kate, thinking of the events earlier in the evening, but they said nothing to the Rossonis, who waited by the front door of the restaurant.

On the way back to Silvertree Farm, Kate and Alex sat in companionable silence while the radio played softly and the full moon glistened brightly. At the entrance gates, Alex slowed the car and then surprised Kate by veering to the left of the house and following the bumpy, unpaved road that led to Morning Cove. When the Jaguar stopped at the edge of the cliff rimming the crescent-shaped beach, Alex turned off the engine, and they sat drinking in the spectacular view that the gleaming path of moonlight made across the frothy waves.

"How could anybody leave this? I have a sailboat that's moored near the school, but I come into this cove often because it's so peaceful." Alex seemed to be talking to himself, but he turned to Kate, whose profiled face was calm and thoughtful in the silvery glow. Gripping the steering wheel tightly, Alex appeared to struggle with some decision and then he exhaled quickly and started the car, backing slowly up the dirt path. "Bad idea," he muttered, looking over his shoulder as he maneuvered through the dark trees.

Kate felt very confused by the man sitting next to her. His jaw was hard and he was clearly troubled by his thoughts. Lulled by the pleasant evening they had shared, Kate suddenly experienced a sinking sensation in her stomach as if she had failed in some way and angered Alex. To her horror, tears began to spill from her eyes, and she covered her face, willing herself to control her emotions until she reached the safety of home. Instead, great wrenching sobs ripped at her body for the first time since Max's death, and she found herself unable to breathe as the grief she had suppressed for so long spewed out like a poison which had eaten away at her body and soul.

Alex stopped the car and stared at Kate helplessly, unsure of the source of his companion's pain. Finally, he gathered Kate's shaking body into his strong arms, murmuring unconnected phrases and patting her heaving back as she rid herself of the nightmare that had been her last year with Max. Finally, cleansed but shaken, Kate turned streaming eyes up toward Alex, who wiped her burning face with his handkerchief as he awkwardly smoothed back her hair.

"I'm sorry, Kate." Alex's voice was rough as he struggled to say the right thing. "I don't know what just happened here, but I hope I didn't do or say anything to upset you." Alex's face was hidden in the shadows as the moon passed behind the clouds, but Kate could hear the pain in his voice. When she didn't answer, Alex put the car in gear and drove up the road toward the distant lights of Silvertree Farm, achingly conscious of the silent woman beside him. At the house, he got out and opened Kate's door, holding her hand briefly as he helped her out of the car.

"Good night, Alex. Thanks for bringing me home," she whispered in a broken voice, cursing the tears that still welled in her eyes as she slipped into the dark back entry.

As he watched the door close behind her, Alex pounded the top of his car. Kate's perfume still filled his senses, as did the memory of her obvious distress. "Shit!" he muttered in frustration and drove away slowly into the night.

THE SHAPE OF DARK- Chapter Six

Opening her eyes on Saturday morning after a restless night's sleep, Kate was aware of a dull ache in her temples and a metallic taste in her mouth. Slowly, she pushed back the covers and sat on the side of her bed reluctantly reliving the last hour that she spent with Alex Stamos. Unpleasant warmth spread through her body as she remembered his discomfort at her tears and her inability to control her outburst.

Determined to shake herself free of the embarrassing memory, Kate padded across the room to the welcome sting of a hot shower and found that the pounding water relaxed the tension in her neck.

A crisp, cool breeze was blowing in her window overlooking the ocean, and as she pulled on jeans and a heathery-green cable-knit sweater, she could see the young man who cared for the grounds at Silvertree Farm guiding his tractor across the big field which led down to Morning Cove.

"Mama?" Jessica's soft voice outside of her bedroom door drew Kate across the floor and into the long hallway that ran the length of the spacious house. "Julia wants to know if you're going to eat breakfast. She's made blueberry pancakes."

Kate was pleased to see that Jessica looked relaxed and calm and that she even had some color in her cheeks as she took her mother's hand and led her down the stairs. Kate had been so concerned about Jessica's withdrawal and silence that a glimpse of her formerly ebullient daughter was enough to drive thoughts of the previous evening out of her mind.

Downstairs, the sun was streaming into the kitchen where Mildred and Tikka were chatting over their second cups of coffee. Kate slid Jessica into her chair and helped herself to a stack of pancakes from the buffet, delighting Julia, who expected Kate to request her usual spartan breakfast.

"My, my, Katie you've worked up an appetite all of a sudden." Mildred looked at Kate's heaping plate. "Did you have a nice time at the dance? I noticed it was quite late when you came in."

Kate flushed at the comment and felt her hunger disappear. She pushed the plate to one side, causing Tikka to lean across Jessica, sitting between them, and fix her hypnotic green eyes on Kate's pale

74

face. "One of our rules," Tikka declared in her rich, accented voice, "is that no detail can be spared concerning social activity, especially when that intriguing Alex Stamos is involved. So begin immediately."

Tikka sounded so serious that Kate almost laughed. "Sorry Tikka, there's nothing juicy to tell. We had a lovely late supper at Rossoni's and them came right home. We did hear a wonderful young guitarist, who happens to be a student teacher in my department, but other than that, the only drama in the evening was when Mrs. Rossoni kicked Big Ed George and his buddies out of the restaurant."

Both Tikka and Mildred looked very interested and demanded to know the details. After Kate explained what had taken place, Tikka shook her head. "Ever since Sheila George had to go into the nursing home, something has happened to Big Ed, especially when he starts drinking. The Rossonis were lucky that he went so peacefully last night. There was one time early last summer when he practically wrecked the Clam Bar in town."

"Who's Sheila?" Kate asked as she reached for the coffeepot.

"This is really a sad story." Mildred leaned forward on her forearms. "About five years ago, Sheila George, Chickie's mother, started to become very confused and absent-minded. She'd be driving somewhere and forget where she was going, and she'd call people by the wrong names. It got worse and worse until Doc Miller told Ed to take Sheila for a full neurological workup at Maine Med. It turned out that Sheila had Alzheimer's Disease at the age of 40. The neurologists said that it was one of the worst cases they had ever seen, and in only a year, Sheila was completely helpless. Ed hired someone to care for her when he and Chickie weren't home, but the woman wasn't very reliable and let Sheila get away one day. Somehow, Sheila found the car keys and drove into Portland, or at least almost into Portland. She lost control of the car on the Casco Bay Bridge and crashed into the concrete divider between the pedestrian walkway and the road. Luckily, nobody was hurt, but Big Ed realized that he couldn't keep Sheila home any longer. So, about three years ago, just when Chickie was going into his sophomore year at Rocky Shore, Ed put his wife into Thornton Oaks, and it's costing him a fortune."

Kate suddenly remembered the conversation she had overheard between Carlo Brito and Chickie about the boy's need for a scholarship, and his father's concern suddenly made more sense in light of the existence of Sheila. "How did Chickie deal with all of this? He seems like such a great kid."

"He is," Mildred sighed. "Sometimes I just want to take that child home and give him the love and support that he deserves, because he certainly doesn't seem to get it from Big Ed any more. Ed's so torn up about Sheila that he's lost perspective. But I know that he really cares about his son, and there isn't a more vocal parent at the soccer games. You'll see this afternoon."

"Yes, he is proud of Chickie's athletic ability, but Ed can get carried away if he's been drinking his lunch." Tikka frowned at Mildred. "Remember the regional baseball playoffs last year?" Mildred nodded and Tikka turned to Kate. "Rocky Shore was playing its big rival, Eastham. They were leading going into the first of the seventh inning, and they were only one out away from winning. Chickie came up to bat with runners on first and second and two out. He hadn't been hitting very well, so nobody thought he had a chance. But, he hit a homerun, putting Rocky Shore ahead by one run. Eric Lundgren hit next and flied out. Then, Eastham came up. The first man walked, the next two struck out, and the fourth man popped up to the pitcher. We went wild, thinking we'd won. But, the umpire ruled that our catcher, Eric, had interfered with the last batter, and let him take first base."

"It was terrible, because Eastham finally won. Our team was so demoralized, but they were gentlemen about it. The parents, on the other hand, were awful, especially Eric's father and Big Ed. He went after the umpire who made the interference call, and if it hadn't been for Chief Wallace and Alex, Ed probably would have really hurt the guy. They found out later that Ed had come to the game after having spent the early part of the afternoon with Sheila and the two hours before the game in a bar. Ed was arrested, and the umpire agreed to drop the assault charges only after Ed promised to stay away from baseball games in the future."

Kate frowned. "I hope nothing like that happens at the game today. Is Big Ed allowed to attend soccer matches?"

"So far. Since this is Chickie's senior year, I hope his father behaves himself, but you can never tell, especially since this Rossoni kid is playing in Chickie's old position." Tikka tapped the newspaper in front of her. "It says here that Jean Pierro is the hottest thing in shorts and that college scouts will be watching him carefully."

"Well, if we're all going to the game, we'd better get cracking." Mildred stood up from the table and consulted with Julia about the day's shopping list, which she then handed to Kate, knowing that one of the few things that Jessica seemed to enjoy doing was going to Dunham's. Tikka hurried off to Avesta, which was scheduled to open on Tuesday, and Mildred disappeared into her study for what she hoped would be a quiet morning's rewriting of her almost completed manuscript.

Dunham's was extremely busy when Kate and Jessica arrived, but Paul Dunham took the time to pick out a rosy apple from the pile he was constructing, handing it to Jessica with great ceremony. With her daughter munching in the seat of the shopping cart, Kate wheeled through the crowded aisles collecting Julia's supplies, and was so preoccupied that she jumped in surprise when a body stopped her progress.

"You're a menace on the roads, Madame!" Flustered, Kate was about to apologize for her clumsiness, when she looked up and saw the easy, lopsided grin of Josh Temple. "And who is this charming young lady?" Josh bowed formally to Jessica, who had streams of apple juice dripping from her chin. Josh produced a clean white handkerchief, and Kate mopped Jessica's face.

"What are you doing here, Josh? Don't the Rossonis feed you?" Kate knew that Josh was staying in a cheap motel nearby, but she assumed that a fringe benefit of his job at the restaurant would be good food.

"I'm just getting something for breakfast," Josh explained, stuffing two boxes of doughnuts under his arm. "Unfortunately, one meal a day doesn't do it for me, especially when I try to work out in the morning."

Josh pulled a box of animal crackers from the shelf and shared them with Jessica. "What keeps you busy besides school?"

Kate consulted Julia's list and opened the freezer containing ice cream and sherbet. "Actually, I share your love for music. I've played the piano forever. But mostly I spend time with Jessie and read a lot. In my youth, I was a dancer, but the old body refuses to cooperate, so I've given in gracefully and just walk and swim. That's one of the joys of living in Maine. There are so many beautiful places to go where there is plenty of air and space." They reached the checkout counter, and Kate began to unload her groceries.

Josh's face lit up at her mention of music. "Maybe you and I can play together sometime. I love doing classical duets for piano and guitar."

Kate felt her spirits lift considerably. "I'd really enjoy that, Josh. Imagine, a stuffy old schoolteacher in concert with a rock star!"

Bob Dunham was filling in for one of the checkout clerks, and he reached across the counter for the sticky apple core, which Jessica was still clutching. Bill squinted at the assortment of food that Kate had taken from her carriage. "You forgot your muffins, Mrs. Hammond. You must have been distracted!" Bob grinned at Josh, who was lounging against the candy rack. "You new in town?"

Kate introduced the two men and they shook hands across the cash register, while one of the students in Kate's freshman study hall bagged her groceries. Josh paid for the few items he had purchased and pushed Kate's cart out of the store into the cool September sunshine.

"Almost noon." Josh opened the trunk of the BMW and unloaded the brown paper bags from the wire carriage. "Are you going to the game?"

To Kate's surprise, Jessica spoke seriously to Josh. "Yes we are. My friend Chickie is playing." Josh chuckled at Jessica's answer as he lifted her from the shopping cart and put her on her feet.

"Well, you've got great taste in men, and it's going to be a terrific afternoon." Josh squatted down until his eyes were level with Jessica's. "Will you sit with me?"

Jessica nodded. "You're nice."

Josh's face softened. "You're nice, too, Jessie. I'll see you later." As he turned to get into his ancient Volkswagen, Josh's eyes met Kate's and she threw him a grateful smile. Josh winked and waved to Kate and Jessica as he guided his wheezing car out of the parking lot.

By the time Kate, Mildred, and Jessica arrived at the game, the Rocky Shore stands were almost full, and most of the students were sprawled on the grass of the natural amphitheater that surrounded the soccer field. Bunches of green and white balloons had been inflated with helium and attached to the light poles that were located at regular intervals around the field and used for the occasional night games during the season. The Lazy River Boys were once again present in their green and white striped blazers, and their bouncy ragtime music danced across the excited crowd as people made themselves comfortable for the game.

"Kate! Jessie!" Josh's rich baritone carried easily over the other voices, and he beckoned them to the seats he had saved in the top row of the spectator stands. Mildred chose to sit in the first row with Alistair Henry, so Kate and Jessica scrambled up and across dozens of warmly dressed people until they reached Josh's vantage point from which they had an excellent view of the game.

No sooner had Kate and Jessica settled into their seats, when a roar went up from the crowd, and the Rocky Shore High School soccer team came running down the hill, led by their captain. As the team ran around the perimeter of the field, the fans whistled and clapped, led, Kate noticed, by Big Ed, who was standing with a group of men along the sidelines. When the players took their places for the start of the game, Ed turned to the crowd and urged them to get on their feet in support of the team.

Even though she was unfamiliar with the finer points of soccer, Kate was immediately impressed with the skills of the Rocky Shore players. The Lake Richmond team seemed to be bigger, but they were unable to keep the ball away from the faster, more graceful boys in bright green and white. Before long, Jean Pierro blasted a shot past the confused Lake Richmond goalie, and Rocky Shore was leading.

Looking around at the crowd in the stands. Kate saw that Arthur Rossoni and Sophia were sitting together a few rows down, and they both jumped up in excitement when Jean Pierro scored his first goal. As the game progressed, the flashing legs of the Italian boy seemed to have a magical power over the white and black ball, and four more times in the first half, Lake Richmond defenders stood by helplessly as Jean Pierro skillfully guided the ball into the net.

With the score 5-0, the two teams went to separate ends of the field at half-time, and Kate and Josh, holding Jessica between them, climbed down to get something to drink at the refreshment stand. As they approached the line of people waiting to be served, Kate saw Alex leaving his position at the scoring table, and her heart tightened as he began to move across the field to where she and Jessica stood.

His progress was stopped, however, by Big Ed and Bill Lundgren, both of whom looked angry and frustrated.

From where she was standing, Kate could see that Ed's face was very red and that Bill Lundgren had the same threatening expression that Kate remembered from her classroom confrontation with him on Thursday. Alex stood calmly and listened to the two men, shaking his head firmly, and when Ed moved menacingly closer, Alex held up his hand in warning, causing the two infuriated fathers to turn on their heels and stalk away.

Alex rubbed his forehead and came over to Kate and Jessica. "It looks like the party didn't stop at Rossoni's, at least for Big Ed." Alex looked very grim, and he signaled to Chief Wallace, who was conferring with one of the referees. As the Athletic Director moved toward them, Alex explained what had just happened.

"Big Ed and that jerk Bill Lundgren are the 'spokesmen' for a group of parents who object to the fact that Carlo replaced Chickie with a 'dumb dago' as they put it so eloquently. The fact that Jean Pierro is scoring the pants off of the other team is unimportant compared to the fact that these parents are afraid that the college scouts will be blinded to anyone else but Jean. I guess that someone from Notre Dame told Chief Wallace that they were only interested in Chickie if he were in the front line. Now Ed is all bent out of shape and mad as hell at Carlo Brito. He says he has no loyalty to his old players, only to other foreigners. Anyway, Ed's been drinking, and Lundgren is nasty enough cold sober to make everyone's life miserable."

"What's up, Alex?" Chief Wallace came up beside the principal, his square, bulky body squeezing through a group of giggling junior high school girls.

"I want you to keep an eye on Big Ed, Chief. He smells like a brewery and he's spoiling for a fight with Carlo over changing Chickie's position. Did you tell him something about a Notre Dame scout losing interest in Chickie?

Chief Wallace looked uncomfortable. "Well, I figured that he had a right to know. Frankly, Alex, I questioned Carlo's decision, too. After all, Jean Pierro is only here for one year and Chickie's college tuition probably depends on his being recruited. But, Carlo's the boss, at least as far as soccer is concerned, and he was determined to start Jean Pierro. Between us, Chickie doesn't look so hot at sweeper, and Eric's playing a terrible game. He can't seem to get any rhythm at all with Jean Pierro. Luckily, we've got a one man scoring machine out there."

The strident blast of the warning horn signaled the resumption of play in one minute, and Alex jogged back to the scoring table, leaving Kate and Josh to make their way to the refreshment booth, where they each bought a cup of coffee and ordered some juice for Jessica. "Let's watch the rest of the game from down here," Kate suggested. "I think Jessie's getting a little antsy, and I can take her for a walk around the campus if she gets really bored."

Josh nodded, and they found a spot on the sloping grass and sat down. Big Ed and his group were directly below them, about halfway between the center of the field and the goal that Rocky Shore was defending, placing Ed nearly opposite to Chickie's originating position on the field.

"Goddamn it, Chick! Will you start hustling out there? You look like you're asleep!" Ed's booming voice could be heard clearly. Chickie looked pained at his father's words, but he stared down at the ground as the referee's shrill whistle split the air.

Jean Pierro acquired possession of the ball almost immediately, and he skated down the field, avoiding defenders with a swerving dexterity that was more dazzling than anything Rocky Shore fans had every seen. Lake Richmond players converged from everywhere, but no one seemed to be able to figure out which direction Jean Pierro would turn next.

"MAN ON!" Chickie's voice screamed as a burly Lake Richmond fullback barreled across the grass and hurled himself at Jean Pierro's legs. There was a sickening crunch, and Jean Pierro fell, screaming in agony. Two of the Rocky Shore players attacked the boy who had downed Jean Pierro, and almost immediately, both benches cleared and there was a full-blown brawl on the field.

The two coaches, their assistants, the referees, everyone at the scoring table, Chief Wallace, and three policemen were required to separate the angry players. Jean Pierro was rolling on the ground in agony, and Chickie knelt beside him, a terrified expression on his face at the odd angle of his teammate's leg. A portly man with a shock of white hair hurried onto the field, having struggled down from the top of the grandstand. As he bent over the stricken player, the sound of a siren could be heard in the distance.

Kate moved down the hill closer to the edge of the field, where she found herself standing behind Big Ed, Bill Lundgren, and two other men she didn't recognize. Ed spoke derisively to the father standing next to him. "There goes Doc Miller. Now the Rossoni kid is cooked for sure!" Ed's comment attracted disapproving stares, but he ignored the disgust of the parents who were concerned with the plight of the injured player, and continued to make disparaging remarks about Jean Pierro and anyone who was attempting to help him.

Within minutes, the Cape Mariana Rescue arrived, and three paramedics immobilized Jean Pierro's leg as much as possible before transferring him to the ambulance. Arthur Rossoni climbed in the back with his nephew, and the truck sped up the hill toward Portland.

After Jean Pierro was removed from the game, the referees, coaches, and captains set about the difficult task of restoring order to the game and assigning penalties. Following considerable debate as to whether or not the game could continue safely, the referees gave the Lake Richmond defender a red card for clipping Jean Pierro, and several other players on both sides, including Eric Lundgren, were given yellow cards for their unsportsmanlike behavior.

The tide of the game turned significantly without Jean Pierro, in spite of the fact that Carlo moved Chickie up to his old position and replaced him at sweeper with another senior who had played there before. The Rocky Shore team seemed to lose its concentration, and before long, Lake Richmond tied the score. In the last minute of the game, Rocky Shore missed three attempts to go ahead, including two corner shots taken by Chickie that were wide of their mark. Lake Richmond, on the other hand, rocketed a long pass down the sidelines with ten seconds left to play, and the Rocky Shore goalie slipped while attempting to block the shot, allowing Lake Richmond to win in the last three seconds of the game.

In the shocked silence that fell over the Rocky Shore fans, Lake Richmond's joyous cries of victory were particularly grating. Chickie and his teammates shuffled forlornly through the obligatory handshaking with their opponents, and then gathered around Carlo, who reassured them they had done their best.

Across the field, Big Ed George stamped around in disgust, muttering obscenities to anyone who would listen. Finally, as the crowd dispersed and the team moved up the hill toward the locker room, Ed grabbed Carlo as he went by and squeezed his arm roughly.

"Do you see what happens when you mix up a perfectly good team with one of your spic superstars? We should have beaten Lake Richmond easy, but you had to screw up the whole thing and all of our boys' college chances too. I ought to..." Ed's florid face was contorted into an ugly grimace, and he drew his fist back.

"DAD!" Chickie grabbed his father's raised arm and ducked as Ed aimed a clumsy punch at his son instead of Carlo. "Are you out of your mind?"

By this time, Alex and Chief Wallace had run over to where Ed was still grasping Carlo's shirt. "I'm warning you, Ed. One more display like this and you're barred from any athletic competition at this school! Now go home and sober up!" Alex's icy voice cut through Ed's rage and got his attention.

"I'll drive him home, Alex." Chief Wallace put his beefy hand on Ed's shoulder and urged him up the hill toward the parking lot. "Chickie, you bring your father's car home."

Chickie nodded and held out his hand to Carlo. "I'm really sorry, Coach. I told you my father was really messed up about this."

Carlo put his arm around Chickie's hunched, sweaty shoulders. "Relax, my friend. Your father's behavior has nothing to do with you, so don't worry about it. You played a very good game, and we just lost the luck. Now, let's go into the locker room. I want to call the hospital about Jean Pierro."

Chickie continued to look embarrassed. "Thanks, Coach. I'd like to go into Maine Med with you, if I can. I'd like to give my father a chance to cool down. Every time he goes to see my mother, he has a couple of drinks to calm his nerves, only he ends up flying off the handle at something."

Kate's heart went out to Chickie as he walked off toward the school building with Carlo, and she saw from the expression in Alex's and Josh's eyes that they were feeling the same kind of compassion. But before any of the adults could say anything, Jessica broke free of her mother's grasp and ran after Chickie and Carlo.

Wordlessly, the little girl took Chickie's muddy, sweaty hand and held it tightly. "I'm sorry your friend got hurt." Jessica piped up at Chickie, squinting in the late afternoon sun.

Chickie's face lightened up, and he tousled Jessica's hair. "Thanks, little buddy. See you at the next game?"

Jessica suddenly became shy and ran back to Kate, hiding her face in her mother's leg. Josh knelt down and touched Jessica's shoulder. "That was really nice, Jessie. Chickie was feeling bad and you made him better." Alex looked thoughtfully at Kate and seemed about to say something when the sound of his daughter's voice ripped across the field.

"Could you drag yourself away long enough to listen to my plans for the evening?" Phaedra was standing with a group of girls staring coldly at her father as he turned toward her.

"Duty calls." As Alex walked away, the venom in Phaedra's gaze shocked Kate. Determined not to flinch, Kate met the girl's stare until Phaedra dropped her eyes, making low-voiced comments to her friends until her father came within earshot.

"That is one mean girl." Josh commented.

As they walked toward the parking lot, Kate remembered the evening in the moonlight at Morning Cove, and although she tried to push her feelings aside, the image of Alex's face swam repeatedly into her consciousness, making her unable to concentrate on Josh's casual conversation.

That night at dinner, Kate tried to be subtle in her questioning of Mildred and Tikka about the Stamos family, but she was unable to fool them. "I don't blame you for being interested," Tikka bubbled. "Alex Stamos is absolutely gorgeous and doesn't deserve that witch he's married to. The trouble is that he's such a gentleman he won't leave her and the daughter from hell."

Mildred agreed. "For a long time there have been rumors about Claire having some kind of relationship in Boston, but Alex seems to ignore the whole thing. I saw her in the Meridian Hotel with a very distinguished looking older man, but she pretended not to recognize me."

Kate looked down at her plate and toyed with her salmon. "One thing I know is that Phaedra hates me with a vengeance for reasons that I can't figure out, unless it has something to do with her father being nice to me—in a professional sense, that is."

"Darling, just look at yourself in the mirror. By your very existence, you are a terrible threat to someone like Phaedra who may sense that her parents are on a rocky road." Tikka folded her napkin and pushed away from the table. "What do you think about our running over to Rossoni's for a little while after dinner to listen to that guitarist that you and the whole town are raving about?"

Kate was about to protest that she had to put Jessica to bed, when Mildred endorsed Tikka's suggestion. "I'd love to read my grandniece a bedtime story. You two go along and have some fun."

Kate gave in and soon she and Tikka were driving along Ocean Road past Half-Moon Beach where several cars were already parked in preparation for the evening's teenage social activity. Although it was illegal to drink in Maine under the age of 21, students in Cape Mariana consumed large quantities of beer, and it was a constant challenge for the teenagers to find a place where they could conduct their evening's entertainment without interference from the police. Half-Moon Beach, which was actually a succession of small coves, was one of the favorite party spots, and it appeared from the cars streaming into the parking lot that this was the location of choice for the evening.

Inside Rossoni's, Josh was tuning his guitar in preparation for his first set, while most of the tables were filled with the same wide variety of people that Kate had observed the night before. From his seat on the small stage, Josh smiled at Kate and Tikka, who were seated in a quiet corner nearby, where they ordered glasses of wine and waited for the music to begin.

"Nice to see you, ladies." Alex's deep voice startled Kate as he approached their table. "Would you allow a lonesome man to join you?"

Before Kate could say anything, Tikka quickly pulled a chair between them and winked flirtatiously at Alex. "Nothing would give us greater pleasure, would it Kate?"

Very conscious of Alex's presence next to her, Kate murmured her agreement, but did not meet his eyes. Luckily, the first rippling notes of music filled the silence, eliminating the need for conversation, and while Alex signaled for a beer, the three of them settled down to enjoy Josh's skill.

"IS THERE A DOCTOR IN HERE?" Before Josh had completed even one song, the door to Rossoni's was flung open and a frightened-looking teenager stood on the threshold, peering anxiously around the crowded restaurant. When he spied Alex across the room, the boy, who Kate recognized as one of the soccer players, raced over and clutched the principal's arm.

"You've got to help us, Mr. Stamos! Something awful has happened to Kelly, and we don't know what to do."

Without a word, Alex flew out of his seat and ran for the door, followed by the distraught boy, Kate, and Tikka. Within a few minutes, the four of them reached the far edge of Half-Moon Beach, where a group of people milled around a body on the wet sand. Kelly Lundgren was convulsed into a tight ball, whimpering with her eyes closed and her breathing labored.

"Kelly! Can you hear me?" Alex touched Kelly's cheek, and her hands flew up to her face as if to protect herself. "Kelly," he repeated, "it's Mr. Stamos and everything is going to be all right." Alex looked up at the white faces of Kelly's companions. "Do any of you know what's going on here?"

Most of the group shook their heads, but one boy finally spoke up in a trembling voice. "About an hour ago, we had just built a fire at the second cove over, and people were beginning to arrive. Phaedra and Eric left to get some more, uh, soda, and the rest of us spread out to look for wood for the fire. Kelly went off behind one of the dunes because she said she had to go to the bathroom."

"We all came back within about ten minutes, but Kelly didn't, so after about a half an hour, we went searching for her. It was dark, so it was hard to see anything and no one had a flashlight. Finally, someone yelled for us to come back into the woods where there's an old storage shed. Kelly was inside, crouching on the floor and making funny noises like she's doing now. She didn't seem to be able to get up off of the floor, so we carried her back to the fire. She was shivering and whining, but she wouldn't tell us what happened."

"We told her we were going to take her home, and she began screaming and begging us not to tell her parents. Since we didn't know what she was talking about, and she began to get hysterical, we thought we'd better get some help."

Alex had knelt by Kelly's side while the boy was speaking, and he beckoned to Kate and Tikka, while motioning the group to move back so they could have more light. "Kate, look!" Alex pointed to the front of Kelly's light blue jeans, where a dark stain was spreading down the legs from her crotch area.

Kate leaned over Kelly and whispered in her ear. "Kelly, do you have your period?" Kelly shook her head and lowered her hands protectively to where the blood was flowing more profusely. Kate glanced up at Alex in alarm. "I think we'd better call an ambulance right away!"

The same rescue team that had transported Jean Pierro in the afternoon arrived within minutes, exactly at the same time that Eric and Phaedra careened around the end of River Road in Eric's battered Jeep. Eric insisted on riding in the ambulance with his sister, who was now nearly unconscious and losing blood fast. Phaedra rode with her father, and Kate and Tikka followed after they made several attempts to contact the Lundgrens who, according to Eric, were having dinner at Antonio's Barge on the Portland waterfront.

While the ambulance screamed its way toward the hospital at speeds that Alex couldn't begin to approach, Phaedra huddled in the passenger seat, refusing to answer any of her father's questions about the evening. It wasn't until the bright circle of lights around the Emergency Entrance to Maine Medical Center came into view that Phaedra spoke up angrily. "What the hell was that woman doing with you at Rossoni's?"

Alex was so stunned by Phaedra's hostility that he didn't have time to answer before his daughter bolted from the car and ran into the Emergency Room. Kelly had been rushed into one of the Trauma Units, and a team of doctors and nurses was frantically trying to determine the cause of the heavy bleeding that had soaked her jeans completely. When they removed Kelly's upper garments, there were scrapes and abrasions on her upper arms, breasts, and back. The trauma team quickly reached the conclusion that Kelly had been the victim of a vicious attack and probably raped.

Although Kelly regained consciousness right after she arrived at the hospital, she was incoherent and unable to answer any of the doctors' questions about what had taken place. As soon as her vital signs were stabilized, Kelly was taken to surgery, where a D&C controlled the internal damage that had caused the profuse bleeding. The procedure was able to be performed speedily, since Eric was old enough to authorize emergency medical treatment for his sister, when the Lundgrens could not be found at Antonio's Barge.

It wasn't until Kelly's parents returned home a little after midnight that they learned of their daughter's situation. Alex had left an urgent message on their answering machine, and frantic with worry, they drove quickly back into Portland and got to the hospital just as Kelly was being transferred from Recovery to a room on the ninth floor.

In spite of her previous unpleasant experience with the Lundgrens, Kate felt a great deal of sympathy for their obvious state of shock in learning that their daughter had been attacked. Kelly's cervix and vagina had been severely torn, and her uterus had suffered some damage, causing the violent hemorrhaging. Kelly's face had been spared the brutality that the other parts of her body had suffered. Kate watched Mona Lundgren's eyes fill with tears while the surgeon described the nature of Kelly's wounds, and Bill Lundgren's face was so mottled and contorted with rage that he had trouble breathing and had to sit down to regain his composure.

"I think I can promise you that Kelly is out of any kind of danger," the surgeon assured the Lundgrens. "She has clearly had a terrible shock, but her condition has stabilized and the bleeding is definitely under control. The police will want to question her in the morning, but right now she needs rest. You may see her for a moment, if you wish."

Everyone was clustered outside the private room in which Kelly had been placed, and the Lundgrens moved through the door to the bed where their daughter was a small, pale form in the pool of light cast by the bedside lamp. As Mona gently kissed Kelly's forehead, Bill took her hand and leaned over her.

"Tell us who did this to you, darling," Bill whispered in a strangled voice. "So help me, I'll kill the son of a bitch."

Kelly opened her eyes and looked up at her father. "It was so dark—I'm not absolutely sure, but I'm almost positive. I think it was that creepy janitor at school, Alf Stanton."

THE SHAPE OF DARK- Chapter Seven

After only a few hours of sleep, Alex found himself sitting in the Cumberland Country Jail across the table from a fidgeting Alf Stanton. "I swear, Mr. Stamos, I had nothing to do with hurting that little Lundgren girl." Alf's greasy black hair hung over his bloodshot eyes, and he pushed it back impatiently with his hand, which, Alex noticed, was covered with small scratches. "When the police came to my room last night, I couldn't believe they wanted to arrest me for raping someone. I wouldn't do that!"

Alex pushed away from the worn table where he and Alf had been told to sit, and he looked at the nervous custodian. "Listen, Alf, I want to believe you, but you must admit that things aren't looking good, especially since they found that picture on the wall down in your storeroom."

Alf banged his fist on the table. "I explained that over and over, but the cops wouldn't listen. I had pictures of all four classes up on my wall, and one day when Kelly came down to get a box of folders, she circled her face in the junior class picture and told me to remember her when she was rich and famous. Other than that, I never spoke two words to the girl, and I certainly didn't hurt her the way they say I did."

"Where were you last night, Alf?"

"I was at the school until about six o'clock. There was a mess after the game, and me and Lenny had a big job to clean it up. Then, Lenny told me to go home, said he'd finish during the evening shift. I picked up some beer and went back to my room where I stayed all night." Alf's eyes shifted back and forth from Alex to the wall above his head as he offered his alibi.

"Did your landlady see you or talk to you at all?"

"No, my entrance is at the back of her house, and unless she was looking out the window as usual, she didn't know when I came home. The police are going to question her today. With my luck, that 'I know everything you do' old biddy will have been minding her own business, for once."

Alex stood up and paced around the small interrogation room, troubled by the fact that he couldn't really tell if Alf was being truthful. Two years before, Alex had hired Alf when he had been released from Thomaston State Prison after serving time for a crime of which he was innocent. Mildly mentally retarded, Alf had been working in a pizza parlor in Bangor when one of his fellow workers, a sixteen-year-old girl, had accused him of raping her. After Alf had been convicted and had been in Thomaston for three years, the girl confided to one of her friends that she had lied to protect her own boyfriend. Luckily for Alf, his accuser felt so guilty that she went to the police and recanted her story, paving the way for Alf's release.

When Mildred Worthington read about the situation in the Portland paper, she decided to interview Alf as a possible character in her forthcoming mystery novel. Mildred found herself troubled by the fact that Alf had been unable to get a job since he had gotten out of prison, in spite of the fact that he had been acquitted of the rape charges. As Chairman of the Board of Trustees for Rocky Shore High School, Mildred convinced Alex to hire Alf for his custodial staff, and Alex had never been sorry, finding Alf to be the most conscientious worker he had ever had. Now, Alex wondered what Alf was really like.

"Well, Alf, I'll tell you this. Bill Lundgren is so bound and determined to hang you that it will be difficult to get a judge to set bail. This story is already on TV and will certainly be in the newspaper tomorrow, so it looks like you'll be sitting in the Cumberland County jail for awhile. I've called the school's attorney and asked him to represent you, but I'm not even sure if that will work. Meanwhile, I'm going to go out to that shack at Half-Moon Beach and see if I can find anything out. The police are there this morning, and at least I'll see what they've dug up."

Alex paused and put his hand on Alf's slumping shoulder. "Hang in there, Alf. If you didn't have anything to do with this, something will turn up to tell us who did!"

Alf rose slowly to his feet and held out his hand. "Thanks, Mr. Stamos. You've always treated me real nice, and I trust you." Alex opened the door and the uniformed officer outside led Alf down the long, dank corridor toward the holding cells.

On the way home, Alex kept sifting through the events of last evening, trying to get a clearer picture of the players in the strange situation. When Kelly mentioned Alf Stanton's name, Bill Lundgren rushed into the dark hospital corridor and startled the sleeping patients and busy night nurses by shouting for someone to call the police. Only the arrival of the hospital security personnel had been able to quiet the enraged man, and they had quickly escorted him back into Kelly's room where he placed a call to the Cape Mariana authorities, demanding that they arrest Alf Stanton.

By 4 a.m., Alf had been taken into custody and Alex collapsed onto his bed. Phaedra had been just as sullen on their return to Cape Mariana, so Alex decided to wait until later to question his daughter about her opinion of the whole episode.

When he got to Half-Moon Beach, Alex found that Cape Mariana Police Captain James Brogan had finished examining the site of the rape and was climbing into his car. Two other officers were carrying boxes of various items they had picked up in and around the storage shack where Kelly had been attacked, and they placed the evidence in the trunk of their cruiser and drove off toward the police station in the center of town.

Jim Brogan, recognizing Alex, got back out of his car and leaned against the door, waiting for the high school principal to join him. "Morning, Alex. I imagine you'd like to know what we found." Jim held out his hand and gripped Alex's firmly. The two men had known each other since Alex had come to Cape Mariana, and they each had deep respect for the other's abilities. As the father of two grown children who had graduated from Rocky Shore High School and a daughter who would soon be a freshman, Jim continued to take an interest in the activities of the town's teenagers.

"I just came from seeing Alf, Jim, and we'd BOTH be interested in your investigation. Alf swears he was home alone all night and that Kelly herself marked that picture on his wall."

"Well, as far as I can see, there's nothing dramatic, one way or another. There are signs of struggle in the shack, but otherwise, all we found were some old beer cans. It looks like the kids have partied in there, probably when it rains. The one thing I can't understand, though, is why the other people didn't hear the attack, especially if Kelly got off a scream or two. The shack is quite close to where the fire was last night, and unless the assailant gagged Kelly in some way, it's pretty likely that she would have made some noise."

"Hey, Jim, you know how those kids are. They probably had music going and were being pretty loud themselves."

"Maybe, but the old lady who lives in that house at the end of the beach and usually calls us when the kids party in the second cove over, said that she saw the fire but didn't notify the police because the kids were so quiet last night."

"Do you mind if I take a walk out there and look around?" Alex knew that the police had probably yellow-taped the shack, and he didn't want to disturb anything.

"Sure, go ahead. I've got some time. Maybe we overlooked something."

Alex and Jim walked through the dune grass to where the remains of last night's fire blackened the sand. After peering into the shack, which had been cordoned off, the two men circled the building slowly, working their way away from the beach toward the woods behind the small weathered building.

About twenty feet from the shack, Alex's foot struck the tip of an object, which was submerged in the sandy soil and covered by a loose pile of leaves. Hastily pulling on latex gloves, Jim brushed aside the gooey layer of vegetation. Grasping what appeared to be the thick knobby top of a stick, he twisted the cylinder, about ten inches long, from the dirt where it had been plunged in vertically. Alex could see that it was a small baseball bat on which was written "The Little Hitter." From the gouges and overall wear on the bat, it was obviously old, and there was a jagged cut in the top of the bat.

As Alex looked more closely at the object in Jim's hand, he could see there was a reddish brown stain in the splintered slit, and he was almost certain that it was dried blood. Frowning in concentration, Jim slipped the object into a plastic bag and walked toward his car. At the entrance to the beach parking lot the two men talked for a moment and then separated, Jim heading into town along Rte 11 and Alex turning left onto the River Road.

When Alex arrived home, the living room was deserted, but the two Sunday newspapers were scattered all over the floor. As Alex began to search for the sports page, his daughter appeared in the doorway, drying her hands on a dishtowel.

"Did you see Alf?" As usual, Phaedra's chin was lifted defiantly, and even the most innocuous comment sounded belligerent. "How is the filthy pervert?"

"Hold on a minute." Alex held his hand up. "Kelly wasn't certain that she was attacked by Alf, and it was only after her father badgered her that she was willing to press charges. What makes you so sure Alf is guilty?"

"Oh, I have lots of reasons for thinking it was Alf. You have no idea what a lech that man is. He's always staring at the girls out at gym, and I swear he has a peephole between his storeroom in the basement and the girls' locker room. Some of the girls think it's funny and purposely do stuff to attract his attention, but I think he's repulsive!" Phaedra plopped down on the sofa and took the comics from the pile of newspapers on the floor.

"Why didn't you say something before this, Phaedra? I need to be made aware of things like that. Now, have you got anything else that you think I ought to know about?" Alex sat down in one of the wing chairs by the fireplace and focused his attention on his daughter.

"Well, you probably don't want to hear it, but a lot of kids are talking about Mrs. Hammond and all of the funny things that have been going on with her, like Eric getting locked in that closet. She's been coming on to Chickie like crazy, and she LOVES to talk about sex and stuff in her classes. I think she has the hots for anything in pants!" Phaedra stared at her father, who flushed in anger but didn't answer immediately.

Finally, Alex controlled himself and responded. "Oh, I imagine you girls are just envious because Kate Hammond is such an attractive woman. What man in his right mind wouldn't admire her?"

Alex stifled a smile as Phaedra's eyes blazed. "You haven't really seen her in action. The first day of school she was all over Chickie, who was her Green Shield aid. Just because he did some nice things for her, she's been flirting with him ever since."

"Don't worry, Phaedra, I think the male population at Rocky Shore will survive the seductive wiles of Mrs. Hammond. The question is, will you?" Perversely, Alex knew he was infuriating his daughter, but he was annoyed with Phaedra and felt oddly protective of Kate.

Phaedra threw down the comics and flounced out of the room, glaring back over her shoulder. "Just don't forget that I warned you, ALEX!" As soon as Phaedra's door slammed, rattling the walls of the whole house, Alex was sorry that he'd baited his daughter and resolved to be more careful in the future.

Before he was able to finish the front page of *The Boston Globe*, the telephone rang and within seconds, Phaedra was leaning over the stairs. "It's for you. Your favorite person, I believe." The disgust on Phaedra's face was very clear, and she purposely didn't move as Alex picked up the phone.

"Alex, I'm sorry to bother you at home, but I was anxious to know if you had heard any news about Kelly." Kate's soft voice made Alex's pulse quicken, but he kept his tone steady and businesslike as he replied.

"Nothing more to report this morning. Kelly is resting comfortably, and Alf is in jail, absolutely insisting that he is innocent." Alex heard Phaedra snort at his last words while finally retreating to her room.

"Oh, well, that's what I really wanted to know." Alex's cool tone was very obvious, and all Kate wanted to do was hang up. "I'll see you in the morning."

"Yes—" Alex's words were cut off by a click on Kate's end of the line. "Damn!" He fumed as he glared at the spot where Phaedra had stood listening.

****

The news of what had happened to Kelly was all over Cape Mariana by Monday morning, making the telephone in Alex's office ring continuously as concerned parents called to complain about the fact that an ex-convict had been hired to work in the school. Alex grew so tired of repeating Alf's story that he finally instructed Marta Stone to take messages and he went looking for a friendly face in the teacher's lounge.

Alex had just poured himself a cup of coffee and sat down at one of the round tables to read the morning newspaper, when the bell ended the first period of the day and the lobby filled with students hurrying to their next class. As was his custom, Alex left his coffee on the table and moved into the center of the school's foyer. He knew nearly every student's name, and he commiserated with several of the soccer players about their disappointing but valiant effort in the game on Saturday.

"Mr. Stamos, could we talk to you for a minute?" Sophia Rossoni and Eve Calvert crossed the lobby to where Alex was standing and handed him a folder. "Would you mind looking this over when you have time?" Sophia seemed to be the spokesperson for the pair, but Eve's shy smile gave her moral support.

"What's this, girls?" Alex was particularly fond of Sophia and was glad that she seemed to have taken Eve under her wing.

"We're taking an Honors Civics course, and each person has to come up with a proposal to help in some community activity. We're supposed to get your approval before we begin, since Mr. Wallace wants to make sure the school is aware of the fact that kids are out in the community, sometimes during school hours. Eve and I would like to volunteer at Thornton Oaks, and we've already called them and talked about some ideas. We want to each adopt a resident and work with them about ten hours a week, depending on what would help the most."

Alex flipped through the neatly typed proposal and scribbled his signature at the bottom of the last page. "I think it sounds like a great idea and I'm all for it. I wish more kids would do things like this." Alex beamed at the two students and watched them hurry away as the bell echoed through the lobby.

When all of the students had found their ways to classrooms, Alex returned to the teachers' lounge to finish his coffee, now luke-warm. Kate and Josh came into the room almost immediately after he had resumed his seat, and he signaled them to join him. After they had sat down, Kate and Josh exchanged amused glances. "What do you think, Kate?"

Kate gave Alex a long, hard stare. "Pure horse. Although there might be a glimmer of muffin around the edges."

Josh nodded seriously, studying Alex. "I think you're right. There isn't an ounce of sparrow anywhere!"

Alex looked from one person to another in complete confusion. "What the hell are you two talking about?"

Kate burst into laughter and pointed to Josh. "This man is now convinced I'm stark raving mad, and so is one of my junior classes. I'm beginning a unit of poetry and I asked them what a metaphor was.

95

Somebody gave a textbook definition, but I would have bet my soul nobody really understood the concept, so I asked them if they wanted to play a game. Well, of course, you mention the word 'game' to any high school kid and you're golden."

Kate's eyes sparkled as she recounted her instructions to the class. "Let's pretend anyone in the world can be described in terms of three qualities—muffin, horse, and sparrow. Now be sure you understand that it's not *A* muffin, but just muffin. Look at the person sitting next to you and decide if you think he or she is pure muffin, pure horse, or pure sparrow. If you think there is a combination of qualities in that person, then describe those. Like mostly muffin with some sparrow. Or largely horse with some sparrow. Get it?"

Josh broke in. "Of course nobody really understood it, but Kate was relentless. She made the kids choose names from a hat and then write how that person fell into the three categories. She collected the slips of paper and read the descriptions, asking the class to guess which person was being categorized. It was incredible how often the class guessed the right name."

"Then the students asked me what I thought about Josh, and you, and Chief Wallace, and even poor old Alf. We all argued about everybody, but I think that they got into the idea of describing one thing in terms of another." Kate leaned back in her chair. "Instant metaphor-making."

"The kids had a great time." Josh looked at Kate with such obvious admiration that Alex felt a twinge of resentment. "You really have a way with teenagers, and the whole idea of getting around to figurative language like that was brilliant. I can't wait to see what you're going to do next."

Kate blushed self-consciously. "Maybe you can come up with a suggestion for me. It won't be long before you're in front of a class yourself!"

"Well, it sounds like you two had some fun. Alex stood up as Susan Moore approached their table. "Fill Susan in on your fascinating experience while I go and see if I can talk the school attorney into representing Alf." Alex took his coffee mug with him and hurried across the lobby.

In a few minutes Kate pushed herself away from the table. "I must run, too. A few seniors are coming in to talk about their writing projects, so I need to get back upstairs."

As she climbed the stairs to the second floor, Kate found herself thinking about the painful moments at the end of her Friday evening with Alex and she colored with embarrassment at her loss of control. Preoccupied with her daydreaming, Kate tried to open her classroom door, and then remembered she had locked it before going downstairs, following Alex's advice to be cautious after last week's incidents.

As she turned the key in the lock, Kate thought she heard movement inside, but the room was empty and dark as she laid her purse on her desk. The pleasant weather of the weekend had given way to a blustery, gray day with rain threatening at any moment, and Kate was glad to be indoors as she walked back to switch on the lights.

CUNT! Kate froze as the sudden illumination made the garish red letters on the blackboard dance crazily in front of her eyes. Thick strokes of crimson formed letters that were at least four feet tall, almost filling the area of the large green square on the front wall. The writing had been done hastily, because paint dripped on the floor from the bottom of the letters, but the angry intention of the message was perfectly clear, if somewhat messy.

Kate went to the door of Carlo Brito's classroom and looked in. To her relief, there was a study hall fidgeting under Carlo's watchful eye, and he rose quickly and came into the hall when he saw Kate's pale, stricken face. "Carlo, did you hear anything in my room a couple of minutes ago?" Kate pointed through her open door, and Carlo could see the word that was spread obscenely across the front wall.

Carlo shook his head and took Kate's cold hand in his. "You sit at my desk for a minute and I'll go get Alex." Carlo watched as Kate disappeared into his study hall and then ran down the stairs two at a time to the principal's office.

Alex was just coming out of his door with a round, balding man carrying a briefcase. "I'm sorry you feel that way, but I understand." Carlo waited impatiently for Alex to complete his conversation and then whispered what had happened in Kate's classroom.

When the two men got to the second floor, they discovered that several students, juniors and seniors who were not compelled to attend study hall, had seen the vulgarity on Kate's wall and were talking excitedly in the corridor, attracting the attention of anyone who passed by. Kate felt a sense of deep relief when Alex appeared in the hallway and dispersed the congregating students, one of whom was his own daughter.

"Get out of here," he growled. "You know that this floor is off-limits on frees."

"What did I tell you?" Phaedra smirked. "She probably paid someone to write this so that she could call a little more attention to her favorite body part!" Everyone standing around Phaedra gasped at her audacity and Alex's face darkened at his daughter's triumphant expression. Barely controlling his temper, Alex said that he would talk to her later, and as he watched the small group of students saunter away, he found that his fists were rolled into tight balls.

"Sometimes I really don't understand what makes that girl say the things she does! But right now I have to deal with this mess! Go and relieve Kate, will you? She must be nearly hysterical."

When Kate walked out of Carlo's room, her knees were shaking and she felt her eyes burn from the unshed tears which she was so rigidly controlling. "Why would anyone do this? HOW was it possible? The door was locked."

"Let's not worry about those things right now. You have some choices to make. We won't be able to remove this paint until later, but we can cover up the board with construction paper or one of those big maps that Chief Wallace has downstairs. Or, you can just leave it up there and let the kids see what kind of harassment is going on. I have the feeling you'll get a lot of sympathy from most of the students, and we might even get some information as to who is doing this stuff to you. What do you say?" Alex put his hands on Kate's shoulders and turned her toward the window so the dim light from outside fell on her face. With a gentle touch, Alex brushed away the lone tear that had disobeyed Kate's steely resolve, and he looked steadily into her pained but still luminous eyes.

In spite of her anguish, Kate felt herself relax in the warmth of Alex's obvious concern, and she nodded slowly. "My seniors come in next, and maybe I can use this—this—thing to teach them something. Anyway, I can't run away from the fact that someone's determined to drive me out of Rocky Shore."

"Not if I have anything to say about it. Now, let me just look around a little while you go to the ladies' room and pull yourself together." Alex pushed Kate gently in the direction of the corridor, and he moved carefully up the center aisle of the neatly arranged desks, noticing that there were a few tiny spots of red on the floor near the back of the room where Eric had been trapped in the storage closet. Alex tried that door and found it locked, but he reminded himself to ask Kate to open it when she returned from the restroom.

By the time Kate reappeared, however, the period had ended and her senior students were filing into the room, visibly surprised by the lewd message on the front board. Alex asked Kate if she wanted him to stay, but she shook her head and he slipped out, noting with admiration that Kate stood by the door, smiling at the entering students and not commenting about the vulgarity in front of them.

When Eric Lundgren arrived and collapsed into a seat in the back corner of the room, Kate walked over to him and inquired quietly about Kelly's condition. He seemed somewhat surprised by her concern, but described the fact that Kelly would be home in a day or two and back to school in a week. "She's really bummin', Mrs. Hammond," Eric commented, "and my father doesn't help things much. I wish he'd leave Kelly alone. He's just making her more upset by talking about that Alf guy all the time."

"Has anyone from the Rape Crisis Center been to see Kelly?

"Are you kidding?" Eric scoffed. "My parents wouldn't let anyone like that anywhere near Kelly. All those shrinks are alike."

Before Kate could respond, the bell rang and she walked toward the front of the room. With the tall red letters emblazoned behind her head, Kate turned to the class, all of whom were sitting expectantly, waiting to see what she would say. As she scanned their faces, Kate could see that a few of the students, including Eric and Phaedra, looked delighted with the unexpected turn of events, but most of the young people in front of her had expressions of concern and sympathy.

"Eric, what is the definition of the word behind me?"

The entire class wheeled around to face Eric, whose feet had hit the ground with a loud thump. As Kate waited for his answer, the room was absolutely soundless as his obvious embarrassment grew and he struggled to respond. "Why do you ask me? Anyway, what kind of a question is that?" Eric's squirming would have been amusing, had Kate's expression been less serious.

"It's a perfectly legitimate question, and I think you know the answer." Kate willed herself to outlast Eric, while Sophia and Eve looked uncomfortable.

"Uh, it's a word for a girl." Eric mumbled his response, but the class was so attentive that every syllable could be heard clearly.

"Oh, is that so? What are some other words for girls?" Kate went quickly around the room, pointing at individual students who offered words like "dame", "lady", and "chick", at which the whole class laughed and Chickie George raised his eyes to the ceiling. "Is there any difference between this word up here and those you have just mentioned?"

"Yeah, there sure is." Sophia Rossoni spoke out with certainty. "That word up there is obscene."

"Or at least laden with sexual connotation." Kyle Monkton's thin voice piped up in agreement, and the rest of the class nodded.

"How many of you agree with Sophia that this expression is obscene?" Most of the members of the group raised their hands, with Eric and Kyle the only people abstaining.

"Eric, why do you think that the word 'cunt' is not obscene?" Kate walked back to where Eric had resumed his semi-reclining position and stood in front of him.

"Because everybody uses it all the time, and it just means a girl, that's all. I always use that word, and so do most of my friends." Eric's arrogant tone made Kate want to grind her teeth, but she continued to question the class..

"O.K., Kyle, how about you? Why do you disagree with most of the group that this word is obscene?"

Kyle looked earnestly at his teacher. "I just think that the whole issue of obscenity is very complicated. If you asked me if I find this word disgusting or repelling, I'd say yes. But even the Supreme Court has a hard time defining what's obscene."

Chickie slowly raised his hand. "I agree with Kyle, Mrs. Hammond. I hate that word when it's used to describe a person of the female persuasion, but I guess that I'd have a hard time being sure that it was obscene."

Kate felt the tension beginning to leave the room. She picked up a book from her desk and held it up. "This is one of the great masterpieces of English Literature. We're going to read it next, and it contains words and phrases that are just as strong, shall we say, as the word on the board." Even Eric looked intrigued by that idea, and they all strained to read the title that was embossed in the smooth leather of the binding.

Chickie, who was sitting near the front of the room, squinted at the volume Kate was holding and read out loud. "*The Canterbury Tales*. Hey, that's Chaucer. I didn't know that he was obscene."

"I'm not sure he is. That's something we have to discuss next week. But meanwhile, this word up here is staring us in the face, and I bet that you'd like to know why it's on the board. Anybody got an idea?"

"Because you wanted us to talk about obscenity, or at least start thinking about it?" One of the quiet girls on the side spoke up courageously.

"I think it's because you want us to know that you're cool and that we can use any language in the class discussions and you won't bag us for it." Eric's suggestion was met with several jeers, and he lifted his middle finger to Chickie, who was one of the critical voices.

Kate ignored the gesture. "Why did you react like that to Eric's comment, Chickie?"

The burly senior lifted his dark eyes to meet Kate's. "I bet some scumbag wrote that up there to insult you." Chickie's voice was quiet, but the genuine outrage he felt was very obvious to everyone in the class. Slowly and deliberately, Chickie turned in his seat to face Eric. "If I ever find out who did that, I'll kill the PRICK."

Before Kate could interfere, Eric had risen from his chair. "Are you accusing me of anything, Romeo, or are you just trying to make points with Katie-baby?"

Chickie's face turned bright crimson, but he stayed seated. "Sit down and shut up, Eric. You're one of the few people around here who calls every girl he meets one of those." Chickie pointed to the offending word on the board. "And we all know that you've been mad at Mrs. Hammond since the first day of school. So chill."

Kate glanced at the clock in the silence that followed and realized that the period was almost over. "Look, everybody, this has been a difficult day. Chickie is correct about one thing. Someone did write this on my board, and I find it highly offensive. I decided, however, to leave it up there to prove a point, not about obscenity, although that was very convenient, but about facing things. I could have covered this up and pretended there was no one who hated me enough or wanted to scare me enough to do something like this. But there IS that person, and I have to face the truth. We all have our own dragons to fight, and the monster that you look for is less scary than the one you run from. Does that make any sense?"

Several of the students squirmed in their seats, and averted their eyes, but Chickie stared hard at Kate, his eyes filled with admiration.

Kate looked around at the young faces in front of her. "Thanks for listening, everybody. Now, how about an early lunch?"

The students got up to leave, several of them stopping to express their outrage on Kate's behalf. When most of the room had emptied, Kate turned to straighten the papers on her desk. "Don't think that your little trick to get everyone's support is going to work." Phaedra's face was a mask of hostility as she glared at Kate. "And keep your hands off Chickie and my father or you'll be very sorry."

Kate watched the girl's stiff back disappear around the corner and looked again at the huge red letters emblazoned across the front of her classroom. What had she possibly done to collect so many enemies so quickly?

THE SHAPE OF DARK—Chapter Eight

"Are you going to be all right, Mrs. Hammond?" Collapsed on her desk chair while the tension drained out of her body, Kate was surprised to see Chickie's face appear in the doorway of her classroom.

"Sure, Chickie. I've been through worse things than this. But I really appreciate all of your support. You have no idea how much it helps to have someone stick up for you."

Chickie burst into laughter. "Are you talking about that stupid remark that Eric made? Don't worry, he's probably jealous that you and I are friends. He thinks teachers and students should be mortal enemies who are out to get each other all the time. That's why I wouldn't be surprised if he had something to do with that." Chickie pointed to the garish lettering.

"Thanks, Chickie, that means a lot. Now, take advantage of that extra time at lunch."

Chickie grinned. "Sure," he said as he obediently trotted down the hall.

Kate stood up and gathered her purse, glancing once more at the word on the board that had caused her so much pain. She carefully locked the door of her classroom and made her way downstairs toward the teachers' lounge, although she had no appetite.

"Mrs. Hammond!" Marta Stone's voice cut through the chatter of the students clustered around her desk in the lobby. "I was about to send this message up to your room. Your daughter's nursery school called, and it seems that Jessica has come down with an upset stomach. Leslie Barton explained that she called Silvertree Farm to find Mildred Worthington, but the cook said that both Mildred and Tikka had gone to Boston for the day. Apparently, the cook doesn't drive, so Leslie hoped you could pick up Jessica during your lunch period."

Kate felt a slight prickle of fear at the message, but shook it off, reminding herself that children got sick all the time. "I'll go right away. If something happens that Jessie is really sick, is there someone who can cover my last class?"

Marta Stone looked flustered. "I'm not sure where I can find someone at this late hour, but I'll try."

Alex came out of his office and smiled at his secretary. "I'm sure you'll be able to solve this problem very effectively, Mrs. Stone." He looked at Kate with concern and walked with her to the stairs. "Don't mind her, Kate. I'll take your class myself, if necessary. Don't even bother to come back. It's been a tough day for you. And try not to take this kind of thing personally. I've heard nothing but support from nearly everyone, and it's clearly the work of a very screwed-up person. Now, go get your little girl, and don't worry about anything here."

Kate ran back upstairs for her bookbag and hurriedly drove to the complex of low buildings that housed the Barton Learning Center. Leslie Barton was waiting in the nurse's office with Jessica, who was huddled on a small cot, looking very pale and miserable.

"She's thrown up twice, Kate, but she has no temperature, so I think that either she ate something that didn't agree with her or she has a little bug. A couple of the other children are out today, so maybe something's going around." Leslie stooped quickly and handed a basin to Jessica, who vomited a small amount and whined that her stomach hurt.

"Do you think you can make it home, Ladybug?" Kate wiped Jessica's mouth with the damp cloth that Leslie passed to her. "It's only a short ride, and then you'll be in your own bed."

"Take the basin with you, just in case." Leslie handed the enamel container that she had just washed to Kate and lifted Jessica carefully off the cot, placing her gently in Kate's arms. Leslie followed them to the BMW parked by the front door and helped Kate buckle Jessica into the back seat.

"Good luck, you two. Hope you're all better tomorrow, Jessie." Leslie's usually lively face was solemn as she spoke through the car window. "Let me know how she's doing, will you? I like to keep track of my little ones."

Kate nodded and drove away quickly, praying that Jessica's stomach would cooperate on the ride home. Luckily, the child was quiet during the five minutes it took to reach Silvertree Farm, and when Kate stopped the car and opened the back door to lift Jessica out, she found that her daughter was sound asleep.

Julia was waiting at the top of the back stairs when Kate carried Jessica into the kitchen and then through the dining and living rooms to the broad staircase leading to the second floor. Once they had settled the child into her bed, Kate turned to Julia. "Did Jessie have anything unusual for breakfast this morning?" Kate had left before her daughter ate, and she wondered if the cook had prepared something that could have triggered one of Jessica's many food allergies.

Julia shook her head. "No. All she had was a bowl of cereal and a banana. She didn't even want orange juice. She said that today was somebody's birthday and that his mother was bringing cupcakes to school. She wanted to leave room."

Kate turned back to Jessica and pushed up the long sleeve of the jersey she was wearing, exposing her tiny forearm, which was covered with hives. Jessica sleepily scratched the reddening bumps and murmured that she itched. When Kate and Julia undressed the child, they found that most of her body showed evidence of the welts that always appeared when Jessica ate something she was allergic to. "Will you get her antihistamine?" Kate watched the cook disappear into the bathroom as she slipped Jessica into a soft cotton nightgown.

Once she had swallowed the liquid Benadryl, Jessica fell into a deep slumber, while Kate hurried to the phone to call Leslie Barton to see if Jessica had eaten anything out of the ordinary at school. When Kate enrolled her daughter, she had carefully explained to Leslie that Jessica had a history of allergies, some of which were very serious and had required prompt medical attention in the past. The worst culprit had proven to be peanut butter, but subsequent tests had shown that Jessica was severely allergic to nuts of all kinds, so Kate was extremely careful to warn anyone who might be serving Jessica food that all nuts had to be avoided.

When Leslie heard about Jessica's hives, she was very puzzled. "Jack's mother asked if she could bring cupcakes, and I told her about Jessie's allergy to nuts. She assured me that she would provide plain white cake with white frosting. Jessie only had a small piece, but come to think of it, it was shortly after our little party for Jack that Jessie got sick. Mrs. Clayton also made peanut butter and jelly sandwiches for the other children, but I know for sure that Jessie didn't touch any of those. Let me ask around and see if any of the others have any ideas. I'll call you right back."

Within minutes the phone rang and Leslie had the answer. "One of the girls from your school who is helping out here on Mondays tells me that she cut the cupcakes in half with the same knife that Mrs. Clayton used to make the sandwiches. A tiny amount of peanut butter must have gotten on Jessie's cupcake. But I'm amazed that it would have that serious a reaction!"

"Don't worry about it, Leslie. Jessie's asleep, and I just looked at her arms. The hives are much better, so there's no real cause for concern. We'll just have to be more careful. Remind me to leave an Epi-pen with you, in case something like this should happen again." Kate, who was severely allergic to beestings, carried a syringe of life-saving epinephrine in her purse, but she had never thought to equip Jessica with one at school.

By the time Jessica awoke from her nap, it was getting dark outside, and Kate went through the big house, turning on lights and making a fire in the paneled library. Jessica curled up in the corner of Mildred's big green velvet sofa to watch *Mr. Rogers' Neighborhood*, and Kate sipped a glass of sherry as she planned the next day's lessons.

The loud ringing of the front door bell startled Kate, but she heard Julia bustling into the foyer, so she stayed put and concentrated on the work in front of her. Soon, however, she heard the deep tones of a man's voice, and she looked up to see the friendly face of Josh Temple in the wide door of the library.

"Hi, sugar plum. How are you feeling?" Josh sat down next to Jessica and began to discuss the intricacies of Fred Rogers' world. "Know what, Jess?" Josh ignored the fact that Jessica had shrunk into the corner of the sofa and continued in a conversational tone. "When my nephew was little, he was afraid of Bob Dog, one of the characters on this show. My sister wrote a letter to Mr. Rogers about the situation, and Fred Rogers sent two notes, one to my sister advising her how to handle the situation, and the other to my nephew telling him that it was O.K. to be afraid and that he was a very special person. Ever since then, we've all been big fans of Mr. Rogers."

Kate smiled at Josh's story and at the adult tone of voice he used in chatting with Jessica, whose shyness seemed to dissipate in the face of Josh's warmth and gentleness. Jessica even looked slightly disappointed when Julia came from the kitchen to summon her for a bowl of chicken noodle soup.

Like most visitors to Silvertree Farm, Josh commented on the beauty of the library, but quickly turned his conversation to the events that had transpired at school after Kate had left to get Jessica. "You should have been there, Kate. You wouldn't have believed it. Virtually everyone in the dining hall was talking about what happened in your classroom, and from what I heard, the entire student body is on your side. Except, that is, for Phaedra Stamos and Eric Lundgren, who made no secret of the fact that they were delighted by your misfortune."

"Then, the next period, when I was observing Chief Wallace's Civics class, Alex came to the door and yanked Phaedra out. I thought our esteemed principal was going to breathe fire. I guess that Phaedra had some rather rude things to say about you, and she was overheard by Marta Stone, who told Alex. Well, Phaedra never reappeared in class, so who knows if we'll ever see that young lady again. Personally, I don't know why Alex puts up with her snottiness. Other than that, everything went very smoothly after you left. How are you doing now?"

Warmed by the sherry and the fire, Kate felt better than she had all day. "I'm fine, thanks. I was worried about Jessie earlier, and that distracted me from thinking about how many ugly things have taken place in the last week! I can't figure out whom I've offended so badly that they'd go to such lengths to insult me. However, I'm kind of glad that it's out in the open, although I'm sorry if I've caused trouble between Alex and his daughter."

"From what I hear, that situation has been brewing for a long time."

Kate refilled their glasses and studied Josh for a long minute. "I'm curious. You are clearly an extraordinary musician. Whatever made you decide to go into teaching, of all things?"

"You'll never believe this, but I almost killed myself while I was touring with a band, and I was just lucky enough to get out in time. After a month of serious drug rehab, I decided to save my own life by getting off the stage. I haven't missed it at all, even the groupies." Josh was so wholesome and fresh-faced that Kate had difficulty visualizing him in the bizarre world of rock and roll. "I would hate to give up performing all together, and this gig at Rossoni's is just enough to satisfy my need to be in the spotlight."

Kate laughed. "Don't let the word get around that you were in a band, or the kids will be so intrigued by your former life that they won't take you seriously as a teacher."

"Hey, mum's the word!" Josh finished his sherry and went into the kitchen to say goodbye to Jessica.

"Take care of your momma, darlin." Josh sang out and bounded down the stairs into the rainy evening.

"He has a happy face, Mama," Jessica observed as Kate came through the kitchen door and sat at the table with her daughter.

"Yes, he does, Jessie, and he really likes you. Now, finish up, cause I want to give you a bath before Mildred and Tikka get home."

"Oh, I forgot to tell you, Miss Kate. Mrs. Worthington called earlier to say that she and Miss Tikka were staying in Boston overnight. I guess they were able to get tickets for the symphony, and since they were down there anyway, they decided to take advantage of it. They'll be at the Meridian if you need to reach them." Julia dusted her hands on her apron and opened the refrigerator door. "Would you like anything special for dinner? I thought I'd save the lamb chops until tomorrow night, when everybody will be here. How about a sautéed chicken breast and a salad?"

Suddenly, Kate realized how tired she was. "Don't bother with anything, Julia. I think I'll take a bath with Jessie and then maybe make myself some soup. I'm really wiped out. Isn't this your Bingo night?"

"Yes, but I usually miss the first part because of cleaning up after dinner. If you're sure that you don't mind, maybe I'll call the woman who picks me up and see if she wants to go early. I feel lucky tonight!" Julia waddled over to the phone, and Kate scooped Jessica up from the table and headed upstairs.

"Have fun, Julia! Be sure to take your key, because I'll lock up right after you leave." Kate heard the cook laughing on the phone as she made her way down the long, dark upstairs hall toward her bathroom.

After an extended, relaxing playtime with Jessica in the steaming bathtub, Kate put on her nightgown and robe and read several stories to her daughter until the little girl could no longer keep her eyes open.

Relieved to see that Jessica's cheeks were rosy once again, Kate tucked her in and kissed her goodnight before settling onto the chaise lounge in her own bedroom to start the new novel that Mildred had given her.

Outside, the wind blew harder and the rain ticked against the windows, rattling the panes on the ocean side of the house and dripping onto the flue of the fireplace in Kate's bedroom. A Mozart symphony was floating out of the CD player on the bookcase when, suddenly, everything went dark and still.

Jessica, who was sound asleep, was unaware that the power had failed, so Kate was relieved that she didn't have to stumble through the blackness to her daughter's room. This was the first time the electricity had gone out since Kate had come to Silvertree Farm, and she wasn't sure if there were flashlight or candles on the second floor. She knew, however, that there was a large flashlight in a drawer in the kitchen, so she cautiously felt her way to the top of the stairs and inched down, feeling each carpeted tread carefully.

When she reached the smooth oak floor at the bottom of the steps, Kate had to move very gingerly across the vast living room with its three sofas, a dozen chairs, and a grand piano until another stretch of bare floor indicated that she had reached the dining room. Just as she was about to work her way through the pantry toward the kitchen, Kate saw some movement out of the corner of her eye.

A shadowy form was standing outside the French doors that led from the living room to the grassy terrace that was elevated over the lawns sweeping to the ocean and to the swimming pool and cabana. Not daring to move, Kate held her breath as the person on the terrace wiggled the handle of the locked doors. It was so dark that Kate could barely see motion, but she could hear the slight squeak of metal as the intruder twisted the brass knob.

Rigidly controlling herself from screaming, Kate heard footsteps descend the stone steps at the far end of the terrace, and she imagined that whoever was trying to enter the house would examine the basement windows to see if any were open. As quickly as she dared, Kate inched through the butler's pantry and into the kitchen, where she found the flashlight after painfully colliding with the oak table in the center of the room.

Fortunately, the batteries in the flashlight were weak but still alive. Outside, Kate could hear rustling at the base of the house, and she quickly went to the telephone and almost cried with relief when she heard the hum of an open line. Cape Mariana did not have 911 service, and the telephone number of the police department was a difficult one to remember, so Kate dialed the operator with shaking fingers. After many unanswered rings, the operator finally came on the line and tersely informed Kate that she could have called information.

Through gritted teeth, Kate whispered that someone was trying to break into her house, and when the Cape Mariana Police Department identified itself, Kate could hardly stammer out her name and address. The dispatcher, recognizing Kate's panic, tried to calm her down by telling her that there were two cruisers in the area, but Kate barely heard him as she recognized the sound of something falling in the basement.

Without hanging up the phone, Kate raced over to the door between the stairs leading up from the cellar and the kitchen and quickly twisted the deadbolt, locking the door securely as heavy footsteps scraped up the rough cement of the cellar stairway. The intruder twisted the knob of the kitchen door, and finding it locked, hurried back down the steps.

Silvertree Farm had been built on ledge that had been partially blasted away, and Kate was amazed when Mildred showed her the gigantic remains of the rock which protruded into the cellar and through which, in heavy rainstorms, a gushing river flowed into a drain in the floor. Also in the basement were bins for storing the wood that fueled the house's five fireplaces, a cumbersome dumb waiter, and a large storeroom stocked with provisions for the kitchen.

In her terror, Kate could envision the prowler discovering the dumbwaiter, and she realized with a sinking heart that she could not lock the door between the small area that housed the dumbwaiter and the library. Foolishly, Kate rushed into the library, intending to push a heavy chair in front of the dumbwaiter door, but halfway into the room, she remembered that there was another door that led from the dumbwaiter to the front hall, eliminating any possibility that she could contain a determined intruder.

Just as Kate thought that she might be in inescapable danger, she looked out of the library windows and saw the flashing blue lights of two arriving police cruisers. Kate flew down the back stairs and unlocked the door to admit the officers, who were surprised to find her house dark, since there was no power outage anywhere else.

"He—he's in the basement, I think." Kate struggled to find enough breath to speak, snapping open the lock on the cellar door, while the officers drew their guns and followed the bright beams of their flashlights down the steep cellar stairs. After about five minutes, the policemen came back into the kitchen, shaking their heads.

"Nobody down there, Ma'am, but there has been a visitor recently. There are wet footprints all over the place, and one of the windows is wide open. Lucky whoever it was didn't notice the dumbwaiter. Somebody had propped a big wooden door against the thing, and I guess that the prowler just went right by it. We'll check outside."

The officers went out into the rainy night, and Kate put her head down on the kitchen table, feeling the onset of a painful headache and wondering how all of this could be happening to her. Within minutes, however, the policemen came back with the explanation of the blackout of Silvertree Farm. Apparently, a large tree branch had fallen on the storage shed through which the power lines fed from the main road, a quarter of a mile away. The officer put in a call to Central Maine Power for an emergency crew to come out immediately.

The two policemen set out again to look around the property adjacent to the house, while Kate found several candles in the pantry and lit up the kitchen and library. Jessica had evidently slept though everything, because Kate stood at the bottom of the stairs and heard only silence from the second floor. So, she returned to the candlelit kitchen and waited to hear what the police had discovered outside.

"There's a single set of footprints all around the base of the house." The young, earnest officer reported his findings to Kate and the other policeman went out to the back of the house to direct the CMP repair truck that had just arrived. "From the size of the foot, it's hard to tell much about the prowler, but I did find this." The officer held up a thin silver chain with a soccer ball dangling from it and "#1" inscribed on the back.

"What's that for?" Kate turned the object over in her palm and vaguely remembered seeing similar bracelets on many of the girls in school.

"The soccer boosters sold these last year after the team won the State Championship. Lots of people in town bought them to support the team. Someone doing work around the yard or delivering something may have dropped this. No way to tell if it belongs to the prowler." The officer paused and put on his hat. "Everything else looks clear out there, but we'll stick around until you get your lights back at least, and then we'll drive through several times during the night. Don't hesitate to call if something else happens."

Just as he finished speaking, the power buzzed on, and the green lights on the microwave clock flashed insistently. Kate reset the controls to 9:25, the correct time according to her watch and thanked the policeman as she locked the back door behind him. Kate blew out the candles she had lighted and trudged upstairs to find Jessica awake, having been startled by the sudden explosion of light in the house.

After she quieted Jessica, Kate slept fitfully until she heard Julia return home close to midnight. From then on, Kate's slumber was punctuated with unpleasant dreams, and it was with some relief that she heard her alarm signaling the beginning of another day.

****

Arriving at school around 7:30, Kate hurried upstairs to her classroom, happy to find that the defaced blackboard had been replaced. Realizing that she had no chalk, Kate unlocked the storage closet and searched the shelves for the box that she had seen on the one occasion that she had entered the small room. To her surprise, Kate saw a few drops of red paint on the floor of the closet, but she was prevented from any further speculation when she heard her name being called.

Eve Calvert, her shiny light brown hair gathered into a tidy French braid, stood by Kate's desk with the same folder that she and Sophia had shown to Alex the day before. "Mrs. Hammond, Sophia and I wondered if you would be willing to serve as our sponsor for a project we'd like to do at Thornton Oaks. Mr. Temple said that he'd help us, but since he's only going to be here for two months, we need a regular member of the faculty to be our advisor. This folder has our proposal and some ideas that we got from talking to Mr. Temple yesterday. I hoped you would look it over and tell us what you think."

Kate accepted the folder from Eve and invited her to sit down while she glanced over some of the preliminary work the girls had done. "This looks like a wonderful idea, Eve. I'd be happy to help you. Just let me know what I have to do."

Eve beamed in relief and explained to Kate that the guidelines for the assignment suggested that the advisors visit the community sites during the students' initial activities and that occasional, preferably unannounced observations be made during the year. It would be the joint responsibility of the advisor and Chief Wallace to assign a grade for the project.

"That sounds easy enough. When do you want to start?" Kate took out her appointment book and looked expectantly at Eve.

"Actually, we were hoping that we could go this afternoon. We talked to the people at Thornton Oaks, and they've assigned a room with two patients to us, so both Sophia and I are anxious to get going. Mr. Temple said that he's free today, if you are."

Kate glanced over her schedule for the day and nodded. "Today will be fine, Eve. Right after school?"

"Great! Thanks a lot, Mrs. Hammond. Some of the teams are having a lot of trouble getting teachers to work with them, so I'm really happy that you'll help us. Shall we meet downstairs in the lobby?"

"Fine. We can double check with Sophia and Mr. Temple, since they'll both be here in a minute. While we're waiting, Eve, is that nice Mrs. Calvert in the town library any relation to you?"

For a moment, Eve looked startled, but then she nodded. "Yes, that's my mother, but when did you meet her? She never mentioned it."

"Oh, she wouldn't remember, I'm sure. I went into the library during the summer, and she was very helpful in locating some material for me. I noticed her name on the desk, but we never discussed the fact that I was a teacher. What does your father do?"

Again, Eve seemed surprised by Kate's interest in her family. "He's an accountant in Portland."

113

"Do you have any brothers and sisters?" Kate had the distinct feeling that Eve was reluctant to discuss her family, but she always liked to know as much about her students as possible, and she thought that it would be useful to learn a bit more about Eve if they were to work together closely during the year.

"Yes, I have one younger brother, nine years old."

"Oh, then he's in the fourth grade?"

"Well, he should be, but he doesn't go to school. He gets tutored at home." By now, the expression on Eve's face made it absolutely clear that she wasn't comfortable talking about her personal life, and Kate refrained from asking any further questions. She made a mental note to ask Sandy Monkton or Alex about the Calverts.

The school day went very quickly, with the class that Kate taught to her juniors being especially effective. Josh sat in the back of the room while Kate led the students through an exercise in synesthesia, the association of one sense with another. After drawing a large chart on the blackboard and instructing the students to do the same in their notebooks, Kate labeled each vertical column as one of the five senses, and at the top of the sixth column she wrote "emotion". Then she asked the members of the class to fill in one word in each column and to try to associate the other senses with that word.

When it was clear that the students were confused and resistant, Kate asked one of the girls to name a color. She responded with "purple" and Kate wrote the word in the top box of the "sight" column. Next, she called on a boy for a smell, and he offered "dead fish" for which Kate thanked him enthusiastically and put it in the second box in the "smell" list. Other students contributed "onion", "siren", "sandpaper", and "hate" to the remaining columns, making a diagonal line of words across the chart, with "hate" at the bottom of the "emotions" row.

"Now, fill in the rest of the chart," Kate instructed the class, which began to grumble at the strange task. "This is easy. What's the smell of purple? What's the taste of sandpaper? What emotion do you associate with dead fish?"

Gradually, the students warmed to the task and began to scribble in their notebooks. After about fifteen minutes, almost everybody's chart was complete, and Kate, who had been roaming up and down the aisles with Josh, encouraging the students' imaginations, went back to the blackboard.

"O.K. Now, we're going to write a poem." Everyone groaned in unison, but Kate persevered. "Take one of the words from the "emotions" column and put it at the top of a page in your notebook. Then, look at the sense impressions that you've associated with that feeling and develop a fuller image from each one. For example, if you thought that the smell of hate was rotten eggs, you might do something like 'the stench of rotten eggs from an overflowing toilet'. Kate watched with satisfaction as the entire class wrinkled their noses and grimaced. "Lovely, strong image! Anyway, you get the idea. Go to it."

For the remainder of the period, the students hunched over their desks, scribbling lines of poetry and then fiercely erasing or crossing out words until their notebook sheet was filled with untidy writing. Just before the bell was about to ring, Kate instructed the class to go home and work on their poetry and make a final copy for tomorrow, when they would critique each other's work in small groups.

When the students filed out at the end of class, Josh got up from his seat in the back of the room and congratulated Kate for another successful class. "It's so hard to convince some of these kids about the beauty of poetry, and you're really doing a great job of introducing them to the importance of imagery. I can't wait to see how they do with the poems themselves."

"Well, in spite of some initial resistance, they really seemed to enjoy themselves."

Josh peered at Kate. "Are you feeling all right today? You look kind of tired."

"You'll never believe what happened last night. I'll tell you about it this afternoon when we go to Thornton Oaks with Sophia and Eve." Kate's freshman study hall was shuffling into the room, and she said goodbye to Josh who disappeared down the stairs towards Alistair's classroom on the first floor.

****

It was almost three o'clock in the afternoon by the time Kate and Josh turned into the long, winding driveway of Thornton Oaks, the stately old house that had been converted into an elegantly appointed assisted care facility with mostly large private rooms that the residents could furnish with their own belongings. One wing of the building housed a corridor of smaller, double occupancy rooms and bore more of a resemblance to a nursing home, providing complete care for twelve patients who were in need of constant supervision and support.

Sophia and Eve were waiting in the large, cool entrance of Thornton Oaks when Kate and Josh arrived. The four of them were then ushered by the owner of the facility into the complete care wing which was brightly lit and had three rooms on either side. The group stopped directly opposite the nurses' station, and the owner spoke to Sophia and Eve in a low tone.

"This is a very interesting pair of ladies. One of them is going to be ninety-five next week, and she's sharp as a tack. The other one is only forty-two, but she has advanced Alzheimer's Disease. I think it will be a tremendous challenge for you to develop ways of helping each of these women to be comfortable and happy. Good luck!"

The first person that the four of them saw was sitting in a large chair by the window. The frail, bright-eyed woman introduced herself as Betty Callahan. On a lap desk across her knees was a worn journal containing unfinished poems and stories that the lively old woman said she was going to get into shape for her great grandchildren. While Sophia and Josh poured over the flimsy pages with growing delight, Kate and Eve were both startled by a sudden loud moaning from the occupant of the other bed in the room. The sound grew in intensity until the dark-haired form in the partially curtained alcove was almost screaming.

"Don't mind her, dearie," Betty said calmly, patting Eve's hand. "She's such a sad little thing, and every once in a while she cries like that. It almost breaks my heart, but she has no idea what she's doing. Pretty soon, she'll curl up and go to sleep, just like a baby. I feel so bad when that big, handsome son of hers comes to see her and she's like this. The last time he came, he felt so wretched that I told him he shouldn't come so often. But every other day or so, he's here, holding her hand and bringing her flowers and those peppermint drops that she likes." Betty stopped and looked at Eve. "You must know him if you go to high school at Rocky Shore. That's Sheila George."

Eve gasped. Although Chickie's fellow students were dimly aware that his mother was very ill, few of them knew what was actually wrong with her, and Eve doubted if Chickie ever talked about her and her condition. As they said goodbye to Betty, who was almost asleep in her sunny corner, Kate and Eve glanced at Sheila George, and Kate felt a deep pang of sympathy for the emaciated woman lying in a fetal position under a bright blue wool coverlet.

****

At Silvertree Farm, Alex's Jaguar was parked behind Mildred's car. In spite of her resolution to remain totally professional in her relationship with Alex, Kate felt her face flush as she hurried inside. Calling out for Mildred, Kate expected to hear a man's deep tones in the library with her aunt. Instead, the mingled sounds of two women's voices floated out into the kitchen, sending a pang of dread through Kate at the thought that Phaedra was waiting to confront her again.

As slowly as possible, Kate put her books on the kitchen table and walked through the pantry into the library, where Mildred was sitting on the opposite end of the sofa from a tall, very thin woman with sharp features and a sleek cap of short blond hair. When she turned her eyes toward Kate, the visitor's gaze was a pale blue and her nostrils flared slightly as she looked over Kate from head to toe.

"Kate, my dear," Mildred began stiffly. "I want you to meet Claire Stamos, Alex's wife."

Claire rose from the couch and offered a limp, cool handshake. "I'm delighted to meet you at last, Mrs. Hammond. I understand from my daughter that we have a great deal to discuss."

THE SHAPE OF DARK—Chapter Ten

Kate was so stunned by the sudden appearance of Claire Stamos that she was speechless, plunging the library into a total, awkward silence. Finally, Mildred coughed uneasily and excused herself to confer with Big Ed George, who was outside digging around on the side lawn. "I think there's something wrong with the septic system, because there's water on the basement floor. Big Ed is going to see what he can find out, but I'd better get out there and give him moral support."

Mildred disappeared into the kitchen before Kate turned to Claire, who had reclaimed her seat on the couch, sitting comfortably with her long legs crossed. "This is quite a surprise, Mrs. Stamos. I've heard a lot about you."

Claire raised an arched eyebrow. "I'm sure you have. When I arrived home from Boston this afternoon, Phaedra was very anxious to tell me about the events of the weekend, and she seems to have some idea that you and my husband are becoming involved."

Blinking at Claire's bluntness, Kate struggled to find a response. "I'm afraid that Phaedra has a very vivid imagination. Alex invited me to have supper with him after we both chaperoned the dance on Friday night, but basically we're colleagues, and there's absolutely nothing for you or your daughter to concern yourself about."

"And what did you talk about during this innocent little evening? Did Alex tell you what a horrible person he's married to?" Claire's expression was icy and hostile.

In spite of herself, Kate was rattled by the other woman's questions, feeling the deep crimson begin to stain her cheeks. "Not at all. He told me a little bit about his life before Rocky Shore, and we discussed some school matters. Mostly, we listened to Josh Temple play the guitar. He's very talented."

Claire rudely shook off Kate's mention of Josh. "What about Saturday night? Phaedra said that you and Alex were together then, too."

Kate felt her patience wearing thin and she struggled to keep her voice low and controlled. "This is really unnecessary, Mrs. Stamos. My friend Tikka and I met Alex accidentally at Rossoni's, and we all responded to Kelly Lundgren's situation. As I said before, I work with Alex and that's all. Now, if you will excuse me, I would like to see how my daughter is feeling. She was ill yesterday."

It was immediately obvious that Claire was furious at Kate's calm reaction. "From what I hear from Phaedra, you are indeed involved in several unpleasant situations, rather an astounding record for someone so new to town. But then, you're no stranger to controversy, are you?" Claire stood up and smoothed down her short skirt.

"Goodbye, Mrs. Stamos." Tight-lipped, Kate led the way to the front door.

With her hand on the brass handle, Claire turned slowly and looked down at Kate, naked hatred congealed on her face. "Let me give you a work of advice, Mrs. Hammond. Stay far away from my husband and treat my daughter very well. Otherwise, you'll be sorry that you ever came to Cape Mariana!"

Kate resisted the urge to slam the door behind Claire and was annoyed to find herself trembling with frustration. It seemed that Alex lived with two very unhappy and vindictive women, and Kate had no doubt whatsoever that each one was capable of vicious behavior.

"Isn't she adorable?" Mildred came up behind Kate and put her arm around her niece. "I told you she was Lucretia Borgia reincarnate, and now you know that I wasn't exaggerating. But do watch out for her. Now, tell me about this intruder last night. When I got home this afternoon, Jim Brogan called to ask if everything was all right."

Grateful to have her attention diverted from Claire Stamos, Kate described the events of the previous evening, while Mildred watched Tikka negotiate with Big Ed as they stood beside his truck. Tikka's silvery hair whipped around her head in the suddenly stiff autumn wind, while the burly contractor laughed uproariously at something she said. Finally, they shook hands and Tikka trotted toward the back door, hugging her arms against the chill.

"Honestly, I feel so sorry for that poor man! I just asked him how Sheila was doing and he could barely answer me. I guess there's absolutely no hope that she'll ever improve, but she's so strong physically that she could last for a long time. I had to make a lot of jokes about the joys of digging for shit to change the subject." Tikka shook her head and went into the library to warm up in front of the fire.

Kate followed Tikka into the richly paneled room. "I know what you mean about the Georges' problem. I was at Thornton Oaks today with a couple of my students, and I happened to see Sheila. It's absolutely pathetic the way she lies there and cries, and it must be terrible for both Ed and Chickie, to say nothing of the huge costs they are facing. I understand that Thornton Oaks has such an excellent reputation that it's very popular and very expensive. How can Ed possibly afford it?"

Tikka sunk into the big velvet sofa and shook her windblown head. "I have no idea, but I imagine he borrowed on his house, on his life insurance, and who knows what else. I just realized out there that he is a very attractive man in a grizzly bear kind of way, and he's only about my age. He must think his whole life is over now, and he's really in his prime."

Mildred swung around from the desk where she was writing checks. "Tikka! Is that a note of interest that I hear in your voice? You know Big Ed does have a sort of primitive charm, but he can also be awful when he drinks. You'd better watch your step."

Tikka laughed. "Don't worry, Millie. He's not quite my type. I go more for the Alex Stamoses of this world. Or how about that charming Howard Calvert who does your income taxes?"

"Now don't be mean, Tikka. Howard may be very uptight AND a religious nut, but he's a great number cruncher. Leave him alone."

Kate looked from one woman to another in confusion. "What's this about your accountant? Is he peculiar or something? I teach his daughter, Eve."

Tikka explained. "When Howard comes here to work with Millie, I have to leave. The guy really gives me the creeps. He and his wife, who's rather nice, by the way, are born-again Christians so fanatic that they wouldn't even let their daughter go to public school until this year. If it hadn't been for Alex Stamos convincing Ruth Calvert that Eve needed the broad curriculum offered at Rocky Shore, the poor child would still be at home, all alone, working with a strange woman from their church. For a long time, Eve had to wear hopeless outfits that looked like the fifties, and you'll notice that even today, you never see Eve in the kind of casual clothes that the kids live in. Every time I see that sweet girl, I itch to do a makeover!"

"You know," Kate said slowly, "I have been aware that Eve dressed differently than the other kids and she suffers some ridicule, but she is so pretty that she even looks good in those long skirts and baggy tops that she wears."

Julia came to the door of the library and informed everyone that dinner would be served in about an hour, so Mildred turned back to her bookkeeping and Kate and Tikka enjoyed a glass of sherry while they flipped through the evening paper. Everyone was so engrossed in what she was doing that the jingling of the phone made all three women jump.

The call was for Tikka, who uttered a few monosyllables into the receiver and hung up quickly. "I have to go out for a little while after dinner. The shipment of silk scarves that I thought was lost has been found in a store in Portland, so I'm going to run in later and pick them up."

"Do you need any help with the display? I could go with you into Portland, since I've already done most of my work for tomorrow." Kate had watched Tikka plan her shop during the summer and really enjoyed working with the beautiful objects and articles of clothing that Avesta carried.

"No, don't bother. You've had some stressful times recently. Take a hot bath and curl up with a good book." Tikka seemed positive that she wanted to work alone, so Kate shrugged and went back to her newspaper until Julia summoned them for dinner.

During a blissfully uneventful evening, Kate found her attention wandering from the romantic novel she was reading, and she was annoyed that the cause of her inability to concentrate was Alex Stamos and the unexpected arrival of his glamorous, if definitely hard-edged wife. In her mind's eye, Kate reconstructed conversations in the Stamos living room, becoming so distracted from her reading that she finally gave up and went to bed about 9:30.

It was close to 1:00 a.m. when Kate heard Tikka come up the stairs, and she was surprised to hear her humming as she made her way down the corridor to her big corner bedroom overlooking the terrace.

****

Wednesday morning dawned clear and sunny with a light breeze blowing off the ocean. It was a welcome relief from the chill of the day before, and Kate noticed as she arrived at school that almost everyone looked cheerful and appreciative of the Indian Summer day.

"Kate!" Josh beckoned to her from the teachers' lounge and handed her a sheet of yellow paper on which he had scrawled a lesson plan. "I got an idea last night about how to follow up on that great poetry exercise you did yesterday. What if we had the kids turn their poems into song lyrics? The class could vote for the best one, and I could put together a tune."

As she glanced at Josh's suggestions, Kate found his enthusiasm contagious. "I think that the students would love this, Josh. Sort of a small taste of the music business. Why don't you formalize the plan, and we'll let you have a go at running the class." Kate chuckled at the look of sheer panic that crossed Josh's face at the thought of handling a room of teenagers on his own. "Don't worry, I'll be sitting in the back row to protect you from the untamed adolescents."

Josh looked slightly sheepish as he collected his papers and stood to leave. "I admit that my years in rock and roll have done nothing to prepare me for that first time I have to dazzle a class. By the way, I was in Rossoni's picking up my check for last weekend's performances, and that woman with the wild blond hair who was with you on Saturday night was there again."

"Was she alone?"

Josh shook his head. "No. I was surprised to see her sitting with the man who made such a fuss at the soccer game last Saturday after getting thrown out of Rossoni's on Friday night. They were having a gay old time, laughing like crazy."

"Big Ed?" Kate's shocked expression made Josh chuckle.

"That explains a lot" Kate muttered as the bell sounded, sending teachers and students to their first class.

The day passed so quickly that Kate had no time to wonder about the peculiar pairing of Tikka and Big Ed until Chickie's presence in her last class of the day reminded her. Just before the bell was to ring at 2:30, Kate interrupted the students' reading of *Beowulf* to remind them to be thinking about their yearlong writing projects. "I suggest that you use your journals for brainstorming during the next week or so. Remember, the quarter ends in early November."

In the back of the room, Eric swung his feet to the ground and looked steadily at Kate. "Mrs. Hammond, how do we know that the material in our journals will remain confidential? I've heard stories of teachers who have had their students keep journals and then have blabbed about what the kids have written. One guy I know swears that his English teacher read his journal to a table of teachers in the lounge."

The group was silent at the serious tone in Eric's voice and the absence of his usual sarcastic wisecracks. Kate walked slowly through an aisle of desks and stood quietly in front of Eric, who was sitting up straight in his seat.

"Eric, if that really happened, I am absolutely appalled. No teacher has the right to violate a student's privacy, especially in journals. However, now might be a good time to tell you about the exceptions to the confidentiality rule." Kate turned to face the rest of the class.

"As far as I'm concerned, your journals are a place for you to express yourselves on many levels. I don't read them as a source of gossip, I look them over to evaluate the energy with which you are approaching such an important writing and mental health tool. However, because I am a mandated reporter, there are three situations in which I feel I must reveal the contents."

"First, if you threaten to harm yourself or someone else, I will take action. Second, if you describe yourself as the victim of abuse, be it sexual, physical, or emotional, I will ask you to talk to the social worker. Finally, you should feel free to discuss your own personal use of drugs. You may have questions, or you may want to ask for help. But, if you offer information about the distribution of drugs, and especially if you mention any names, I will go immediately to Mr. Stamos." As she spoke, Kate noticed that every student shared Eric's seriousness, and she sensed that her words had penetrated the afternoon fog in which classes often drifted.

Just then the bell rang ending school, and Eric and Chickie came to the front of the class talking in low tones as they approached Kate's desk. "Thanks for that explanation, Mrs. Hammond. I feel better about the whole journal thing." Eric's sincerity surprised Kate, but she smiled warmly at the two boys.

"I'm glad, Eric. It's a tricky thing for a student to trust a teacher enough to share personal thoughts. However, don't forget that you can also use your journal as a writer's notebook. Mr. Temple was telling me that he used to scribble first drafts of his song lyrics in his journal. Maybe that's something that would interest you."

Eric raised his hands in surrender and backed out of the room. "Not me, Mrs. Hammond. I'm absolutely tone deaf. But the Chickster here has a great voice!"

Chickie looked intrigued. "Well, I used to sing a lot. My mother has a real pretty voice, and she loved to harmonize with me and my father on these old songs like 'Shine on Harvest Moon.' But since she's been sick, there hasn't been much music around our house."

"I'm sorry about that. I saw your mother yesterday, and I know how difficult it must be for both you and your father. Have you ever thought of making a tape for your mother of the songs that you used to sing together? Maybe the music would reach her somehow."

Chickie's face brightened up immediately. "Hey, that's a great idea. She likes to have me talk to her, I think, but I hate to leave because she just lies there. A tape would be something that the nurse could play for her. Do you think Mr. Temple would play the guitar for me?"

"I'm sure he would,"Kate replied. "But if not, I can struggle along on the piano. O.K.?"

"Fantastic. Can we do it soon?"

"Anytime you want. Make a list of the songs that you and your folks sang together, and give them to Josh and me. Maybe both of us could help you." Kate's throat ached at the eager look on Chickie's face.

"You're the best, Mrs. Hammond. Did I ever tell you that I love you?" The twinkle in Chickie's eye made the innocently affectionate implication of his words very clear to Kate, but Phaedra, standing in the hallway outside, got a different impression entirely.

Alex, climbing the stairs toward the second floor, passed his daughter and was struck by the unusually smug, yet also angry expression on her face. He was about to speak to her, when Chickie came running down the hall and nearly knocked Alex into the wall.

"Oops, sorry Mr. Stamos! Late for practice!" Chickie disappeared down the stairs and Alex continued on toward Kate's room, shaking his head at the boundless energy of teenage boys.

Kate was just shutting off her light when Alex stuck his head in the door. "Got a minute?" he inquired as she locked the room securely.

"Sure, Alex. What can I do for you?" Kate looked up at the principal and felt the same tingle of excitement that she experienced each time she was with the imposing, powerful man. His tan was still glowing from the sailing trips he continued to take each weekend, and Kate was annoyed with herself that she wondered how his lips would feel on hers.

"Is there any way I could convince you to have dinner with Claire and me this evening?" Kate opened her mouth to reply and Alex held up his hand. "Wait, there's a catch—a big one. I understand that you met my wife yesterday and that Claire gave you the third degree for which she's so famous. Well, when I got home last night, she pumped me for more information about you, using the excuse that Phaedra was worried I had more than a professional interest in you."

Alex paused and looked down at Kate with such a warm smile that she felt her knees quiver. "Claire doesn't really want me, you understand, but she also is driven crazy by the fact that I might ever be attracted to someone else. Apparently, Phaedra's been telling tales of all kinds of supposed romantic stuff between us, and Claire is determined to make us both squirm."

Kate was puzzled. "Why would either one of you want me to have dinner under such awkward circumstances? We'd all be miserable!"

"That's what I thought, but Claire insists that since you and I are simply colleagues, it would be an opportunity to clear the air. She SAYS that she wants to make amends for coming on so strong at your house. I'm not so sure, but she's very insistent. Also, she has asked me to invite Josh as a surprise for Phaedra, who has discovered his former career and is most anxious to ask him about life in the world of rock and roll!" Alex looked so beleaguered that Kate took pity on him.

"All right, I'll come, but I'll wear my bulletproof vest." Kate shifted her interview materials to her other arm. "Where do you live?"

"That's another plus. Claire insists that we go to the Half-Moon Inn, which has a terrific chef. Can you meet us there at seven?" Alex walked downstairs with Kate to the nearly deserted lobby. "I promise it won't be terrible."

Kate was very tired when she left the high school grounds about five o'clock but she remembered that she had promised to pick up some chutney for Julia, so she drove quickly to Dunham's and then decided, on impulse, to stop by Tikka's boutique, hoping to find things ready for the opening at 10:00 the next day

Tikka herself was swathed in brilliantly patterned silk scarves when Kate arrived, and it was easy to see why she wanted to surround Susan Moore's jewelry with the oriental motifs and shimmering fabric. A pair of large, round earrings, which had intricate carving in the gold and silver and were studded with jade, amethyst, and lapis lazuli, particularly attracted Kate. After admiring them at length, she reluctantly put them back in the window where they shone against a jade scarf shot with gold thread.

"Good taste, my love," Tikka approved. "Those are my favorites, too, and they're quite reasonable, considering the material and work that went into them. Mark my words, Susan Moore is going to be a superstar someday, and her things will be worth ten times what you have to pay today."

Kate looked wistful. "You have a terrific sales pitch, Tikka, but I'll have to do without for now. Max's mother has contested his will, and who knows when things will be settled. If it weren't for Millie…"

"And you've got me, too, and don't you forget it!" Tikka studied Kate, who was glancing at her watch and moving toward the door. "Any more crises today?"

"No, not a one. But there was one puzzling thing. Josh Temple said that he saw you and Big Ed at Rossoni's last night. I thought you were going in town to get those scarves and that you were going to work on the display."

Tikka's face turned bright red at Kate's words, and she began to speak very rapidly. "Actually, it was the funniest thing. I was in the

Old Port picking up my package, when I met Big Ed outside of that new bar, Sail Inn. Ed asked me if I wanted to have a drink, but I said that I needed to get back to the Cape. So he invited me to Rossoni's. We really had a nice talk, and he drank very little."

Kate had the strange feeling that Tikka wasn't telling the whole truth, but she said nothing except that she had to get home and get Jessica bathed and fed before she went out for the evening. When Tikka's eyebrows raised in surprise, Kate mumbled that she would fill her in later.

It was a little after seven when Kate drove up to the Half-Moon Inn, a sprawling complex of luxurious suites situated on a high bluff overlooking Half-Moon Beach. The hotel had been bought recently by a Japanese conglomerate, and the original, somewhat dilapidated inn had been renovated completely so that it was now the accommodation of choice for most people visiting the Portland area. The seaside dining room, presided over by a temperamental but talented young chef, attracted customers from all over southern Maine who put up with the inconvenience of waiting weeks for reservations.

In early September, the Inn was relatively quiet, allowing Kate to slip into a convenient parking space next to Alex's Jaguar. Inside, the plant-filled lobby was deserted, but a young bellman, whom Kate recognized as one of the students at school, stepped forward to greet her.

"Mrs. Hammond? Your party is already seated in the dining room. Will you please come this way?" As they passed through the airy reception area, Kate caught a glimpse of herself in one of the floor-to-ceiling mirrors that lined the walls, pleased that she had chosen to dress very simply but elegantly. Her black silk suit had a short skirt that revealed her slender legs, and the fitted bodice of the jacket flattered Kate's trim figure. After much deliberating in front of her jewelry case, Kate had selected a double strand of creamy pearls and some antique diamond and pearl earrings that her mother had left her. The total effect was stylish but understated, and Kate felt the approval in Alex's and Josh's eyes as she made her way through the dining room to a large round table by the windows overlooking the ocean.

The men rose as Kate approached the group, seating her between them, across the table from Claire, who wore a blue and white checked Chanel suit and ropes of gold chains. Her short blond hair was swept away from her face, emphasizing her high cheekbones and bright red lips, which were pulled back in the imitation of a welcoming smile.

"I'm so glad you could join us, Mrs. Hammond. I wanted to apologize for being rather grumpy yesterday. May I call you Kate?" Once again, Claire's eyes remained cold and aloof, in spite of the supposed warmth of her greeting. Kate felt an involuntary chill run down her back, but she forced herself to nod and look pleasant while trying to relax into the thickly upholstered chair.

Obviously relishing the role of hostess, Claire looked around the table. "What shall we have? A drink first, perhaps. I'll have a dry Martini, straight up, with olives…"

Kate ordered dry sherry, Alex and Josh had beer, and Phaedra reluctantly asked for a coke, after her father shook his head at her initial request for a glass of wine. Claire made a face at her daughter, and they whispered something to each other while looking at Alex, who did his best to ignore both of them.

When their drinks arrived, Claire turned to Josh on her right and began to question him about his former band, which had released a best-selling album the previous spring. At almost the same moment, Phaedra put her hand on her father's arm and engaged him in a conversation from which he was unable to extricate himself. Each time that he tried to include Kate, Phaedra renewed her chattering and physically demanded Alex's attention by flecking an imaginary speck from his jacket or grasping his hand.

Sipping her sherry, Kate was almost amused by the obvious way in which the Stamos women had isolated her from the group. Josh kept sending her sympathetic glances, and Alex looked increasingly pained, but it was not until the waiter came to the table to take their orders that Kate was included in the discussion.

After the wine steward left with their choice of a white Bordeaux to accompany their dinner, Claire finally spoke across the table to Kate. "Tell me, Kate, how did you happen to come to Maine so suddenly?" Although the question seemed casual, the intense expression on Claire's face suggested that there was a definite reason for her inquiry.

"Mildred Worthington is my father's sister, and when I wanted to relocate after the death of my husband, she offered my daughter and me a place to stay. I must say that we have enjoyed Cape Mariana very much, and I especially feel right at home, since I went to college in New England." Kate spoke smoothly, but her palms were sweaty.

"When did you lose your husband?" Claire's eyes bore into Kate's and there was an edge to her voice.

"At the end of last spring. It was very sudden, and Jessie and I are just now adjusting to life without him." Kate tried to phrase her answers to give a general kind of information that would provoke no further curiosity from Claire.

"I think you're adjusting very well!" Phaedra's sudden comment was heavily laced with sarcasm, but Kate chose to ignore the venom in her voice.

"Thank you, Phaedra, I'm trying." When Kate refused to take Phaedra's bait, Alex smiled and lightly pressed his knee against hers under the table. Alex was interrupted by the arrival of their salads, and for the next hour, the dinner table conversation was curtailed by the excellent food for which the Half-Moon Inn was justly renowned. Finally, when coffee was being served, Claire turned once again to Kate.

"I'm especially glad to have you with us, Mrs....Kate. Next week is Phaedra's birthday, and I've decided to give her a special present this evening. I know you've become friends with the other members of my family, and I thought you'd like to share the occasion with them." In light of the rude behavior that Phaedra had displayed toward her, Kate found Claire's statement particularly ironic, but she simply settled back in her chair and waited.

Claire produced a long, slender box from her purse and handed it to Phaedra. "I had this made especially for you by that woman who is teaching art at your school, although she's really too talented to be wasting her time in a classroom!" Ignoring the possibility that she was insulting practically everyone at the table, Claire handed the package to Phaedra.

"Oh, Mummy, this is gorgeous!" Phaedra squealed as she lifted an intricately carved silver hair clip from its nest of cotton and examined it closely. "Look, the pattern is made with little "P's" embossed on the surface."

Claire looked pleased with her daughter's reaction. "I know. Put it on, darling, and let's see how it goes with your hair."

Glowing from the attention she was receiving, Phaedra fastened the ornament in her hair and accepted compliments from her father and Josh, while throwing a superior smirk in Kate's direction. "How do you like it, Mrs. Hammond? Does it meet with your approval?"

Kate refused to be goaded by Phaedra's contemptuous tone. "I think you look wonderful, and I'm so pleased that more of Susan Moore's jewelry is going to be available at Avesta. It's really special to own something so unique."

For a moment, Phaedra was disarmed by Kate's genuinely complimentary words. But then her face hardened, while her tone became artificially sweet. "Thank you for those nice words, but then we all know how easy it is for people to fall under your spell."

Everyone at the table except for Claire seemed surprised by Phaedra's blatant insolence. Alex pressed his knee against Kate's once more before he turned on his daughter. "What the hell do you mean by that?"

Kate saw to her horror that Claire was sitting erectly in her chair, an expression of triumph on her pointed features. She fixed a chilly gaze on Kate, but didn't say anything, preferring to let Phaedra mount the surprise attack.

Feeling her mother's support, Phaedra tossed her head defiantly, the silver clip glinting as it caught the light of the chandelier above the table. "It's no secret that Katie-baby here, as all the kids call her, has hypnotized most of the men in the school, including the younger ones. Admit it, Mr. Temple, you worship the ground this woman walks on, and so does my father. But you're both out of luck, because she's into robbing the cradle and has managed to steal my boyfriend!"

"If you don't shut up right now, Phaedra, I will not be responsible for what I do. Your behavior toward Kate has been inexcusable, and I have been very patient, but I'm through. One more word and you'll find out how sorry you can be." Alex spoke in a low voice through tight lips, but other people in the dining room were looking up in curiosity at the drama being played out in the corner of the room.

"Now Alex," Claire interjected, "you're sounding like an abusive parent. Phaedra is simply expressing her opinion, and it seems to me she has the right to do so, even if she is a bit strong in her wording." Phaedra sniffled, glaring at Kate, who was sitting stunned and silent.

Alex turned his attention to Claire, fixing her with a piercing glare. "You know, Claire, it seems outrageous to invite someone to dinner and then to support your daughter's ridiculous attack on that person. It doesn't say much for your skills as a hostess or as a mother."

Claire narrowed her eyes at both Alex and Kate. "You can defend your 'colleague' all you want, my dear, but it would be interesting indeed to see how the community would react to one of their teachers seducing a young boy."

"WHAT? You're as nutty as ever, Claire. Kate wouldn't have anything improper to do with a student and we all know that." Alex turned apologetically to Kate, who was huddled in the corner of her chair. "I'm so sorry about all of this, Kate. I had a hunch this dinner was a bad idea, and I should have followed my instincts. You've been treated very badly."

Kate rose from her chair and struggled to control herself. "Thank you for the delicious dinner, Alex. I hope you can calm Phaedra down and convince her that she doesn't know what she's talking about." Kate shook her head at Josh's offer to walk her to her car, and as she started to cross the dining room, she heard Phaedra's strangled voice rise above the murmuring in the room.

"Then, Mrs. Hammond, the next time that Chickie George tells you that he loves you, I suggest that you remind him of the slight difference in your ages!"

Kate's breath caught in her throat, but she forced herself to pretend she hadn't heard Phaedra's last remark. Unfortunately, in her haste to retreat and somewhat blinded by the tears that began to flood her eyes she failed to see Mona and Bill Lundgren sitting at a secluded table nearby.

THE SHAPE OF DARK—Chapter Ten

In a way, Kate was relieved the next morning when she saw that Chickie's seat was empty during her first period class. After Phaedra's angry accusation in the Half-Moon Inn the previous evening, Kate was uneasy at the thought of facing the young man.

The other person Kate could have done without after a sleepless night was Eric, but he arrived in class right on time and chose a desk in the middle of the room, instead of lying on several of the chairs in the back.

"O.K., folks, today we're going to wrap up our study of *Beowulf,* and tomorrow there will be a test in class. Does anybody have any questions before we start grappling with the themes of the epic?" Kate sat on the high stool beside her desk and waited while the students shuffled through their notes. Finally, Sophia raised her hand.

"I've noticed that there is almost nothing about women in this story, Mrs. Hammond. Besides the queen of Denmark and Grendel's mother, everybody else is a man. Is that just the way the story goes, or should we know why?"

"Excellent question, Sophia. Does anybody have an idea?"

One of the girls in the back spoke up. "I don't think that women were very important in Anglo-Saxon society. Didn't you tell us that it was a rough, warrior civilization?"

"Yes, I did, and I think you have a point. People tend to write about what they value, especially in epic poetry. One of the interesting things to watch for as we read the literature of various periods in England is the way that attitudes toward women change and how those shifts are reflected by the writers." Kate turned to the blackboard and picked up a piece of chalk "Now, are we ready to list themes, or does anyone else have a question or comment?"

Eric put both feet on the chair in front of him and stretched. "Actually, I kind of liked the scene where the queen went around and served everyone. That's my idea of how women ought to behave!" A few people giggled in the class, and Eric sat up straighter in his chair and looked directly at Kate. "It seems there were rules in those days that kept women in their place."

Kate returned Eric's stare and debated with herself whether or not to let the conversation go any further. Clearly, Eric was expressing his own male chauvinism, but there was something in the tone of his voice that warned her he had other issues on his mind.

"And what exactly IS a woman's place, as far as you're concerned?"

"I was thinking about the fact that some women today think they can mess with any guy and get away with it. For example, teachers who come on to their students..."

Kate felt an invisible hand clutch her throat. When she arrived at school, she had glimpsed Phaedra surrounded by a knot of students, but she hadn't seen Eric in the group.

Kyle Monkton turned around in his seat and blinked at Eric. "What are you talking about?"

"If you weren't such a geek, you'd know what everybody else does. The professor here is having a thing with Chickie. Phaedra saw them making out, and she confronted Katie-baby about it in the middle of the Half-Moon Inn dining room. I know, because my parents were there!" Eric leaned back in his chair and looked pleased with himself, while the rest of the class turned to Kate, who was gripping the edge of her desk.

"I hesitate to dignify such a ridiculous statement with a reply, but I'll take a moment to set the record straight. Chickie's a wonderful boy, but he's just that—a boy." With an iron will, Kate forced herself to straighten up and move to the blackboard once again. Although her fingers were shaking, she wrote the word "THEMES" on the top of the board and began to question the class.

It wasn't until just before lunch that Kate saw Chickie coming out of Alex's office, and she turned quickly into the teachers' lounge so she could avoid what she feared would be a very embarrassing meeting for both of them. To her surprise, Chickie followed her across the lobby and caught her just as she was about to sit at a table with Alistair Henry.

"Mrs. Hammond, could I see you for a minute?" Chickie spoke from the doorway of the lounge. From the attentive looks on the faces of the other teachers in the room, Kate was certain that Phaedra's story was in full circulation throughout the school. Excusing herself, Kate followed Chickie out into the lobby, which was now virtually deserted.

When Chickie turned to face her, Kate was dismayed to see that his face was white and haggard. Kate had a sinking feeling in her stomach, but she forced herself to meet the anguished eyes of the clearly troubled boy. "You look as if you have been up all night."

"I guess you could say that. Mr. Lundgren found it necessary to call my father last night, and he wouldn't stop yelling at me. He wouldn't listen to anything I said, and he had been drinking. I was able to hold my own pretty well, so he's as tired as I am this morning. I'm sick of letting him push me around." Chickie's mouth was set in a straight, determined line.

"Listen, Mrs. Hammond, don't blame yourself for any of this. Mr. Stamos just told me what happened at the Inn last night, and I think he'd like to give Phaedra a good spanking, but he's not that kind of guy. Ever since I broke up with Phaedra, she's been trying to get back with me, and it drives her nuts when I pay attention to any other girls, or women. She swore that she'd get even, and it looks like she's keeping her word."

"Oh, Chickie, I feel terrible about this. You have enough to contend with as it is, without these kinds of rumors going around. I'm sorry to say that something like this happened in another school where I taught, and it was a real mess until we found out that the boy himself was spreading the stories to make himself look important." Kate could barely look at Chickie without wanting to cry.

"Don't worry about me. We both know Phaedra's story is way off base, so that's all that matters. My father loses it real easily these days, but I don't think he'll try any rough stuff with me. Friends?" Chickie held out his hand and Kate grasped it firmly.

"Ah, Chickie, if you were only twenty years older!" Kate joked and turned to go back to lunch, but the smile left her face as she watched Chickie stride toward the stairs.

Alex walked from his office to where Kate was standing, looking thoughtfully after Chickie. "Great guy, isn't he?" Alex's voice was rough and he put his big hand on Kate's shoulder.

"Come into my office for a minute, will you? We need to settle something." Alex led the way past Marta Stone's empty desk and closed his door. Before Kate realize what happened, Alex grasped her face in his hands and kissed her with such longing and tenderness that Kate's knees began to give way. Feeling her tremble, Alex gathered

Kate into his powerful arms and kissed her again, this time with a slow, deliberate urgency.

"I couldn't stand it another minute, Kate. You looked so sad and lonely out there in the lobby that I had to let you know how I feel, even if we both know what an impossible situation this is." Alex's dark eyes studied Kate's face for a long moment before he claimed her soft lips again.

"I…" Kate struggled to find words but fell silent as Marta Stone's voice was heard on the other side of the closed door.

"I think he's in a conference, Mrs. Stamos. If you'll have a seat, I'll buzz him."

Claire's annoyance was evident at being prevented from entering her husband's office. "He's always available to me, Mrs. Stone. If you don't mind."

The door swung open and by the time Claire Stamos came into the office, Kate had collapsed into the chair in front of Alex's desk. Claire's icy glance swept over the room while Kate looked flushed and breathless. Alex stood behind his desk and glared at the intrusion.

"Having a *conference,* Alex? Is this sort of thing a regular occurrence around here, or is Phaedra right about Mrs. Hammond's irresistible attraction?" Claire moved to the second chair in front of Alex's desk and sat down in a fluid motion.

"If you must know, Claire, I was apologizing to Kate for Phaedra's abominable behavior last evening. Apparently, your daughter has spread her ridiculous rumor around the school, and she succeeded in getting Chickie George in trouble with his father." Alex turned to Kate leaving Claire to stare at his broad back. "Again, Kate, I am so sorry for the way you were mistreated at the Inn." Alex's expression was serious and tender as he looked into Kate's eyes.

"Please, Alex, let's forget about it. I'm far more concerned about what happened to Chickie, but he thinks the situation with his father is now under control. If you'll excuse me, I have only a few more minutes of lunch before my next class." Kate turned to Claire, who looked cool and crisp in a tailored red linen blazer and short navy skirt, while Kate was conscious of her own tousled hair and the streak of yellow chalk across her gray cashmere sweater. "Goodbye, Mrs. Stamos."

Claire ignored Kate's departure. Alex frowned at his wife and followed Kate out of the office and closed the door between them and Claire. Marta Stone was away from her desk and Alex touched Kate's arm to stop her progress across the lobby.

"I'm going to deal with Claire right now, but I really need to see you tonight. Could we meet at Morning Cove late this afternoon? I'm going to bring my sailboat around so that Slayton Marine can pick it up tomorrow, and I should get there sometime around five." Alex's eyes pleaded with Kate, and she nodded, shaken by the memory of his lips on hers.

"Having a nice day, Mrs. Hammond?" Phaedra stood in the lobby just outside her father's office and sneered openly at Kate, while pronouncing her name with mock formality.

Kate wheeled on Phaedra, meeting the hostile look in her eyes with an expression that was equally angry. "The question is, Phaedra, are YOU satisfied? Talk to Chickie and see what your asinine accusations brought him." Kate snapped her mouth closed and left the petulant teenager to watch her rigid back march up the stairs.

In the second floor hallway, students were milling about waiting for lunch to be over. As she unlocked her classroom door, Kate sensed someone behind her, and when she turned around, she found Eve Calvert standing a few feet away.

"Can I help you with something?" Kate noticed Eve's face was very pale and her eyes were ringed with dark circles. "Are you all right?" Kate beckoned Eve to follow her into the classroom.

Eve shuffled her feet and looked down at the ground. Her baggy brown sweater hung over a long skirt, and only her delicate features and shiny hair were hints of the beauty that was hidden beneath the layers of unbecoming clothing. "I'm afraid I'll have to be excused from any personal writing assignments." Eve's voice was so soft that Kate could barely hear her, and slow tears were starting to trickle down the girl's cheeks.

"I'm sorry to hear that, Eve. I've found that journal keeping and the year-long assignment really engages students, but I'll certainly honor your wishes and come up with an alternative. You seemed so enthusiastic the other day. Did something happen to change your mind?"

Eve shook her head. "No, that's not it. My father doesn't think it's a good idea for strangers to read about my life." As Eve was speaking, Kate noticed her rubbing a large bruise on her arm.

"Would it help if I talked to your father and explained that this isn't the kind of project he should be afraid of? After all, you don't have to write about personal things."

Momentarily, hope lightened Eve's face. "Would you do that? I know that my father does a lot of work for Mrs. Worthington, so maybe she could say something, too."

"I'm sure she'd be happy to put in a good word. After all, she's a professional writer. Don't worry. We'll figure something out." Kate smiled encouragingly. "By the way, what did you do to your arm?"

Eve turned away from Kate's concerned expression. "Nothing. I must have banged it somewhere. Thanks, Mrs. Hammond."

"Listen. If you need someone to talk to, I'm always around. Promise you'll remember that?" Kate laid her hand on Eve's shoulder and was surprised to find the girl trembling. "Promise?"

"Yes," Eve whispered and fled out of the room, leaving Kate puzzled and vaguely troubled. Directly after school, Kate raced over to Avesta, which was filled with chattering women by the time she arrived close to three o'clock. The fragrant interior of the boutique glowed with the brilliant colors and textures of the clothing and accessories Tikka had assembled, and soft piano music was accompanying the informal modeling of exquisitely cut wool suits.

Tikka herself, dressed in a royal blue silk dress and several pieces of Susan Moore's jewelry, met Kate at the door, her blond hair swirling wildly as she greeted potential customers who had eagerly awaited the opening of the shop.

"It's better than I ever imagined!" Tikka twittered, indicating the two saleswomen who were frantically trying to help stylishly dressed women select from among the many tempting items. "Thank God I decided to go ahead and open, even if some things haven't arrived from Europe. If this keeps up, I'll be reordering almost immediately."

Kate was impressed by the number of people gathered on the sidewalk waiting to get inside the packed store, pleased for Tikka that her obvious sense of design and flair for presentation was so well received. After the opening, Tikka planned to offer a personal image shaping service, and Kate was certain that it would be hugely successful as well.

After spending an hour browsing through the racks and shelves of luxurious merchandise, Kate got home just as the bright blue Barton Learning Center van pulled into Silvertree Farm and Jessica climbed out. The child was unusually excited about a field trip the children had taken to a farm in West Cumberland. There had been horses and cows and sheep, Jessica explained breathlessly, and the children had been able to pick their own apples for lunch. Kate was so distracted by the thought of meeting Alex at 5:00 that she barely responded to her daughter's enthusiastic description, but Jessica didn't seem to notice and found a more receptive audience in Julia, who was kneading bread dough in the kitchen.

"Do you mind if I leave Jessie with you for a little while? I've got an appointment at five, and I'm not sure how long it will last." When Julia agreed, Kate rushed upstairs to change her clothes, finding she was as nervous as she had been on a first date at fifteen.

Muttering at herself to stop being ridiculous, Kate dressed carefully but casually in a soft pink turtleneck sweater, snug, pressed blue jeans, and a brown and pink tweed jacket. As she fastened thin gold hoops in her ears and brushed her hair until it shone, Kate found her lips curving in an involuntary smile at the glowing woman who looked back from the mirror.

"Mama, you smell really pretty!" When Kate came through the kitchen door, Jessica looked up from the counter where she was standing on a stool.

"Thanks ladybug. You be especially good for Julia, and I'll be home before you know it!" Kate slipped out the back door and ran through the thick carpet of bright leaves that was beginning to cover the ground between the house and the rippling waves of Morning Cove.

When she arrived at the edge of the bluff overlooking the rocky beach, Kate saw Alex tying up his boat at the end of the pier. A pickup truck was parked close to where the long wooden ramp met the land, and two men were walking out to meet Alex. From where she stood, Kate could see that one of them was as tall and powerfully built as Alex, although much younger. The trio talked for a minute and then walked back to where Kate stood.

"Kate Hammond, meet Deke Slayton and Timmy Brogan. These guys are going to haul out my boat tomorrow, and then the summer will really be over." Alex spoke so mournfully that the two other men chuckled.

"You can always come fishing with me, Mr. Stamos." Timmy Brogan's broad smile contrasted with his deep tan, and Kate thought she had never seen such an attractive young man.

"Thanks for nothing. I've heard stories about how you work your sternmen." Alex was obviously fond of Timmy, whose longish brown hair had been bleached by long hours in the sun and salt water. "Kate, this guy graduated the first year that I was at Rocky Shore, and I barely lived through his senior year. Now, he's a respectable lobsterman with 800 traps."

"Except on stormy days, when he works for me!" Deke Slayton clapped Timmy on the back. "One of him is worth six other people, so I pray for rain."

Timmy looked embarrassed and kicked the dirt with his heavy boot. "Don't listen to them, Mrs. Hammond. Do you live around here?"

Kate indicated the big house on the hill behind them. "I'm Mildred Worthington's niece."

"Mrs. Worthington's the best. Say hello to her for me." Timmy grinned. "I worked for her in the summers before I started fishing." While he was speaking, Timmy's eyes swept appreciatively over Kate.

"Anything more you need to tell us about the boat?" Deke Slayton was obviously anxious to be on his way, and when Alex shook his head, Deke pulled Timmy's arm. "Come on, buddy. Stop admiring the scenery."

Reluctantly, Timmy followed Deke to the truck, and they slowly backed up the hill. Alex beckoned Kate to follow him out onto the pier, leading the way down the creaking weathered boards to the deck of his sailboat. "You've really made a conquest now, Kate. Half the women in Portland would turn handsprings to get his attention."

"He's absolutely gorgeous, but about ten years too young, I'd say." Kate stepped onto the boat, balancing as the waves rocked it. "You must be really sorry when the sailing season is over."

Alex sat down on the railing in the stern. "I am. Claire and Phaedra hate the ocean, but I feel really at peace on the water. I've had this boat for a long time, and I refuse to give it up."

Kate settled alongside him and watched the gulls wheel and screech around Angel Rock. "I know what you mean. This cove has been responsible for a lot of healing for me, and I know Millie could never live anywhere else." Kate glanced up at Alex. "What did you want to talk to me about? Claire's unfortunate timing?"

"Everything about Claire is unfortunate these days. We're just going from bad to worse."

Kate looked at Alex in surprise. "That's the first time you've really said anything against your wife. I've seen you angry at her, but I've never heard you criticize her to someone else."

"Actually, I think you're right. I always figured she was Phaedra's mother, and the more civilized we could be to each other, the better Phaedra would be able to handle things. But now I find that Claire has been encouraging Phaedra in her dirty tricks, and I'm so mad that gallantry is out of my reach right now." Alex's eyes clouded over and his jaw hardened.

"How did you make out with Claire after I left your office?"

"To be honest with you, I don't know. I expected more vitriol, but she only said that no matter how I felt about you or any other woman, she would never agree to a divorce. She thinks our estrangement is seriously harming Phaedra, and she said she was going to do everything she could to reconcile our differences. She went on and on about not throwing away eighteen years of marriage. I didn't know what to say. The last thing in the universe I care about is resuming any kind of real relationship with Claire, and she knows it. She must be up to something."

Kate shook her head. "Well, I'll tell you one thing, Alex. My female intuition, if there is such a thing, is screaming at me that Claire is a dangerous person to have for an enemy. If she is manipulating Phaedra to achieve her own purposes, it's the worse kind of psychological abuse."

"I agree. But I'm not sure what to do about it. Every once in a while I see this terribly sad expression on Phaedra's face, but when I ask her about it, she replaces it immediately with that wise-ass rudeness. But I didn't ask you here to talk about Claire and Phaedra.

I want to find out how you're doing in all of this. I really feel responsible for a lot of the hassle you've been getting since you started school."

Kate shrugged. "It's been an experience, that's for sure. I had no idea so many bad things could happen in such a short time, but I'm doing fine, really. I feel rotten about what happened to Chickie. Those Lundgren people are sweet, aren't they? Rushing to tell Big Ed that his son was being seduced by a teacher?"

"As soon as I heard what happened from Chickie, I called Big Ed and read him the riot act. From what I could tell, he was feeling very bad about the whole thing. Big Ed really loves Chickie a lot, but he has a hard time showing it." Alex took Kate's hand and held it in both of his own.

"Lots of us have that problem. I remember the night we came down here after Rossoni's..." Kate's voice trailed off and her sea-green eyes were fixed on Alex's face. She smoothed her hand over the arm of his blue chambray shirt. She noticed that dark hair curled from the open neck of his collar, and she had an almost irresistible urge to press her lips to the spot on his throat where she could see his pulse beating.

As if he sensed her thoughts, Alex moved so their thighs were touching, and he gently gathered her into his arms, enfolding her pliant body against his chest. Kate inhaled sharply at his touch and smelled the clean, masculine scent of bay rum on his slightly rough cheek.

Alex looked down to see Kate's satiny lips, and he deliberately brushed his mouth across hers until her ragged breathing raced with his beating heart. "Is this what you really want?" Alex whispered.

Kate's answer came in the darkening of her eyes. Unable to hold back any longer, Alex devoured her lips, while their intermingled tongues united them in a long, searching passion that deepened and grew in intensity.

Alex felt her body strain against his as he moved his hand slowly up her slender side to her breasts. At Alex's touch, Kate's nipple hardened under his palm, and she felt a delicious stab of desire deep within her body.

"Oh my God, Kate, you're so beautiful!" Alex's voice was husky as he gazed down at the exquisite woman whose skin glowed, even in the gathering dusk. "But I can't stand to make any more trouble for you."

Kate shook her head. "The way I feel, I really don't care about anything except here and now."

Alex groaned and drew away for a moment, watching as Kate stood up and walked to the side of the boat. Her hair was tumbled around her flushed face, and Alex thought she looked like a teenager.

As if she had read his mind, Kate giggled and reached over to fix the collar of his shirt. "I feel like some high school kid who's been making out on her mother's couch. This is silly."

Alex took Kate into his arms again and held her gently while he smoothed her hair back. "There's a cabin below. Would you like to see it?" Alex's voice was rough and his arms trembled slightly.

"I know I should run up that hill as fast as I can," Kate whispered, burying her face in Alex's shoulder. "But I don't want to leave."

His arm holding Kate close to his side, Alex opened the hatch and led her below deck where there were two bunks covered with bright blue sailcloth. Large plaid cushions were strewn here and there and a hanging brass lantern swung from the ceiling as the boat swayed in the rising tide.

"Sit here for a minute." Alex closed the hatch, plunging the cabin into soft, bluish-gray shadows, lit only dimly by the last rays of the setting sun. He reached into a cabinet and brought out a bottle of wine and two plastic glasses. "Not too fancy, I'm afraid, and the wine's not chilled."

Leaning against the cushions on the bunk, Kate felt herself grow warm in the small enclosure, and she shrugged out of her wool blazer while Alex struggled with a corkscrew. When he turned toward her, Alex's eyes widened at the rosy softness of Kate's sweater.

He handed Kate a glass of wine and sank to the bunk beside her. "I always used to hate the day that I took my boat out of the water. Now I'm beginning to have an entirely different perspective."

"This is so weird, Alex. This is all wrong, but I feel as if we're alone in the world and all of those awful things that have been happening don't really matter." Kate's voice was barely audible, and Alex had to bend close to hear her words.

"We really are safe here, Kate, but nothing will happen between us unless you want it to. The last thing I want to do is make your life more difficult and complicated. It's just that you are so incredible." Alex put his hand under Kate's chin and lifted her face until she could feel his warm breath on her cheek. Slowly and with great care, he lowered his lips to hers, tasting the sweetness of her mouth in the deepening kiss.

Kate felt her head spinning, and she wasn't sure if it was the wine or Alex's hard body against her. "Kiss me again." She held out her arms, and Alex felt his heart lurch as he gathered her close to his chest. This time, Alex's lips were hot and insistent as he explored her face and neck.

In spite of the fever racing through her veins, Kate stiffened as Alex reached for her breasts. She knew that one step further into intimacy would be the end of any resolve she had to resist plunging into an affair with a married, if unhappy, man.

Alex sensed Kate's hesitation and held her face in his hands, kissing her tenderly as he moved away. "We can't do this, can we? At least, not now."

Reluctantly, Kate nodded. "There's nothing I would like more than to fall into your arms and say the hell with the rest of the world. But my life has been such a mess recently I'm terrified to add another variable that might affect a lot of people. Can you understand that?"

"Of course I can," Alex assured her. "At least we agree on what we'd LIKE to do." Alex grinned at Kate and wrapped his arms around her waist as he drew her to her feet. "Who knows, something magic may come our way yet."

While the last sprinkles of sun glimmered on the lapping waves, Alex looked wonderingly at the exquisite woman who stood before him, her face only faintly visible in the dim light. His hand traced a feathery path across her velvety cheek and she sighed at the gentle touch.

"You didn't mention, Mr. Stamos, that there would be such incredible fringe benefits to this job." Kate cuddled against Alex's heavily muscled body. "Remind me to commend your administrative talents at the next faculty meeting."

"Wouldn't Marta Stone have a field day with that little bit of news?" Alex grinned at the thought of his prim secretary's reaction, but his expression darkened as Claire's face flashed across his consciousness. "I hate to think what Claire would have to say."

"You're not going to tell her that any of this happened, are you? She'll make your life miserable, and she'll probably blow up Silvertree Farm!"

Alex frowned. "I suppose you're right, although I am certainly not ashamed of loving the most perfect woman in the world. Perhaps, though, the timing is bad, and it would be wiser to wait and see what Claire's next move is going to be. I just don't want you to worry."

"Who, me? I could float all the way home. But let's not complicate our lives any more than they already are." Kate mounted the narrow steps to the deck and breathed the cool evening air. Alex followed her, marveling at the slender grace of her lithe body.

"Just remember how it felt to be together, and hold the thought," Alex said as he caught up to her and walked up the field toward the house, keeping his arm around her shoulder oblivious to anything but her fragrant softness. "Could I beg a ride back to the marina?" As he opened her car door, he cupped her face in his hand and kissed her hard. "You're very special to me, Kate, and don't you forget it."

Kate slipped into the driver's seat and started the engine. "I feel exactly the same way, Alex, and don't YOU forget it." The BMW crunched across the gravel and spun out of the driveway toward the marina.

Someone else was watching the boat in Morning Cove, and when Kate and Alex drove away from Silvertree Farm, another car emerged from a clump of trees and sped off in the opposite direction.

****

Jessica was still awake when Kate came into the house, so she said hello quickly to Mildred and Tikka and went upstairs to kiss her daughter goodnight. After Jessica's favorite story and a long snuggle with Kate and Cynthia the bear, the little girl stuck her blanket in her ear and slipped into a peaceful sleep.

Watching Jessica's face in the moonlight, Kate wondered if Phaedra had ever looked that angelic and what kind of person Jessica would grow to be. As she walked downstairs to see what was left from dinner, Kate was filled with a sense of sadness for Alex at his daughter's hostility, but she was also keenly aware of her own increasing need for him.

With her cheeks flaming by the thought of the early evening, Kate welcomed the cold air that issued from the refrigerator as she took out a covered bowl of chicken stew, still warm from the evening's meal. Quickly reheating her plate in the microwave, Kate took a small tray into the library to join Tikka, who was lying in an exhausted heap on the sofa in front of the fire.

"Where's Millie?" Kate set her tray down on the coffee table and discovered she was ravenous, as she smelled the delicious aroma of Julia's hearty stew.

"Another one of those historic preservation meetings. I guess they're putting together a book about the man who designed a lot of the houses around here, including this one and Rocky Shore, and they want Millie's input. She should be home soon. How was your day?" Tikka set aside her book and peered closely at Kate. "You look different. Anything special happen?"

"Besides attending a world class opening of what will clearly be the hub of Maine fashion, nothing much. How are you holding up?"

Tikka mumbled something incoherent and rubbed her feet. "I'll be fine as long as no one makes me move from this spot. Ever."

"I'll get rid of this tray and come back with a ton of papers to correct," Kate laughed as she gathered her supper dishes and disappeared into the kitchen. The big wooden clock on the pantry shelf struck ten just as Kate was returning to the library with her bookbag, and she settled at Mildred's desk, intending to grade a set of essays that her junior class had written that day. Instead, Alex's lips and arms floated into her consciousness, and she found herself staring into space and reliving the time they had spent together.

"You're not making much progress. Something on your mind?" Tikka's amused voice cut into Kate's reverie, and she tried to get back to work but was distracted again when Mildred returned from her meeting.

"There's something big going on in town," Mildred wheezed as she turned on the television. "There are police cars all over the place, and two ambulances passed us on Route 11 when we were headed into Portland. Let's see if there's anything on the late news."

The three women waited through the last steamy minutes of a nighttime soap opera and then several commercials before the familiar face of the local newscaster appeared.

"Good evening, ladies and gentlemen. This is Ron Draper reporting for Channel 5 news. Our top story this evening is a tragedy in Cape Mariana where a nine-year-old boy has shot and killed his father and seriously wounded his mother. Dead on arrival at Maine Medical Center was Howard Calvert, 38 years old, an accountant with the firm of Mason and Towell. Calvert's wife, Ruth, also 38, is in critical condition. The child, Wilson Calvert, has been taken to Juvenile Hall, where he remains in protective custody, pending an investigation of the incident. The Calverts' other child, Eve, was apparently not home at the time of the shooting and has not been located. Cape Mariana Police are asking for any information concerning the whereabouts of Eve Calvert."

As the voice of the newscaster droned on, reciting the latest economic indicators, Kate looked at Mildred and Tikka in stunned disbelief. Kate spoke first, breaking into the shocked silence. "I can't believe this. I saw Eve just this afternoon. Where do you suppose she is at this hour of the night?"

Mildred thought for a minute. "You know, I've had the funniest feeling about those Calverts for a long time. Nobody seems to know much about the family except for the few people who are members of that crazy church they belong to."

"What crazy church? I thought you said they were Christian Fundamentalists or something." Kate's confusion was growing by the second.

Mildred sank back into her chair. "There's this little building way out in the marshes where about twenty-five families go and spend most of the day on Sunday. No one except the members is allowed in the place, and there's an odd man who lives in the back of the building and seems to be a sort of leader. I think they call him Brother Able. One of the Portland newspapers tried to do a story on the church last year, and Brother Able drove the reporter away with a shotgun."

Tikka and Kate were about to question Mildred further on the Calverts' peculiar religious habits when they heard the back doorbell ring. All three women looked at each other in alarm, because it was nearly 11:30, but Kate, who was sitting closest to the kitchen door, got up and moved to the head of the back stairs, where she had a good view of the service entrance. Bathed in the light that illuminated the small porch below, a slight figure leaned against the door and rang the bell again.

As quickly as she could, Kate raced down the stairs and unlocked the door, catching Eve Calvert in her arms just before the girl collapsed. "Tikka, come quickly!" Kate struggled to support Eve's weight, and in a few seconds she and Tikka half-carried, half-dragged the limp teenager up the stairs and into the library, where they laid her gently on the big velvet sofa. Eve's eyes were closed, but after she had been on the couch for a minute, they fluttered open.

Kate knelt down beside Eve. "Are you all right, Eve? Everyone's looking for you." She didn't say anything about the shooting, because it looked as if Eve were in shock, and Kate didn't want to upset her any further.

Eve turned over on her stomach and groaned. She had on a thin yellow windbreaker, and it looked as if there were rusty brown stripes here and there on the fabric.

"Get a blanket, Tikka. The child must be frozen, and her jacket's wet. Let's get it off her." Kate lifted Eve's arm carefully and began to remove her damp outer clothing. When she peeled part of the jacket back, she stopped and stifling a cry, pointed to Eve's back. Clearly visible on her white blouse were crisscrossed lines of dried blood covering most of the area from her shoulders to her waist.

When Mildred saw what Kate was pointing at, her hand flew to her mouth, and she looked away in horror. Even through the clothing, it was obvious that the girl had been badly beaten, and as they carefully lifted the hem of her long skirt, they could see that her legs had lacerations like those on her back.

"Eve, who did this to you?" Kate gently touched her tear-stained cheek. "You can tell us. We'll protect you."

The young girl began to shiver uncontrollably, turning her head away from Kate mumbling something about Willie and having to get him out. When Tikka laid a lightweight blanket across her, Eve flinched from its contact with her wounds, but her shaking slowed, and she began to sob.

"We'll have to notify the police right away, Eve. There are cruisers all over town searching for you." Kate spoke gently but firmly, and Eve looked puzzled.

"Why are they looking for me? My parents know that I always come back."

The three women surrounding the girl exchanged glances, and Kate spoke reluctantly. "Eve, are you aware of what happened in your house tonight?"

Eve sighed and closed her eyes again. "Of course I am. The same thing that always happens when HE thinks that I've disobeyed or sinned in some way. When I tried to explain that there was nothing evil about keeping a journal, he got madder and madder until I knew that there was no way out except to run. But he caught me and dragged me to the room where we get our whippings."

Tears ran down Eve's cheeks, and Kate wiped them away, fighting the urge to hug the girl's scourged body. "Are you talking about your father, Eve? Is he the one who beats you?"

"He did it this time, but sometimes its Brother Able who does it. If Willie or I have done something really awful, my father calls Brother, and he comes to the room and hits us with this special belt that he says was blessed by God."

Kate felt her stomach turn over. "Where is your mother while all this is happening?"

"She's so scared of both my father and Brother Able that she never says or does anything, even when she hears us screaming. And she always thanks Brother Able for coming after he's beaten one of us and gives him a tin of cookies or something."

"Where did you get that bruise? From your father?"

"Yesterday he came home furious because someone in his office had told him about the dance after the bonfire last Friday. I hadn't mentioned I'd been there, so he twisted my arm until I swore that I didn't dance. If he'd ever known what Eric made Jean Pierro do, he probably would have killed me." Eve's voice was scratchy, and Tikka went to get her a glass of water.

"Go on about what happened tonight. Did you run away?"

Eve nodded. "Usually, after I get my beating, my father locks the door of the room and makes me lie down on the bare floor all night, unless my mother comes and lets me out. But tonight he forgot and I snuck away. The only trouble is that Willie was standing outside the door while my father was whipping me, and he was yelling at my father to stop. I'm afraid that when my father finds that I'm gone, he'll take it out on my brother."

Kate looked down at the distressed girl. "Eve, I think there's something you should know…" Kate's words were interrupted by the ringing of the front door bell, and Tikka hurried to answer it, reappearing a minute later with a detective in street clothes and a uniformed officer. Mildred followed the men into the library and whispered that she had called Captain Brogan because she knew he would be careful in his treatment of the injured girl. Before he could say anything, Kate stood in front of the couch protectively.

"Captain Brogan, Eve has been cruelly beaten tonight, and I think she's in need of medical attention right away. She left her house right after her father did this to her, and she doesn't know anything about the events of the evening. I was about to tell her when you arrived." Kate stepped aside so that Jim Brogan could see the bloodstained back and legs of the girl on the sofa.

Brogan felt his throat tighten at the sight of Eve, and he motioned the officer with him to move away so Kate could continue to talk to Eve. "I'll put in a call to the station and let them know we've found her, and I'll see if I can get Doc Miller over here right away."

Eve's eyes were large in her face as she realized from the appearance of the police that something was terribly wrong. "Tell me, Mrs. Hammond. What's going on?"

"There's no easy way to say this, Eve. For some reason that we don't know for sure, your brother shot your parents after you left the house tonight. Your mother is in critical condition in the hospital, and your father is dead."

"What's happened to Willie?"

"The police are taking good care of him, and we can ask Captain Brogan exactly where and how when he comes back." Kate could see the slight amount of color that had come back into Eve's face begin to drain out, and she held the girl's hand. "Hang in there, Eve. This has been an awful night for you, but you need to be strong."

Jim Brogan strode back into the library and saw that Kate was leaning over Eve and grasping her hand, obviously having told her about the shooting. Eve's skin had a pasty, gray-green cast.

"Jim, Eve's worried about her brother. Can you reassure her that he's being taken care of?" Kate stood aside and let the detective kneel down beside Eve, whose breathing had become shallow and labored.

"Willie's in good hands, Eve. Apparently, your father was going to give him a beating, too, when Willie squirmed away and got your father's rifle from the hall closet. For some reason it was loaded, and Willie fired. He hit your father at close range, and when your mother tried to help your father, it seems that Willie fired again, not at your mother, but because he was afraid that your father would get up and come after him. The neighbors heard the shots and called the police. We've taken Willie to a psychiatric hospital nearby. You know, Merton House. A social worker will stay with him until we have a chance to talk to him in more detail."

The front doorbell rang again, and Doc Miller followed Tikka into the library, shaking his head at the sight of Eve's injuries. "Can she stay here, Mildred, at least for tonight? I'd like to get her into bed before I treat those lacerations, and I want to give her something to help her sleep." The doctor turned to Captain Brogan. "Is that all right with you, Jim?"

"That's fine, Doc. But I do need to talk to Eve in the morning. I can come here to do it. O.K. Eve?"

Eve nodded and seemed to relax a bit, flinching only when the burly young police officer picked her up in his arms. Doc Miller followed the pair up the stairs, and Kate came last, leaving Tikka and Mildred to make arrangements with Jim Brogan for his visit in the morning.

When they reached the landing on the stairs, Doc Miller turned to Kate, who was behind him, and whispered back angrily. "I told Howard Calvert that if he ever beat his children again, I would call the authorities. He swore to me he wouldn't, and I believed him. I guess some of us are born fools."

THE SHAPE OF DARK- Chapter Eleven

Before Kate left for school the next morning, she looked in on Eve and found the exhausted girl sleeping soundly. During the night, either Kate or Tikka checked on Eve every hour, and they were relieved to see that the mild sedative Doc Miller had given her seemed to have let her slip out of her nightmare and into a healing slumber. Friday had long been scheduled as a Teacher's Workshop, so Kate's own fatigue from the long night before wasn't as much of a concern as if she had to face five classes of active students.

Once she had hastily dressed herself and Jessica, Kate hurried down to the kitchen and found Mildred and Julia sitting at the table watching "Good Morning America," waiting for the local news which came on at twenty-five minutes past the hour. "I shudder to think of the gruesome details that were found overnight," Mildred commented. "Those poor children lived in Hell, and the story is really going to shock everyone who thought they knew the Calverts."

Just then the local news segment came on, spelling out many of the sordid details of the Calvert family's secret abuse of their children. The announcer reported that Eve Calvert had been found and was resting in satisfactory condition in a safe place.

"Thank God they didn't say where she was," Mildred commented. "I wouldn't put it past Brother Able to come looking for them."

"I never thought of that, Millie. Are you sure you'll be all right here? Do you want me to stay home from school?" Kate was truly concerned for her aunt's welfare, as well as Eve's, but her offer was met with a firm refusal.

"Absolutely not, Kate. Julia is here and can be very ferocious if provoked. Also, Lester Jordan will be working on the terrace gardens today, and I'll alert him to keep his eyes open. Jim Brogan is coming at ten o'clock to talk to Eve, so I think we're well covered."

"Do you know what this Brother Able looks like?" Kate began to gather her materials for the teachers' meeting at school, and she also grabbed a warm jacket, since there was a blustery wind which made Morning Cove a frothy slate-gray.

"Actually, I did see a picture of him once, when that Portland reporter tried to do a story on his church, but all I can remember about him was a black beard and wild dark eyes. Don't worry, Katie, if worse comes to absolute worst, I have a whole cabinet full of guns in the attic." Mildred walked over to Kate and pushed her toward the door. "Now, scoot, or you'll be late."

At Rocky Shore, the campus and lobby were teeming with reporters and photographers. Alex was standing in the middle of a sea of microphones, trying to answer the journalists' questions with some kind of calm logic, but the shouted inquiries and snapping cameras created an instant sense of chaos.

"Ladies and gentlemen, PLEASE." Alex held up his hand to ward off any further quizzing from the media. "I don't know any more about Eve Calvert's condition or whereabouts than you do. The police have her in their protection, and I imagine they'll make some kind of a statement as soon as they can. Meanwhile, I know nothing about Wilson Calvert or Ruth's Calvert's situation. I suggest you wait for news from Captain James Brogan of the Cape Mariana Police Department."

Grumbling a bit, the newspeople gathered their equipment and slowly left the building, but Kate noticed as she walked toward the teachers' lounge that most of them remained on the school grounds, shooting commentary by various reporters against the backdrop of the handsome façade of the building. Alex disappeared into his office, but most of the other teachers were in the lounge, drinking coffee and chatting, while they took seats at the round tables and waited for the meeting to begin.

It was not long before the principal strode into the room and glanced quickly around the group, checking to see who was present. In spite of the fact that several people were missing, Alex called the meeting to order.

"Well, folks, in all my years in education, I have never seen ten days with as much happening. I think we're all terribly upset by what has happened to the Calvert family, and I know that the media is not going to go away. I'll just ask you to be discreet in discussing the matter, and as soon as I have more information about Eve, I'll let you know. Meanwhile, let's turn our attention to some other matters."

The rest of the morning was spent discussing the upcoming accreditation of the school, which was scheduled for the following year. At lunch time, most of the faculty left the school grounds, taking advantage of the full hour that Alex had given them, and Kate had the opportunity to catch him alone before she hurried home to see how Eve was doing.

Kate was glad that Alex's back was to Marta Stone's desk when she approached because the expression on his face was unmistakable in its tenderness and warmth. Kate blushed a bit, but fought to keep her own features composed as she spoke to him in a low voice. "Would you like to come to Silvertree Farm for lunch? There's someone that you might like to see."

Alex looked surprised, but he turned to Marta and asked her if he had any appointments during the next hour. When she said no, Alex told her that he would be off campus for lunch, and as he and Kate walked out of the building together someone was watching them closely.

Captain Brogan's car was parked in the circular driveway when Alex and Kate came into the kitchen. Julia informed them that the police had been with Eve for almost two hours. During the drive from school, Kate had hastily filled Alex in about Eve's arrival last night and about her story of the extensive abuse she and her brother had suffered. Alex's reaction had turned from shock to anger, especially when Kate told him about Doc Miller's knowledge of the situation.

"I could tell you so many stories of things that Doc Miller has done that should land him in front of the medical board, but somehow he gets away with it in this town. People seem to protect him, and I can't figure out why." Alex was obviously disgusted with the local doctor, but his real rage was directed toward the Calverts.

"How could that mother allow her husband to abuse her own children like that? This Brother Able thing sounds like a cult to me, and we have a couple of other kids in the high school from that church. You can bet that I'm going to check on them."

Alex and Kate were just coming through the dining room when Jim Brogan came down the stairs, scowling and muttering to himself. "Peters," he said to the uniformed officer who was with him, "Get on the radio and see what you can find out about Ruth Calvert's condition. Then get ready to take a little ride with me out to that crazy church the Calverts belonged to. This Brother Able has some explaining to do!"

Brogan sat down in a chair in the corner of Mildred's vast living room and took out a notebook on which were scrawled pages of smudged words. "Well, Mrs. Hammond, I got basically the same story from Eve that you did last night, except in more detail. If what she said is true, the abuse was so bad that her brother's actions were clearly in self-defense, especially since the father still had a vicious looking strap in his hand when he was killed."

"How did Eve hold up under the questioning, Jim?" Alex asked as Kate excused herself to go upstairs and see how Eve was feeling.

"Amazingly well, considering the fact that she and her brother are orphans, for all intents and purposes. I can't imagine that the courts will let their mother have custody of them, after her complicity in the father's brutality. When I asked Eve if they had any relatives, she would only name her maternal grandmother, saying that everybody on her father's side was as crazy as he was. Evidently, Eve's mother got into some kind of trouble when she was a teenager, and this group that Howard Calvert was associated with took her in. Eventually they got married." Jim paused and flipped a couple of pages in his narrow notebook.

"According to Eve, this whole group, led by Brother Able, used to live near the north shore of Massachusetts in a commune known as Ledyard Hill. Wilson was born here in Maine, but Eve remembers her father working for an accounting firm in Beverly and the three of them living in a house with another family. Even then, and Eve was only four or five years old, she was brutally beaten by both her father and Brother Able for wetting her pants or spilling her milk."

Alex sighed and looked at the back of his hands. "I'm not sure I want to hear all of this, but go on."

"All the time Eve was little, she recalls her mother getting letters from her grandmother and hiding them from Howard, who had forbidden Ruth from having any contact with her family. Then, one day, one of the children in the other family in the house died, probably from severe abuse, and the little town they lived in threatened Brother Able's whole group of people. I guess it was a kind of vigilante justice because the building that was serving as a church was burned down, and rocks were thrown through the church members' windows."

"Brother Able decided the group had to move, and someone had a contact here in Maine. Several of the men, including Howard, came up to see what was available for housing and jobs. While Howard was out of the house, Eve remembers her mother calling her grandmother and telling her she wanted to get away from the group. The grandmother flew to Boston and met her daughter at a motel so the other church members wouldn't see them and report to Howard."

"Eve and her mother stayed overnight with the grandmother, and Ruth told the family they lived with that she had taken Eve on the bus to Boston to go to the Science Museum. Eve remembers how happy Ruth was to be reunited with her mother, but she finally refused to go home with her and hurried back to Ledyard Hill before Howard got home from Maine. Shortly after that, the whole bunch moved up here where they seemed to have hidden their child-rearing tactics well enough to escape attention from the authorities."

Alex let his breath out slowly and shook his head. "What about this grandmother? Has she been contacted?"

"Not yet," Captain Brogan replied, "but that's my next step. Eve gave me her name and the city where she used to live, so I hope she's still alive and I can track her down. Those kids need someone."

Both Alex and Jim looked up in surprise to see Kate assisting Eve down the stairs. Eve had put on some of Kate's clothes, and in spite of a very pale face, she looked remarkably well for the ordeal she had undergone.

"Eve would like to see her brother, and then she wants to stop in at the hospital, if her mother can have visitors." Kate kept her arm around the slender teenager as she spoke. "She asked me if I would go with her, if it's all right with you, Alex."

"Absolutely. No problem." Alex looked compassionately at Eve, who was standing with her eyes lowered. "Eve, I want you to know how sorry we all are that no one knew what you and your brother were going through."

"My mother knew." Eve's quiet voice was matter-of-fact, but her lower lip trembled. "And Doc Miller knew, too."

Alex's jaw tightened. "I'm aware of that, Eve, and I intend to do something about it. Meanwhile let's find out what we can about your mother."

Officer Peters came in from the kitchen and handed Brogan a slip of paper. "Here's the word from the hospital, sir." Peters glanced sympathetically at Eve.

Jim Brogan frowned as he read the report, and then he turned to Kate and Eve, who were both sitting on one of the living room couches. "Eve, it doesn't look good for your mother. She's lost a lot of blood, and it seems she has a very rare type that the hospital is having trouble locating. She needs surgery right away, but they don't dare go in without some blood on hand. She's still unconscious, and they've downgraded her condition to extremely critical."

Eve sat quietly for a moment and then turned her clear gray eyes up to Brogan, who was standing in front of her. "I have the same blood type as my mother."

"But Eve, honey, you're still weak from that beating. I don't know if they'd even let you donate." Kate took Eve's hand and found it to be cold and clammy. "Are you sure you want to do this?"

"I have to, Mrs. Hammond. I have no choice." Eve got up from the couch and accepted the arm that Alex put around her in support.

"Well, then, let's go, Peters. Get there as fast as you can." Captain Brogan watched Alex and Officer Peters help Eve and Kate into the cruiser, and after the police car had sped away toward Portland, siren screaming and blue lights flashing, Brogan got into his own unmarked car and followed, dropping Alex at the entrance to Rocky Shore.

When they arrived at Maine Medical Center, the physician who was taking care of Ruth Calvert was waiting in the Intensive Care Unit to speak to Eve and he agreed to let her donate blood for her mother. "Would you like to see her?" he inquired, pointing to a draped form in one of the unit's machine-filled cubicles.

Eve stared in her mother's direction. "No thank you." The solemn politeness of the girl's voice startled the doctor. "I never want to see her again." Eve turned toward the door, allowing Kate to lead her into the corridor. As soon as Eve's blood was taken, Ruth Calvert was wheeled into surgery and Eve and Kate got back into Officer Peters' car to go to Merton House, where Wilson Calvert was being held.

Kate could tell from the taut planes of Eve's face that she was very nervous about seeing her brother in the psychiatric hospital, but she sat calmly in the cruiser with her hands folded in her lap. Kate put her arm around Eve's shoulders, and as they came to a stop under the front portico of the hospital, Kate felt Eve's body tense and become almost rigid.

"Relax, Eve," Kate whispered. "I'm sure they're taking good care of Willie." As soon as they saw the boy, however, Kate realized that Eve's apprehension had been well founded. Evidently, Howard Calvert had landed a few blows before Willie had twisted away, because there were two angry-looking bruises on the youngster's cheek, and his eyes looked huge and haunted in his small, freckled face.

"Willie! Oh, Willie!" Eve rushed over to her brother and gathered him into her arms. The boy, small for his age, clung to Eve's waist as she patted his thin back and murmured to him. "Are you all right?"

Kate felt the tears welling while she watched the reunion of brother and sister, and as she glanced at Officer Peters next to her, she saw that his eyes were suspiciously moist. A white-haired, kindly looking nurse had brought Willie into the reception area, and Kate turned to her for information.

"How is he, really?"

The nurse shook her head. "The poor baby has been completely traumatized, and someone had to hold him all last night to keep him even remotely calm. They gave him a tranquilizer, but I'm afraid it didn't do much good. He's afraid to close his eyes, because he thinks God is so angry with him that he will die if he goes to sleep. Honestly, in thirty years of nursing, I've never seen a child so wounded both physically and emotionally."

"What will happen to him now?" Kate watched as Eve talked to Willie, and he gradually curled up in her lap and stuck his thumb in his mouth.

"I don't know. Our staff is doing everything we can, but it looks to me as if the best thing would be for him to be with his sister." The nurse took off her glasses and wiped them clean after blowing her nose.

"I couldn't agree with you more. Do you suppose they'd let Willie come home with me? Eve is staying at our house, and there are two beds in the room she's in. I can't bear the thought of separating them again." Kate wondered briefly if Mildred would object, but she dismissed that notion.

Jim Brogan, who had just come through the door, overheard Kate's idea. "Suppose I call the District Attorney and see what he says. We haven't charged Willie with anything yet, and this whole mess is so complicated that I doubt if there is much precedent. I wonder what the doctor in charge of Willie's case would think."

As they spoke, Kate and Brogan were approached by a balding, gentle-looking man in a long white coat who introduced himself as Dr. Ephron, the psychiatrist who had been given the responsibility of evaluating Willie's condition. Watching Eve comfort her brother, the doctor enthusiastically endorsed the idea of their remaining together, and he was particularly impressed by the police captain's willingness to provide security for Silvertree Farm until the District Attorney decided whether he was going to bring any charges.

Kate and Brogan crossed the waiting area of Merton House to where Eve sat in a comfortable chair, still holding Willie on her lap. The little boy had fallen asleep, clutching Eve's hand, and the peaceful look on his face reminded Kate of Jessica when she settled down for the night. "Eve," Kate whispered, "I just called my aunt, and they are going to let us take Willie to Silvertree Farm, and he can share your room with you. Perhaps he'll be able to rest if he knows you're right there."

Eve looked down at her brother's bruised face and tightened her arms around him. "Thank you, Mrs. Hammond. This really means a lot to both of us. I don't think we could stand to be separated right now."

Kate beckoned to Officer Peters, who lifted Willie from Eve's lap and carried him out to the waiting police cruiser. Dr. Ephron followed them to the door and stood watching while Eve climbed in beside her brother and laid his head on her lap. "That child is absolutely exhausted, and the best thing that can happen is for him to feel secure enough to get some sleep. I'll give you a call later and see if Willie is up to talking to me. If not, we'll wait until tomorrow."

The doctor accompanied Kate down the steps of the hospital and helped her into the passenger seat of the cruiser. "Be sure to let me know if you need any help or advice for either one of them. This is quite a responsibility you've taken on."

As the cruiser drove down the long, winding driveway of Merton House, Kate looked back as Dr. Ephron climbed the stairs leading inside, his shoulders slumped, and his head shaking.

Back at Silvertree Farm, Mildred bustled through the house, checking on the bedroom Eve and Willie would share and informing Julia about the imminent arrival of the little boy. "Just think of it, Julia. Less than three months ago, it was only three women rattling around in this big old house, and even I wasn't here for a lot of the time. Now two tragedies have filled these rooms with children and my beautiful Kate. But we must be very careful not to tell anyone that Willie and Eve are here until the police decide it's safe to do so."

Tikka heard Mildred's last words as she came through the door into the kitchen, and she agreed. "The press is everywhere in Cape Mariana, and the slightest hint about the Calvert children will bring them out like vultures. Mildred, I'm going back to the shop for a while. Is there anything you want me to pick up on my way home?"

Julia opened the refrigerator door and looked inside. "No, Miss Tikka. Thanks, but we've plenty of everything."

"Then I may drop by Susan Moore's studio for a minute. She has some new pieces to show me." Tikka tossed a bright, hand-woven shawl around her shoulders and gathered up her purse. "Don't worry about me for dinner. I might grab a bite somewhere, or I'll eat leftovers later. You'll have your hands full with the Calverts and Jessie!"

As Tikka left the house, she saw Jessica's school van turning into the gates, and she passed several police cruisers on her way into town, one of which, she surmised, was bringing Kate and her charges back to Silvertree Farm. Traffic around the little shopping center where Avesta was located seemed to be double its usual volume, a result, Tikka was sure, of the intense media interest in the Calvert murder case.

One of Tikka's salespeople was showing a piece of Susan Moore's jewelry to a woman when Tikka came into the main room of the boutique, entering as usual from the back, where she had a reserved parking space. The customer, whose face Tikka recognized as one of the local television anchorwomen, held the large beaten-silver brooch up to her shoulder and studied herself in the gold-framed mirror behind the counter.

"That looks wonderful on your cranberry jacket," Tikka commented. "This jewelry is quite extraordinary, don't you think?"

"Yes, it is. There are several pieces here that I like. Is this the work of someone local?"

Tikka nodded, taking several of the bracelets and pins out of the display case and laying them on a bright silk scarf for the woman's perusal. "Yes. Susan Moore teaches art at our local high school."

"Then you live in Cape Mariana?"

"Just around the corner. Why do you ask?"

"Because it seems funny in a small town like this that no one knew what was going on in that house where the man was killed by his son. I know the networks are going to be all over this very soon, and I'd love to get a jump on them. Do you have any idea where the children are now?"

Tikka shook her head. "But I'll tell you an angle of this I did hear about. Apparently there's some crazy church the Calverts belonged to that advocates this kind of child abuse. Why don't you take your cameras out into the marshes and find that Brother Able person who is supposed to be the leader?"

"We've already thought of that. Somebody at the studio remembered when he scared off the newspaper reporter, but we went anyway. The place was locked up and he was gone. The room behind the church where he lived was stripped of everything, clean. Then we heard that most of the members of this group lived in the same neighborhood out in the marshes. When we arrived, all of their houses were deserted, although it looked as if some of their things were still there." The reporter decided on the original brooch, and Tikka rang up her purchase. "Here's my card. Would you give me a call if you hear anything. I'd really appreciate it."

Tikka looked at the name on the small piece of cardboard. "Surely. And come back soon. Susan Moore is bringing in some more pieces next week." The journalist smiled and walked out the curtained front door of Avesta as Tikka turned her back and began to straighten a pile of sweaters which had become untidy during the day. As she worked, she looked at her watch and was surprised to see that it was almost 5:30 and time to close. When she moved toward the front to lock up, the door opened and Big Ed George came in.

Tikka hadn't seen Ed since the night they had gone to Rossoni's, so she wasn't prepared for the shadows under his eyes, even though Kate had told her about the argument between Chickie and his father. "When was the last time you got any sleep, Ed?" Tikka decided to play dumb and see what the big man would say.

"Oh, come on Tikka. Kate Hammond must have filled you in on the little disagreement my son and I had about his relationship with your cousin. That's what I wanted to talk with you about. Are you closing up?"

"As a matter of fact, I am." Tikka moved around the shop turning off lamps and adjusting the chairs in the little seating area she had created for the comfort of her customers. "What's on your mind?"

Ed looked down at the floor. "Actually, I was hoping you might have dinner with me, maybe at Antonio's Barge in town?" Tikka was so used to seeing Big Ed in his work clothes and signature cap that the fact he had obviously dressed carefully in pressed chino pants, a blue striped shirt, and a corduroy sports coat was strangely touching.

"Well, when somebody looks as good as you do, Big Ed, how could a lady refuse?" Tikka laughed at the embarrassment that flooded Ed's face and allowed him to drape her shawl across her shoulders as they walked out of the shop toward his car.

Antonio's Barge was one of Portland's most popular restaurants, located on the waterfront in a floating, charming old ferry that had been carefully converted into an elegant, candlelit dining room and lounge. All of the tables were full when Tikka and Ed arrived, so they put their name on the waiting list and went into the lounge, which overlooked a wharf full of picturesque lobster boats.

"See that boat over there, the *Special K*?" Ed pointed to a neat, blue and white vessel that was just pulling up to the wharf. "The kid who owns that boat lives in Cape Mariana and fishes about 800 traps out in the bay and along the shore."

Tikka looked across the wharf and watched a burly young man with sun-bleached hair and a deep tan. The fisherman was only about 6'2", but he was so solidly built and heavily muscled that he looked bigger. "Great looking guy. Who is he?"

"That's Timmy Brogan, the police captain's oldest son, and one of the nicest people you'll ever meet. He's worked for me off and on, but now he's a full-time fisherman and trap builder. The funny thing is that he was one of the brightest kids at Rocky Shore and probably could have gone to any college he wanted. But, he's always loved the ocean."

As Timmy Brogan heaved large trays of green-black lobsters onto the pier, Tikka caught Ed watching Timmy with a thoughtful expression on his face.

"You know, Tikka, when Timmy decided not to go to college, Jim Brogan and his wife supported his decision and never stopped telling people how proud they were of their son, the fisherman. But look what I do when somebody repeats some gossip about my boy that probably isn't true!" Ed's eyes were full of pain as he watched Timmy's powerful young body swing a heavy stack of bait trays onto the dock. "I don't even have enough faith in Chickie to ask him what the story is before I start hollering at him. And this isn't the first time this has happened."

Tikka put her hand on Ed's arm. "Do you think that it has anything to do with your drinking?"

Ed shrugged. "I almost wish I could blame it on the booze, but I've gone after Chickie when I've been cold sober. Somehow when Sheila was around, it never got out of control, and I could always stop myself before it was too late. But since she's been away, things have gotten really tense.'"

"Ed, have you ever sat down with Chickie and tried to tell him how you feel about this?" Tikka's emerald eyes were serious as she looked steadily at Ed.

"That's part of my problem, Tikka. I have a hell of a time telling people stuff like that, and I'm afraid he'd laugh at me. But I'll tell you one thing, after what's happened to the Calvert kids, things are going to change around my house."

With the sun almost set, Ed's profile was illuminated by the hurricane lamp that flickered in the center of their table, and Tikka was aware of the strong lines of his battered but compelling face. Suddenly ill at ease, Tikka turned her attention back to the activity on the wharf, looking up in relief as the hostess informed them that their table was ready.

Tikka was still thinking of Ed's comments about Chickie when she drove through the gates of Silvertree Farm shortly after nine o'clock. A police cruiser was parked unobtrusively beside the garage, and she recognized Jim Brogan's car behind the BMW that Kate used. Lights blazed all over the house, and as Tikka made her way up the back stairs into the kitchen, she heard Brogan's deep tones mingled with Mildred's gravely voice as they talked in the library.

"It's the damnedest thing, Mrs. Worthington. The bunch of them has simply vanished into thin air. We searched everywhere out by the church and in a couple of empty barns in the marshes, but we didn't find a trace. All of the church members' houses are locked up, and there isn't a sign of Brother Able anywhere." Jim Brogan was sitting on a wing chair beside the fire with his elbows on his knees and his hands clasped together in frustration.

"I know what you're talking about!" Tikka breezed into the library and plopped down next to Mildred on the couch. "That woman from Channel 7 came into the shop today and told me they had been out with a news team to interview Brother Able, but he was nowhere to be seen."

"Yeah, but what I'd like to know is WHERE they've gone. With psychos like that, you can never be sure what they'll do, especially when all the sordid details come out of Brother Able's role in abusing the Calvert children. That poor boy upstairs is scared to death, and no matter how many times I tell him that he would have police protection around the clock, he's afraid to close his eyes. Kate's up there now, trying to reassure him." Jim's craggy face showed his obvious fatigue, and as he slowly got to his feet to leave, he looked down at Tikka and Mildred.

"If anything, and I do mean ANYTHING seems strange or out of the ordinary to you, I want you to let the officer outside know immediately. Also, feel free to call me at home." Jim scribbled his unlisted number on a sheet from his notebook and handed it to Mildred. "Are you sure you don't want someone to stay inside the house tonight? I could call my son Timmy. He'd be glad to help out, as long as he's gotten the smell of fish bait out of his pores."

"No, thanks very much, Jim. We'll be fine, and just to be sure, I've brought this down from the attic." Mildred went to her desk and unlocked the bottom drawer, from which she took a revolver. "The ammunition is in the cabinet over the fireplace, and believe me, I am a crack shot with this thing."

Jim grinned at the spirit in Mildred's voice, and he watched as she replaced the gun and locked the drawer securely, hiding the key in a secret compartment in the Queen Anne desk. "Well, then, ladies, I think I'll head home. Say goodnight to Kate for me and thank you all again for helping these poor kids." Brogan let himself out the back door, locking it behind him.

Upstairs, in one of the bedrooms, Kate struggled to keep her voice steady as she talked to the little boy who was huddled in the middle of one of the twin beds, while Eve lay on the other. "Willie, honey, you simply must close your eyes and try to sleep. Eve is right here beside you, and I'll sit in this chair all night if you want me to. Just let me turn down a couple of these lights..." Kate moved to the bureau and switched off one of the tall brass lamps that flanked the mirror.

"NO!" Both Eve and Kate jumped as Willie's terrified voice cut through the quiet house. "Please leave on the lights!" Tears streamed down the youngster's face and he began to tremble so hard that the bed shook.

Eve moved from her bed and pulled her sobbing brother into her arms. As she rocked him, she looked over his head at a puzzled Kate and explained his reaction.

"Willie's always been afraid of the dark, but my father wouldn't ever let him have a light on at night. One time, Willie found a flashlight outside and smuggled it into his room so he could turn it on after my father had shut his door, but my father discovered the light and whipped Willie for disobeying him. When my father told Brother Able what had happened, Brother locked Willie in a dark storeroom at the church and left him there all night to teach him to mind his elders. Poor Willie was so scared he wet his pants and worse, and then got punished for that."

Kate swallowed hard. "When did all of this happen?"

"About six months ago, and because Willie stopped asking for a light at night, my father thought he had cured Willie of a sissy habit. I heard him bragging to someone in church about the whole thing."

Kate strode over to the bureau and snapped on the lamp. "Willie, you can have every light in the house on if you want to. Jessie used to be afraid of the dark, and so was I when I was a little girl, so I understand what you mean. Do you want to know what made Jessie feel a little better?"

From his sanctuary in Eve's arms, Willie nodded. Kate could see that the child had stopped shivering, so she told him she would be right back with something to show him.

When she returned, Kate was carrying one of Jessica's stuffed animals, a black, furry kitten with a tiny pink tongue and bright blue glass eyes. "Jessie told me that the dark had a scary shape, and I asked her what she meant. She said it was big and like a monster with eleven arms, and that only the light would keep it away. Is that how you feel, Willie?"

Willie blinked and wagged his head.

"Well, I told Jessie to try to think about the dark having other shapes, like her favorite black velvet hair ribbon or a delicious piece of licorice."

"I don't like licorice," Willie whispered in a tiny voice. "It's yukky."

"O.K., let's try something else. How about those smooth black stones that you find on the beach? Or a shiny black toy car? Or this kitty here? Jessie and I talked about how soft and cuddly she is, in spite of the fact that she's black like the night. Touch her, Willie."

Willie slowly reached out his hand and patted the silky fur of the toy cat. "She's nice."

"Try to think of her as one shape of dark that won't hurt you, and maybe if you sleep with her tonight, she'll make you feel better." Kate handed the stuffed animal to Willie and watched him tuck it under his chin and run the soft fur against his face.

"Thanks, Mrs. Hammond. Willie was never allowed to have things like that." Eve tucked in her brother and moved back to her own bed. "These lights won't bother me, and I think Willie is settling down now."

Kate came around the side of Willie's bed and smoothed his blanket before stooping to kiss his forehead. "Goodnight, Willie. You're perfectly safe here. I want you to try and get some sleep. My room is right next door, so you have Eve call me if you get scared. O.K.?" Kate moved across to Eve's bed and kissed her cheek. "Hang in there, kiddo. This is going to get a lot better for both of you."

Leaving the guestroom door ajar, Kate began to move toward her own bedroom when she heard Willie speak to his sister. "Eve, no matter what anyone says, he's out there, waiting in the dark."

There was a moment of silence before Eve answered. "I'm afraid you're right."

165

THE SHAPE OF DARK—Chapter Twelve

The house was shaking from the buffeting of a strong northeast wind when Kate awoke on Saturday morning. Looking out her window, she could see the violence of the gray ocean as it roared in and out of Morning Cove, and a cold rain lashed the tall oaks behind the house, driving the falling leaves into soggy brown piles.

One of the clocks in the living room struck eight, but Kate could hear no other activity in the house. After peeking in at a soundly sleeping Jessica, she allowed herself the long, hot shower that early school mornings curtailed. Since the house felt chilly after Kate came out of the steamy bathroom, she dressed in jeans, a turtleneck jersey, and a cozy handknit sweater Max had brought back from Norway shortly after they were married. Kate walked by the bedroom where the Calvert children both lay in exhausted slumber and padded down the back stairs to the kitchen, finding Julia in the midst of making Jessica's favorite apple cinnamon muffins.

"Morning," Kate yawned. "What's new today?" The newspaper had been delivered at dawn and lay on the kitchen table, still in its blue plastic sleeve. Shaking open the front page, Kate saw a familiar face.

"SCHOOL CUSTODIAN INDICTED FOR RAPE OF TEEN." Alf Stanton's surly scowl did nothing to improve his looks, and the picture of him in handcuffs and leg irons made him look sinister and mean. The grand jury, which had met the day before, had agreed with the District Attorney that Kelly Lundgren's positive identification of the ill-kempt janitor was more than enough reason to hold him for trial. In spite of Alex's efforts to find a good lawyer, the inexperienced public defender the court had assigned had been unable to convince the judge to grant bail.

The other picture accompanying the story about Alf was that of Kelly leaving the hospital with her parents. Mona Lundgren, stylishly dressed in a fitted wool coat, held Kelly's right hand, while Bill Lundgren, looking grim and powerful, had his arm protectively around his daughter's shoulders. Kelly herself had a sad, vulnerable look that, juxtaposed with the belligerent frown on Alf's face, made him appear even more menacing.

"I wonder if Alex has seen the paper this morning," Kate mused. "He's bound to be very discouraged for Alf." Julia poured a cup of strong black coffee for Kate who had just started to read the rest of the news when the phone rang.

Kate waved Julia off and jumped up to answer the call herself, remembering that Dr. Ephron was going to come by and talk to Willie sometime this morning. The call, however, was from another doctor, the surgeon who had operated on Ruth Calvert the day before. He informed Kate that the operation had gone as well as could be expected, considering there had been severe damage to the base of Ruth's spine. As a result, it was highly unlikely she would ever walk again.

Kate replaced the phone and turned to Julia. "If Ruth Calvert is going to be an invalid, this whole situation is more complicated than ever. I just hope that Jim Brogan can find the kids' grandmother."

Accepting a warm muffin from Julia, Kate sat down at the table again, this time with a glass of freshly squeezed orange juice. Before she could open the paper a third time, there was a knock at the back door, and Kate looked down the stairs to see the blue uniform of a police officer.

"There's a landscape gardener out here in the driveway, Mrs. Hammond. He'd like to talk to the owner about doing some work on the lilacs." The policeman, who had just replaced the evening shift, indicated a large gray van parked on the circle, and he waved over one of the men who had climbed out into the rain.

"I'm sorry," Kate said as she stood under the sheltering roof over the back door. "Mrs. Worthington is still asleep. Did she have an appointment with you?" There was no name on the side of the van, so she looked carefully at the slight man in work clothes.

"No, ma'am." The gardener pointed to the border of lilac trees near the circular driveway. "I'm new in this area, and my helper and I have been driving through some of the estates to introduce ourselves and to see if there are any special projects people would like done. I noticed that these lilacs are badly in need of pruning, and I wanted to talk to Mrs. Worthington about the possibility of our doing them for her."

Kate took the card the man offered and put it in her pocket. "Well, I'll certainly give this to the owner and tell her you came by. If she's interested, she'll give you a call, I'm sure."

The man touched the visor of his cap, and after glancing at the police cruiser parked by the garage, drove away. Automatically, the officer on duty wrote down the license number of the van before it turned out of the Silvertree Farm gates, reassuring Kate that the police were being very thorough in their screening of visitors.

When Kate went back up into the kitchen, Tikka had come down from upstairs, her face devoid of makeup except for a bright slash of lipstick. "I forgot that one of my salesladies is going to Boston today, so I have to open the store. Thank God Jessie woke me up, talking to that blue bear of hers." Tikka threw on a raincoat and accepted the coffee that Julia had ready. "Thanks. I'll drink this in the car. Oh, Kate, while I was getting dressed I heard that the soccer game has been postponed because of the weather."

As the back door slammed behind Tikka, Kate made her way upstairs and found that Jessica had wandered down the hall to the bedroom where Eve and Willie were just waking up. Jessica had brought her blue bear, Cynthia, with her and Kate was surprised to see that her daughter had climbed onto Eve's bed, where Willie had also landed, snuggling the black plush kitten. Eve was between the two younger children, conducting an imaginary discussion between the bear and the kitten, raising and lowering her voice to fit each character, and Kate's throat constricted once more at the sight of the innocent youngsters.

"Good morning, everybody!" Kate perched on the end of the bed and was delighted to see that color was beginning to come back into the faces of the Calvert children. "How did you two sleep?"

Eve looked considerably stronger. "I can't believe how much better I feel this morning. I think Willie slept through the night for the first time in his life." Willie clutched the kitten, patting its soft fur.

Jessica looked up at her mother. "Mama, can we give Blackie to Willie for his very own? Cynthia gets very mad when I pay attention to anyone else."

"I think that's a wonderful idea, Jessie. Willie, would you like to have Blackie to keep?"

Willie's fingers tightened on the stuffed animal and he looked up to Eve for permission. Just then, Julia appeared in the door with the clothing she had washed for Willie, and Kate left with Jessica to get her daughter dressed for the day.

By the time everyone finished breakfast, Dr. Ephron called from Merton House to ask if he and Dr. Adler, a specialist from Boston who dealt with seriously abused children, could come and talk with Willie and Eve. At the same time, Jim Brogan drove up outside and stood in the driveway talking to the officer on duty while making a few notations in his book.

"It looks like this is going to be a busy place this morning, Julia. Why don't you give me your list, and Jessie and I will go to Dunham's early so we can get back here before the doctors arrive." Kate bundled Jessica into a bright yellow slicker and was about to put on her own raincoat when Mildred came into the kitchen carrying a box which had been carefully wrapped for mailing.

"Here it is, Katie, finally. I stayed up last night and rewrote the last few pages. Would you mind dropping this at Dunham's so that UPS can pick it up?" Mildred handed her manuscript to Kate and sat down between the Calverts, who had each consumed two of Julia's muffins.

"Sure thing, Millie. Another bestseller, no doubt. By the way, a landscape gardener stopped by this morning to see if you wanted to have the lilacs pruned." Kate gave the card to Mildred and urged Jessica down the stairs. "We'll be right back, everybody, but in case we're held up, Dr. Ephron is bringing a Dr. Adler by at eleven."

Dunhams's was already busier than usual when Kate and Jessica arrived, but they hurried through the store and were headed up the last aisle when they saw Chickie George and Josh Temple talking beside the display of blank audio tapes by the checkout counters. As soon as Josh spied Kate, he beckoned to her and she wheeled her carriage in their direction.

"Well, if it isn't my best girl!" Chickie lifted Jessica out of the carriage and hugged her before setting her on his shoulders, where she grabbed onto his hair and beamed. "Thanks to the weather, there's no game, so Mr. Temple is going to help me make that tape for my mother."

Josh studied the various brands of tapes on the rack. "If we were really going to do this right, we should use a professional studio, but time and money are a problem, so we're trying to find a place that has good acoustics. Any ideas?"

Kate barely hesitated. "The living room at Silvertree Farm has particularly low ceilings for a house its size, and Mildred tells me there have been several benefit concerts for the Portland Symphony there. Also, there's a beautiful Mason and Hamlin piano and a state-of-the-art stereo system." Kate considered the wisdom of letting two more people know the whereabouts of the Calvert children, but she quickly decided that the comforting presence of both Chickie and Josh would help to take Eve's mind off of the recent events. "I'll check with my aunt, but I'm sure this afternoon would be fine."

Josh selected the tapes that he wanted and followed Kate to the checkout counter, while Chickie paraded around the store with Jessica bouncing on his shoulders. "That would be wonderful, Kate. Chickie is really anxious to get this done, although he's not sure how his father might feel about it."

"What Big Ed doesn't know..." Kate paid for her groceries and waited at the door while Chickie and Jessica came from the back of the store, the little girl clutching an apple that Paul Dunham had given her. Groaning because the rain was heavier than earlier, Kate ducked her head against the storm and raced across the parking lot.

It was almost eleven when she drove into Silvertree Farm, and Kate could see that a strange car was parked by the front door. Jessica and Kate shed their rain gear and went into the library where a fire was burning and Mildred was talking to Dr. Ephron and a little, pear-shaped man with kind eyes and a white beard.

"Dr. Ephron has filled me in on most of the background of this case, Mrs. Hammond, but I wanted to talk to you before I saw the boy. Is there anything else you can tell me that will help in my understanding of his condition?" The earnest concern on Dr. Adler's face reassured Kate that Willie would be treated gently, and she told him about his fear of the dark and their conversation of last evening.

Dr. Adler's face clouded over. "You know, it's not unusual for severely abused children to be so arrested in their development that they never progress to the point where they can begin to form value systems or ethical structures. I suspect both Eve and Willie are going to need a lot of help to heal properly."

The two physicians rose when Eve came into the room leading Willie by the hand. The little boy had a haunted look on his slight features while Eve had a calmness about her that was almost ethereal.

"Willie, I'm Dr. Adler from Boston, and I've come up here to talk with you. Is that O.K.?" The specialist put his hand on Willie's shoulder and Kate noticed that the child shrank from the contact. "Perhaps we could find a quiet place by ourselves."

Mildred suggested they use her study on the second floor, and as she led the doctor and the boy out of the library, Willie looked back at Eve in alarm. "It's all right, Willie. I'll be right here if you need me." Eve sat down on the library sofa and looked at Kate and Dr. Ephron. "I hear that my mother made it through the surgery, but Mrs. Worthington said her legs are paralyzed. Is that right?"

Kate nodded. "I'm afraid so. I guess there was a lot of injury to her spine. Would you like to see her?"

Eve looked straight at Kate. "No, Mrs. Hammond, at least not yet. Is that awful?"

"Of course not, honey. After what you've been through, I'm astounded you had enough compassion for your mother to donate your blood so she could have the surgery. Take your time about everything now."

Kate heard Julia open the back door, and Jim Brogan soon appeared in the library, followed by the young man Kate had met at Morning Cove. Seeing father and son together, Kate was struck by their resemblance to each other, although Timmy's flashing smile dominated the room in which they were all gathered.

"I've got a bit of disturbing news," Jim began. "It seems that those landscape people who visited Silvertree Farm this morning were in a stolen van that was taken from the parking lot of Compton's Tree Service last night. Thanks to the fact that Officer Elliott wrote down the plate number, we ran a check, and as soon as we discovered it was stolen, we began to look for it. We found the van, deserted, over in Lake Richmond, and I have a weird feeling about who those gardeners may have been."

Kate tried to remember the face of the man she had talked to, but all she could recall were pale eyes and a freckled, balding forehead. "O.K., Jim, let's have it. Who do you think they were?"

"I'm afraid those two this morning may be connected with that crazy church. It's possible they watched Merton House and saw you leave with Eve and Willie yesterday afternoon, and when they spotted the police here this morning, they must have been pretty sure they had found the Calvert kids. If half of what Eve and Willie have told us about Brother Able is true, I wouldn't put anything past him. That's why I brought Timmy with me." Jim Brogan drew his son farther into the room.

"Dad would like me to stay around the house, if that's O.K." Timmy Brogan's plaid shirt strained across his broad back as he sat on the edge of a chair, his big, callused hands resting on his knees. "It's fine to have an officer outside, but Dad feels uneasy leaving only women inside to protect the kids."

"Well, I, for one, would welcome your presence, Timmy. Less than a week ago someone tried to break into the house, and I've been kind of spooked ever since." Kate rose and crossed the room as the telephone rang.

When she hung up after a short conversation, Kate turned back to the group assembled in the library and commented that this was going to be a busy day at Silvertree Farm. The caller had been Josh Temple, and they had made arrangements to record Chickie's tape in the middle of the afternoon when the doctors were finished talking with Eve and Willie.

"I heard Josh Temple at Rossoni's the other night," Timmy spoke up. "I don't understand why he wants to be a teacher, when he's a professional musician. Uh, oh, sorry Mrs. Hammond. I meant…"

Kate laughed. "Don't apologize, Timmy. I've heard the story of your love affair with school, so I completely understand your viewpoint. I think Josh wants to cover all his bases, since making a living as a musician can be difficult."

"Do I hear a familiar voice?" Mildred came through the library door and hugged Timmy. When she heard about the stolen van, Mildred readily agreed it would be nice to have Timmy around.

"Do you have anything you want done while I'm here, Mrs. Worthington? How about that firewood out in the back that needs to be split?" It was clear to everyone that Timmy needed to be busy, so Mildred sent him out into the cold drizzle, where the sound of the energetic cracking of logs could soon be heard.

Almost as soon as his son had left the library, Jim Brogan excused himself, saying that other matters awaited his attention at the station. He assured them, however, he would be back later in the day to make sure all was going well. Shortly thereafter, Dr. Adler reappeared with Willie, who seemed much more relaxed than he had earlier, and he even agreed when the psychiatrist suggested they have another meeting before his return to Boston on Monday.

The two doctors said goodbye to the Calvert children who followed Mildred into the kitchen to see what Julia was cooking for lunch. Kate accompanied the men out to their car and was greatly relieved to hear Dr. Adler say that with therapy, Willie should be able to recover from the traumas he had suffered. He also suggested that Dr. Ephron talk to Eve, especially when it was decided who was to be responsible for the welfare of her and Willie.

"The important thing, Mrs. Hammond, is for both Willie and Eve to feel perfectly secure in their surroundings. They have been terrorized for so long that the best immediate relief for them is to be absolutely certain they are safe from harm."

"Don't worry, Dr. Adler. One way or another, we'll watch out for those kids until a permanent solution can be found." Kate waited while the car drove away, and was unaware, as she slowly walked back to the house that someone was watching.

Everything was quiet for the early part of the afternoon, after Julia served tomato soup and grilled cheese sandwiches to everybody, including Timmy Brogan, who came in, red-cheeked, from his wood chopping to devour two bowls of soup and three sandwiches. "Do you always eat like that?" Kate asked, since there wasn't an ounce of fat on Timmy's muscular frame.

"Nope," Timmy answered between mouthfuls. "I usually eat more." Willie, sitting next to the strapping fisherman, was obviously fascinated by both his size and his cheerful good humor, and he gazed up at Timmy in adoration, drawn by the gentle kindness in his eyes.

"Hey Willie." Timmy wiped the last crumb of grilled cheese from his lips and grinned down at the boy by his side. "How would you like to help me in the woodpile?"

Kate thought she would cry at the ecstatic expression on Willie's face, and Mildred swallowed hard. "Actually, Willie, I have a box of old clothes in the attic from when my son was young. I think there are some warm things that would fit you. Would you like to try to find something to wear so you could go outside with Timmy?"

Willie's enthusiasm was evident as he followed Mildred out of the kitchen toward the second floor. As soon as they'd gone, Eve turned to Timmy, gratitude shining in her eyes. "I can't thank you enough for being so nice to Willie. Most of the men in his life have caused him nothing but pain."

"I know, my father filled me in." Kate could see the muscles knot in Timmy's jaw.

When Mildred reappeared with Willie, the boy was wearing clothes that were a bit too big, but with the sleeves and pant legs rolled up, he was adequately protected from the chilly wind. The drizzle had finally stopped, and Timmy excused himself and held out his hand to Willie.

"Come on, pal. Get the lead out. We men have a lot of work to do." As the back door closed, Eve commented in a choked voice. "That's the first time I've ever seen Willie look completely happy. It's almost too good to be true."

Kate got up from her seat and patted Eve's back, but she suddenly had a chilling flashback to the last encounter between Jessica and her father, and the memory made her shudder. Eve, feeling the tremor in Kate's body, looked up questioningly, but Kate moved quickly to the kitchen window, which framed the distant picture of Timmy placing one log in Willie's arms, while he picked up eight and stacked them neatly on the growing woodpile.

The ringing of the front doorbell diverted everyone's attention, and Kate, glancing at the clock, realized it must be Josh and Chickie, ready to make the tape for Sheila. Josh, his guitar case under one arm, gestured toward the police car near the garage. "What's going on here, Kate? That cop really gave us a grilling before he let us stop."

"Oh my gosh, Josh, I'm sorry. I forgot to tell him you were coming. We've got sort of a complicated situation here, but I'll explain in a minute." Kate locked the front door behind Chickie and led the two into the living room where a fire crackled at one end of the room and lamps warded off the gloom of the gray skies outside. Chickie carried several books of music, which he set down on the polished grand piano, and Josh began to undo his guitar.

"Hello Chickie, Mr. Temple." Eve stood in the doorway between the dining room and the living room, her body slender and frail looking in the wide opening.

Josh straightened up and Chickie's mouth fell open in surprise. "So this is where you've been!"

"I knew Mrs. Hammond would help me, and she even arranged for my brother to stay here, too." Eve pointed to the French doors leading to the terrace, and Chickie saw a small boy toiling alongside a husky young man.

"That's why all the police protection." Josh came to join the group looking out at the woodpile, and then he turned to Eve. "I'm so glad that you're in a safe place."

"Me, too!" Chickie said immediately, and then looked embarrassed at his outburst.

Josh began to tune his guitar, and he beckoned Chickie over to the piano. "Now, which songs do you want to record? You said there were several you used to sing with your mother?"

Chickie nodded. "Yeah, she loved it. Even my father used to join in sometimes, but that would never happen now."

"Why not, son?" Big Ed George's bulky frame filled the dining room doorway, with Tikka just slightly behind him. "Tikka told me what you were planning to do, and I think it's a great idea. I only wish you had felt able to talk to me about it." Big Ed walked over to Josh Temple and put out his hand. "Hi. I'm that obnoxious guy from Rossoni's who made it so hard for you to play on your first night. I'm really sorry."

Josh took Ed's hand and shook it firmly. "No problem, Mr. George. We all have those moments. You've got a great kid here with a heck of a voice."

"I know I do, and call me Ed. It's been an awfully long time since Chickie felt like singing around me, but I hope that will change."

175

Chickie hadn't moved since his father had walked into the room, but now he sat down hard on the piano bench and shook his head. "Sometimes you confuse me, Dad."

Big Ed put his hand on Chickie's shoulder. "I know I did a lot of stupid things, but I hope you'll be able to understand that it wasn't because I wanted to. When your mother got so sick, I just went kind of crazy, and I thought the booze would help the pain. It only made things worse. I know that now."

"Come in the kitchen, Ed, and have a cup of tea." Tikka motioned to Big Ed, who squeezed his son's shoulder before he followed through the dining room to the kitchen where the teakettle was whistling.

Kate sat down on the piano bench next to Chickie and put her hand on his arm. "Are you all right? You look like you're in shock."

Chickie's eyes were slightly reddened, and he cleared his throat before he could speak. "That's the LAST thing I ever expected my father to say, and the funny thing is that I think he means it."

"Well, Tikka's a very kind, loving woman who knows a good person when she sees one. As long as I've known her, she has said your father was in a special kind of agony and that his drinking and outbursts were only symptoms. Evidently, she was right." Kate smiled at Chickie, who struggled to regain his composure as he flipped the pages of a book of music.

"These are pretty old-fashioned songs, Mr. Temple. I hope you don't mind. This first one was my mother's favorite, and I remember her singing it to me when I was a little kid."

Josh began to strum the opening chords of "Whispering Hope," and Chickie's true, strong baritone rose above the silvery sound of the guitar, sending a rich melody throughout the room. Kate relaxed in a large sofa by the fire and listened with admiration as the pair worked out various aspects of the music and perfected the recording.

After they had done the first song to their satisfaction, Josh and Chickie asked Kate to join them on the piano for "Greensleeves" and "Flow Gently Sweet Afton." They even persuaded Eve to sing "Love's Old Sweet Song" with Chickie, a duet that sent chills through Kate.

As the afternoon wore on, Kate went into the kitchen to talk with Timmy and Willie, who had come in from outside to warm up with a cup of hot chocolate. Tikka and Ed settled in the library and were drinking their tea in front of the fire, listening to the music float in from the living room. When the last tones of "Love's Old Sweet Song" died away, Ed got up from the library sofa and walked through the dining room to where his son was standing by the piano. Josh was rewinding the tape so they could listen to all the songs, when Big Ed spoke awkwardly to his son.

"That really sounded great, Chickie. Your mother is going to love it, I'm sure. But there's one song you forgot, and I think it would mean more to her than anything."

Chickie looked puzzled. "I don't remember any others. Which one do you mean?"

"'Baby's Bed.'" Ed looked a little embarrassed, but he didn't move away from the piano. "That's the one you used to sing to me at night." Chickie, too, had a strange expression on his face. "I remember I wouldn't go to sleep until you'd gone through it about eight times."

"Want to try it together?" Ed's face was bright red now, and he avoided Chickie's eyes. "If it's no good, you can leave it off the tape."

"Sure, Dad. Let's give it a shot." Chickie moved closer to the piano and picked out the melody with one finger. "Think you can play that, Mr. Temple?"

"No problem." Josh stroked his fingers across the guitar strings, and the lovely melody of the old lullaby echoed in the room.

"Baby's bed's a silver boat, sailing in the sky..." Big Ed's deep bass voice began to sing, and Chickie joined in, lending his lighter, but equally true tones to the simple tune. "Sailing on a sea of dreams, while the stars go by..." The two voices blended so harmoniously that Josh's eyebrows lifted appreciatively as he accompanied the song. "Sail, baby sail. Sail across the sea. Only don't forget to come home again to me."

When the last notes faded, Big Ed looked at his son for a long moment and then walked slowly back into the library where Tikka sat on the couch dabbing at her eyes. "That was the most beautiful thing I've ever heard, Ed. Listen." The playback of the lullaby rang in through the library door as Ed stood motionless by the fireplace.

BANG! The gentle tones of the music were obscenely shattered by a loud sound from the back of the house. As everyone rushed to the doors and windows that overlooked the back yard and pool, four people, one carrying a gun, could be seen running from the poolhouse toward the woodpile. One man, who appeared to be at the head of the group, screamed loudly at Timmy, who picked up Willie and ran toward the garage.

As soon as he saw what was going on, Big Ed wrenched open the French doors between the living room and the terrace and hurtled down the stone steps toward Timmy, whose strong legs were outdistancing his pursuers, even carrying a terrified Willie. Chickie and Josh followed Ed toward the group of invaders, and while Julia frantically dialed 911, Mildred ran into the library and quickly loaded her gun.

When Timmy neared the police car, he heard a shot ring out and felt a sharp pain in his side, but he tightened his grip on Willie and kept on running. Officer Peters was crouched behind the cruiser, waiting to fire as soon as Timmy and Willie were out of the way. The policeman's aim was true, and he was able to fell the man leading the attack, while Big Ed picked up the maul that Timmy had been using to split wood and went after the others in the group, who had stopped at the sound of gunfire and now turned toward the woods behind the pool.

Several shots rang out from the terrace. Big Ed looked up to Mildred standing above them with a revolver aimed at the bodies that were rapidly swallowed by the dark trees. A dark-haired man lay writhing on the ground, his face contorted in pain, but as Officer Peters approached him, he screamed once and was still.

Several police cruisers arrived almost immediately, spilling out armed policemen who began to search the woods where the band of trespassers had gone. Mildred came slowly down from the terrace, pointing the gun she held toward the ground, while Peters, his eyes intent on the body on the lawn, moved toward the elderly woman and carefully took the gun from her hand. Mildred seemed to stagger at the sight of the form on the lawn, and Officer Peters caught her arm. "Don't worry, you didn't hit this one. I did."

Eve ran around the side of the house and took Willie from Timmy, who sagged against the police car. Cuddling her whimpering brother, Eve looked at Officer Peters. "Did you get him?"

"I don't know; you'll have to tell us."

Kate came up behind Eve and held a sobbing Willie in her arms as Eve walked slowly down the lawn past Mildred and Officer Peters. She looked quickly at the man who lay spread-eagled on the leaves, his eyes wide open, and swallowing her nausea, she turned stricken eyes toward Kate and the others. "This isn't Brother Able."

THE SHAPE OF DARK—Chapter Thirteen

Cradling a shivering Willie in her arms, Kate could hear the sirens approaching from all directions. Timmy Brogan lay on the driveway in a widening pool of blood, while Tikka knelt beside him, pressing a folded dishtowel against a gaping wound in his side. Jim Brogan's car roared into the yard just ahead of the two ambulances, spraying gravel everywhere as it screeched to a stop near the body of his son.

Timmy was conscious and groaning when his father knelt over him, and when Timmy tried to speak, all color drained from his face. He passed out just as the paramedics came running toward him with their equipment.

As soon as he saw the EMTs lift his son onto a gurney, Jim walked over to Officer Peters, who was standing next to the man who had wounded Timmy. Peters had shot the man in the chest, and after they checked unsuccessfully for any sign of life, the paramedics pulled a blanket over the entire body.

"What the hell happened here?" Jim tried very hard to control his rage at the man who had tried to grab Willie and had hurt Timmy in the process. A dusty black hat lay on the ground near the stretcher where the dead man was being placed, and Jim noticed Eve looking at it with disgust.

"That hat is just like the horrible thing that Brother Able wears all the time, but this man is just one of the people in the church. I can't even remember his name. Brother Able must have told them to get Willie." Eve shuddered as she thought of the possibilities had Timmy not saved her brother.

"Unfortunately, this guy isn't going to be able to tell us anything, but maybe the men found something in the woods after following those others. Did you recognize any of them?" Jim questioned Eve.

"No, everything happened too fast. I couldn't even tell what sex they were, although most of Brother Able's disciples were cruel men, just like he was." Eve turned away from Jim and stumbled over to where Kate was still standing holding Willie. "How are we going to keep him safe, Mrs. Hammond?"

Before he climbed into the ambulance with Timmy, Jim instructed two of the officers who were returning from their search of the woods to remain at Silvertree Farm in case Brother Able's followers returned. "We're going to double the guard, Mrs. Worthington, although it looks to me as if you are quite able to defend yourself. It's getting dark now, so you need to stay inside and make sure everything is locked securely." Jim took Mildred's gun from Officer Peters and handed it back to the stalwart old lady. "Keep this handy, just in case."

Kate ran alongside Jim as he headed toward the ambulance, concern filling her eyes. "I'm so sorry Timmy got hurt. He was wonderful in protecting Willie that way, and he made Willie feel really special all day. I pray he's going to be all right."

Jim nodded, his eyes stinging. "I agree, Kate. If anything should happen to Timmy I'd... "Jim broke off and coughed. "I called my wife from the car, so I'm sure she's at the hospital by now. I'll let you know about Timmy's condition as soon as I can."

Kate watched the ambulance roar through the stone gates at the end of the driveway before she slowly made her way back into the house. Eve and Willie were huddled together on the couch in the library, while Big Ed made a fire to brighten the darkening room. Tikka, Mildred, Chickie, and Josh all sat helplessly on various chairs around the room, frantically trying to think of something to say to diminish the Calvert children's obvious fear.

When Kate came into the library, Josh offered her his chair, apologizing that he had to leave for his evening's performance at Rossoni's. While Tikka saw him to the door, Big Ed stood in front of the fire and looked seriously at the children on the couch. He twisted his big rough hands together, but he spoke slowly and calmly.

"Now I want you kids to listen to me. What happened out there was very scary, especially for you Willie, and I know you're frightened that some of the people got away. You need to remember that those people are only ordinary men. They may seem bigger than life to you now, but the facts are that Timmy and Officer Peters were more powerful than they were, right Willie?"

Willie, clinging to Eve, nodded.

Ed went on, speaking primarily to Eve, whose face was a white mask of barely concealed fright. "How do you feel about all of this, Eve?"

Eve spoke so quietly that the people in the room had to strain to hear her. "I don't know where we can go to be safe."

Big Ed came over and sat on the couch next to Eve and Willie. "Would it make you feel better if both Chickie and I stayed here tonight?" The expression of relief was so instantaneous in both Eve's and Willie's eyes that Ed looked questioningly at Mildred. "I know this sounds patronizing, Mrs. Worthington, but maybe a couple of fairly good-sized men in the house would make these kids relax a little. That is, if you have room for us."

Mildred didn't hesitate. "I've got nine bedrooms, Ed, and I think we'd ALL sleep better knowing you're here. Just let me tell Julia about dinner. Are you sure that you don't have other plans, Chickie?"

"Not me, Mrs. Worthington. I'd be glad to stay. The only thing I'd like to do is deliver the tape we made over to my mother at Thornton Oaks. It'll only take about a half hour." Chickie glanced at his father. "Do you want to come, Dad? You usually visit on Saturday afternoon."

"Actually, I think it would be better if we go one at a time. You leave now, and I'll run over after supper." Big Ed had taken Willie into his lap, and the youngster had begun to doze off in the warm shelter of the burly man's arms.

Chickie agreed and was about to leave the library when Eve spoke up. "Would you do me a favor, Chickie? I promised the woman in your mother's room, that I would visit her this weekend. I'm sure she has no idea why I haven't come, unless she reads the newspaper. Could you explain for me? Tell her I'll come as soon as I can."

Tikka spoke up. "Why don't you go with Chickie, Eve? I've got a blond wig upstairs you could wear as you leave the house, and if anyone is watching he'll think I'm the one getting into the car. It might do you good to go for a little ride and think about something else. Besides, you helped make that tape, and you might like to see Sheila's reaction."

Eve's face lit up as she turned to Kate. "What do you think, Mrs. Hammond? Is it too much of a chance to take?"

"To be honest, Eve, I think it's a great idea, although I suppose there is a little risk involved. Still Chickie will be with you."

As Tikka left left the room to find the wig, Kate went to the front hall closet and took out Tikka's bright purple coat and a multicolored cashmere scarf. When Tikka returned and adjusted the wig over Eve's brown hair, the transformation was remarkable. "I like you better the old way," Chickie whispered as he helped Eve into Tikka's coat. "But this is sort of fun."

Big Ed struggled to get his keys out of his pocket without disturbing the now soundly sleeping Willie, and the two teenagers walked as nonchalantly as they could past the police guard by the back door. When the officers failed to question her, Eve realized her disguise must be effective, and she relaxed into the front seat of Ed's truck.

The ride to Thornton Oaks passed quickly, with Eve and Chickie sitting in companionable silence, neither one feeling the need to make idle chatter. As they got out of the car at the nursing home, Eve took off the blond wig, realizing that Betty Callahan might not recognize her. As she was attempting to pat her own hair into some semblance of order, Chickie reached over and smoothed a wayward strand into place. His hand brushed across her cheek, and Eve's face burned, making her very glad that the interior of the truck was dark.

Inside the lights in the central corridor of the extended care wing reflected brightly on the polished linoleum floor, but the lamps were dim in the room that Sheila George and Betty Callahan shared. Both women were lying in their beds, and Eve left Chickie talking quietly to his mother, while she went over to Betty, who was engrossed in a romance novel.

"Eve, you precious thing! I didn't expect you to come after what you've been through!" Betty pointed to the morning newspaper that was neatly folded on her bedside table. "But I'm awfully glad to see you. Come and sit down and tell me how you and your brother are doing."

"We're going to be all right, I hope, but we had a real scare today." Eve described the attempted abduction of Willie, and Betty sighed at the mention of Timmy Brogan's name. "I love that boy. He used to deliver my paper, and when my husband died, he'd come twice a year to do my screens and storm windows. I certainly hope he's not hurt badly."

While Betty and Eve were chatting, they heard the faint sound of music, and Eve explained about the tape so Betty would understand who was singing. At their request, Chickie turned up the volume, and the songs they had recorded earlier reached into the corners of the large, square room.

At first, there was no response from Sheila, but gradually Chickie felt an increase of pressure from the hand he was holding, and as he looked down at the frail form of his mother curled in the center of the bed, he saw a softening of the vacant grimace that had become her usual expression. When the final song came on, with the strong voices of Big Ed and Chickie blended in the lullaby, Sheila looked up at her son and smiled faintly for the first time in several months.

Betty's kind face wrinkled into a broad smile. "What a wonderful idea for Sheila to have that tape! Now whenever she gets restless or unhappy, I'll make sure someone puts it in for her. But I'm telling you, Eve, after seeing how this terrible disease has affected Sheila and her family, I'd kill myself if I thought I'd be like that."

"I know, Mrs. Callahan. I feel the same way." Eve patted Betty's delicate, papery hand. "The trouble is that by the time you realize your mind is going, it's already too late to take control of what happens to you."

"Well, folks, how's everybody tonight?" The overhead light in the room turned on and Doc Miller strode in, followed by the charge nurse who carried a pile of metal-jacketed charts. "Chickie, my boy. Visiting your mom? How does she seem to you?" Doc's shock of white hair flopped up and down as he shook Chickie's hand and bent over Sheila.

Chickie shrugged and turned off the tape recorder as Doc listened to Sheila's heart and lungs. "She's all right, I guess. Not much different, except that she doesn't have any idea who I am now. She used to recognize me once in a while, but not anymore."

"I know. That's one of the hardest parts of this disease." Handing Sheila's chart back to the nurse, he walked around to Betty's bed. "And how are you, Missy? Sassy as ever?" Doc's eyes widened as he recognized Eve, but he didn't say anything.

Betty chuckled. "There isn't anything wrong with me that a good stiff drink wouldn't cure. How about you and I take a little spin over to Rossoni's and have a party?"

Doc Miller smiled and shook his head. "Sorry, honey. You'll have to make do with Geritol. Now, let's have a look at those legs."

Eve said goodbye to Betty as the nurse began to draw the curtains around her bed. "See you next week, Mrs. Callahan." Chickie kissed his mother, and he and Eve made their way back through Thornton Oaks to the parking lot.

"I think your mother looked better tonight than the last time I saw her." Eve repositioned the blond wig on her head as they headed back to Silvertree Farm. When they drove past Half-Moon Beach, it was almost seven o'clock, but there were no cars.

Suddenly, Chickie jerked the wheel to the right and drove over to the edge of the beach where he shut off the engine. When he turned toward Eve, she could see that tears were forming in his eyes as he looked desperately at the girl next to him. "I don't know how much longer I can stand this, Eve. My mother's not better. She's worse, and there's nothing my father or I can do about it. If I could have one wish it would be for my mother to die peacefully in her sleep, because she'd hate the way she is now."

Eve moved closer to Chickie and put her arms around him. "I'm so sorry, Chickie. I wish there was something I could say to make you feel better."

Chickie laid his head on top of hers and drew in a long, shuddering breath. "You probably think I'm a real wimp, Eve, especially after what you've been through. I always thought men were supposed to be tough about stuff like this." When Eve raised her head to answer him, Chickie tilted her chin up and kissed her lips gently. "Thanks for listening."

Eve could feel Chickie's warm breath on her face, and his wet, slightly rough cheek brushed her soft skin. "We'd better get back," Eve whispered raggedly. "Mrs. Worthington said dinner was at seven."

For a moment, the inky clouds covering the moon parted, letting a path of silvery light fall on the ocean and reflect in Eve's clear, gray eyes. Chickie studied the delicate features of the girl beside him and then straightened his shoulders. "Right." He said, turning over the engine.

Julia was just lighting the candles in the dining room when Eve and Chickie came up the back steps, after having been stopped twice, first at the stone entrance gates and again by the back door. "That's reassuring," Chickie commented. "Old Brother Able is going to have trouble getting through those guys."

185

Everyone was gathered in the library watching the evening news when the smiling face of Timmy Brogan flashed across the screen, file footage taken from a news story that had been done earlier about the difficult time that the lobstermen were having all along the Maine coast.

"There is another tragic twist to the story which began Thursday evening when young Wilson Calvert fatally shot his father and wounded his mother in order to stop what has been described as extensive and serious abuse of both him and his sister. Timmy Brogan, 21, was killed this afternoon while attempting to protect the Calvert boy from abduction by members of a religious cult of which the Calvert family were a part. According to police, who killed the man responsible for Brogan's death, the leader of the group, a Brother Able, had instructed his followers to find and punish Wilson Calvert for the death of his father. At this moment, both Calvert children are under police protection. In other news..."

For a moment, there was absolute silence in the library. Kate, playing a game of checkers with Willie, looked over at the boy, who was bent over the game board, his hand still resting on the piece he was about to move. Then, slowly, he raised his head and stared straight ahead, his eyes round and glassy. "I killed Timmy, too," Willie mumbled, the anguish so naked on his face that the adults in the room were at a loss for words.

Big Ed recovered his voice first and went quickly to the boy's side. "No, Willie, you're wrong. A bad man shot Timmy, and you were in no way responsible, even if you were with Timmy when it happened. You must understand that."

Willie closed his eyes and sat absolutely still, as if he were in a trance. Then, he began to rock back and forth, seemingly oblivious to everything around him.

"I hoped I'd never see him do that again," Eve said in a choked voice. "The last time he acted like this was after Brother Able and my father locked him in the dark closet at the church. When they opened the door, this is the way they found him."

"I think he's escaping from his pain," Kate answered as Willie continued to retreat from the people around him. "The poor child has had so much to contend with in the last few days he must have short-circuited when he heard about Timmy. I'm going to call Dr. Ephron right away."

Eve went over to her brother and spoke to him, but there was no response, in spite of the fact that Willie opened his eyes. He continued to sway rhythmically and to make meaningless sounds, refusing to answer either Eve or Big Ed on either side of him.

"Dr. Ephron and Dr. Adler are on their way over," Kate reported, hanging up the library phone. "They think it would be wiser and safer to take Willie back to Merton House, especially since this Brother Able is still on the loose."

"I hate the thought of Willie being there alone," Eve said. "But, I guess they're right. I think he needs a lot more help than we know how to give him." The tears that had been brimming in Eve's eyes spilled onto her cheeks, and Big Ed reached across Willie to squeeze her hand.

"Don't worry, honey. Chickie and I will still stay here overnight in case those nuts come back. I'm sure the police will find it easier to guard Willie at Merton House, and Brother Able won't know if Willie is here or there." Big Ed's face was grim and his jaw was set, but his touch and voice were gentle as he spoke to the distraught young girl.

Mildred looked gratefully at Big Ed and shook her head slowly. "I can't even begin to think what Jim Brogan and his wife are going through right now. Everybody who knew Timmy thought the world of him, and my heart just breaks for his family."

Kate felt her eyes welling with tears as she thought back to the events of the afternoon. "Willie had so little time to be happy before his world turned upside down again."

By the time the doctors arrived, examined Willic, and left for Merton House, it was after nine o'clock, and Julia came to the door of the library. "Mrs. Worthington, you folks still haven't had supper yet, and you need to keep your strength up. Why don't you come into the dining room and eat what you can?"

Mildred stood up stiffly and beckoned to the others. "She's absolutely right. Even if we're not hungry, let's make Julia happy." The fire had been lit in the dining room and there was a big tureen of leek and potato soup on the sideboard along with crusty French bread, thin slices of Virginia ham, and a mixed green salad. In spite

187

of their numbing grief over the loss of Timmy, everyone found the appetite for something.

While they were eating, Big Ed looked across the table at his son, sitting next to Eve, their backs to the warm fire. "It doesn't look like I'll get over to see Mom tonight, Chickie. How was she when you were there?"

"I think she was about the same, although she really did respond to the music. Somebody had combed her hair, so she looked better than the last time I saw her, but she had absolutely no idea who I was. Doc Miller came in for his weekly examination, and he spent all of thirty seconds looking at Mom."

"That goddamn pill-pusher! I still can't figure out why a fine place like Thornton Oaks would have him for its doctor!" Ed snorted.

"I thought nearly everyone in town went to Doc Miller." Sitting at one end of the table, Kate tried to reconcile Doc Miller's apparent popularity with the growing evidence of his questionable practices.

"That's what's so strange about it," Ed replied. "He'll prescribe sleeping pills and tranquilizers like they're candy, and he was even involved in giving a depressed high school kid enough dope so she almost killed herself a couple of years ago. But somehow, he never gets called on that kind of thing, and almost everybody in town seems to protect him."

Eve's eyes darkened in anger. "My parents didn't believe in going to doctors, but one time they had to take Willie for treatment after a bad beating. Doc knew all about what was happening in our house, and as far as I know, he never said anything. He claims he threatened my father, but it didn't do much good."

The steeple clock on the mantle chimed ten times, and Mildred pressed the floor buzzer for Julia to clear the food away, most of which had been eaten, in spite of everyone's subdued mood. "Let's move into the library and have a brandy while we wait for the eleven o'clock news. There may be some more information about Timmy or Brother Able."

"Do you mind if Eve and I light a fire in the living room? It might take our minds off of everything that has happened today." Chickie helped Mildred out of her chair, and she quickly gave her permission for the two teenagers to have some time to themselves.

Unfortunately, there were no more details about the Calvert case on the late evening news except for a heart-wrenching glimpse of Jim Brogan and his tearful wife leaving the Maine Medical Center. The reporter waiting outside attempted to question Jim about the case, but the police captain brushed him aside and hurried to his car, his arm around his wife's shoulders.

At the conclusion of the news broadcast, Mildred declared she was going to bed with her gun in her bedside table. Big Ed and Chickie were given guest rooms at the end of the long second-floor corridor, and Kate, too, decided to take a book to bed, glad once more that Jessica had spent the night with her school friend, Chrissie Barton..

Tikka and Ed were both still wide awake, so they decided to take a walk around the grounds before going to bed. As they passed through the living room on their way to the terrace doors, they saw Chickie and Eve huddled close to the fire, talking in low tones, their faces barely visible in the dying glow of the embers.

Big Ed called to his son across the room. "Chickie, you keep an eye on everything. We'll be back in a few minutes."

The evening had cleared, and the moon was almost full, with only a few wispy clouds trailing across its light. As they stood on the grassy terrace overlooking the field that led to Morning Cove, both Tikka and Ed were struck by the dazzling splendor of the trail of light that gleamed along the ebony ocean.

Tikka shivered in the chilly dark, and Big Ed moved closer to her and put his arm around her shoulder, sharing the warmth of his powerful body. Involuntarily, she leaned closer to him as they stood in comfortable silence watching the stars sparkle overhead.

"Funny, isn't it? Just a few hours ago, there was nothing beautiful about what was happening around here." Ed looked down at Tikka and was surprised to see tears in her eyes. "Is it the good stuff or the bad stuff that's making you cry?"

Tikka reached in her pocket for a handkerchief. "A little of both, I think. I just have to believe a God who gave us all this beauty had a reason for taking Timmy away, just as I had to accept the death of my husband two years ago."

Big Ed tightened his grasp around Tikka's shoulders. "I wish I could think that way, but I can't. I'm mad as hell at a God, or whatever you want to call Him or Her or It, that would permit children to be hurt in his name, my sweet wife to become a vegetable, or a strong, loving boy like Timmy to be taken so early."

"I know, Ed. I felt the same way when I came to live with Millie after John's death. He had so much life and energy it seemed impossible he was gone so suddenly. I spent months wallowing in self-pity and moaning about how unfair life had been to me. I'd stay whole days in my bathrobe, and I even got into trouble with pills and alcohol for a little while, thanks to the generosity of Doc Miller."

"How did you get yourself squared away?" Ed's eyes were sympathetic and extremely interested in what Tikka was saying.

"Millie did it. One day, when I could barely get out of bed because of the pills and liquor I had consumed the night before, she handed me a full bottle of pills and a fifth of vodka. She said I might as well kill myself all at once instead of a little at a time because she was sick of watching me abuse myself. And she was serious. I was so shocked that I stopped everything cold turkey, and after a few very rough days, I was O.K. That's when I started to think about opening a boutique, something I had always wanted to do. And, as they say, Avesta was born."

"Well, Mildred's shock treatment obviously worked for you. Now, if you could come up with something that would do the trick for me..." Ed broke off and gazed out over the ocean. "The trouble is there's no way out of this thing. The neurologist told me Sheila could go on like this for years, or she could die tomorrow. There's simply no way to tell. I just know Sheila would slit her throat if she knew what she was like now."

"I know. It's awfully hard to watch someone you love deteriorate, especially since you're still young and attractive and deserve a life of your own." Tikka was conscious of Ed's body pressed against hers, and she offered no resistance at all when he drew her into the shadows at the end of the terrace and buried his face in her jasmine-scented neck before claiming her lips with a fierce urgency that left them both breathless.

"Tikka, may God forgive me, but it's been so long, and I need you so much." Ed lowered his head again and kissed Tikka slowly and deeply, holding her slender body against his broad chest. "How do you feel about this?"

"Come to my room when everyone is asleep, and I'll show you." Tikka's deep, accented voice was throaty with desire as she rubbed her hands up and down Ed's back. She was about to say more when the terrace light went on and Chickie and Eve came out of the French doors into the moonlight.

"We just came to say goodnight." Chickie frowned a bit at the sight of his father and the beautiful blond woman standing so close together, but he didn't comment. Ed and Tikka followed the young people back into the house and locked up securely before turning off the lights.

At the top of the stairs, Tikka went left to one of the big corner bedrooms overlooking Morning Cove. Eve disappeared into the room she had shared with Willie the night before, and Ed and Chickie continued down the long hall to two smaller bedrooms at the end of the corridor near the back stairs. The very last room on the hall was Julia's, but her door was tightly shut, so Ed and Chickie separated silently into their own rooms.

As Ed looked out the window into the darkened driveway, he could see the outline of the one police car which remained after Willie was taken back to Merton House. Small red lights glowed inside the cruiser where the officer struggled to stay awake. Across the hall, Chickie stretched out on the bed and covered himself with the quilt that was folded at the bottom of the counterpane. It was so quiet outside that every noise was magnified, and the owls, raccoons, and other night creatures could be heard against the muffled rhythm of the distant ocean.

Chickie had just started to doze off when the faint squeaking of hinges jolted him awake. Opening his own door a crack, Chickie saw his father disappear down the back stairs into the dark below. Had Chickie been vigilant any longer, he would have seen his father reappear at the other end of the hundred-foot corridor after climbing the front stairs to knock softly on Tikka's door. She answered immediately, admitting Ed to her darkened bedroom where a single candle glowed on her dressing table.

Wordlessly, Ed ran shaking hands over Tikka's silky bare shoulders, on which tiny straps supported the weight of her sleek satin nightgown. Even in the dim candlelight, the rosy peach of the form-fitting gown embraced Tikka's delicate breasts and curving hips, and

Ed felt his own body harden almost immediately when he lowered the straps, leaving Tikka bare to the waist...

"I'd almost forgotten what it's like," Tikka whispered as she lay cradled in Ed's arms.

Without warning, the candle on the dressing table burned out, and the exhausted lovers found themselves bathed only in the silvery moonlight that streamed in through the window. Somewhere in the house a telephone could be heard ringing, but Tikka was only dimly aware of the sound as she snuggled against Ed's warm body.

The thudding footsteps running down the long hall gave a few seconds warning before Tikka's door flew open. At first, Kate was too distracted in her panic to notice Ed's presence, but she quickly became aware Tikka was not alone. Gripped by hysteria she tried desperately to control, Kate switched on the light on Tikka's dresser and attempted to speak calmly to the surprised couple in Tikka's bed.

"That telephone call was from a man who said he was Brother Able. He claims he has Jessie!"

THE SHAPE OF DARK—Chapter Fourteen

Tikka's eyes widened in surprise. "How could he possibly have Jessie. She's staying overnight at the Barton's on the other side of town."

Kate seemed to snap out of her frozen state at the sound of Tikka's voice. "I've got their number in my room! I've got to call them."

When Kate rushed from the room, Ed pulled on his pants and shirt as Tikka fumbled with her robe. Ed yanked open the door of Tikka's bedroom and ran down the hall to where Kate was frantically dumping things out of her purse, her hands shaking violently.

"OH GOD!" The scream ripped from Kate's throat and the color left her face. "What if that monster has my baby!"

Tikka sat down beside Kate and put her arm around her friend's shaking body. "Try to be calm, Kate. We've got to check this out right away."

Ed was already around the side of the bed to the small table where Kate's phone was located. "What's their number?"

Kate opened her address book with trembling hands and gave it to Ed, who held it at arm's length, squinting to see the notation in Kate's fine handwriting. "Goddamn old age, I can't see a thing!" Ed passed the book to Tikka, who read the number out loud and was forced to repeat it when Ed's big fingers slipped onto the wrong buttons.

Ed frowned as he listened for a moment. Then he slammed down the receiver. "The number is not presently in service, whatever the hell that means. Come on, Kate, get dressed. We're going over to the Bartons. I'll call the police to meet us there."

"Why don't we get the officer outside to take us? It will be much faster." Kate disappeared into her bathroom and came out less than a minute later, fully dressed.

"Do you think it'll be all right to leave this house without a guard?" Tikka's face was furrowed with concern.

"We'll call another cruiser, once we're on our way to the Bartons. Just make sure you stay calm and lock the doors." Ed took Kate's arm and they ran down the front stairs into the darkened living room. Before long, the blue light of the police car in the yard began to flash and tires squealed on the gravel driveway.

"What's all this noise about?" Mildred, who was slightly deaf, hadn't heard any of the original commotion, but now she was fully alert and standing in Kate's bedroom door, holding her revolver. Chickie and Eve stood in the door, having been awakened by the activity.

Tikka went over to her mother-in-law and took the gun from her hand. "We're afraid Brother Able may have Jessie, and Kate and Ed have gone with the officer on guard to find out. Let's put this up on the mantle here and calm down a bit." Tikka reached for Kate's phone and listened for a minute. The quizzical look on her face was replaced with one of fear as she replaced the receiver. "The phone is dead."

At that moment, there was a loud explosion from the back of the house and a sudden burst of flame shot into the air from beside the cabana next to the swimming pool. Through Kate's window overlooking the terrace, rapidly spreading fire could be seen, casting a lurid gleam over a large section of the back yard. Strange black shadows were created by the flickering glow, and it was hard to tell if there were human figures moving around or if the shapes were those of trees and bushes swaying in the wind.

"How can we reach the fire department?" Mildred stood wringing her hands as she watched the spreading destruction below her. "What can we do?"

"There's a phone in my father's truck. I'll go call from there." Chickie bolted down the stairs to the back door, where Ed's pickup was parked near the garage. Upstairs, the three women huddled together and watched the flames spread into the pool cabana, feeding on the pool furniture, Ping-Pong table, and beach equipment that had been stored inside for the winter.

Within minutes, Chickie returned, having contacted the police and fire departments, and the sound of sirens could be heard as help raced toward Silvertree Farm.

****

On the other side of town, the police cruiser drew up in front of the modest house where Leslie and Steve Barton lived. The dwelling was entirely dark, but as Kate and Ed, followed by a young officer, approached the front door, they could hear a dog begin to bark. Before long, their insistent knocking was answered by a sleepy Steve Barton, who looked shocked to see his late night visitors.

"Where's Jessie?" Kate's voice was shrill as she looked past Steve into his toy-strewn living room.

"I don't know what this is all about, Kate, but the girls are sound asleep. Leslie checked on them just before we went to bed, and they were both out like lights." Steve looked slightly annoyed as the police officer went past him and picked up the phone to see if it had a dial tone.

"It's a very long, ugly story, Steve, but I need to see Jessie immediately. Would you mind if I peeked in on her?" By this time, Leslie Barton had joined the group, anxiously gathering a worn woolen bathrobe around her. Kate turned to her apologetically, and anxiety was so clear in her eyes that Leslie took her hand and led her down a short hall to the bedrooms.

"Look," Leslie whispered, "There they are." The two little girls were sprawled out on the double bed, each with a tattered blanket snuggled under her chin. Leslie crept in and adjusted the quilt, which had fallen off her daughter.

Kate shook her head. "I don't understand this at all." Leslie closed the bedroom door, and the two women went back to the living room where the men waited. "We just had a phone call from that horrible Brother Able, telling us he had Jessie. We couldn't get through on the phone, so we raced over here to see what was happening."

Steve looked embarrassed. "I'm sorry about the phone. There was some mix-up about the bill, and the company shut off service yesterday. It's all straightened out, but the line won't be restored until tomorrow morning. But this Brother Able thing is weird, because it's been very peaceful around here, at least after that birthday party zoo this afternoon."

While Steve was speaking, Ed looked at the police officer, and both of their expressions changed at the same time. Watching them, Kate felt a chill at the base of her spine.

"The only trouble is he could be playing some sort of elaborate cat and mouse game. Perhaps once we leave here, thinking Jessie is safe, he'll cause trouble for the Bartons. We need to take Jessie back to

Silvertree Farm." Ed spoke firmly as he and Kate headed down the hall toward the bedroom where the two little girls slept.

"Thanks for everything, Leslie. I'm awfully sorry to have awakened you, but I wouldn't rest a minute unless Jessie were with me." Kate spoke softly as Ed carried a still sleeping Jessica down the front walk, now brightly lit by a tall lamppost.

Even before the cruiser reached the stone entrance gates, Kate and Ed could see the whirling red lights of the fire engines, and two additional police cars that were parked by the front door. Most of the activity was in the back of the house, and as Ed guided Kate across the dark lawn, they could see that the pool house was in smoldering ruins. A small knot of people stood well apart from the fire while the smoke rose in ghostly clouds toward the towering oak trees above the pool. From a distance, Kate recognized Tikka standing with her arm around Mildred, while Eve and Chickie hovered nearby. Several policemen were talking to the firemen, who struggled with the heavy hoses, their black coats lit by fluorescent strips.

Kate was surprised to see Jim Brogan standing beside the remains of the dark-green propane tank that held the gas for heating the large pool. Shards of metal in a ghastly sculpture could be seen illuminated by Jim's flashlight as he walked back and forth between the tank and the demolished poolhouse, inspecting the ground.

"Tikka! Millie! Are you all right? How did this happen?" Kate grabbed Mildred's hands and found them to be ice cold.

"Right after you left, the propane tank exploded," Tikka explained. "Then the poolhouse caught fire. The telephone lines had been cut, but Chickie called for help from Ed's truck."

"What's Jim Brogan doing here? If my son had been killed today, this is the last place I'd want to be." Ed shook his head and walked down to where the firemen were standing beside the humming pumper truck. Jim was off by himself, frowning in concentration as he scribbled in his notebook, using the light cast by the fire engine's headlights. Ed put his hand on the police captain's shoulder.

"God, Jim, I don't know what to say to you. Timmy was such a great kid." Ed coughed around a lump in his throat.

"Thanks, Ed. I know how good you were to Timmy when he worked for you, and I always meant to tell you how much my wife and I appreciated it. As soon as I heard on the scanner that Silvertree

Farm had been attacked, I had to come and see for myself." Jim's face was strangely composed as he closed the notebook and put it in his pocket before walking over to where Mildred waited.

Before anyone could say anything, Jim spoke matter-of-factly. "Someone definitely blew up that tank, but we'll have to wait until daylight to do a thorough investigation. My concern is that this person is so unpredictable. I'm going to leave plenty of protection here tonight while I try to figure out what Brother Able is going to do next."

"Let's go inside," Mildred said, her voice shaking with cold. "There's not much left of the night, but maybe we can all get a little rest." The group moved up the hill toward the stone steps leading to the terrace. As they came into the cavernous living room, the area was in deep shadows, lit by only one small lamp on the piano.

Tikka was the first one through the terrace doors, and she was immediately aware of a strong odor. She swept her eyes around the perimeter of the room, and caught her breath suddenly as she focused on the large rectangular mirror over the fireplace. Screaming from the center of the beveled glass were large, blood-red letters spelling out the word "DIE", followed by a cross, which dripped thick globs of paint onto the elegant mantelpiece.

Looking into the dining room, everyone stared in horrified fascination at the elaborate mirrored clock over the buffet on which was scrawled "GOD'S WILL BE DONE." Drops of red smeared the top of Mildred's polished dining room table, and there was a trail of crimson out through the kitchen.

"Oh my God!" Kate's voice was rusty with fear, and Eve clung to Chickie in mindless terror. Still carrying a now-whimpering Jessica, Ed strode to the terrace door and yelled for Jim Brogan, who was talking to the fire chief. The detective covered the distance to the house very quickly, and after a cursory glance at the vandalism, called for two of the officers in the yard.

On Brogan's orders, the policemen drew their guns and began to search the premises. After the officers had gone upstairs, Jim turned his attention to Eve, whose eyes were dark holes of panic in her white face. "I think we'd better move you to a safer location, Eve. Apparently, this guy is going to stop at nothing to get you and your brother, and Merton House is very easy for us to protect, compared to a place like this."

Kate moved closer to the pale young girl. "Actually, Eve, they can probably make you very comfortable there, and you can see Willie whenever you want."

"I know, it makes sense. May I take a few of the clothes that you lent me, Mrs. Hammond? I don't want to go back home yet."

"Of course. Let's go upstairs and pack a bag for you. I promise I'll visit you tomorrow, or rather today."

"So will I." Chickie took Eve's hand and held it in both of his. "This will be over soon."

After Eve left with Jim Brogan and the police found the house to be secure, it was 4:00 a.m. and everyone wandered into the bedrooms exhausted, to try to get a little sleep. Kate was so tired she curled up into a ball in the middle of her bed and fell into a black, dreamless sleep from which she struggled, grainy-eyed when the telephone beside her bed rang at 7:30.

"Hello, Kate." Leslie Barton's pleasant voice didn't sound at all tired, in spite of having been awakened so abruptly the evening before, and she listened to Kate's description of the fire and vandalism with growing concern. "Well, all the more reason for you to agree to our plans for the day. My mother lives in Freeport, and we have been promising to drive up for Sunday dinner for several weeks now. Would you let Jessie come with us? We'll take the girls to Bean's or maybe to the State Park. That'll give you some time to sort things out there without having to worry about Jessie getting all upset."

Kate thought she would weep in gratitude. "I can't thank you enough. I feel very secure having Jessie with you and Steve. I just looked out the window, and the damage is horrible-looking in the daylight. Poor Jessie is so upset that an outing might distract her."

"We'll probably be home around seven o'clock, and I'll call you to see if you want us to bring Jessie home, or if you want us to keep her another night." Leslie assured Kate it was actually easier having the two girls to keep each other company than it was to take Chrissy anywhere by herself, and Kate recognized the sincerity in Leslie's voice.

Thoroughly awake by now, Kate heaved herself out of bed, careful not to awaken Jessie. Aware of a nagging pain in her lower back, she quickly pulled on the same clothes she had worn to the Barton's the night before. On her way into the bathroom, Kate glanced out the window at the still-smoldering poolhouse and was surprised to see Officer Peters walking around the yard, pausing every once in a while to pick something off of the ground.

Curiosity aroused, Kate hurried through the living room, averting her eyes from the hateful writing on the mirrors and joined the policeman beside the twisted wreckage of the propane tank. Officer Peters had one plastic bag full of bits of metal, string, and plastic, and was holding another bag in which there was a matchbook and something silver.

"Good morning, Mrs. Hammond." Officer Peter's friendly, freckled face looked tired but determined as he measured different sets of footprints in the soft, muddy grass between the propane tank and the poolhouse.

"There's no doubt about it. Someone fired a high-powered rifle at the tank, probably from those woods over there. The funny thing is that it looks like at least one of the people in those bushes was a woman, unless there's a man around here with very small feet." Officer Peters took an item from his collection of evidence. "I also found this in the same area. We'll see about prints, but I doubt we'll have much success."

Kate peered at the shiny purple matchbook and saw that it came from Hu Xuan, a large, garish Chinese restaurant on Route One, about fifteen minutes north of Boston. "I suppose anyone could have dropped that. Sometimes kids come and drink in these woods."

"I guess so," Officer Peters replied," except there's no other debris in that area. No beer cans, no cigarette butts, nothing except those matches and this." He held up a silver button. "We'll just keep all the pieces and see how they add up."

"How are Captain Brogan and his wife doing?" Kate could hardly believe it had been only the day before that Timmy had died. There had been a businesslike calm about Jim in the early hours of the morning, but Kate was sure Timmy's mother was having more trouble maintaining her control.

"She's in pretty tough shape, I'm afraid." Officer Peter's eyes clouded over, and he sighed as he put the bag of evidence in his pocket. "Captain Brogan told me that he needs to keep busy, but that Ellen just sits in Timmy's old room and cries. Her mother is with her now."

Kate's eyes stung at the policeman's words, and she was unable to speak for a moment. "Please let us know if we can do anything for either of them. How about a cup of coffee? It's cold out here."

For the rest of the morning, the kitchen at Silvertree Farm was the center of activity as policemen came and went, the fire chief stopped in briefly, and Big Ed and Chickie devoured stacks of Julia's blueberry pancakes before leaving for their own home.

"I'll be happy to come back any time you ladies are nervous," Ed offered as he and his son headed for home.

Tikka put her arm through Ed's and walked with him to the truck. Chickie, trailing behind the pair, narrowed his eyes as his father bent low to hear what Tikka was saying, and he felt the core of resentment he had felt the night before harden into a certainty.

Kate, standing beside Chickie in the driveway, caught the flash of anger in his eyes as he watched Tikka and Big Ed, and she put her hand on the boy's arm, causing him to stop and look down at her. "You know, Chickie, this may be none of my business, but both Tikka and your father have lost someone dear to them before they were ready to let go."

Chickie's dark eyes were troubled. "I don't have difficulty accepting friendship for my dad, but this thing is more than that." Kate watched as Chickie walked away and climbed into the truck, averting his eyes from Tikka.

"See you, Chickie!" Tikka leaned down and waved through the closed window.

"Later," Chickie mumbled as he stared out at the ocean in the distance.

Kate waited for Tikka at the back door after Big Ed drove away. "You know Chickie's on to you, don't you?"

Tikka looked alarmed and slightly guilty. "What do you mean?"

"Come on, give me a break. Chickie is aware of the, shall we say, vibrations between you and his father."

Tikka sighed. "I guess some things are hard to hide, but I certainly don't want Chickie to feel bad. It was really only a one-time thing, so it's not too late to put on the brakes."

"Not so fast. I think it's wonderful that you and that poor suffering man can give each other some comfort. You'll have to be very discreet, that's all. In spite of the fact that Sheila George has no idea of what's going on around her, she's still breathing, and her son may not be able to accept the idea of another woman in his father's life." For some reason, Alex Stamos's face flashed across Kate's mind as she spoke, and she wondered how he had been during the tumultuous weekend.

As if by telepathy, the telephone rang and Alex's deep voice lifted Kate's spirits, especially when she heard how concerned he had been for her safety. "Timmy Brogan was a special favorite of mine, as I guess he was of everybody," Alex said as they discussed the young man's tragic death. "It certainly makes you appreciate the time you have on this earth, doesn't it?"

"Speaking of time," Kate said. "I'm going over to see Eve this morning. Would you like to come along, or are you tied up? Millie's got workmen swarming all over the inside of the house, cleaning up the disgusting graffiti from last night, so I think she's surrounded by plenty of people. Can you have lunch?"

"There's nothing I'd like better, Kate, but I may get stuck with Claire. Phaedra and she left unexpectedly for Boston yesterday afternoon, but she left me a note asking me to be here this morning so we could discuss our future. Depending on how understanding she's feeling, which is probably not at all, I'll try to get away by one o'clock. Is that too late?" Alex's voice pleaded for Kate's agreement, and she did so quickly, caring only that they'd have some time together.

It was actually closer to one-thirty when the aged Jaguar drove through the gates and Alex stepped out into the clear sunlight, which had broken through the cold fog only a little while before. When he saw the damage that had been done to the poolhouse, Alex put his arm around Kate and held her close. "Thank heavens no one was hurt."

Kate shivered, glad of the rough warmth of his tweed jacket. "I know. The fire chief told us this morning that if there had been more propane in the tank, there's no telling what would have happened to the main house."

Alex looked down at Kate's buttery yellow sweater, trim gray slacks, and black cashmere blazer. "Well, it's clear you're all in one piece." Alex stopped and held Kate by the shoulders. "If you had been hurt, I would have been homicidal." He lowered his head quickly and kissed her hard. Keeping his arm tightened around her, Alex's expression darkened. "Now let me fill you in on Claire's latest foolishness."

During the fifteen-minute ride to Merton House, Alex described the tense, disagreeable discussion that had just taken place between him and his wife. According to Claire, their marriage was basically a strong one that had been affected by "outside influences" such as her work and Alex's new interest in Kate Hammond. For the good of their daughter, Claire had insisted, they should set aside their differences and try one more time to reconcile.

"I had the strangest feeling the whole time Claire was pleading her case," Alex commented. "It was as if she had some other reason for needing to appear to be happily married, because I'd bet my life on the fact she's not really interested in being my wife again, especially if she had to compromise her work."

"Maybe she really does mean what she says about Phaedra's welfare," Kate offered. "Your daughter doesn't seem to be very happy with things as they are."

"There again, I think both Claire and Phaedra are blaming our marital difficulties for other problems that each one has. I've always wanted Phaedra to see a counselor, but Claire has refused, saying that it would stigmatize Phaedra." Alex turned into the driveway of Merton House and came to a stop near the wide portico. "I'm afraid for Phaedra if she doesn't get some help, and Claire knows it. She even tried to use my feelings about that to twist my arm by saying she would consider therapy for Phaedra if we were both able to give her support. Meaning, of course, that we'd have to be living in the same house and sleeping in the same bed."

Kate shook her head. "What kind of a mother would use her own daughter's mental instability as a pawn in her game?"

"An evil one, that's who. And the horrible part of the whole thing is that Phaedra's problems stem from so long ago that she may not even remember them herself. Claire covered everything up at that time, and she's still doing it, except when it suits her purposes to do otherwise."

"I'm afraid I don't follow you on that one." Kate looked up at Alex as they approached the big glass doors leading into the lobby of Merton House.

"It's a long story. I'll tell you more later, after we see Eve." Alex pulled the door open and they walked across the shiny marble floor to where Dr. Ephron stood talking to one of the policemen on duty.

"Mrs. Hammond!" The psychiatrist came forward and shook Kate's hand. "Eve will be so glad to see you. The George boy has just left, and his visit really cheered her up. Mr. Stamos. Nice to see you again. How long has it been?"

Alex smiled broadly and then turned to Kate. "Dr. Ephron and I scandalized the parents at Rocky Shore about two years ago when we presented a lecture series on families coping with teenage sexuality. The first session was so explicit and accurate that several adults walked out in the middle, led, of course, by Mona and Bill Lundgren."

"As I recall, however," Dr. Ephron continued, "every single kid stayed and so did most of the parents. I had several patients come to me as a result of those lectures."

"I remember," Alex replied. "And I wanted my daughter to be one of them, but her mother put her foot down."

"Unfortunately, Mr. Stamos, a lot of people are still terrified by the idea of a stranger probing into a family's life, and they think by avoiding discussion of problems, they will miraculously go away." Dr. Ephron led Kate and Alex to the elevator, where another policeman was standing.

When the elevator doors slid open on the fourth floor of Merton House, Kate and Alex found themselves in a large room that looked like the lobby of an elegant hotel. The thick carpeting, comfortable couches, and soft lighting made an inviting environment in which small knots of people were scattered around, talking.

"This is a separate part of the hospital from the areas where we provide concentrated, continual care for people who are seriously ill. We call this floor 'The Penthouse.' We have ten rooms we use for all different kinds of people, none of whom requires nursing care or monitoring. There is one nurse who is available, but she is seldom needed. What we do have up here is complete safety, although you'd never know it by the appearance of things." Dr. Ephron pointed to a group of people playing bridge at a table near the broad, tinted windows. "Two of those people are guests, and two are security people."

Alex and Kate looked around, struck by the serenity of the atmosphere. Mozart played in the background, and there were bouquets of fresh flowers on the low tables in the seating area and on the small desk where a receptionist sat, speaking into a telephone.

"Dr. Ephron, there's a call for you. Meanwhile, shall I take Eve's visitors down to her room?" The smartly dressed young woman beckoned to Kate and Alex, who followed her into a wide corridor on either side of which were large doors with brass knockers and peepholes, much as one would find in a luxury hotel.

About halfway down the hall, the receptionist stopped and rapped on one of the doors, which was opened after a moment's pause by Eve, dressed in the clothing Kate had lent her the night before.

"Wow, Eve, this is some place!" Alex peered into the room where the girl was staying. Bright floral chintz was at the windows and on the queen-sized bed, and there was a cozy armchair in the corner facing a built-in unit containing a television and a stereo system.

"I know. I was surprised when I got here. Everyone is so nice, and it's very quiet and restful, especially after what happened yesterday. For the first time in a long while, I feel really safe." Eve looked very tired, but the anxious frown that had lined her young face since Thursday had almost completely disappeared.

"Where's Willie? Have you seen him?" Kate sat down on the bed next to Eve and took her hand. "I know he needs more care than they could give him up here."

"Yes, he does. Dr. Ephron told me he is quite heavily medicated because he was so upset about Timmy. I went down to see him this morning, but he was still sleeping, and I could only peek in at him. The rooms are very nice downstairs, but it looks like a hospital, and there are lots of nurses and orderlies around." Eve stood up and looked out the window at the Portland waterfront in the distance.

"Did you know you can't see in through these windows and they're bullet-proof?"

Eve turned back and looked steadily at Kate. "How long am I going to be here? I know I should be very grateful, and I am in lots of ways. But, I also feel like I'm in sort of a prison."

"I honestly don't know, Eve." Kate rose and put her hand on the girl's slender arm. "Just take the time in here to gather your strength for what lies ahead. I'll make sure you get your schoolwork, and I'm sure Chickie will come often, judging from the look on his face when he asked about you this morning."

Eve's shoulders sagged as she sighed at Kate's comments, but she turned to Alex with an expression of steely resolve. "There's one place I have to be, even if it puts me in danger, and that's Timmy Brogan's funeral. I'd never forgive myself if I didn't say goodbye to the man who saved Willie's life."

"Actually, those arrangements haven't been finalized yet," Alex replied. "I talked to Ellen Brogan this morning, and she said Timmy requested to be an organ donor, so there will be some kind of memorial service, but it's not set up yet. I'll come and get you myself with a whole army of guards if necessary, because I think you should be there."

"Thanks, Mr. Stamos, that means a lot to me." Eve sat down on the bed again. "The other thing I suppose I should do is visit my mother. Dr. Ephron told me she's out of danger and is asking for me, but I just can't bring myself to see her."

"That's completely understandable, Eve." Kate saw the pain etched in the girl's face. "Wait until you feel ready. You gave your mother her life back. There's plenty of time for the rest later."

A knock at the door interrupted any further comment Kate might have made, and Dr. Ephron hurried into the room looking harried. "Eve, your brother is awake now, and he'd like to see you. Do you feel up to coming downstairs?"

Eve got slowly to her feet, following the doctor down the long hall toward the elevator. Kate and Alex came behind, intending to say goodbye, but Eve asked if they would stay with her while she saw Willie. "I don't know why, but I'm afraid."

"Don't be alarmed, Eve, by anything Willie might say or do. He's really out of touch with reality now and has spent the last twenty-four hours hallucinating and having sort of waking dreams. Part of this is caused by the medication, but it's also the way he's escaping from the memory of the awful things he's so recently experienced."

The elevator purred to a stop, and Dr. Ephron punched in the security code that opened the doors. This time, the big central room was more brightly lit, and the furniture was more functional, although still very attractive. Bright green hanging plants dotted the waiting area, in which a few people were reading magazines or watching the big television set in the corner. Nurses bustled in and out of the rooms that stretched along the corridors that fanned out from the central area. Dr. Ephron led the way to the first room on the hall to the left of the nurses' station.

As he pushed the door open, Dr. Ephron pointed to Willie's small body, which was curled up in the center of the hospital bed, its metal sides pulled up for protection. "He may still be asleep, although the nurse told me he had awakened not long ago."

Eve walked over to her brother's bed and leaned over his frail form. "Hi, Willie."

Willie opened his round blue eyes and stared at Eve. "Are you an angel?"

"No, honey, it's Eve and you're in a hospital." Eve looked at Dr. Ephron.

"You're wrong." Willie's voice was high and clear as he looked at his sister. "I've died, but I didn't go to the bad place like Father said I would. I'm in heaven. See the lights?"

Kate felt her heart tighten at the little boy's confusion, and she saw Eve was at a loss for words.

Dr. Ephron stepped around Eve and looked down at the bed. "Now, Willie, you remember me, don't you? You know I'm a doctor and this is where you were before. O.K.?"

Willie shook his head firmly. "No, you all must be angels. Do you know why this is heaven?" The little boy's freckled face was earnest as he looked at the people standing around the bed.

Eve spoke in a tight voice. "Tell us, Willie. Why do you think this is heaven?"

Willie closed his eyes, and when he opened them, tears were gathering at the corners. "Because Timmy Brogan is here."

THE SHAPE OF DARK—Chapter Fifteen

"That poor little kid!" Alex said, holding Kate's arm as they crossed the parking lot in front of Merton House. "He actually believes he's dead and in heaven with Timmy. I only hope they can help him in there."

Kate's eyes were concerned as she looked up at Alex. "I was as upset for Eve as I was for Willie because I think she's afraid her brother's really retreated from reality. You know, you read about abused children developing multiple personalities to cope with the anguish of their lives. Maybe this fixation of Willie's is something like that, since Timmy was so genuinely kind to the boy."

"I'm not sure what's going on in Willie's mind, but the whole situation makes me more determined than ever to get some help for Phaedra." Alex opened the car door for Kate, and she slid across the smooth leather seat.

"You were going to explain what you meant about some early trouble of Phaedra's perhaps being responsible for the way she behaves now. But maybe you'd rather not discuss it."

"No, actually, I think it would help me to have your opinion if you don't mind. But, before I start. Do you have time for a drink at the Teller's Cage? They have great jazz piano on Sunday afternoons, and those nice private alcoves." When she agreed, he turned the car toward Portland, where the popular bar was located in the Old Port section of the city.

"Where to begin?" Alex mused as they drove over the bridge across the Fore River. "Do you remember I told you Claire and I lived with my parents in Newton after Phaedra was born and we were finishing up at Harvard? Well, when Phaedra was two, Claire was completing her third year at law school, and I was working part-time for an educational consulting firm in Cambridge. Right before Christmas, Claire's older brother came to stay at the house because the place he was living in burned down, and the engineering firm he was working for out on Route 128 went bankrupt."

Kate looked over at Alex as he spoke, and she was alarmed by the rigid anger she saw in his face, but she listened silently as he continued. "For a while, Uncle Buddy was everybody's pal, and Phaedra adored him. In spite of some depression, which he medicated with booze, he tried to help my mother by taking care of Phaedra whenever she needed to run an errand or go to her weekly bridge game. One day, however, my mother noticed Phaedra's genital area was irritated, and when Ma asked Phaedra what had happened, she was able to say Uncle Buddy stuck his finger in there when no one was home. To make a long and painful story short, Uncle Buddy's finger was not located on his hand." The muscles in Alex's jaw were knotted, and he gripped the steering wheel with whitened knuckles.

Kate stared straight ahead at the road. "What did you do?"

"Well, I'm not proud of it, but I beat the shit out of Buddy. I swear I would have killed the guy if my mother and Claire hadn't intervened. The worst part was that Claire actually defended Buddy, saying children often made up stories. She refused to take Phaedra to the doctor, probably because she wanted to protect her brother's reputation. I did get my way about Buddy, however, and he left town. I heard he died a couple of years ago in Seattle, after getting married and having a couple of children."

"Poor Phaedra. Did she ever mention the experience again?"

"Not directly, but I'm sure it's festering around in there somewhere, and I just wish Claire would agree to some help." The car rolled to a stop at a red light, and both Alex and Kate were silent, each lost in his own thoughts.

The light turned green, and they continued down Congress Street, turning right onto Exchange Street in the handsomely renovated section of Portland's waterfront. The Teller's Cage, one of the newer bistros in the Old Port, was housed in the three rooms of the second floor of a former bank where the architect had cleverly incorporated the teller's cage motif into the booths built around the periphery of the restaurant, affording the patrons an unusual degree of privacy.

When Alex and Kate climbed the carpeted steps to the second floor, they could hear the melodic sound of Gershwin's *Preludes* being played on the grand piano that stood in the center of the room. A graceful arrangement of autumn flowers stood on a pedestal by the piano, and the tinkle of ice cubes mingled pleasantly with the music, creating a relaxed, convivial atmosphere.

All of the tables were full, except for one alcove by the window. In a few minutes, Kate and Alex were seated, able to see the bustling waterfront in the distance through the filmy curtains that diffused the strong sunlight into a golden glow.

"This is more like it," Alex sighed as he stretched his long legs under the table and ordered sherry for Kate and a beer for himself. "What a hell of a week it was, and a worst one to come, I'm afraid."

Kate happened to glance toward the door, and she saw Tikka and Big Ed standing by the maitre d', who was looking around the crowded room for an empty table.

"Do you mind if we ask them to join us? I know you've had some trouble with Big Ed on occasion, but after yesterday, I feel as if he's a part of the family." Kate wasn't sure what Alex's reaction would be, and she was relieved when he jumped up and motioned to Tikka and Ed.

Alex stood and took the seat next to Kate, while Ed pulled out the chair across from Kate for Tikka. "Thanks for letting us barge in. This place is really busy. What are you two doing in town?"

Kate quickly described her visit to Eve and the sad condition of little Willie. "How about you folks? I'd have thought you'd still be catching your breath from last night."

Tikka looked down at her hands. "Ed took me along while he visited Sheila at Thornton Oaks. Actually, I waited in the car. I needed to tell Ed what Chickie said to you, Kate, and it was difficult getting any privacy at home with Millie's army of cleaners around."

Alex looked puzzled at Tikka's comment about Chickie, and Ed explained, looking embarrassed, but also boyishly pleased. "You know better than anyone, Alex, how it's been since Sheila has been sick. Well, Tikka and I have become friends, GOOD friends, and Chickie is feeling rather resentful." Ed took Tikka's hand as he spoke, and his face softened visibly as he looked at her.

"You know, Ed," Kate commented, "I don't think there's anything more difficult for teenagers to comprehend than the fact that their parents have sex lives. Give Chickie a little time to get used to the idea."

Ed's face reddened. "I actually told Sheila about Tikka. There was no one elsc in the room, and Sheila had no idea what I was saying, but I felt better."

"I guess we both have some difficulty with our children and our love lives, Ed. At least you aren't hurting Sheila, and Chickie will come around. With Claire and Phaedra on either side of me, I feel like I'm in a trash compactor!" Alex looked pained as he spoke.

Kate glanced at her watch and stood up. "Would you excuse me for a minute? I need to call Millie and see if the Bartons have brought Jessie back. If they have, I need to get going."

Five minutes later, Kate was back with a big smile on her face. "Reprieve. They won't be in Cape Mariana until after eight, and Millie is going to bed with a tray. She says that all's well at home. Except for the war zone at the pool, everything else is cleaned up."

Alex insisted on everyone staying in town for dinner, in spite of the fact that Claire was probably furiously waiting for him. "I told her I was driving up to Brunswick and wouldn't be back until later tonight, so let her stew!" He declared as they sampled the contents of a Pu Pu platter in the bustling Chinese restaurant across the street from the Teller's Cage.

By the time Kate and Alex returned to Silvertree Farm, the Bartons' battered station wagon was disgorging a very tired but contented Jessica, who fell asleep in Alex's arms as he carried her upstairs.

Kate undressed her daughter without waking her, and as Jessica lay peacefully in the moonlight, Alex and Kate watched her innocent face, wrapped, as usual, in her ever-present blanket. "How could anyone purposely hurt a child?" Alex voiced both of their thoughts, and Kate recognized the same pain in Alex's eyes she had seen in the afternoon when he told her about Phaedra's molestation by her uncle.

"You're thinking about your daughter, aren't you?" Kate whispered as she led Alex downstairs and into the library. "Isn't there some way you can convince Claire Phaedra needs help?"

"Damned if I know, but I've got to try. I've talked until I'm blue in the face, but maybe one more time..." Alex reached over and snapped off the lamp beside the sofa, leaving the room lit only by the lingering embers in the fireplace.

"I've wanted to do this all day," he murmured, brushing his warm, searching lips across Kate's silky mouth, slightly parted as she breathlessly awaited his kiss. Kate reached up and grasped Alex's powerful shoulders, clinging to him in the dark as she molded her body against him, inviting him to deepen his exploration of her soft lips and tongue.

A groan of frustration escaped from Alex as he saw the sweep of headlights around the circular driveway and heard the slamming of a car door, followed shortly by the steady ringing of the front doorbell.

"Shit!" Alex groaned. "The fates are definitely conspiring against us."

Kate switched on a small lamp and went through the darkened living room. Through the glass panels on the sides of the front door, she could see two uniformed officers, and when she pulled open the door, a young policeman touched the brim of his hat.

"Good evening, Mrs. Hammond. Sorry to bother you, but Captain Brogan asked us to check in before you folks went to bed. Anything unusual going on?" As Alex came up behind Kate, the officer's face brightened. "Hey, Mr. Stamos. How are you doing?"

"Scott Dean! I'm glad to see you." Alex shook hands with the officer, whose older partner swept his flashlight across the bushes in the front of the house. "I just heard you joined the force."

Scott grinned. "I'll bet I was the last person you thought would be a law and order guy. Remember the hot water I used to get into?"

Alex laughed. "Do I ever! As long as I live, I'll never forget the picture of you and Timmy Brogan streaking across the dining room at school wearing only ski masks and jock straps. Too bad your friends double-crossed you and locked you outside in the freezing cold." Alex turned to Kate. "That happened the first year I was principal, and it was all I could do to keep a straight face while I suspended those two. What a pair!"

Almost immediately, Scott's face fell into an expression of deep sadness. "Hell of a thing about Timmy. I just had a beer with him the other night, and he was telling me about all the new traps he was building and how his boat was almost paid off. Half of the guys on the force would like a crack at that Brother Able."

"I know, Scott. We all feel the same way, but I really believe evil is its own worst enemy. Something will break." Alex clapped the officer on the shoulder. "Are you boys patrolling the whole area, or is someone staying here tonight?"

"We'll be in and out," the older policeman answered. "Now that the Calvert children are gone, there doesn't seem to be the same urgency for round-the-clock protection, but we're not far away in case anything happens."

Kate yawned. "Well, I for one am wiped out after last night. Here comes Tikka, so I think we'll all turn in." Another set of lights turned into the gates and pulled up behind the police cruiser.

Alex said goodnight to the policemen and solemnly shook hands with Kate. "School tomorrow, Mrs. Hammond. See you in the trenches." He winked as he followed Scott Dean down the front steps. "We'll have to continue that discussion we were just having."

Kate and Tikka locked up the house and climbed up the front steps to their bedrooms. "I've got one of Father Worthington's guns in my nighttable," Tikka confided in a low voice. "I learned to shoot when I was young, so don't worry about security. We'll be fine. Sleep well."

The moon was nearly full as Kate walked through her dark bedroom to the window overlooking the pool. The ugly wreckage of the propane tank was a jagged shape against the silvery mountain laurel, but the ocean was calm and the path of light across the waves sparkled in the distance.

As Kate gazed in the direction of the pool, her peripheral vision caught flashes of light from the woods where the matchbook and button had been found. Although she strained to focus on the shadowy trees, they were too far away for her to be able to recognize anything distinctly. It was clear, however, that at least two and maybe three lights were moving in the shelter of the trees, skirting the moonlit field where identification would have been easier.

Kate picked up the phone and dialed the police, reporting what she had just seen. The dispatcher assured her he would notify the officers in the area, and within minutes, Kate heard the cruiser drive up and saw Scott Dean and his partner running across the field toward the woods. The long beams from the policemen's flashlights were very different from those Kate had seen before, and she saw them flashing back and forth, searching the ground at the edge of the field and then moving farther back into the woods.

After about fifteen minutes, the two policemen emerged, their lights waggling up and down as they walked toward the cruiser. Scott Dean was carrying something in his hand, but Kate couldn't make out what it was.

****

In spite of the puzzling incident in the woods, Kate slept well and awoke before her alarm sounded in the morning. It was another clear blue September day with a nippy breeze and bright sunlight, and Kate noticed as she drove to school that even the oak trees had started to turn gold.

The lobby of Rocky Shore was deserted except for a small group of students clustered around Sandra Monkton's desk with permission slips for a field trip that the Art History class was taking to the Boston Museum of Art. Susan Moore stood in the center of the milling students looking confused while she checked off names on a clipboard.

Spying Kate near the bottom of the stairs to the second floor, Susan called out wistfully as she juggled the notes that students were waving in her face. "Kate! Help. This is my first excursion away from school, and I'm losing my mind."

Kate chuckled at the flustered expression on Susan's beautiful face, noting that her usually impeccable person looked disheveled. "Here, Susan, let me give you a hand. The most important thing is to get an accurate list of the kids who get on the bus so that you can make sure you've got them all when you leave Boston. There's nothing worse than getting back to school and discovering that you've left one of the gremlins in the museum coffee shop."

Susan looked terrified at the prospect. "Has that ever happened to you?"

"Unfortunately, yes, in Georgia. And it was a mighty long trip back to Jacksonville to retrieve the student. Needless to say, my principal was less than thrilled, since he was thc one who had to go. It was his son who went AWOL."

"Oh well," Susan sighed, "at least most of these kids are pretty reliable." Kate glanced over the list and recognized the names of most of her senior class.

"You've made my day a lot easier. My last class will have about three kids in it."

Susan checked off the last permission slip and smiled at Kate. "Then you owe me one. Wish me luck! Kate, hearing the warning bell sound, headed through the lobby toward the second floor. Before

213

she reached the bottom of the stairs, however, Alex's deep voice came over the loudspeaker and everyone stopped to listen.

"As most of you know, some very tragic events have taken place since last Thursday. In order for everyone to be equally informed and to give some of you a chance to express your concerns and thoughts, there will be an assembly during first period. After homeroom attendance, please proceed directly to the dining hall."

Normally, an unexpected assembly was cause for celebration at Rocky Shore, but there was no jostling or joking among the students as they looked expectantly toward the front of the room where Alex stood waiting for the last stragglers to find seats. Most of the faculty stood around the perimeter of the room, although active supervision of the students on this occasion was unnecessary.

Kate noticed Kelly Lundgren had returned to school, pale, but seeming to be recovering from her traumatic experience. She sat about halfway back in the room surrounded by her friends, including Phaedra, who glowered at Kate the one time their eyes met. Most of the soccer team sat together toward the rear, and Kate was upset that Chickie had turned away from her when they accidentally met at the door of the dining hall.

"Let me have your attention, everyone." Alex raised his voice above the hum in the room, and the students quieted down immediately. "You know I believe in telling you the truth about what's going on around here, and today will be no exception. A lot of very ugly things have transpired over the weekend, and since some of you will be affected directly, I think you deserve to know the facts. There are a great number of national media teams in town, and although we've barred them from the Rocky Shore campus, I'm sure they will approach you in other places to find out what you know about the situation."

There was a slight murmuring among the students, and Alex waited until it was silent again. "As you know, Eve Calvert's brother, Willie, shot his parents last Thursday and killed his father. The reason he did this was because Eve had been badly beaten by Mr. Calvert. Apparently, serious abuse had been going on for a long time, and Willie finally snapped. Mrs. Calvert is recovering from her wounds, but it's uncertain what will happen to the children. At the moment, Eve is in protective custody, but she is very anxious to return to school." Alex took a deep breath and continued.

"Meanwhile, a group of religious fanatics, led by a man called Brother Able, is determined to get their hands on the Calvert kids and punish them, especially Willie. These people have made several attempts and will probably try again, which is why I want you to be on your guard. If you see anyone you don't recognize, notify Mrs. Monkton or me immediately."

Several people in the audience looked around in alarm, and there wasn't a sound in the room except for Alex's deep, serious voice. "The people who are after Eve and Willie are sick, dangerous, and evil. They condone the torture of innocent children in the name of God, and I'm afraid they'll stop at nothing to complete what they consider to be a holy mission of revenge."

Alex paused and cleared his throat as the room buzzed. "Now that you know the basic facts, I hope you will use good judgment in talking to the press, and once Eve comes back to school, you will cooperate in whatever safety precautions we feel it necessary to take."

A hand shot up in the back of the room. "Mr. Stamos, where are Eve and Willie now?"

"I'm sorry, but I can't tell you that. They are safe and being well taken care of. After Eve was beaten on Thursday, she sought the help of one of our teachers, Mrs. Hammond." All eyes swung toward Kate, standing next to Susan Moore by the far windows. "Mrs. Hammond also took in Willie, but this Brother Able sent his hit squad to Silvertree Farm, and it was only because of the heroism of one of our finest graduates that Willie is still alive."

Alex glanced over at the door and saw that Jim Brogan and his wife were paused at the threshold. Jim was holding his wife's hand, and when Alex looked at him, he nodded slightly. "This is going to be the hardest part of what I have to say today." Alex felt his throat tighten, but he swallowed and carried on. "Willie Calvert was saved by the extraordinary strength and courage of Timmy Brogan, who was tragically shot to death in the process. I know those of you who are seniors now were freshmen when Timmy graduated, and I thought there might be people here who would like to remember Timmy in some way, because he was a very unusual young man who touched many lives."

215

Hands began to raise immediately throughout the audience, and Alex motioned to Kyle Monkton, sitting directly in front of him. Kyle got to his feet and stood next to Alex with his hands shoved deep into his pockets.

"When I came to Rocky Shore High School, I was eleven years old and really small for my age. During the first lunch period of my freshman year, some sophomore boys decided to dump me head first into one of those big trash barrels over there." Kyle pointed to the line of steel drums along the wall. "Nobody tried to stop these guys, and everyone in the dining hall was laughing. That is, until Timmy Brogan came through the door and saw what was happening. He lifted me out and brushed all the garbage off me, but I couldn't stop crying. I remember Timmy put his arm around my shoulders and held up his other hand until the room was quiet. Then he said that if anyone ever bothered me again, that person would have to deal with him. 'From now on, this kid is under my protection,' he said, and nobody ever caused me any trouble as long as Timmy was here in school."

Kate looked across the room at Sandra Monkton as her son was speaking, and saw that tears were flowing unchecked down the older woman's face. After Kyle sat down, a hand went up from among the faculty.

Hal Gibson, a small, bespectacled Latin teacher shuffled forward, limping from the wound he had received in Vietnam. "When I first began to teach here, Timmy Brogan was a junior. I remember him as this gentle giant of a kid who hated Latin, but always tried to be polite and cooperative, unlike most of the other students in his class. There was one particular boy who always gave me trouble and even threw things at me when my back was turned. He stole my grade book and generally made my life so miserable that it interfered with my ability to teach the class."

Hal blinked behind his round glasses. "Later on, the kids told me Timmy Brogan finally got fed up with this kid and warned him to lay off me because nobody was learning anything. I guess the boy didn't take Timmy seriously, because the next day he was at me again. I'll never forget what happened. Timmy got out of his seat and said 'Excuse us, Mr. Gibson, but we have business to attend to.' He lifted the boy out of his chair by his belt and the back of his shirt and hustled him out into the hall. We heard some loud voices and then what sounded like something crashing into the lockers. Soon, however, Timmy and the boy came back and the kid never caused me any more difficulty. The rest of that year was actually pretty easy for me."

There was a slight wave of laughter as Hal left the front of the room. Kate had heard stories of how the sweet, dedicated man continued to be persecuted by unkind students, but after his story, she saw several people surreptitiously wipe their eyes.

"Anyone else? We've got time for one more story, I think." Alex pointed to a pretty, petite senior girl wearing a cheerleading uniform for the soccer scrimmage that afternoon. "When I was a freshman, one of the senior boys asked me to a dance, and I thought I'd died and gone to heaven. But when we got to the dance, all this boy did was drink and dance with other girls. It turned out his mother and mine were friends, and they had arranged the date. Anyway, I sat in the corner wishing I could disappear, especially during the slow dances, when this boy I came with would drape himself all over someone else. I was sure everyone was laughing at me. Then, Timmy Brogan came over and asked me to dance, even though I'd never dared to speak to him. He was the most popular boy in the senior class, and I thought the most handsome. It also turned out he was the nicest, because he kept dancing with me, even when the boy I came with decided I was cool enough for him." As the girl spoke, unshed tears glistened in her eyes.

Alex stood up again. "I'm sure there are others of you who were touched in one way or another by this wonderful young man. His parents are here with us today, and I want to end with a story I don't think even they know. During my first year as principal, Timmy was captain of the soccer team and an outstanding player. Somehow, he accidentally injured a player from Lake Richmond in the opening game, and a feud broke out between the two towns with all kinds of threats being exchanged. I got wind of the fact that a gang from Lake Richmond was coming to Cape Mariana on a Saturday night to fight with our kids, but none of the adults could find out where this was going to take place."

Alex looked over at Timmy's father. "Jim, you were away that weekend at some kind of convention in Boston, and I remember the chief considered calling you, since Timmy was involved, but he decided against it."

"Evidently, the rendezvous place was in a big field over on the River Road. The two crowds of kids, about fifty in each group milled around, exchanging threats. There had been some drinking, and a couple of kids had picked up sticks to use instead of their fists. The story is that Timmy stepped out of the Cape Mariana crowd and offered to fight anybody from Lake Richmond to settle the problem. He said that it was stupid for a lot of people to get hurt, since he was the one who had been responsible for starting things, although he hadn't meant to."

Alex paused and looked around the room, seeing that several students were nodding in recollection of the incident. "No one came forward from Lake Richmond, so Timmy hollered, 'If we're not going to fight, let's party!' They built a bonfire and probably had a keg, but it was typical of the way Timmy used his strength."

Timmy's mother was sobbing when Alex finished his story, and there was complete silence in the room. Kate watched as Alex fought to stay in control, speaking in a tight voice. "God bless you, Timmy. We'll miss you."

Alex walked over to the Brogans and led them out of the room while the faculty and students followed. Many of the teenagers and most of the adults had tears in their eyes. There was someone watching, however, whose face was contorted in anger at the outpouring of emotion for Timmy Brogan. Unrecognized by anyone in the room, hidden rage fed on itself and resolved once again to punish without mercy.

THE SHAPE OF DARK—Chapter Sixteen

After the assembly, Alex returned to his office to find Mona Lundgren waiting to speak to him about Kelly's return to school. As usual, Mona was impeccably dressed in a forest green blazer and slim tan wool slacks with a Hermes scarf tossed casually around her shoulders. When Alex came into the room and shut the door, Mona was already seated by his desk, nervously picking at some threads on her jacket, which was missing one of its silver buttons. Mona peered on the floor around her feet, but then shrugged in frustration and complained about the liability of having a daughter who could wear her clothes.

"You know, Alex, Kelly has come back to her classes today after a terrible experience. She had to give a deposition to the District Attorney on Friday, and it was an awful ordeal for her. I'm concerned she not be put under further strain."

Alex sat back in his chair. "Of course, we'll try to do anything we can to make Kelly's adjustment easy for her. Do you have something specific in mind?"

"She's quite apprehensive about one of her classes, English, with your Mrs. Hammond." Mona watched Alex to see if her remark had hit a nerve and was annoyed when his expression didn't waiver. "Kelly feels there is a personality conflict with Mrs. Hammond, and she'd like to be placed with another teacher."

"Well, ordinarily, we don't make lateral transfers without a solid reason, Mona. As you'll recall, I witnessed the episode between Kelly and Mrs. Hammond, and your daughter was clearly at fault. Otherwise, I wouldn't have suspended her. However, I'll talk to Kate and see if she would approve such a move. Personally, I think it would be good for Kelly to work things out with Mrs. Hammond, who, by the way, is a fine teacher."

Mona looked unconvinced. "I'd think that you'd be having the same concerns that we are, Alex. I understand from Claire that Mrs. Hammond picks on Phaedra mercilessly. At least Kelly has been absent and working with a tutor, so she hasn't suffered the way your own daughter has!"

Alex's face flushed, but he kept his voice calm. "Our daughters, Mona, are not widely known for their gracious behavior, and I for one am not going to make it easy for Phaedra to get away with rudeness. If she has a problem with one of her teachers, then it's up to the two of them to solve it reasonably, if possible. I only get involved when one or both of the parties is abusive to the other."

"There are many kinds of abuse, as you put it, and I think simply being in the same room with someone like Kate Hammond is cruel and unusual punishment for your daughter. After all, that woman is responsible for your unwillingness to heal the problems in your family." Mona fluffed the back of her hair and looked at Alex with an expression of smug superiority.

Forcing himself to keep his voice even, Alex leaned forward in his chair and stared at Mona. "You have no idea what you're talking about, and I fail to see how my family is any of your business."

Mona looked a bit surprised at Alex's icy tone, but she persevered in spite of the warning in the principal's eyes. "Claire and I had lunch on Sunday, after you had dismissed her attempts at reconciliation. She was crushed, and personally, I think your tawdry little liaison with Kate Hammond is in very bad taste, considering your position."

Alex stood up. "I think we've concluded our discussion. I will talk to Kelly today. Goodbye." Alex opened his office door and watched Mona flounce out, nearly colliding with Marta Stone, who had obviously been listening to the conversation.

Flustered, Marta hurried back to her desk and handed Alex a pink telephone message. "Susan Moore called in to say she'll be late, AGAIN. Do we have any substitutes who would be available to take the class that meets next period?"

"I don't know, Marta, that's Sandy's department. Ask her." Alex's annoyance was spilling over, and he longed to barricade himself in his office.

"She's left the building for a while. Some kind of meeting at Portland High School."

Alex rubbed his hand across his brow. "That's right. Well, see if there's anyone around to cover. If not, I'll go down myself." Alex watched Marta walk toward her desk and retreated to his own office.

Within minutes, however, Alex was headed for the basement, where the Art Department had its studio. Everyone was impressed with the range of activities Susan was offering her students, as witnessed by the large display case in the lobby, which was already filled with completed projects.

The studio was dark and silent, but when Alex switched on the overhead light, a delightfully confusing jumble of color and form sprang to life in the large room. Easels, two potters' wheels, several long tables holding rough pieces of sculpture in progress, and another bench devoted to jewelry making were all covered with the creative chaos that nurtures the artist. Alex regretted there was no natural light in the room, but he had promised Susan to find space on the third floor for portrait work.

The bell rang, signaling the end of the second period, and students began to trickle into the studio for their third period class. Most of the people donned aprons and smocks, beginning to work without instruction, after a moment of surprise at seeing the principal in charge. Alex circled the room, fascinated by the talent of the young people, and he was particularly impressed with the heavy sterling silver hair clips two of the girls were making.

"Sally, that's really beautiful. I think Phaedra has one that looks similar. Where did you learn how to do this kind of work?" Alex picked up the clip and admired the intricate carving across the gently curving top of the ornament.

"I studied with Ms. Moore this summer. She does a lot of pieces like this and sells them to boutiques around town. Recently, most of her work has been going to Avesta." Sally glowed at the attention from the principal as she continued to polish the hair clip.

The table where the girls were working was in the far corner of the room, and there was a door directly behind them. Curious, Alex tried the handle and found it locked. "What's in here? Do you know?"

Sally frowned. "I'm not sure. Ms. Moore keeps it locked all the time. It must be a storage closet of some kind, maybe for supplies. See, there are some drops of paint on the floor by the door."

Alex looked down and saw some red blotches on the threshold, and he nodded to Sally in agreement. "I think you're right. It pays to lock up paint in a high school, especially during soccer season. Remember last year?"

Sally laughed. "I know, the rock wasn't good enough for the state championship. It had to be the side of the building!"

A long-standing tradition in Cape Mariana centered around a large rock which was located on Route 11 between Half-Moon Beach and the center of town. With the tolerance of the police, different groups of students, and sometimes even adults, would whitewash the rock and paint slogans in support of a sports team in the midst of a tournament. Occasionally, the rock would contain message of other kinds, including slanderous comments about an individual's sexual activities, but that kind of graffiti was quickly covered over.

Last year, as Cape Mariana was heading into the final game of the state soccer championship, some overly zealous fans painted the side of the gymnasium building, and when the culprits were discovered, they spent the better part of the fall laboriously removing the bright green paint.

"Let's hope THAT doesn't happen again!" Alex left the girls to their jewelry and wandered over to where Jean- Pierro was frowning in concentration as he bent over a spinning potter's wheel.

"How are the legs feeling?" Alex clapped a large hand on Jean-Pierro's shoulder, and the boy looked up, startled.

"Oh, Mr. Stamos! I am, as you say, in the fog when I do the pottery. It makes me dizzy. My legs, they are good. I will play this Saturday." The Italian boy's liquid brown eyes reflected his enthusiasm as he gazed up at Alex.

"That's great, Jean-Pierro. Looks like we're up to speed. Carry on!" The potter's wheel began to spin again, and Alex spent the rest of the period chatting informally with each of the people in the class. When the hour was nearly over, Susan Moore rushed in the door, full of apologies and clearly taken aback that the principal had been forced to cover for her.

"Never again! I promise! My morning got all twisted up because I had intended to make my delivery to Avesta during first period. Once I got involved in the assembly, I forgot I had promised Tikka Worthington some special pieces for a private show she is having today. I really appreciate your doing this. Any problems?"

"No. I'm really blown away by the nice work you're doing down here." Alex's compliment was so obviously heartfelt that Susan beamed. "But I was wondering about that door over there by Sally. What's in there?"

"I haven't the faintest idea." Susan shook her head and shrugged her shoulders. "Nobody seems to have a key that fits. I even asked Alf to open it for me, but he had his trouble before he could get to it. Now that poor Lenny is the head custodian, he'll never have time."

"It's probably just stuffed with old junk," Alex said, dismissing the closet from his list of problems. "Maybe in the next century, we'll get the thing open." The bell rang and the students scrambled to clean up their workstations, while Alex left the supervision to the art teacher and climbed the steps to the lobby.

"Marta, see if you can find out when Kelly Lundgren has a free period. I'd like to see her." Alex accepted another pile of messages from his secretary.

By the time Alex worked his way through six phone calls, Marta Stone announced the arrival of Kelly Lundgren. At the sight of the girl's pale face, Alex felt an initial tug of sympathy, but when she sat down and he saw the familiar petulant set of her mouth, he looked at her dispassionately.

"I understand from your mother you'd like to transfer out of Mrs. Hammond's English class. What seems to be the problem?"

Kelly shrugged. "We just don't get along, that's all. She's always on my case, and I think I'd do better with someone else."

Alex swiveled in his chair a moment. "But Kelly, you've only been around for a few days. The rest of the time, you've been out of school. Don't you think you should give it a little longer?"

"I won't feel any differently, no matter how long I'm in that stupid class." Kelly's expression was sullen, and she refused to meet Alex's eyes.

"Well, I'll tell you what. You stay with Mrs. Hammond for the rest of this week, and we'll talk again on Friday. If you still have the same opinion, then perhaps we can work something out. Meanwhile, I have something else I'd like to ask you about." Alex reached into his safe and took out the bat that he and Jim Brogan had found at the scene of the attack on Kelly. Jim had delivered the object earlier in the day after discussing Alex's plan to show it to Kelly. "Do you recognize this?"

223

Kelly's eyes widened in obvious shock, and her voice trembled as she answered. "Where did you get that?"

"That doesn't really matter right now. I'm just curious as to whether you have every seen it before." Alex turned the bat over in his hands so the "Little Hitter" label was visible to Kelly.

"I don't think so, unless Eric had one of those when he was learning to play baseball. I don't remember." It was so obvious Kelly was lying that Alex had difficulty keeping his questions calm and matter-of-fact.

"O.K., Kelly, I just wondered. Now, do you need a pass?" The dismissal was clear in the principal's voice, and Kelly muttered she had a free period. As she backed out of the office, Alex noticed Kelly's eyes were focused on the bat he still held in his hand. At the door, she turned suddenly and almost ran across the lobby to the dining hall, where a group of her friends were chatting at one of the round tables.

Alex locked the bat in his safe and asked Marta to locate Phaedra and ask her to come to his office whenever she could. As his secretary walked to Sandra Monkton's desk where the student schedules were kept, Alex saw Officer Dean cross the lobby and speak to Kate, who had just come down from the second floor. The policeman had something in his hand, and when he showed it to Kate, she shook her head. Curious, Alex left his office and walked over to where Kate and the officer were in serious conversation.

"Anything wrong, Kate?"

"No, just puzzling. Last night after you left, I thought I saw flashlights moving over in the woods beyond the pool. I called the police and they investigated right away. They didn't see anybody there, but they did find this." Kate handed a silver hair clip to Alex, and as he examined it closely, he saw it was very much like the ones the girls were making in art class. "Officer Dean wanted to know if it was mine, but it's not, although I've often looked at similar ones in Avesta."

Alex turned the hair clip over, and in the smooth silver on the back, he saw the initials "SM" engraved in the middle of a triangle. Puzzled, he showed the letters to Kate, and she knew immediately it was Susan Moore's trademark, since an identical symbol was on the back of a pin Kate had bought a few weeks earlier. "Tikka told me when I bought my pin that no two pieces of Susan's jewelry are alike, so it would be interesting to find out who owns this hair clip. It looks strangely familiar."

"Do you mind if I borrow this for a little while? I'd like to ask someone about it." Officer Dean handed the clip to Alex, after Kate assured him she would take responsibility for returning it, and Alex returned to his office.

Phaedra was seated in the chair facing his desk when Alex came in and shut the door behind him. Since the unfortunate dinner at the Half-Moon Inn, Alex had said very little to his daughter, and he was somewhat taken aback by the amount of makeup she was wearing and by the provocative effect of her short skirt and navel-baring sweater.

Alex restrained himself from saying anything critical and vowed he would remain calm, no matter how irritating Phaedra became. "I had an interesting morning," he began conversationally. "I took over Susan Moore's art class and watched Sally Prentice making some lovely silver jewelry. I gather Ms. Moore gave lessons this summer, and some of the students are producing real masterpieces."

Expecting a lecture from her father about any number of topics, Phaedra was taken by surprise when he seemed to have no agenda, and she visibly relaxed in her chair, allowing her skirt to ride up, much to Alex's discomfort. "I know. I love the stuff Ms. Moore makes. Remember the clip Mother gave me for my birthday?"

Alex watched his daughter closely. "Yes, I do. It was beautiful, but I've never seen you wear it."

Phaedra's face fell. "That's because I can't find it anywhere."

"Is this it?" Alex took the hair clip from his pocket and showed it to his daughter.

"Great! Where did you find it?" Phaedra reached for the clip, but Alex held it firmly in his hand.

"Take a good look at this one. Are you sure it's yours?" Phaedra reached across the desk and took the clip from her father, examining it carefully.

"I'm positive. See the little 'P's' engraved in the design?" Phaedra was about to put the clip into her hair when Alex held out his hand.

"Sorry. I can't let you have this right now, but I'll take good care of it." Alex felt slightly sick to his stomach as he replaced the clip in his pocket. "Phaedra, have you been up to anything recently you think you ought to talk to me about?" He was somewhat uneasy about using his most effective interrogation technique on his own daughter, but he felt he had no choice.

"What do you mean?" Phaedra's face congealed into its most defiant mode, and she sat up straight as she faced her father.

"I mean some mighty strange things have been going on around here since the beginning of school, and I want to know if you're involved in any of it." Alex directed a stony stare at Phaedra and refused to waver, causing her to drop her eyes.

"I don't know what you're talking about, unless Mrs. Hammond has been complaining about me again. Honestly, Dad, she's such a bitch. Why can't I transfer to another class?" Phaedra's voice had taken on the whining twang that Alex detested, but he remained calm as he watched the stormy expression on her face.

"Tell me the truth. Do you think Kate Hammond is coming between your mother and me?"

Phaedra was taken aback by Alex's blunt question, and she stammered for a moment before answering. "Yes, I do. Even though you and Mother weren't getting along well before, HER arrival on the scene made things much worse."

"Honey, there's something you need to understand for once and for all. I just don't love your mother any more, and it has nothing to do with Kate Hammond or with you. This is strictly between Claire and me, and the sooner everyone realizes that the better our lives will be. We BOTH love you and always will, but I have to level with you and tell you I'm finding it difficult to even *like* your mother these days, and I have no desire to share my life or my home with her. I'm sorry if this hurts you, but I can't help how I feel."

Alex could see the tears beginning to well in Phaedra's eyes, and he slid a box of tissues toward her. "Try to understand. These things happen in some marriages, and even though the kids blame themselves, there's nothing they can do about it. When it's over, it's over, just like Yogi Berra said, sort of." Alex tried to smile at Phaedra, but she wouldn't meet his eyes.

"Now, Phaedra, this is hard for me to ask you, but I want an answer. I know you blame Kate Hammond for my lack of feelings toward your mother. Have you done anything to get back at Mrs.

Hammond?" Alex leaned across the desk and looked earnestly at the unhappy young girl opposite him.

"Yes." Phaedra's answer was so soft Alex could hardly hear her. Then her tone became filled with rage. "I hate her, and I wish she'd go away and never come back!"

"What did you do?" The pit of Alex's stomach had fallen toward his feet as Phaedra admitted her guilt, and he dreaded facing the reality that his daughter could have been involved in the terrible things that had been directed toward Kate.

"I can't tell you." Phaedra cringed against the back of her chair as she shook her head.

Alex recognized the resolution in his daughter's voice, and he realized Phaedra was probably not responsible for her own actions. There was a flickering glow in Phaedra's eyes that made him shudder and all the more desperate because he knew with certainty she needed help immediately.

"O.K., honey, let's leave it here. Perhaps we'll talk about this more later, but right now, I'll have to accept your right to remain silent." Alex got up from his seat and came around the desk, helping Phaedra out of her chair and steering her toward the door. "Would you like to go home and rest?"

Phaedra nodded and Alex kept his arm around her as they passed through the lobby and into the parking lot. The little Honda Alex had bought for Phaedra the previous summer was at the end of a row of cars, and as he helped her into the driver's seat, Alex looked down at her hand, which trembled as she tried to insert the key into the ignition.

"Do you want me to drive you home? You seem a little unstrung."

Phaedra looked up at her father, much more composed than she had been in his office. "No, really, I'm fine. I'll go home and take a nap. I want to come to the soccer scrimmage this afternoon, so I'll be back."

As the car drove away, Alex stood looking after it until it passed out of sight. Then, shaking his head, he walked back into the school, wondering how he was going to be able to convince Claire how very troubled their daughter had become.

Most of the school attended the soccer scrimmage in the afternoon, enjoying the warm sunshine and purple-blue skies of a perfect September day. Rocky Shore won easily, even though Jean Pierro only played part of the game, and as the victorious team streamed up the hill toward the gym, the spectators followed more slowly, faculty and students mingling in their mutual enjoyment of the game.

Alex turned to see Kate and Big Ed walking toward him, their heads together in an apparently serious discussion. As they approached, Alex could see Big Ed's broad face was lined with concern, and Kate looked sympathetic as she listened to what he was saying.

"Hey, you two. What's up?"

"Poor Ed," Kate explained. "Chickie hasn't spoken to him since yesterday, and just now when Ed tried to congratulate him on the good game, he just sort of shook his father off and stalked away."

"It's a bummer," Big Ed lamented. "I've been feeling lousy for so long, and Chickie has been the one who's kept everybody's spirits up. Now that I'm beginning to feel and behave like a human being again, he's down in the dumps because of his old man. Oh well, I'll just keep on trying. See you later!" Ed jogged off toward his truck, and Kate smiled up at Alex, her heart softening in the warmth of his eyes.

"Are you through for the day?" Kate hoisted her bookbag onto her shoulder and looked at her watch. "I've got to run because Jessie is home by now, but you look like you have something on your mind."

"I do, but there's not time to go into it all right now. Suffice it to say my daughter has been involved in what's been happening to you, and I've just started to get to the bottom of it."

"I'm sorry, Alex, truly I am. I can understand why Phaedra might resent me, but I wish it didn't put you in such a bad position. It's frustrating when you know she needs help, but you can't give it to her. Call me later if you'd like to tell me more." Kate squeezed Alex's hand and moved toward her car, leaving him standing looking after her.

When she turned into the gates at Silvertree Farm, Kate noticed there was an unfamiliar car parked behind Mildred's, and as she hurried up the back stairs, she could hear voices coming from the library. Mildred's gravelly tones mingled with Jessica's high-pitched chatter, and a third, soft southern accent sent a tremor of apprehension through Kate as she put her things down in the back hall and moved toward the library.

At first, the visitor's back was turned toward the door through which Kate entered, but even from that angle, Kate recognized the severely elegant French twist that was her former mother-in-law's trademark. Marissa Hammond sat on the sofa holding Jessica in her lap, while Mildred looked expectantly at Kate, waiting for her reaction to the newcomer.

"Hello, Marissa," Kate said. "What brings you to Maine?"

Jessica climbed off her grandmother's lap, holding a Madame Alexander doll dressed in an elaborate Victorian costume. Kate murmured a few words to her daughter before approaching the sofa. She couldn't forget Marissa's hostile attitude after Max's death, and she wondered what possible reason there could be for her arrival at Silvertree Farm.

Marissa rose from the sofa and took both of Kate's hands in hers. "I know this must be a shock after the way I behaved in Georgia, but I had to see you. I have some information about what's been happening recently, and I'm afraid for you and Jessica!"

THE SHAPE OF DARK—Chapter Seventeen

Kate found herself unable to move after Marissa's frightening announcement. Mildred, too, was silent, and only Jessica whispered to her new doll. Finally, Kate found her voice and called to the cook, who was chopping vegetables in the kitchen.

"Julia, could you let Jessie help you for a few minutes? I need to talk with her grandmother."

Jessica started to resist, but when Julia appeared in the library door with a chocolate chip cookie in her hand, the little girl changed her mind and scampered out of the room.

"Now, Marissa, what's this all about?" Kate sat down on the sofa and concentrated her attention on her mother-in-law, now sitting erect, her face a mask of fear.

"First, Katie, I need to tell you how sorry I am about the way I acted when Max died. Something just collapsed inside me when I realized you had killed the only child I had left, and the fact you were only defending you and Jessie against his brutality didn't seem to matter. I was awful to you, and I only hope you can find it in your heart to forgive me. I don't want to lose you and Jessie, too."

Kate reached out and grasped Marissa's hand. "It was a dreadful time for all of us, and we don't want to be cut off from you, either."

Tears of relief welled up in Marissa's eyes, but she brushed them aside and opened the envelope she was holding. She took out a stack of photographs and letters and shuffled them.

"Do you remember what I told you about Max's father and sister?"

When Kate nodded, Marissa handed her several pictures.

"These were taken just before Clinton left." The black and white photographs were a bit fuzzy, but Kate could recognize younger versions of both Marissa and Max standing with a tall, dark-haired man who was holding a little girl with blond curls.

"And here's what came in the mail the other day." Marissa gave Kate a plain piece of white paper with a brief message scrawled in red crayon. "THE BITCH WHO KILLED MY SON AND THE CHILD SHE BORE WILL SUFFER THE TORTURE OF GOD."

"Actually," Marissa continued, "when this arrived, it didn't make a lot of sense in itself. The envelope was postmarked 'Boston', and I had this horrible feeling it was from Clinton, but I had no idea where to begin trying to find him, or Samantha, who would be in her twenties, if she were still alive. Then I saw this in *USA Today*." Marissa showed Kate the page from the popular newspaper in which brief stories from each state were presented. Under "Maine" there was a summary of the Calvert shooting. Although the dateline was Portland, the account ended with the fact that Cape Mariana police were investigating the incident and protecting the Calvert children from retribution by Brother Able and his followers.

"Kate," Marissa eyes were dark in her ashen face. "Max's father's name was A. Clinton Hammond, and the 'A' stood for 'Able'!"

Mildred arose immediately and went to the phone, while Kate sat in stunned disbelief. "Captain Brogan, please. Mildred Worthington calling." There was a pause, and Mildred shifted from one foot to another in frustration. "Well, the minute that he comes in, will you please ask him to call?" Mildred hung up and turned to the two other women. "Surely the police have copies of the picture of Brother Able the Portland newspaper took a couple of years ago. I can't remember it clearly enough to tell if this is the same man."

"My gut tells me it is," Kate breathed. "There has been so much hatred heaped on me and on us for no apparent reason. This makes sense, in a horrible sort of way, and your description of Clinton helps me understand Max's behavior at the end."

Julia came into the library carrying a silver tray with a pot of tea. "From the looks on your faces," she fussed, "you might like some of this."

Mildred poured the fragrant liquid into delicate Spode cups, commenting she would really rather have a nice stiff drink. Jessica came back into the library and curled up next to her mother on the sofa, lending a small ball of warmth to Kate's numb body. Marisa seemed to be exhausted by her revelations as she sipped on her tea.

"If Brother Able is Clinton Hammond, he's probably just as anxious to get his hands on me as he is to punish the Calvert children, and now that they are relatively safe, it makes sense that he's going to direct his energy toward his son's killer." Kate avoided mentioning Jessica's name as a possible target for Brother Able's revenge, and the little girl, absorbed in examining her new doll, seemed oblivious to Kate's comments.

The telephone rang beside Mildred, and she picked it up quickly, recognizing Jim Brogan's voice on the other end. "Jim, we've had some startling news about Brother Able. Do you have a fairly recent picture of him?" Mildred nodded as she listened to Jim's affirmative answer, and she urged him to come to Silvertree Farm as quickly as he could.

Almost as soon as Mildred hung up the phone, it rang again, and this time it was for Kate. It was Alex, and the panic in his voice was palpable. "Kate, it appears Phaedra has run away, and I just called the police station to talk to Jim Brogan, but he's on his way to your house. Is it all right if I come over and talk to him there?"

"Of course." Kate wondered how many crises could occur in one afternoon, but she deliberately kept her tone smooth, recognizing the fear in Alex's words. "Are you sure she isn't visiting one of her friends?"

"No, she left a note and took some of her clothes. Claire isn't home, and she's not answering her cell phone. But I've checked around with Phaedra's buddies, and no one saw her at the soccer scrimmage. It's clear from what she says in the note she doesn't want to be found. I'd like to talk to Jim, in spite of the fact they can't help officially for twenty-four hours."

When Kate hung up, Mildred was at the front door admitting Jim Brogan, whose haggard face suggested both a lack of sleep and a profound sadness. The police captain had a copy of the picture the photographer had hastily snapped of Brother Able. In spite of its poor quality, Marissa was able to positively identify the wild-eyed man with one fist in the air and a large gun under one arm.

"Even with the weird costume and long hair, I'm sure that's Clinton. His eyes look dark in the photo, however, Clinton's were blue. Marissa could barely bring herself to look at the man who had stolen her baby so many years before. Then she expressed a thought they all shared. "If he's here, where is my daughter?"

Jim leafed back through his notebook until he came to his scribbled record of his conversation with Eve on the morning after Willie shot his parents. "Eve described her early life in Massachusetts with Brother Able, but she never mentioned his having a child with him. Perhaps she might be able to remember more about those days."

Kate spoke up immediately. "I promised Eve I would bring her schoolwork out to Merton House, and I was planning on going after Jessie went to bed. Would it be all right for Marissa to come with me and ask Eve a few questions?"

Looking out the library windows, Kate saw Alex's car drive in, and she went to the front door to meet him. His tie was loosened as if he had yanked it away from his neck, and he ran his fingers through his rumpled hair as he followed Kate into the library.

Alex acknowledged Kate's introduction of Marissa as politely as he could before snatching a piece of pink stationery out of his pocket and handing it to Jim. "This is the note Phaedra left on her bed this afternoon."

"Did she have any money that you know of?" Jim scanned the paper Alex had given him and wrote a few notes in his book.

"Only her allowance for this week. She begged me for an advance last weekend because she had spent everything she had on some CD she wanted. Unless Claire gave her something, she only had about twenty dollars."

"In a way, that's good. She has her car, but that small amount of money won't take her far. Why does she say in the note she's done some bad things she'd be punished for if she stayed in Cape Mariana?"

"I'm not sure, exactly. This morning I asked her if she had been involved in the harassment Kate has received, and she said 'yes', but she wouldn't tell me what she had done. I got the feeling there was someone else involved, but I decided not to pursue it at that moment, because I had just dumped a lot of pain on Phaedra by telling her how I felt about her mother. Maybe I should have tried harder to find out what her role has been in all of this, because she certainly must have felt guilty to run away like this."

Jim looked steadily at Alex. "Or scared. Maybe she was afraid you would find out who else was involved. Anyway, I'll ask around."

After Jim and Alex left, the women ate a hasty dinner in the kitchen, and Jessica went willingly to bed, abandoning her new doll for the soft familiarity of Cynthia the blue bear. Mildred settled in the library at her desk while Kate assembled school materials for Eve and set off for Portland with Marissa.

The windows in the psychiatric hospital glowed as Kate guided the BMW up the winding driveway. Eve looked more rested than she had the day before, but there was profound pain on her face as she described her brother's condition. "He's absolutely convinced he's dead, and nothing anyone can say will change his mind. He thinks Timmy's here and they have long conversations where Timmy assures Willie God will protect him from harm. Willie has this peaceful look that's scary. I'm so frightened for him. Do you think he'll ever come back to reality?"

"I don't know, Eve. That poor child has been through so much he may not be able to reconnect. But speaking of strange connections, my mother-in-law has come to Maine because she has realized Brother Able is probably her estranged husband, Clinton Hammond. Marissa wants to ask you a few questions about your first recollections of Brother Able during the days when you all lived in Massachusetts, because he abducted their baby daughter when he left Georgia."

Eve sat down on the edge of the bed and Kate took a seat beside her with Marissa facing them in the desk chair. "I know this may be hard for you, but I would really appreciate any information you could give me. Do you remember anybody else living with Brother Able when you were little? A child, maybe? Samantha would have been about eight years older than you."

"I think Brother Able lived alone in a room behind the house they used for a church, just the way he did here. He was only at Ledyard Hill on the weekends." Eve wrinkled her brow as she tried to dig into her memory. "There was a girl who came to visit during the summer, and she stayed with another family next to the church, but I remember she spent a lot of time with Brother Able. She had blond pigtails and told us she lived near the ocean. We all liked her a lot, and Brother Able was always nicer when she visited. But then I think something weird happened the last summer she came to Ledyard Hill. A lady in a fancy car came to pick her up, and had a big fight with Brother Able. After that, we never saw her again.

Marissa sat motionless, listening to Eve's recollection. "That girl could well have been Samantha. Clinton's sister was supposed to have married someone from Massachusetts, and he may have sent Samantha to live with them. I tried to call Alice right after Clinton disappeared, but the family she had worked for in Marblehead had no idea where she had gone. Maybe it would be worth trying to contact them again."

On the way home to Cape Mariana, Marissa apologized again to Kate for her behavior in the time that immediately followed Max's death. "When I visited him at the Holt Institute after he had assaulted you and Jessie, I saw the same look in his eyes that used to be in his father's after he had done something violent. It was a sort of flat, stony anger, and I should have been more aware of what could happen."

Kate reached over and patted her mother-in-law's hand. "Don't torment yourself about something you can't change. I'm just glad Jessie has her only grandparent back!" Then the realization dawned on both of them and they looked at each other in horror. "Oh my God, Marissa. Brother Able is Jessie's grandfather!"

"I'd lie down in front of a train before I'd let that evil man near Jessie. I want to see this thing through with you, Kate. Is there a hotel nearby where I can stay?"

"I'm always inviting people to stay at Silvertree Farm, but I know Millie would insist, and Jessie and I would love it. Actually, it would make me feel better to know that someone else is here who cares about Jessie. Ever since that awful time with Max, she's been so quiet and withdrawn. Every once in a while, there'll be a glimmer of her old sparkle, especially around a couple of young men at school, but most of the time she seems to be in her own little world." Kate sounded genuinely glad for Marissa's presence, and the older woman found herself smiling in the dark, relaxed for the first time in a long while.

As it turned out, Jessica awoke the next morning with an upset stomach, so Kate was relieved that Marissa was pleased about the prospect of taking care of the child, since Mildred had to go to Boston. When Kate left for school, grandmother and grandchild were cuddled in a big chair in Jessica's bedroom, reading *The Velveteen Rabbit*.

Coming through the entrance doors to Rocky Shore, Kate saw Alex standing in the door of his office watching the movement of the students, most of whom were clustered around the bulletin board in the lobby. When she walked over and asked him if he had heard anything from Phaedra, he shook his head. "Not a word, but I certainly got an earful from Claire. She accused me of driving HER daughter away and of every other crime you can think of, including adultery!" For a moment, Alex's expression lightened. "How ironic is that! Anyway, she's insisted on hiring a private detective, and Jim Brogan is doing his best. We'll just have to wait and see."

Kate saw from her watch that the warning bell was about to ring, so she made her way toward the stairs, only to be nearly knocked down by Eric Lundgren, who had just come bounding down from the second floor. "Wait till you see your room, Mrs. Hammond! The phantom painter has been at it again."

Hearing Eric's words, Alex pushed his way through the milling students until he reached Kate's side. "What do you mean?"

The gleeful expression on Eric's face infuriated both Kate and Alex, but they listened calmly as the boy described the pictures and captions that now adorned the walls of Kate's classroom. His voice was so loud nearly everyone in the lobby heard him, and crowds of students pushed their way up the stairs to see for themselves.

Since the classroom was securely locked, the only view the fascinated audience had was through a pane of reinforced glass in the door. Bright red stick figures could be seen in various lewd positions, and in each case, the names "Kate" and "Alex" were printed in the appropriate places. Only one wall was visible, but it was enough to make Kate feel nauseous, and it was only Alex's reassuring bulk next to her that helped her keep her composure.

With shaking hands, Kate opened the door and she and Alex slipped inside, leaving the curious students frustrated in the corridor. All of the walls had been decorated in a similar fashion, displaying the artist's vast knowledge of deviant sexual behavior. On Kate's desk was a pile of photographs, with a sheet of paper next to them on which "WHORE!" had been scrawled in red crayon.

Rifling through the pictures, Kate caught her breath and handed them to Alex, who swore. A telescopic lens had captured the two of them embracing on the deck of Alex's sailboat, and even from a distance, their passionate involvement was obvious.

"Who is doing this to me, Alex? And why?" Kate felt tears close to the surface, but she willed them back.

"Damned if I know," Alex muttered. "Are you sure you locked this door last night? After we had the locks changed, I made sure there were only three keys. You and I each have one, and Lenny has the third. Have you lost your keys recently?"

"No, I'm certain they've been with me all the time. What about you?"

"The same with me. I'll double check with Lenny to find out if he saw anyone in here last night, and I'll also arrange to have these walls painted. Look at the bright side. These rooms haven't been spruced up for years, and now you'll have instant redecoration." Alex pulled Kate out of the line of vision from the corridor and gripped her shoulders. "Stay strong, Kate."

Alex slipped out of the room, closing the door behind him. "O.K., everyone, go to your homerooms, please. Mrs. Hammond's students, please go down to Mrs. Monkton and sign in with her."

Left alone in the room, surrounded by the ugliness on the walls, Kate suddenly felt very tired. "There's been too much, all at once," she thought to herself, and she put her head down on the desk and let the tears flow, releasing the tension that had been building inside.

"Are you all right, Mrs. Hammond?" Kate lifted her eyes to the sympathetic gaze of Sophia Rossoni. "I knocked, but you didn't hear me, so I thought I'd come in and see if there was anything I could do for you. This is such a sick stunt for someone to have pulled!"

Sophia's compassion touched off a new wave of sobbing in Kate, and she struggled to regain some degree of control while fumbling in her purse for a tissue. "I feel like a fool, Sophia, but I don't seem to be able to stop crying. I should be getting mad instead of feeling sorry for myself."

"I think you have a right to do both. The trouble is, though, that a few nasty people have made your life miserable, while everybody else here thinks you're a wonderful person and a terrific teacher. I hope you know we all appreciate what you did for Eve and how much you've helped in lots of ways. Some of the teachers who have been here for twenty years won't do a thing except teach their classes and beat the kids out the door in the afternoon." Sophia's brown eyes were warm and steady, and Kate felt the girl's sincerity.

"That means a lot, especially now. Thanks, Sophia." Kate drew a deep breath and stood up. "I'd better go and find a classroom that's a bit less colorful for next period. Poor Eric will be so disappointed." Kate managed a watery smile for Sophia and they walked out into the hall together.

When Alex came back to the defaced room with the custodian, they began a concentrated search to see if they could find anything unusual. "I swept this floor real good about 4:30, and I know the door was locked." Lenny's small, wiry body bristled with anger at the idea someone had invaded his territory, and he peered around the room, rubbing his hand along the thick strips of paint on the walls.

"This stuff is real dry, so the creep must have been in here last night. Hey, Mr. Stamos, look here. I'm no art critic, but does it look like the same person did all of this drawing?" As they progressed around the room, Alex and Lenny found clear evidence that at least two different artists had been at work.

"Here's something else." Lenny stood close to one of the walls and pointed to a long hair sticking out of the paint. "Looks like at least one of these jokers might have been a woman."

Alex came over and examined the hair intently. It was impossible to tell what color it was, as it was completely covered in red, but as much as he resisted it, Phaedra's long, dark hair floated into his consciousness. Could his missing daughter have possibly been responsible for this disgusting display?

"I suppose I'd better get the police over here before we repaint these walls, Lenny. But as soon as they're through looking around, I'd like you to get busy and get this stuff covered up. Do you have any paint on hand?"

"Alf told me there is some stored in that closet in the art studio, but nobody has a key that will work. Do you want me to take the door off its hinges?"

"Yes, you can do that right now. Ms. Moore has taken her students to the museum in Boston, so the room will be empty all day. Let me know what you find."

Lenny ambled away, whistling to himself, and Alex locked the door and headed for the stairs, noting that Kate had installed herself in Carlo Brito's classroom and was conducting a lively discussion with her senior class. In the lobby, a student aide handed Alex a sheaf of messages, and he headed for his office, feeling somewhat guilty at how peaceful it was in Marta Stone's domain without her presence. His secretary had called in earlier to say that she had a touch of the flu, and was a bit put out when Alex immediately urged her to stay home as long as she needed to.

The first call he returned was to Jim Brogan, who had some surprising news he wanted Alex to pass along to Kate. "It looks like Brother Able has gotten cold feet and is heading south," Jim informed Alex with mixed frustration and relief. "He was spotted in a gas station in New Hampshire by a reporter who recognized him from that old file photo they kept showing on television. By the time the police arrived, Brother Able had disappeared. The reporter who saw him said there seemed to be a group of cars traveling together, but he didn't get license plate numbers because he wanted to call the cops right away."

"Well, if that's true, it will be the best news we've had for a long time. I talked to Eve this morning, and she's very anxious to get back to school, but she doesn't want to cause us a lot of trouble. I'd like to get the kid back to normal as soon as possible, and if it's true Brother Able has given up the ship, then I'll begin to make some arrangements." Alex scribbled a few notes on his appointment calendar as he talked to Captain Brogan. "Let me know if you hear anything else, will you?"

"Absolutely. Now, the second order of business. We've alerted police in the surrounding states about Phaedra, and we've shown her picture at the bus station, airport, and any other possible points of departure from Maine. We've also circulated a description of her car. Nobody has seen her, but we'll keep trying." Jim's voice registered his sympathy for Alex's concern.

"Thanks, buddy. This is a lot on your plate at the same time you're trying to hold yourself and Ellen together. How are you doing?"

"We're O.K. Ellen would like to hold off for a little while on a memorial service for Timmy, because many of his friends from the waterfront are away on the big fishing boats. That assembly you had yesterday did a lot for both of us. I know Timmy would have loved hearing those stories people told."

Just before noon, Alex completed his calls, and he hurried across the lobby to catch Kate at lunch. Her reaction to the possibility that Brother Able and his followers might have left Maine was as joyful as her dismay at the defacing of her classroom. "Does that mean it would be safe for Eve to come back to school? She'd be more than welcome at Silvertree Farm."

"Jim seemed to think another sighting of Brother Able, hopefully farther south, would mean she could start to resume a normal life. I only wish we could say the same thing for Willie." Alex took a bite of his roast beef sandwich. "With all that you've been through, are you sure you want to take on the responsibility of another person? Jim hasn't been able to contact Eve's grandmother, and we don't even know if she's alive or well. This could be a big commitment on your part."

"I know what I'm getting into. What would have become of Jessie and me if Millie hadn't brought us up here? In spite of all that's happened, I'm so glad we came to Cape Mariana." Kate colored at the wide smile that lit Alex's face, and she turned her attention to the corn chowder cooling in front of her.

"Then let's see what we can do about getting Eve sprung!" Alex finished his lunch and pushed his chair under the table. "Drop by at the end of school, and I'll tell you what Dr. Ephron had to say."

As Alex hurried by Sandra Monkton, she stopped his progress. "Lenny wants to see you in the art studio right away. Something about a closet he's opened."

Downstairs the familiar damp smell of the basement greeted Alex as he turned into the brightly lit art studio, even more cluttered than it had been the day before. Lenny had removed the locked door and he was pulling out unopened cans of paint, peering at the labels to find the right color for Kate's room.

"No ghosts or skeletons?" Alex's voice boomed through the empty room as he made his way through the colorful disarray to where Lenny bent into the dark interior of the closet. "Isn't there a light anywhere? You can't see what you're doing."

"There's a flashlight in my tool kit, over there. Maybe you could hold it, and I can look at the labels so I don't have to drag all these cans out into the room." Lenny pointed to the gray metal box on the pottery table.

When Alex switched on the powerful lamp, the small closet was clearly illuminated, and Lenny quickly found enough pale yellow paint to repair the damage upstairs. While the custodian replaced the rest of the cans in the closet, Alex shone the beam around casually. "Did you see this switch inside the doorjamb, Lenny? Do you suppose there's a light in here after all?" Alex flicked the switch, which was almost hidden from view, and both men jumped when they heard the sound of a motor whirring in the wall. The back of the closet slid slowly to one side, gradually uncovering a narrow stairway.

"Holy shit!" Lenny's eyes protruded as he stared at the hidden passage. "Where did that come from?"

"Who knows?" Alex shoved aside the pile of paint cans in the middle of the closet and squirmed through the small opening, barely able to maneuver his large body so he could climb the stairs, which were very dusty except for several sets of footprints in the center of each.

Lenny was clearly reluctant to follow his boss, but he squared his shoulders and moved through the closet until he, too, was on the stairway. "You sure this thing will hold us both, Mr. Stamos?"

Alex recognized the fear in the custodian's voice, so he called back. "You stay down there and catch me if I fall." Looking over his shoulder, Alex saw the relief on Lenny's face as he backed down to the bottom step. "Hand me the flashlight, will you?"

With the light pointed upward in his jacket pocket, Alex's face was illuminated from underneath, as he made his way slowly up the stairway, pausing to test each step before he put his full weight on it. Cautiously, he held onto the railings on both sides of the stairs, stopping periodically to shine the light up what appeared to be an endless succession of steps into darkness.

After climbing for several minutes, Alex looked back and saw Lenny's tiny form at least thirty feet below him. Just ahead, the stairs ended against an apparently solid dark wall. Balancing on the second to top step, Alex flashed his light around the partition in front of him, puzzled, until he discovered a well-concealed device similar to the one in the closet below. Engaging the switch, Alex jerked back, but caught himself as the movement of the wall to one side startled him.

241

The room in which Alex found himself was lined with shelves on which were stacked papers and classroom supplies. There was a door opposite the hidden staircase, and when Alex turned the knob, he found himself inside Kate's classroom.

THE SHAPE OF DARK—Chapter Eighteen

Alex closed the sliding panel in Kate's storage closet and worked his way back down the steep stairs to where Lenny stood, anxiously peering into the darkness. "Buy two sturdy padlocks and put one on the closet door in Mrs. Hammond's room and one on this door. Then bring me all the keys."

The custodian looked astounded as Alex flipped the switch controlling the lower concealed door. "I knew these old houses were full of odd things, but hidden staircases! I'll bet there's a good story behind why this one was built."

"Probably, but we'll never know. Meanwhile, we're going to keep this little discovery between us. Got that?" Alex's serious expression elicited a quick promise of secrecy from Lenny, and the custodian began to replace the door as he had been instructed.

Upstairs, Jim Brogan was waiting in Alex's office with more good news about Brother Able. "A toll collector at the Hampton tolls near the border with Massachusetts recognized his picture. She said he was driving an old black van full of people, so it looks like our psycho is headed out of town. At least Kate and Eve can breathe easier for a while."

"I'm glad, because we really want to get Eve out of Merton House. But now, let me tell you what I just found..." Alex described the hidden stairway to Jim, who hurried down to the art room to see for himself. While the policeman was gone, Alex called Dr. Ephron and found the psychiatrist heartily in favor of Eve's resumption of as normal a life as possible.

"You know, Mr. Stamos, I've dealt with a lot of abused children in my practice, and they're usually scarred very deeply by their experiences. There is something otherworldly about Eve, though, that I've only run across once before. She's a remarkable young woman, and I think she's going to be all right, but I'm not at all sure about her brother."

Alex sighed. "Let's take them one at a time, Doctor, and be grateful Eve seems to be on the mend. I wish to God that I could have gotten my own daughter to you before she ran away." Alex was completing arrangements for Eve to be picked up later in the afternoon when Jim came back from the art studio.

"Quite a mysterious building you have here. Any more secret passages you know about?" Jim settled into the chair in front of Alex's desk.

"Not yet, but nothing would surprise me." Alex looked out into the lobby and saw Eric walking toward the dining hall. "Jim, do me a favor. I'm going to show that bat we found on Half-Moon Beach to one of the students, and I want you to watch his reaction." Alex went to the door of his office and hailed Eric, who shuffled over to where the principal stood.

"Come on in, Eric. I have something I want you to look at." Alex reached into his safe and took out the small baseball bat he had shown Kelly the day before. "Have you ever seen this?"

Eric eyed the object warily. "Yeah! That's mine. How did you get it?"

"I found it near Half-Moon Beach. Do you have any idea how it might have gotten there?"

"Well, that bat is usually on top of my bookcase at home, but it's been missing a couple of weeks. I figured the housekeeper got tired of dusting around it and threw it away, or it fell behind the bookcase. I was too lazy to look. But I'm glad to have it back. It's sort of a good luck thing for me." Eric reached for the bat but Alex held it back.

"Sorry, Eric, but I'll have to keep it for a while. I can't explain now, but it will become clear later, I hope. Thanks for identifying it." Alex opened his safe and replaced the bat, as Eric started to protest. "That'll be all for now."

Alex closed his office door after Eric left. "What do you think? Was he telling the truth?"

"Hard to tell. I've seen Eric lie many times, and he always has a stupid 'who me?' expression on his face. I didn't see that this time. What does all of this mean?"

"When I showed the bat to Kelly, she looked positively ill. Alf's case is going before the Grand Jury soon, and I think this 'Little Hitter' is the key to the whole story. But there's no evidence Eric is involved beyond a certain gut feeling." Alex got up and handed the bat to Jim.

A call for Jim from headquarters sent the police captain hurrying away while the final bell of the day emptied classrooms throughout the building. Kate dropped by Alex's office and then headed for Portland when she learned Eve could come home with her.

****

Upstairs, Carlo Brito had a big problem. During lunch, one of his students had given him a note informing the coach that several of his players had been drinking before the last game. The message was unsigned, but mentioned the names of four players, one of whom was slouched in a desk at the front of Carlo's classroom.

"Well, Eric, what do you have to say for yourself? Is this information true?"

Eric's face registered his rage at the anonymous author of the charge against him. "Someone must have it in for me, Coach. There's no way that I'm going to get wasted when I have a responsibility to the team. Why doesn't whoever wrote that have the courage to face me in person?"

Carlo almost smiled at Eric's righteous indignation, but he kept his face devoid of expression. "You need to know, Eric, that I've already spoken to two of the other boys mentioned here, and they both admitted it was true and separately named you as one of the people involved. In fact, one of the boys even said that you provided the booze. I'm going to talk to the fourth person, but until I can straighten this out, you're barred from practice."

When Eric opened his mouth to protest, Carlo held up his hand. "Don't waste your breath, Mr. Lundgren. See me in the morning." Muttering under his breath, Eric stomped from the room, slamming the door behind him, while Carlo trotted down to Alex's office to warn him of possibly repercussions.

Outside in the parking lot, Eric cursed as he stumbled on a rock on the way to his car. When the car seemed to drive itself to Half-Moon Beach, Eric parked in the empty lot and strode out onto the sand, annoyed to find the tide so high there was very little room to walk comfortably. As he set out toward the jutting rocks at the south end of the beach, he saw that one other person was braving the chill of the afternoon sea breeze. Far ahead of him, a dark-haired girl bent into the wind, and when he came closer, Eric recognized Sophia Rossoni, her plaid wool jacket turned up at the collar and buttoned around her neck. Sophia's face was down, and she seemed to be watching her feet as she walked.

"Sophia!" Eric called her name when he realized she would pass by without looking at him. Startled, she lifted her head, and Eric could see tears streaming down her face. Sophia swiped her hands across her eyes, but her cheeks were wet.

"Hi Eric." Sophia seemed about to continue on when Eric took her arm.

"What's wrong?" Eric was struck by the intense sadness in the girl's face, and although he didn't know her very well, he felt the need to help her.

Sophia shook her head but seemed unable to speak. She put her hand up to her throat as if something were blocking her voice, and then she sat down on the damp sand and buried her face in her palms.

Eric knelt down next to her and put his arm around her shaking shoulders. "Come on. Talk to me. You might feel better."

Sophia drew in a shuddering breath and looked up at Eric. "My mother just found out she has cancer."

"What do you mean? How do you know?" Eric didn't know what to say.

"When I came home from school today, my father told me the lump in my mother's breast has turned out to be malignant. I can't lose her, Eric. She's my best friend!" The anguish was so jagged on Sophia's face that Eric felt her pain.

"I'm so sorry, Sophia. Isn't there something the doctors can do?"

Sophia bit her lower lip as she tried to control herself. "My father says she has a very good chance, but it involves those treatments that make people so sick, and I'm not sure she could go through them. My grandmother died of breast cancer when she was only fifty years old, and my mother's going to be fifty-one next month. It's killing my father, because he's like a teenager around Mom." Sophia smiled thinking of her parents' continued passion for each other. Then her face saddened again. "My father told me he wants to send Jean-Pierro back to Italy before my mother has to go through chemotherapy and radiation, but she wants him to stay because she knows how difficult his home was in Europe."

Huddled on the sand, Sophia looked fragile and helpless, and Eric felt a sudden urge to protect her. "Come and walk with me and tell me a little more about your family." Eric held out his hand and pulled Sophia into the crook of his arm, thinking she was much smaller than he had assumed. The two set off down the beach, dodging the incoming waves and jumping over the rivulets of water that made deep troughs in the gray sand.

Watching from the deck of his restaurant, Arthur Rossoni had no idea who the tall young man was with his broken-hearted daughter, but he was thankful Sophia had found a friend during her lonely flight from the truth about Maria's condition. Arthur turned back to go inside, skirting the stacked tables, chairs, and umbrellas that were waiting to be stored underneath the deck until next summer.

The restaurant was empty except for three waiters who were setting up tables for the evening's meal. Tuesday was a "Twofer" night at Rossoni's and the prospect of one free meal lured people from the entire Greater Portland area, making the restaurant unusually crowded in the early hours of the evening. Knowing what was ahead of him, Arthur sat down at the bar and poured himself a cup of coffee, adding the three heaping teaspoons of sugar that so annoyed his wife.

What would life be like without Maria to fuss at him constantly, smothering him, Sophia, and now Jean-Pierro with her relentless, full-bodied love? The specter of Sophia's stricken face floated across his consciousness, and Arthur sipped at the scalding coffee, hoping to sear away the memory.

"Hey, Uncle Arthur!" Jean-Pierro came noisily through the front door, dirt and sweat staining his body, and his soccer cleats slung casually over his shoulder. "I have some news for you and Aunt Maria. Is she here?"

Arthur turned on his stool, and seeing the enthusiasm in Jean-Pierro's clear brown eyes, forced himself to smile. "She's taking a nap, Jopo. Tell me before you explode!"

Jean-Pierro plopped down at one of the tables and clapped himself on the head. "You know how I am supposed to be here for this year only? Well, today at practice, a man from a big private school in New Hampshire talked to me and Coach Brito, and if my season keeps on good, they will give me a free time for next year. I would not have to go back to Italy."

Arthur saw Jean-Pierro's expression cloud over at the thought of his home in Naples, and he knew how badly the boy had been treated by his stepfather, leading his sister to beg him to allow her son to come to the United States. Now, with the news of Maria's health, Arthur's mind whirled in confusion, happy for Jean-Pierro's prospective scholarship, but reluctant to have the added responsibility at this time.

"That's great, Jopo! Everyone will be so proud of you." Arthur pushed the possibility of sending his nephew home to the back of his mind and concentrated on bolstering the boy's confidence. "You'll just have to play even better now!" The back door of the restaurant opened, and Sophia came in from the deck, causing the salt wind to ruffle the tablecloths near the door.

"Sophia!" Jean-Pierro bounded over to his cousin and hugged her. "It may be that I can stay in America for a very long time!" Sophia looked at her father, who shook his head slightly, warning her to say nothing of their earlier conversation.

"Shall I start the veal now, Mr. Rossoni?" Antony, the sous-chef peered out from the kitchen, where pots boiled and several white-capped men chopped vegetables and prepared salads.

"I'll be right there. Sophia, can you help out tonight for a little while? Your mother should rest, but knowing her, she'll be in here any minute now." Arthur climbed down from the barstool and put his hands on his daughter's shoulders. "I can depend on you, can't I?"

"Sure, Papa." Tears glistened in Sophia's eyes, but she reached up and kissed her father's cheek. "Jopo and I will both be here for you, won't we?" Jean-Pierro looked on, somewhat confused, but aware that more was being said than the words Sophia was using. Knowing he was missing something, he simply followed Sophia out of the restaurant toward the shingled house next door where the family lived.

After Eric watched from the sand as Sophia climbed the steps to the deck of her family's restaurant, he continued in the direction of the dunes that separated the main part of the beach from the coves where the bonfires were usually built. At the second cove over, Eric sat down on a big piece of driftwood to rest for a minute before heading back to the car. As he watched the waves fold onto the beach, Eric was surprised to hear his sister's voice behind him.

"Did Mr. Stamos show you something today?" Kelly's voice was shaking, and she looked terrified.

"I told you to get rid of that thing, you little slut! He'll probably have it tested for fingerprints or something, and we're both dead meat!"

"Well, it was your idea in the first place, and I'm sure I buried it so that none of it showed. Besides, you were supposed to help me. I wasn't in the best shape, you know."

"I couldn't help it. Phaedra trapped me and I couldn't get away from her.".

"You realize I could have died out there, and all you care about is making sure there's nothing else around for someone to find. What could there possibly be?" Kelly spoke crossly to her brother, who stopped and glared down at his sister.

"I don't know, but it was worth planting that glove of Alf's near the shack. The police will think they overlooked it when they first searched the area, and if there are any more questions from Herr Stamos, there'll be something else out here to nail Alf. Everything depends on this, Kelly. If anyone found out what really happened, we'd both be screwed," Eric growled.

"Oh, that's very funny, brother dear. If you hadn't been drunk when you so rudely entered my bedroom, you'd have known what trouble we could get into." Kelly's hair was being whipped by the cold wind as she angrily faced her brother.

"Hey, baby, don't be a little miss innocent with me. You were begging for it, and you know it. The minute Mom and Dad go out of town and leave us alone, you hop into your sexiest Victoria's Secret and just happen to leave your bedroom door open. You knew I'd been partying, and it's not as if we haven't fooled around before."

"But you know we agreed it was O.K. to have a little fun, but never to go too far. You just wouldn't stop." Kelly's tone infuriated Eric and he grabbed her shoulders roughly.

"You come on to me all the time and you know it. Don't you dare blame me for this whole thing, because it takes two."

****

At the same time Kelly and Eric argued about their dilemma, Kate hung up the phone in the library of Silvertree Farm after receiving the news that Brother Able had been spotted again, this time in a rest area off of the Massachusetts Turnpike near Sturbridge. Apparently, he was switching vehicles as he traveled farther south, because the person who identified him, a truck driver from Biddeford, described the group as being in two battered station wagons, both bearing Massachusetts plates. In spite of a diligent search, the cars had not been spotted again on the turnpike, and although local police had been notified in the surrounding towns, there was no sign of the fugitives.

"Still," Kate explained to Eve, who was sitting comfortably with Jessica in a large, overstuffed chair by the fireplace, "the fact that they seem to be traveling away from Maine is a good sign. I just hope they don't change their minds."

Mildred spoke up from the sofa, where she was squinting over a piece of needlepoint. "I would think you'd be delighted so many people recognize that crazy person and are cooperating to keep track of him. He'll find it hard to remain anonymous with that heavy black beard and the big hat he insists on wearing."

Eve spoke up. "In all of the time I've known Brother Able, I've never seen him without that awful hat. He's very superstitious about a lot of things, and he thinks the hat brings him good luck. I remember one time when it blew off of his head, and he nearly went crazy. It began to symbolize fear for a lot of the children he helped to, ah, counsel, and I remember Willie drawing a picture of Brother Able once, and the whole thing seemed to be an oversized head and hat. My father thought it was wonderful Willie drew the picture and was so pleased he gave it to Brother Able. Willie told me it was a picture of the devil."

"Poor Willie," Kate lamented. "He goes from one extreme to the other. Now he thinks he's with the angels."

Everyone in the library looked up as Marissa Hammond came through the door with a strange expression on her face. She had gone upstairs nearly an hour ago to telephone for some information about Clinton's sister from the family she had worked for in Marblehead, and it was hard to tell by the look in her eyes if she had been successful.

"Any luck?" Kate wished her mother-in-law looked more encouraged.

"I'm not sure. The people still live in the same place, but they're very old and quite hard of hearing. The woman sounded senile, but her husband got on the phone and was able to understand my questions. He said Alice left their employ almost thirty years ago, but he heard she had married a wealthy man on the North Shore. He thought that he had seen her one evening at the Marblehead Yacht Club, but he couldn't be sure." Marissa had dark rings under her eyes and appeared to be very tired, and she accepted the glass of sherry Mildred offered her and sank into a chair by the fire.

"What I'd like to do, if I could, Mildred, is borrow one of your cars and go down to the North Shore tomorrow. I have an old picture of Alice, and maybe if I show it around, someone will remember her."

Mildred agreed immediately and even offered to keep Marissa company on the two hour trip. "I haven't been down that way since George died, and I'd love a change of scenery."

****

The next day was so uneventful that both Kate and Alex remarked at lunch how boring things seemed without at least one crisis per hour. Eve's return to school was accomplished with little disruption, in spite of the fact that a few news teams were still camped on the road opposite the entrance to Rocky Shore. Tikka had lent her blond wig for the occasion, so the cameras paid no attention to Kate's BMW arriving at its usual time with a tousled-haired passenger who bore no resemblance to the quiet, frightened-looking girl whose picture had been splashed across the front page.

Once inside the building, Eve was greeted warmly by most of the students, with Kelly Lundgren and her small group of friends the only exceptions. Chickie took it upon himself to serve as a constant escort, still not trusting that Eve was safe. His gallant behavior made him the butt of many good-natured jokes from his teammates, while Eve received envious looks from the many girls who would have killed for even one moment of such treatment.

Eve had allowed Kate and Tikka to convince her to borrow a gray-green turtleneck sweater and trim black jeans, while using more makeup than she was used to. The effect was that her already pretty but pale face acquired a more vibrant color, her clear gray eyes were

251

subtlely defined, and her lips were tinted with a soft rose gloss. When Chickie first caught sight of Eve walking across the lobby with Kate, his eyes widened in surprise at the transformation that had taken place since the last time he had seen her in Merton House. Eve's cheeks flamed when she saw his reaction to her new looks.

Kate's classroom had been repainted a cheerful yellow that seemed to draw the sun into the formerly dark space, and a heavy padlock secured the storage room door. A clear glass bowl of chrysanthemums was on her desk, and a little card propped against the vase simply had a smiley face on it drawn with one eye closed in a wink. Without asking, Kate knew the colorful blooms were from Alex, who looked pleased with himself when she thanked him.

When she was ready to leave for the day, Kate stopped at Alex's office to thank him again for the flowers and found him frowning over the telephone, obviously very annoyed with the person on the other end of the line. Waving Kate into the chair opposite his desk, Alex growled "over my dead body!" into the receiver and slammed down the telephone without saying goodbye.

"Guess what Claire is telling me now?" Alex was positively fuming as he banged his fist on the desk in frustration. "She has decided Phaedra has gone to Boston, since she's so familiar with the city and Claire is sure she can find her. She wants me to promise her I won't have anything to do with you while she's gone, because, as she so sweetly puts it, my tomcatting around was responsible for Phaedra's leaving. The big excuse for her ultimatum is that we should be ready to present a united front in case OUR DAUGHTER comes home. Bullshit!"

"Have you had any information about Phaedra?"

"Not a word," Alex sighed, "but I have this strange feeling she's not far away. Meanwhile, what am I going to do about Claire?"

"I haven't a clue, but at least you won't have to look at her smiling face over dinner." Kate stood up and lifted the heavy bag of books onto her shoulder.

"Actually," Alex said as he walked Kate to the door of his office, "I have no intention of listening to what Claire has to say. What's your attitude toward Greek food? There's a terrific new place in town."

In spite of a warning voice in her conscience, Kate hesitated only a minute. "Give me until seven o'clock to put Jessie to bed and I'm yours. I would betray my country for baklava and moussaka."

"See you then!" Alex glanced furtively around, and seeing no one in the lobby, bent swiftly and kissed Kate's cheek.

Outside, Kate hummed as she trotted to her car, enjoying the sight of the soccer and field hockey teams swarming over the distant playing fields where the late afternoon shadows were slowly spreading their cool darkness. Setting her bookbag on the hood of the BMW, Kate rummaged through her purse for her keys and was about to unlock the door, when she looked up to see a tall figure moving toward her, his back to the brilliance of the setting sun.

As the man came closer, Kate squinted into the light, trying to define the features of the eerily familiar person who was wearing a slouch hat and aviator sunglasses, one long arm swinging a briefcase by his side. The stranger's other hand was shoved into his faded blue jeans, causing him to walk with a peculiar rolling gait Kate recognized immediately.

All at once, the ground began to slip away from Kate as she gripped the handle of her car door and she swallowed hard to resist a wave of sudden nausea. The man was nearly even with her car when the screaming in her ears was so loud she wasn't sure whose voice it was that split the cool autumn air before she slipped into a long, black well.

THE SHAPE OF DARK—Chapter Nineteen

"Miss? Are you all right?" Kate was aware of a dull ache in the back of her head where she had hit the pavement, and the voice of the man who hovered anxiously above her was distant and blurred, sounding as if it were coming through water.

"Max?" The sun was still in Kate's eyes as she looked up at the dark form who was now waving frantically in the direction of the school. "Is that you?" Kate could hear feet pounding on the ground before Alex and Chief Wallace stepped in front of the stranger and lifted Kate carefully to her feet.

Alex picked a few leaves from Kate's hair and brushed the dirt off her back. "Did you fall? Does anything hurt?" Chief Wallace, who was also the school's sports trainer, looked closely at Kate's chalk-white face where beads of sweat were gathering on her forehead.

"She looks really woozy, Alex. Let's take her back into the building and have her lie down." Alex scooped Kate into his arms and carried her limp body into his office, laying her on his leather couch. The man who had startled Kate trailed behind the group stunned by her reaction to his appearance in the parking lot.

"Can you tell us what happened?" Alex knelt beside Kate, glad to see the color slowly coming back into her face.

Kate looked up at Alex, her eyes round and frightened. "Alex, Max is alive. How can that be?"

"Where did you get an idea like that?" Alex was alarmed by Kate's haunted, slightly dazed expression.

"I saw him. He was walking toward me in the parking lot and then I must have fainted." Kate swept her eyes from Alex to Chief Wallace before she caught sight of a very distinguished looking man who appeared to be in his early sixties with longish silvery-gray hair and a tanned, ruggedly-lined face.

Alex beckoned for the stranger to come closer to the couch so Kate could see him more clearly. The man's sunglasses were hooked casually into the open neck of his checked shirt, and he clutched the briefcase she had seen him carrying before. "Is this the person you thought was Max?"

Kate examined the worried face of the newcomer and nodded, feeling very foolish. There was some resemblance between her dead husband and the man before her, but he clearly was not Max. "It must have been the hat and sunglasses, which are just like the ones Max always wore. Also, there was something about the way he walked…"

"I'm really sorry to have frightened you, Mrs. Hammond, especially since you were one of the reasons I came to Cape Mariana." The man's light blue eyes were disturbed when he saw that Kate's hands were still trembling. "I'm Adam Loring, and I used to work with your husband before he died. Many of his paintings have gone through my gallery in Boston." The man handed a business card to Alex, who glanced at it and gave it to Kate, adding to her embarrassment.

Alex laughed. "We don't usually greet our visitors this way, Mr. Loring, but we've had a tough few weeks, and we're all a little bit on edge."

Adam Loring pressed Kate's hand. "I'm glad you're all right, but I'm going to pretend it was the power of my personal charm that made you swoon like some Victorian damsel. It's quite flattering, you know."

Kate appreciated the man's charming reaction to her hysterical outburst, and she gave him a weak smile. "Thanks for making me feel less of a fool, Mr. Loring. Max spoke of you often, and I'm very happy to meet you after all this time. How can I be of help?"

"Actually, there are two reasons I'm here. First, I'd like to try to convince you to let me organize a retrospective show of Max's work, most of which is in the hands of Appleton Kingsley. And second, there is a young artist in Portland whose jewelry interests me very much. I understand she teaches here, and I'd like some help in persuading her to allow me to show her things in Boston." Adam Loring's manner was easy and relaxed, allowing Kate's heart to slow to normal as she thought about his first request.

"As a matter of fact, Susan is downstairs as we speak, working with some students. While Kate gathers her wits about her, why doesn't Chief Wallace take you down to the art studio? I'm sure she'd enjoy some attention from a big city art dealer."

Adam's face lit up in anticipation, and he eagerly followed the Athletic Director to the stairs at the end of the lobby, while Kate sat up slowly and shook her aching head. "This is too weird. Only last night I dreamed about Max's paintings, and here's Adam Loring in person. No wonder I keeled over."

"Maybe it's too soon for you to think about dredging up Max's memory by allowing a showing of his work. Your reaction to Adam's slight resemblance to your husband indicates the wounds are still raw." Alex sat beside Kate and held her hand. "Why don't you let this guy focus on Susan while you take your time deciding about the other issue?"

"I think you're right. Even the thought of Max still makes me feel strange. There's no hurry to gather all his work in one place."

"Let me get you to your car, and I'll tell Mr. Loring you didn't feel up to talking about his retrospective idea right now. I'll find out where he's staying and get his number." Alex helped Kate up from the sofa, and they walked to the front door as the Chief came back upstairs.

"Don't be surprised if Mr. Loring is never seen again! He took one look at Susan and forgot I was even standing there. Those two are deep in conversation."

"Alex, I feel like such an idiot! How could I have mistaken that nice man for Max? I must be losing my mind." Kate rubbed her head, which still throbbed from her fall. "I was so sure."

"With the sun in your eyes like that, any familiar mannerism or similarity in dress could have triggered a major flashback, especially considering what's been happening around here lately. I'm surprised you haven't freaked out before this." Alex's soothing tone and sturdy arm around her waist help Kate relax as they walked out of the school and approached her car. "Do you feel well enough to drive?"

"Of course. Nobody ever died of mortification, although I certainly felt like it. Thank the Chief for me, will you, and apologize again to Mr. Loring." Kate slipped into the driver's seat and turned on the motor. "Do you dare to be seen with a certified loony-tune tonight?"

"You bet," Alex grinned. "I understand you crazies have highly developed libidos, and Greek food is very stimulating."

"Well, you know what they say about olives..." Kate left Alex standing in the parking lot as she drove away.

Mildred's car was parked beside the garage when Kate turned into Silvertree Farm, so she hurried into the house to hear the results of the trip to Massachusetts. Marissa and Mildred were sitting at the kitchen table sipping hot cups of tea where Kate joined them, allowing the warm liquid to soothe her jangled nerves.

"O.K., ladies, what did you find out?" Kate decided not to tell anyone about her experience with Adam Loring in case her behavior might alarm her already tense mother-in-law.

Marissa tucked an imaginary stray hair into her flawless French twist and opened a small, leather-bound book in which were pages of notes written in a tiny, immaculate script. "Mildred and I were just trying to make sense of this whole story so we could figure out where to go from here."

"It was fascinating," Mildred offered. "Like being in one of my own novels. We followed the trail of this Alice Hammond from Marblehead all through the North Shore."

"Let me start from the beginning," Marissa began. "Otherwise, it's impossible to untangle. We found the house where Alice worked before she was married. By the time we arrived, the old man had been able to find the address of the apartment where she moved after leaving their employ. Luckily, the same person still owned the building, and he recognized Alice's picture, only he said she left after six months, saying she was going to get married. Apparently, she left no forwarding address." Marissa got up from the table and came back with a hot pot of tea.

Mildred picked up the story when Marissa paused for a moment. "We went to almost every town on the North Shore and showed Alice's picture to the local merchants. It was the strangest thing. Many people commented that Alice looked familiar, but no one could actually identify her by name. A drugstore clerk in Beverly Farms thought at first that Alice resembled a wealthy woman who lived on an estate nearby, but then he changed his mind."

"Unfortunately, it was time to come home, so we didn't go to Prides' Crossing, where this Alice look-alike was supposed to have lived. The clerk was pretty sure she had died several months before, because she was supposed to have been in the last stages of cirrhosis of the liver." Marissa drooped in her chair from exhaustion, and Mildred also looked worn out.

Kate was intrigued by the saga of Brother Able's sister and amazed that Marissa and Mildred had been able to uncover so much information. "I'd say you two are pretty good detectives. Remember poor Max and the Wentworth saga?"

Marissa looked surprised. "Of course. I never really connected all of the places we visited today with his experience. Wouldn't it have been odd if Alice had lived in Prides Crossing and Max had come across her at some party without knowing she was his aunt?"

"Stranger things have happened!" Mildred got up and switched on some lamps as the afternoon grew darker.

"I'll say!" Kate sighed. "Wait until I tell you about the dumb stunt I pulled after school today." Kate stood up and stretched, aware of the fact that she had fallen not long before. "But first, I think I'll run up and take a shower before Jessie comes home. I'm going out to dinner with Alex, so I'll see if Julia will feed Jessie early."

While Kate was letting the hot water release the tension from her neck and back, she heard the phone ring, and when she came downstairs, Marissa was standing in the library triumphantly brandishing a piece of paper.

"That call was from the man we talked to in Beverly Farms. I left him this number in case he recalled anything else, and he just telephoned to say the woman he thought looked like Alice hadn't died after all. She was an alcoholic, but she simply disappeared one night, and nobody has been able to find any trace of her. And here's the really weird part. Her name was Alison Wentworth!"

****

Later, the wrought-iron street lamps were lit along the brick sidewalks of Peal Street when Alex slid his car into a parking space in front of a long row of connected townhouses, each with a graceful bowed window and fanlighted doorway. Glowing lamps in the lower windows of several houses revealed silhouetted figures moving behind filmy curtains. The two townhouses at the end of the block had been combined to form Euripedes' Garden, a small but extremely popular restaurant that had just received four stars in the local newspaper.

Over mouthwatering plates of moussaka and dolmathes, Kate and Alex chatted, content to enjoy each other's company in the flickering candlelight. After strong, aromatic coffee and delicate honey-laced pastries, the couple drifted back onto Peal Street where the evening had remained surprisingly warm.

"Look!" Kate pulled at Alex's sleeve, and they both ducked behind a van that happened to be parked next to the restaurant. Halfway down the block, one of the townhouse doors opened and a tall, familiar figure came down the steps, pausing at the bottom to throw a kiss to two women who were standing in the open square of light. Adam Loring said something unintelligible, and the older of the women disappeared into the house, returning with a package, which she handed to her companion. Susan Moore ran down the concrete steps and handed the parcel to Adam, standing on tiptoe to kiss his cheek before ascending the stairs again.

"What do you suppose that's all about? I thought Susan had a studio and loft in the Old Port." Kate looked at Alex, confused. "And it looks as if Adam and Susan have become mighty chummy in a very short time."

Alex narrowed his eyes in thought as the front door of Number 24 closed, and the light over the entrance was extinguished. "I wonder if there's a name on the door." He began to move along the sidewalk toward the spot where Adam had stood. Kate was rooted in one place as Alex glided up the steps and ran his fingers over the brass plate that was screwed into the front of the building. Hunching over, he squinted in the dark and was able to decipher the name "Smith".

When the voices in the house began to sound louder, Alex backed down the stairs and came to where Kate was waiting. "Could you see anything?" she whispered.

"No, but I'm intrigued by the whole situation. Of course, it could be perfectly innocent, and Adam and Susan might have just hit it off. Then, on the other hand…" Alex left his sentence unfinished as the door opened again and Susan Moore hurried down the steps to her car. Once again, the older woman stood in the doorway and waved goodbye, while another girl hovered in the background. From where Kate and Alex were standing, the faces in the townhouse were indistinguishable, but there was something vaguely familiar about both people.

About fifteen minutes later, as the Jaguar purred across the Casco Bay Bridge, another car passed them, speeding in the opposite direction. Barely hesitating at the four-way stop streets that created a staccato traffic flow all the way along the West End of Portland, the car screeched to a stop on Peal Street, and its driver knocked on the shiny black door of Number 24.

This time, an agitated young girl answered. "I called you as soon as I knew who it was," Phaedra stuttered. "You promised me I was safe here, but somehow he's found me. What am I going to do?"

"Not a thing," was the calm reply. "We'll let Alex tip his hand first. Meanwhile, let's try and figure out what he was after."

As they were turning into Silvertree Farm, Kate and Alex passed Chickie on his way out, obviously having spent the evening with Eve. When Alex switched his engine off, he turned to Kate. "I'll take a rain check on those libido-revving olives. It's a school night."

"Story of my life," Kate smiled, and wrapped her arms around Alex's neck. He held her and brushed his mouth across her soft lips, feeling them part. "Resist Claire with all your might," she whispered against his kiss.

"I'll lock my door." Alex hugged Kate carefully, remembering her accumulation of bruises earlier. "Sleep tight."

By the time he reached home, Alex had rehearsed several speeches with which he could discourage interaction with his wife, if she were lying in wait for him. Instead, there was a note on the kitchen counter from Claire, saying she had been unsuccessful in Boston in finding Phaedra, but that there had been new developments in the matter of their daughter. Tonight, the note continued, she was having a working dinner with one of her law partners. Alex felt his heart sink at the failure to find Phaedra in Boston, and as he tried to think of how he should go about looking for her, he collapsed into his favorite leather chair and opened the evening newspaper.

In the second section, a regular Wednesday feature on business, Alex was startled to see his wife's picture featured on the first page, her face floating above the caption, "PORTLAND LAWYER TO RELOCATE". The story below informed the reader that Claire Stamos, formerly a partner in the prestigious law firm of Harrison, Black, and Nye, was leaving the large group to open her own practice specializing in divorce and custody cases. The writer went on to enthuse about Claire's credentials and concluded with the statement that Mrs. Stamos's office would be located in Cape Mariana, where she resided with her husband and daughter.

"What the hell is she up to now?" Alex threw the newspaper down and realized he was very tired. Just as he had decided to go to bed and avoid all contact with Claire, the front door opened and she walked in, throwing her keys on the hall table and handing Alex an envelope.

"Nice of you to come home, Alex. I waited as long as I could for you, but I guess your little girlfriend had other plans for your evening!" Claire's eyes were hostile as she faced her husband. "This note came today, and I think you'd better read it."

Alex looked at the handwriting on the front of the unstamped envelope and realized it was his daughter's. The "Mother and Dad" were scrawled in round, childish letters with Phaedra's characteristic wavy line bisected with two vertical slashes underneath.

After he had skimmed the message, Alex looked at Claire. "She certainly knows how to turn the screws, doesn't she? I wonder where she learned that! Did you give her the idea she could blackmail me into reconciling with you if she came home?"

"Don't be ridiculous!" Claire grabbed the note from Alex and pointed at the last line. "This is your song that she's singing here. 'I know I have problems and will go to a therapist if you two will see a marriage counselor.' She's aware that I'm against this whole shrink thing."

Alex willed himself to be calm and rational. "At least we know she's safe and in the area. She says she'll call for our decision tomorrow."

Claire sat down on the sofa and crossed her legs, swinging her foot back and forth as she stared at Alex. "Well, what are you going to say to her? Do you want your daughter wandering around God knows where, or do you want her home safe with us? It's up to you, but I warn you I will not stand for you having anything to do with that bitch you've been seeing if you tell Phaedra she should come back. Our daughter simply cannot stand the strain."

Alex folded the note and put it in his pocket. "I'll have to think about this Claire. Naturally, I want Phaedra back home, but I'm not sure I can be hypocritical enough to tell her I could even live in the same house with you." Without saying good night, Alex turned his back and went up the stairs to the guest bedroom. Later, he heard Claire close the door of the master bedroom.

****

When the sun rose, Alex still had not been asleep, nor had he made a decision.

With his head pounding, Alex slipped out of bed and put on his jogging clothes, hoping an early morning run by the ocean would clear his brain and help him think more rationally. The sun was rising over Half-Moon Beach when he turned out of the River Road, and the black shapes of gulls following a lobster boat toward open sea wheeled and turned in the soft pink sky.

Alex waved to a couple of passing motorists who honked and shouted encouragement, but his thoughts were entirely on the dilemma in which he found himself. Had there ever been a time when he and Claire had been happy? Try as he might, Alex couldn't remember any protracted periods during which he and Claire had what he would characterize as a 'peaceful' marriage. From the beginning, Claire was frantically possessive of both him and their daughter, creating enormous friction between her and Alex's mother, whose help she needed, but resented.

As the miles passed under his feet, Alex recalled how jealous Claire had been of his family, ameliorated somewhat by the short residence of her brother, but then sharpened into loathing when Alex and his parents had forced Buddy to leave after his molestation of Phaedra. As soon as she graduated from law school, Claire refused to have anything to do with Alex's family, and he had to take Phaedra to visit her grandparents by himself. Gradually, Claire's attitude toward the elder Stamoses seemed to influence Phaedra, and by the time she entered grade school, she, too, refused to visit Alex's parents. Although his mother tried to be understanding about the situation, Alex knew she suffered greatly from the loss of her namesake.

Estrangement from her husband's family and an astonishing success in her law practice did little to diminish Claire's need for constant reassurance, an emotional neediness that she masked with an overbearing, arrogant style of dealing with people. She became increasingly irritable with Alex and only seemed to take pleasure in her daughter and her many trips to Boston.

With the sweat stinging his eyes as he turned back onto the River Road, Alex thought about the difference between Claire and Kate, whose sweet face and manner filled his dreams and waking thoughts. How could he give her up as Claire demanded? But, as Phaedra's father, how could he refuse to do so?

Alex walked slowly around his front yard to cool down as the paperboy pedaled down the street and flung a folded bundle, which Alex caught casually in one hand. As he opened to the front page, the bold black letters of the headline caught his eye. "RUNAWAY TEEN FOUND MURDERED."

Although he was reassured by the accompanying photograph that the dead person was not Phaedra, the tragic situation clarified Alex's priorities, and he reached a firm but reluctant decision as he mounted the steps to his front door.

Claire was sitting in the kitchen when Alex came in, and she wrinkled her nose at the sight of his soaking wet shirt and dripping face. "You look disgusting, darling. There must be an easier way to exercise."

Alex ignored her comment and poured himself a glass of orange juice, which he finished in three thirsty gulps. "It's warm out there this morning. Lots of people out running." He looked steadily at Claire. "What are your plans for today?"

"I'm going to sign the lease for my new office space, and then I intend to come back and wait for Phaedra's call. What shall I tell her?" Claire fixed her chilly blue eyes on Alex's face, but he avoided her glance by reaching down and untying his running shoes.

"Ask her to come home." Alex's voice was muffled with his head bent, but Claire heard him.

"Do you mean you will stop seeing Kate Hammond and you will give our marriage a real try?" Claire's tone had a strident edge to it that made Alex's teeth itch, but he finally met her eyes.

"If you will keep your promise and let me get some help for Phaedra and maybe some family counseling for all of us."

"Plenty of time for that. The most important thing is to be sure our daughter is safe. You understand, of course, you're to move back into our bedroom and we will have to convince Phaedra that we are genuinely trying to rebuild our lives."

Alex hoped his expression didn't communicate his distaste at the thought of sharing a bed with Claire. "We'll have to take that part slowly, too. But you're right that the most important objective is to get Phaedra back on track." He stood up and moved toward the stairs. "Now I have to take a shower and get to school."

"When will you tell your girlfriend that she's history?" Claire's voice followed him until he turned around and stared at her.

"I'll take care of that in my own way and on my terms."

Not far away, Kate watched the sunrise over Morning Cove with a sense of exhilaration and anticipation. Marissa seemed to be making progress toward finding her daughter. Eve was relaxed and settled into life at Silvertree Farm, and her own relationship with Alex filled her with a giddy joy she had feared she would not experience again.

"Why are you singing, Mama?" Jessica toddled through the door between their bedrooms and crawled up on Kate's bed, watching her mother shrug into a becoming lavender wool tunic and skirt. "You look pretty."

"Thanks, ladybug. I'm happy and it's a beautiful day. Isn't it time for you to get dressed? I laid out your school clothes." Kate fastened an amethyst and gold necklace around her neck and slipped wide gold hoops into her ears.

"I'm sick today." Jessica's mournful tone was so exaggerated that Kate looked around in surprise.

"And what's wrong with you?"

"I think it's my tummy." Jessica held her stomach and groaned.

"Any particular reason you don't want to go to school?" Kate crossed the room and sat on the bed next to her daughter, feeling her cool forehead.

"I just want to stay with you. Can't I please?" Jessica abandoned all pretense of illness and turned pleading eyes up to her mother. "Just this once, won't you take me to school with you?"

Kate thought it over quickly. Jessica had spent long, uncomplaining days at nursery school, and there had been a great deal of turmoil in their lives recently. Although she had been a silent, withdrawn shadow of a child when she first came to Maine, Jessica had gradually opened her heart to all of the love that surrounded her, and she had begun to trust the adults in her life once again. "All right, miss, special treat! You go and put on your most grown-up outfit, and I'll call Mrs. Barton and tell her you're going to help me today."

Jessica squealed in delight, a sound Kate heard very seldom, and flew into her own room, where Kate could hear her opening drawers and rummaging in her closet. Any slight feeling of guilt Kate might have had about indulging Jessica's whim vanished when she saw how carefully her daughter had chosen to dress in a pleated plaid wool skirt, white turtleneck jersey, and tiny navy wool blazer. Her little face was lit up with such anticipation that Kate found herself looking forward to watching Jessica interact with her high school students.

When Kate, Eve, and Jessica came into the crowded school lobby, the first person who approached them was Chickie, showing none of his recent coolness toward Kate in the exuberant way he swept Jessica off her feet and twirled her around in circles. The other members of the soccer team standing with Chickie responded to the little girl with equal enthusiasm, and soon Jessica's face glowed with all the attention she was receiving from the big, good-looking boys.

Across the lobby, Alex watched Kate and her daughter with a sinking heart, realizing his hope for a future with them was gone. His depression deepened when Jessica spotted him and ran over, flinging herself against his legs and looking up at him with sparkling eyes. "Mr. Stamos!" Jessica sang out. "I'm here for the whole day!"

As he reached down and lifted Jessica into his arms, kissing her velvety cheek. Jessica put out her hand and patted Alex's face. "Why do you look so sad? Aren't you glad to see me?"

"Of course I'm happy you're here. What a treat for all of us. I'm just sorry I'm tied up all morning," Alex set Jessica down on her feet. "But maybe we can have lunch together. Would you have time for that?"

"We'll have to see how our latest Rocky Shore student holds up!" Kate laughed as she came up to Alex and Jessica. "I thought Mildred could take her home after the board meeting this morning, because I'm not sure this one will make it through the whole day."

Jessica scowled at her mother and put her hands on her hips. "I'm a very big girl now, and I don't need to go home early!"

"We'll see, ladybug. Now, it's almost time for the first class, so let's go and get ready. Kate took Jessica's hand and was weaving her way across the lobby when she saw Susan Moore and Adam Loring talking intently by the stairs leading down to the art studio.

"Mr. Loring!" Kate veered over to the man she had mistaken for Max and held out her hand. "Please let me apologize again for my foolishness yesterday! You must have thought I was crazy."

Adam Loring took Kate's hand in both of his. "No need to even mention it, Mrs. Hammond. Are you all right today? You took quite a fall when you passed out."

"Absolutely fine, thanks." Kate turned to Susan, who was looking very confused. "Have Mr. Loring fill you in on my ridiculous behavior, Susan. By the way, have you met my daughter? Jessie, this is Ms. Moore, the art teacher, and this is Mr. Loring who buys and sells beautiful things, including your daddy's paintings."

Jessica shook hands with both Susan and Adam, staring intently at them. "Do I know him?" Jessica looked up at her mother.

Adam shook his head at her question. "I'm afraid not, Miss Hammond, because I certainly would have remembered such a lovely young lady. But evidently, I have a very common face, because your mother mistook me for someone else, too."

The ringing of the warning bell interrupted their conversation, and Kate grasped Jessica's hand as they were swept up the stairs by the surge of students heading for their homerooms. Unlocking the door to her classroom, Kate looked down at her daughter standing in the middle of a group of teenagers waiting in the corridor. "Why did you think you knew Mr. Loring, Jess?"

Jessica thought hard for a moment, and then said confidently, "He reminds me of my daddy when he used to be nice."

THE SHAPE OF DARK—Chapter Twenty

Kate didn't have time to react to Jessica's statement about Adam Loring because several students were lined up at her desk to pass in absence notes. By the time the first class filed in, Kate was completely preoccupied with adjusting her lesson plans for the day so her daughter could participate with the high school students.

The seniors were happy to see Jessica, confident her presence would distract Kate's attention from the difficult reading material she had assigned the previous night. Few of the students had been able to understand Jonathan Edwards' fiery sermon, "Sinners in the Hands of an Angry God", which Kate chose from American Literature to show some of the religious attitudes existing in the world during the eighteenth century. Most of the students dreaded the possibility that they would be given a quiz.

"How many of you got the point of last night's reading?" Kate looked around the room and was not surprised that only a few students raised their hands. One of the people who tentatively lifted her hand was Sophia, and Kate walked over to her desk, struck by the despondent look on the girl's normally vivacious face. "What did you get out of it, Sophia?"

Sophia's voice was low and without energy as she replied. "I think he's saying God is powerful in a big, frightening way, and he's just toying with us but is ready to punish us without warning. If you're not perfect, God can destroy you and probably will."

The bitterness in Sophia's answer was so raw that Kate realized there was more going on than just a response to an academic question. When she saw Sophia's lip begin to quiver, Kate turned to Eve, who was holding Jessica on her lap. "Do you agree with Reverend Edwards, Eve? Do you think God is essentially angry and without mercy?"

"I used to, Mrs. Hammond. All of those years that such awful things were happening to my brother and me in the name of God, I dreamed about a big, scary man sitting on a huge black throne in the sky. He had yellow eyes that glowed when he was mad, and he sent people like Brother Able to punish sinners." Eve's voice was calm and steady as she answered Kate. The room was completely silent.

"How do you feel now?" Kate saw that even Kelly Lundgren was listening intently for Eve's reply.

"Now, I'm not so sure. There have been so many kind people who have helped us that I'm more and more convinced the REAL God lets these bad things happen for a reason, and if we can understand Him, things will work out for the best."

"How can you believe that?" Sophia's strangled voice cut through the quiet class. "How can a God that's good punish people without reason?"

Eve swung around to look at her friend and was surprised to see tears gathering in her eyes. Eric, sitting behind Sophia, patted her shoulder awkwardly. "I have to believe that way, or I can't survive," Eve explained, "but that doesn't mean I'm right."

Kate made a mental note to speak to Sophia after class and turned to the rest of the group. "What do you think? Do you each have a sense of how you really feel about God? Not what your religion or parents tell you to believe, but what you personally picture in your mind when you think of the concept of a higher power?"

Kelly spoke up from the back row. "Are we supposed to be talking about this kind of thing in school? Isn't there a law about not discussing religion?"

Kate recognized Kelly's familiar antagonism, but she answered seriously. "You have a point, Kelly. In the context of studying literature, I think almost anyone would say it is justifiable to talk about God, since religion is one of the main themes that writers have explored over the ages. However, were I to try to convince you to share my beliefs about God, I would be absolutely out of line in a public school."

Kelly accepted Kate's polite reply with a bored expression, but one of the other students raised his hand. "If we can't talk about things like this in school, why bother to read literature? Aren't we trying to find connections between what was written in the past and how we think now?"

"Yes, that's what I believe, but there are lots of teachers who don't share my opinion. Several colleagues of mine are firmly convinced students should simply read and hopefully understand the great works of our culture without trying to make sense of what they might mean today."

Eve shifted Jessica to the other side of her lap and looked up at Kate. "What do you think about God, Mrs. Hammond? Do you believe in things like heaven and hell?"

Kate leaned against the edge of her desk and looked at the class. "Remember in the beginning of the year I told you I would answer anything that was asked thoughtfully and seriously? Eve's question is a highly personal one, but I think it deserves a response, even though it's important for you to understand this is only my opinion, and should have no influence on your ideas."

Even Jessica was listening closely to what her mother was saying, and Kate looked down at her daughter. "Jessie, what do you think that I believe about God?"

The class was startled by Kate's inclusion of the little girl in their discussion. They had expected a highly philosophical answer from their teacher, and they looked expectantly at Jessica, sitting comfortably on Eve's lap.

"God is great, God is good. Let us thank him for our food." Jessica solemnly pronounced the words of the Grace they said at dinner each night, setting off a ripple of laughter in the classroom.

"Well, that's certainly one place we talk about God in our house. What else do we do?" Kate smiled encouragingly at Jessica, who sat up straight and looked seriously at her mother.

"I always say prayers at night, we sing God-songs, and you believe in angels." Jessica was clearly very pleased with her answer as she fixed her round green eyes on her mother.

Jean-Pierro's hand shot up. "Do you really think there are angels?" His question was obviously sincere, but Kate could see that several of the students, including Kelly, had scornful looks on their faces.

Kate took a deep breath. "I know most of you will think I've gone around the bend here, but I actually do believe there are paranormal experiences, including the appearance of angels. In fact, I've actually seen one."

"Oh, come on!" Kelly's disbelief burst out rudely. "You aren't serious."

"Yes, Kelly, I am, and many other people, not mental cases, but intelligent, pragmatic, reasonable individuals, have had similar things happen to them."

"I'd be fascinated to hear about your angel, Mrs. Hammond. Did it carry a harp?" Sarcasm dripped from Kelly's question, but Kate ignored the tone, seeing the rapt attention on the faces of the rest of the class.

"My mother and father died unexpectedly in a plane crash when I was a sophomore in college. On the night of the accident, I dreamed they came into my dorm room and stood beside my bed. My mother told me she and my father had to leave, but they would always be with me and would come back if I ever needed them. When I woke up the next morning, the House Fellow called me into her office and told me that my parents' plane had crashed in a thunderstorm outside of Philadelphia." Kate paused and frowned, finding the story difficult to tell in spite of the many years that had passed.

"That could have just been a coincidence," Kelly scoffed.

"Yes, I suppose that's possible, except for a couple of things. I remember exactly what my mother was wearing when she was in my room at school, and it turned out she was dressed in the same clothes when she died. Then, ten years later, she came back one night and warned me not to take an airplane trip I was planning. She said the plane would crash and it wasn't my time yet. Even though people thought I was nuts, I canceled the trip, and the plane did go down, killing eight of the thirty-four people aboard."

Even Kelly didn't know what to say at the conclusion of Kate's story, but the bell interrupted the silence. "Read the Edwards piece over again, and we'll talk about extended metaphor tomorrow." Everybody groaned in unison as they got up to leave, but several students stayed behind and questioned Kate further about the experience she had described.

Sophia, in particular, seemed extremely interested in the details of Kate's relationship with her mother, and when the bell sounded, she left the classroom looking far less upset than she had before.

The next period was free for Kate, so she and Jessica went downstairs to get something to drink. As they were crossing the lobby, Susan Moore came out of the teachers' lounge and suggested that Jessica come downstairs to the art studio and paint a picture for her mother. Jessica seemed delighted with the idea, so Kate relinquished her daughter to the art teacher and continued into the book-lined lounge where she helped herself to some coffee. The only other person in the room was the Latin teacher, Hal Gibson, but he was engrossed in a stack of papers he was correcting, so Kate sat down by herself and flipped the pages of *The New York Times.*

"Licking your wounds?" Claire Stamos's metallic voice cut into Kate's concentration, and without an invitation, Claire slid into another seat at the table and tossed her short blond hair back in a strangely triumphant gesture.

"I beg your pardon?" Kate stared at Alex's wife, who leaned back in her chair and examined her long, polished fingernails. "Did you have something to say to me?"

"I assume you've talked to Alex this morning." Claire's bright red mouth was curved into the semblance of a smile, and her pale blue eyes had a haughty glint.

"Not really. I brought my daughter to school with me, so I've been pretty busy."

"How sweet. Well, from now on, you'll have plenty of time to focus on your own little family without disrupting mine." The naked animosity on Claire's face sent a chill through Kate. "Alex has decided that we're going to try to put our lives back together for Phaedra's sake, and he's promised to do everything he can to heal our marriage, including sharing the same bedroom!"

Kate felt her cheeks grow hot as she listened to Claire's smug pronouncement. There had been no hint from Alex of any such reconciliation, but what reason would Claire have to lie? Kate willed her voice to remain smooth and controlled as she responded.

"I'm certainly aware of how worried Alex has been about Phaedra, and I'm sure he would do anything to help her be safe and strong." Kate stood up from the table and kept her movements deliberate, although she wanted nothing more than to flee from the triumph that oozed from Claire's expression. "Good luck to all of you, and especially to Phaedra."

Turning her back on Claire, Kate walked across the lobby, blinded by tears she was determined would not fall in public. Sandra Monkton watched her as she went into the ladies' room and closed the door before releasing the emotion she had so carefully controlled. Then Sandra saw Claire strut confidently out of the teachers' lounge, and she knew something had transpired between the two women that had made Kate terribly upset. Worried, Sandra was about to follow

271

Kate, when Alex came out of the conference room next to the library where the Board of Trustees was about to meet.

"Sandy, Marta is out again today, and I need someone to take notes at our meeting. Could you help us out?" Alex seemed flustered, so Sandra's intention to find out what was bothering Kate had to be set aside.

By the time the bell rang for the next period, Kate was ready to face another class, most of whom were already seated when she arrived in the classroom with Jessica. The little girl was carrying a big sheet of poster board Susan Moore had helped her cover with bright splashes of color.

At the beginning of the first lunch, Jessica was yawning and visibly tired from the excitement of the morning, so Kate decided to see if Mildred's meeting was over. Downstairs, the members of the Board of Trustees were just filing out of the conference room and mingling with the students in the lobby when Kate spotted Mildred standing with Alex near the front door. Reluctant to trust herself to speak to Alex, Kate caught Mildred's eye and motioned her over, relieved that Alex didn't follow her. Jessica put up some resistance to leaving with Mildred, but Kate noticed the little girl's feet dragged as she walked through the parking lot.

Two hours later, Kate felt as tired as Jessica had looked as she packed up her books and papers and locked her classroom. Ordinarily, Kate stayed in the afternoon to have writing conferences with students or to help with some extracurricular activity, but today she wanted nothing more than to go home and take a walk or pound out her frustration on the piano. Claire Stamos's nastiness had drained Kate's energy, and she didn't even have the strength to confront Alex about his decision.

The lobby was nearly empty as Kate made her way toward the front door, but a familiar voice rang out behind her as she reached for the handle. "Kate! Can I speak to you for a minute?" Alex stood in the archway near Marta Stone's desk, and Kate turned and moved back toward him.

"Come on in. I have something I need to talk over with you." Alex gestured toward his office, but Kate stopped outside the door and looked up at him, her eyes dulled with a pain that threatened to blind her.

"Never mind, Alex, I already know about your decision. Claire came to see me this morning, and she told me you're going to give your marriage another try for Phaedra's sake. I can understand that." Kate turned her back on Alex and moved toward the front of the lobby, but his explosive response startled her into stopping short.

"SHE DID WHAT? What exactly did she tell you?"

Kate repeated Claire's comments as accurately as she could, and Alex's face contorted more violently with each word that Kate could remember. "So help me, I'll kill her. I specifically told her that I wanted to talk to you myself, but she couldn't wait to run over here and rub your nose in what she considers to be her victory. Honestly, Kate, I don't know what else to do. I'm scared to death for Phaedra, and all I want to do is get her home and find her some help.'

The raw vulnerability in Kate's eyes stung Alex as she spoke in a low tone. "I know you have no choice, believe me. Don't forget that I killed a man to protect my daughter, so your decision is perfectly understandable. It's just hard for me to think of what you and I will never be to one another."

Alex ached to take Kate into his arms and forget his promise to Claire, but he knew if he touched Kate, he would never be able to let her go. "I wanted things to be so different."

"I did too." Kate smiled sadly and lifted her briefcase to her shoulder. "I'll always remember." Alex felt a lump grow in his throat as he watched Kate walk out of the building. Then he went into his office and closed the door.

When Kate arrived home, she stopped in the kitchen to kiss the top of Jessica's head while the little girl shelled peas into a large bowl under Julia's watchful eye. Then, with the cook's assurance that Jessica would be occupied for at least an hour, Kate dragged herself upstairs and closed her door before allowing a crack in the iron control she had exercised for most of the day. At first, her pain was concentrated in an angry knot in her chest, but gradually, the iron bands loosened, and Kate sobbed into her pillow as if her heart would break.

At dinner, no one commented on Kate's swollen eyes, but the table was unusually quiet. As soon as they had finished eating, everyone found a reason to leave—Eve to do homework, Tikka to return to Avesta, and Mildred to attend a performance at the Portland

Stage Company. Kate put Jessica to bed and curled up alongside her daughter, who begged for a "princess story". Before Kate was through the first part of *Sleeping Beauty*, Jessica's regular breathing allowed her mother to steal silently out of the room.

Kate was about to say goodnight to Eve and tackle some student essays at her own desk, when she heard the sound of the front bell. Eve hurried out of her bedroom and dashed down the stairs to answer the door before the caller could ring again and perhaps awaken Jessica. Curious, Kate followed more slowly, surprised to see the tall form of a man illuminated by the heavy brass lamp above the entrance.

"Hi, Mr. Temple." Eve's voice floated up the stars to the landing where Kate stood. "I forgot to tell Mrs. Hammond you were coming, and I hope she doesn't mind."

Josh Temple strode up the three stairs leading into the living room shook his head in appreciation of the vast room, only partially revealed by the half dozen lamps that were lit. "This house continues to amaze me, Eve. It's hard to think that Timmy Brogan was killed here."

Eve nodded slowly. "I know. I think it really bothers Mrs. Worthington that so many ugly things have been happening in this beautiful place."

"What brings you by, Josh?" Kate's voice floated over the railing from the second floor.

Kate continued down the stairs and she gave Josh a brief hug, noticing that he was holding some papers.

Josh's face crinkled into a wide grin, and he ruffled Eve's hair affectionately. "I saw Eve after school and she told me about the class you had with your seniors today. I just wish I had been there because I'm really interested in this angel business that you told the kids about. When I was in the band, some of us had a reading with a medium, and I swear that my father communicated with me. I brought some stuff that I wrote after the session, and I thought you might like to tell the kids about it."

Kate found herself intrigued by the idea and beckoned Eve and Josh into the library where the remnants of a fire still burned. "I know the kids thought I was crazy today, Josh, but I honestly believe things happen that we can't explain rationally."

"Will you excuse me, Mrs. Hammond? I have a ton of homework, and Mr. Temple really wanted to speak with you." Eve backed out of the library at Kate's nod and vanished up the front stairs.

Josh shook his head. "I can't believe that girl. She has been through such hell and comes out of it with this luminescence."

Kate settled on the couch and motioned Josh to the other end. "I would give anything to see Eve get some happiness. She's so concerned about her brother Willie, and she intends to visit her mother in the hospital tomorrow for the first time. It just doesn't seem fair…" Kate's eyes shone with unshed tears as she spoke about Eve, making them look like clear green pools in the dim lights and flickering fire.

Kate and Josh spent the next half hour exchanging stories about their experiences with the paranormal. As Josh stood to leave, Kate suddenly had an idea. "Josh, why don't you teach the senior class tomorrow and continue the discussion about angels and communicating with those who have passed over? The kids would love to hear about your reading, especially since it was in your rock and roll days."

Josh looked apprehensive. "Are you sure Alex would approve of the subject? That whole religion in schools thing is a hot issue."

The light in Kate's eyes dimmed at the mention of Alex's name, but she shook her head. "No, I think it's entirely appropriate because we're talking about various attitudes towards death. I bet it will be a really interesting discussion."

"O.K., then, I'd like to do it. I'll think up a writing assignment to follow up the class." Josh began to walk out of the library toward the front door and hesitated under the archway between the dining and living rooms. "Kate, do you mind if I ask a rather nosy question?"

When Kate shook her head, Josh cleared his throat. "Ah, there's been some talk at school about you and Alex. Then I happened to be in the Teachers' Lounge this afternoon and I overhead Kelly Lundgren telling her cronies that Phaedra would be coming home now that she had broken up, as Kelly put it, the 'nasty little affair between her father and that bitch.' I assume she was speaking about you, so I just wanted to make sure that you're all right."

Kate felt her self-control beginning to unravel as she looked up into Josh's concerned face. "Whatever was between Alex and me is a thing of the past, Josh. And I'm going to be fine. But thanks for caring."

Josh moved toward Kate and folded her in his arms. "Alex doesn't know what he's losing, Kate. Every man and most of the boys at school think you're the best. Don't forget that."

The tenderness in Josh's tone loosened Kate's steely resolve to keep her feelings in check, and she found herself sobbing while Josh rubbed her back and whispered comforting words. Finally, a knot of sorrow loosened in Kate's chest and she stepped back from Josh, whose denim shirtfront was soaked with tears.

"You're some guy, Josh. I guess I really needed to do that. Now I really am feeling better."

"Great." Josh offered Kate a clean white handkerchief and she loudly blew her nose. "Now, how about a little diversion to take your mind off your troubles?"

Kate found herself smiling at Josh's flirtatious tone. "What did you have in mind?"

"Rossoni's for dinner tomorrow night. I'm performing, but not until after nine, and you can make up your mind if you want to stay. Come on, Kate, It's the least I can do after all of the help that you've given me."

To her great surprise, Kate agreed without hesitation. The prospect of a companionable, stress-free evening was very appealing, and she found herself humming as she closed the front door behind Josh.

****

The next morning, Kate avoided Alex entirely, in spite of the fact that he approached her several times and started to speak. Phaedra was back in school, trailed as before by Kelly Lundgren and a small group of girls, all of whom shot triumphant looks at Kate, indicating by their behavior that Phaedra had broadcast the conditions under which she had agreed to return home. Kate dreaded meeting Phaedra face-to-face in English class, but was spared much of that discomfort by the fact she was able to sit in the back of the classroom while Josh conducted a lively discussion, to which even Eric contributed.

When Kate came out of lunch, she felt strained from having kept herself cheerful all day. Heading through the lobby for the last class of the week, she found Adam Loring and Susan Moore standing at the top of the basement stairs, deep in conversation which seemed to border on argument with Susan looking annoyed in response to something Adam was saying.

As she grew closer, Kate heard Susan's normally melodic voice slide into a whine. "No, it's too risky. We've got to take our time."

"And I told you that I can't wait much longer." Kate could only see the back of Adam's head, but it was clear from his tone he was not happy. As Kate drew near, Susan put a warning hand on Adam's arm, and their discussion stopped.

"These dealers!" Susan complained as she turned to Kate. "I've warned Adam you can't hurry the kind of work I do, but he wants an entire collection yesterday." Adam looked embarrassed at having been caught harassing Susan, and he shrugged.

"I'm just anxious to get back to Boston, but it looks as if I'll be spending some more time here. Would you have a few minutes to chat with me about that other matter that I mentioned to you?"

"Let me see how the weekend goes," Kate suggested, and I'll call you. Are you at a hotel in town?"

"No, I'm staying with a friend, and the number is unlisted." Adam took out a business card and jotted down a telephone number. "I'd be glad to come out to the Cape at your convenience."

Kate slipped the card into her pocket. "I'm sure we can arrange something. I'll be in touch with you."

When she got home from school that afternoon and thought about the possibility of talking about Max's paintings, her feeling of depression was so profound that Kate realized she still wasn't ready to face the issue of a retrospective exhibition, so she placed a call to Adam as soon as she made up her mind. The telephone rang several times, and she was about to hang up when there was a click at the other end of the line.

"Hello?" The voice was so unmistakable Kate found herself stunned into silence. "Hello? Is anyone there?" Kate hung up the phone, certain she had dialed the wrong number.

Carefully referring to the card Adam had given her, Kate redialed. This time, a different, unfamiliar woman's voice answered, followed after a few minutes by Adam's deep tones. He received the news of Kate's desire for more time to think about the exhibit with regret, but thanked her for at least considering the project.

After she hung up, Kate stared at the telephone. Had she dialed the wrong number the first time? Otherwise, why would Claire Stamos have picked up the phone in a Portland location where Adam Loring was staying?

THE SHAPE OF DARK—Chapter Twenty-One

Kate was still thinking about the odd coincidence of hearing Claire's voice on Adam Loring's line when she and Eve approached the broad glass front doors of the Maine Medical Center, where Ruth Calvert was recovering from her wounds. It had taken Eve a full week before she asked Kate to accompany her to the hospital, and even now, Eve's face was pale and frightened as she approached a pink-smocked volunteer for the number of her mother's room.

"Don't be scared," Kate whispered. "It won't be as bad as you think it's going to be. Things never are." Kate cringed at the banality of her comment, but Eve didn't seem to hear her.

"What if I hate her?" The elevator doors whirred open, and Eve and Kate wedged themselves beside a gurney carrying a shriveled old man with several tubes attached to hanging bags of fluid. "What if I can't stand the sight of my own mother?"

"You'll know what to say, Eve." Kate felt helpless in the face of Eve's misery as they both stared up at the lights blinking above them. When the number five illuminated, the doors parted again, and they stepped out into the bustle of the medical/surgical floor where Ruth Calvert had been moved from Intensive Care.

"By the way, Mrs. Hammond, Captain Brogan called today before you got home to say he thought he had found my grandmother. I guess she had moved into a small apartment outside of Baltimore a couple of years ago, but he was able to talk to one of her former neighbors who had her new address. So far there's been no answer, but he said he'll keep on trying." Eve's voice trailed off as they approached Room 520. A nurse was just coming out and she stood aside for the visitors.

"Go ahead in. Mrs. Calvert is awake."

Inside the large double room, only one of the beds was occupied. The form stretched out on it was partially hidden by the curtains that hung from the circular track over the bed. Recognizing her mother, Eve pushed the material back and approached.

Ruth Calvert opened her eyes. "Eve? Is that really you?" A thin hand connected to loops of tubing and a dripping intravenous bottle reached out tentatively and then retreated, as Eve remained motionless. Standing slightly apart, Kate felt suffocated by the warmth of the room and by the tension radiating from Eve's rigid body.

"How are you, Mother?" There was no inflection in Eve's tone as she spoke, but Kate could see tears beginning to gather in the eyes of the frail woman in the bed.

"I'm alive, thanks to you." Ruth spoke laboriously, still in a great deal of pain. "Sometimes I wish I could have died too, but that might mean I would be where your father is, and I couldn't bear that any more."

Eve's body relaxed slightly at her mother's words, and she took Ruth's hand. "Don't say that, Mother. Willie wasn't shooting at you. It was Father who did such dreadful things. And Brother Able."

Ruth closed her eyes. "But I let them hurt you and Willie. I should have been strong enough to stop them. It's just that I was so afraid all of the time." Tears were now streaming unchecked along Ruth's cheeks, and Eve wiped them away carefully with a tissue from the stand next to the bed.

"I know, Mother. But thank God it's all over now. Brother Able has been seen pretty far south of here, and it appears his followers are with him. Willie is being cared for at Merton House, and I'm staying with Mrs. Hammond at Silvertree Farm. You have nothing to worry about except for getting well."

Kate swallowed hard at Eve's compassionate response, impressed once again by the girl's strength and maturity. Ruth took Eve's hand in both of hers and kissed it. "I don't deserve a daughter like you, Eve. I just hope I can make it up to you. If, that is, they let me keep you and Willie."

"Let's worry about that later. Now you need to concentrate on regaining your strength. Soon we may have some good news about Grandma, and perhaps she can come and live with us."

A young nurse bustled into the room and checked Ruth's pulse and IV. "I think Mrs. Calvert has had enough for one day. Maybe you could come back tomorrow."

Eve nodded and kissed her mother on the forehead. "Is there anything you'd like me to bring you?"

"Nothing," Ruth wheezed, "except yourself and your forgiveness. If I live to be a hundred years old, I'll never be able to make up for what you and Willie have suffered. But I'll try."

On the way out of the hospital, Eve looked relieved and almost happy. "I didn't feel angry at all, Mrs. Hammond. She looks so pathetic that I really believe she couldn't stop my father or Brother Able. But at least she'll testify against them on Willie's behalf."

"Let's hope it doesn't come to that." Kate steered her car out of the crowded hospital parking lot and onto the Western Promenade. As they drove along the broad avenue, lined on one side with some of Portland's largest and most elaborate mansions, both Kate and Eve were immersed in their own thoughts while the sloping Western Cemetery on the right skimmed by the car windows.

"Do you have any plans for this weekend?" Kate turned the car away from Portland as they headed for Merton House and Eve's planned visit with Willie.

"Well, sort of," Eve replied. "Chickie has asked me to go out with him tonight, and I'm not sure if it's a real date. Is it all right with you if I go? My parents never let me do something like that."

Kate laughed. "Of course you may. I can't think of a nicer pair to be spending time together. You like Chickie, don't you?"

"Yes I do—a lot. But I feel really strange being alone with a boy, unless it's to do something like visiting his mother. I don't know what to say."

"Just relax, and it will come to you, I'm sure." They arrived at Merton House, and Kate parked the car near the entrance. "Anybody who's been through the ordeals you've endured can handle one boy quite effectively."

By the time Kate and Eve got back to Silvertree Farm, it was almost six o'clock. They had spent about an hour with Willie, concerned to find him still convinced he was in heaven, but relieved his confusion had produced a kind of peaceful acceptance of where he was and what had happened to him. His imaginary friend, Timmy Brogan, still visited with him daily, and Dr. Ephron reported that Willie's anxiety level had decreased significantly.

The lights were all on when Kate drove up behind Tikka's car, making the big old house a welcome sight in the autumn darkness. As usual, Jessica was in the kitchen with Julia as she prepared small salads for Jessica and Eve to accompany the delectable turkey casserole that was bubbling in the oven. Two places were set at the big oak kitchen table, a practice Julia usually followed when the adults would not be dining at home.

Kate dropped a kiss on Jessica's head and left her conducting a serious conversation with Eve and Julia about the chipmunks that lived in the terrace wall. Upstairs, Kate indulged herself in a foamy bubble bath and dressed in black slacks and an aquamarine mohair sweater the same color as her eyes. She found herself really looking forward to dinner with Josh at Rossoni's.

Big Ed George was sitting at the kitchen table with Eve and Jessica when Kate came downstairs, and he whistled appreciatively while she fastened a pair of long, antique earrings, which sparkled against her burnished hair. "Boy, oh boy, Alex Stamos is a mighty lucky man tonight!" Ed's booming voice bounced off the kitchen walls, making Kate wince at the sound of Alex's name.

"Wrong fella, Ed. Alex and I are, as they say, going our separate ways."

Ed looked extremely embarrassed. "Once again I have inserted my foot and chewed. Sorry Kate. I didn't know. I thought the guy was crazy about you."

"He is," Tikka interjected as she followed Kate into the kitchen. "He's just in the clutches of that witch he's married to and her nasty little daughter. Poor Alex. I really feel for him. He'd cut his throat if he could see you tonight. You look sensational."

"You really do, Mama." Jessica got up and came over to Kate, who backed away hastily from the sticky little fingers that stretched out toward Kate's legs.

Eve followed Jessica and scooped her up before she could reach her mother. "Mr. Temple is going to be blown away." Eve scrubbed Jessica's fingers with a wet paper towel and set her back on her feet. "Would you like me to put this person to bed before I go out?"

"Thanks, honey, I'd appreciate that, and I'm sure Jessie will be thrilled, especially if Chickie says goodnight to her as well."

Ed looked surprised. "I didn't know you were going out with my son, Eve. In fact, I don't have much contact with Chickie these days. He's kind of miffed at me, so we steer clear of each other."

"I'm sorry, Mr. George. Chickie's so protective of his mother it must be hard for him to understand your life goes on." Eve picked up

Jessica and started to head upstairs. "Give him a chance to get used to the idea you're not just his father."

Tikka shook her head in wonder. "That girl is wise beyond her years, Ed. Maybe Eve can reason a bit with your son."

The ringing of the front door bell interrupted the conversation in the kitchen, and Kate excused herself to let in Josh Temple, whose eyes widened in admiration at the sight of his stunning dinner companion. "You look sensational, Kate."

Kate chuckled at the expression on his face, but she found herself enjoying the flattery. "Before we go, Josh, I'd like to say goodnight to my daughter."

"How is Jessie? May I say hello?" Josh had a sort of boyish charm, and as Kate led him up the stairs to Jessica's room, she found herself thinking how attractive he was.

Later, as they entered Rossoni's candlelit dining room, it was apparent that the other diners appreciated the young couple's appearance. While they were shown to a table by the windows overlooking the dark sweep of Half-Moon Beach, conversation ceased as they passed by one group after another, and Kate found herself feeling quite self-conscious by the time they were seated.

"Do you always make that kind of entrance?" Josh leaned over the table toward his companion, noting with approval that the stones in Kate's earrings exactly matched the blue-green of her eyes.

"Hardly," Kate murmured. "I think that the people are looking at the star of the show."

Josh grinned. "As long as *you're* intrigued by ex-rockers, I'm happy."

For the next several hours, Josh's stories of life in the music world fascinated Kate as they sipped crisp chardonnay and ate Arthur Rossoni's delicious veal Marsala. In response to his questions about her own background, Kate surprised herself by telling him the true circumstances of her arrival in Maine, and she understood how he had been able to elicit such powerful and honest responses from the students in the class he had taught that afternoon.

"You have a way of finding out a lot about people, don't you?" Kate leaned her chin on her hand and looked steadily across the table at Josh, his lanky frame leaning casually against the back of his chair.

"Thanks for saying so," Josh drawled, acknowledging the compliment. "I'm fascinated by what makes people do the things they do. For instance, if you and Alex Stamos are finished, why is he glaring at me?"

Startled, Kate swiveled around and saw that Alex and Claire were sitting at a nearby table with Mona and Bill Lundgren. The two women and Bill were chatting companionably, but Alex's eyebrows were drawn together in a deep scowl as he watched Kate and Josh lean toward each other in an apparently intimate conversation.

Kate turned back immediately and found Josh's calm gray eyes studying her reddened cheeks. "You look even more incredible when you blush. Are you embarrassed and uncomfortable because he's here?"

"What Alex Stamos does is no concern of mine." Kate kept her voice steady and low.

"Then maybe you'd like to have another glass of wine while I play my first set." The challenge in Josh's invitation was unmistakable, and Kate made up her mind when Claire's brittle laughter rang from the neighboring table.

"I'd love to, Josh. It's been a long time since I've been a groupie."

At their table, Claire leaned over to Mona Lundgren and commented that it looked as if Mrs. Hammond had gotten bravely over her infatuation with her husband and had gone on to younger and hipper men. The triumph in Claire's voice scratched Alex's raw nerves so painfully that he gripped the arms of his chair to keep from losing his temper.

"That's none of our business, Claire," Alex grunted as he signaled the waiter for another drink.

"Then why are the veins bulging on your forehead, my dear?" Claire ignored the rage on Alex's face and continued to smirk, while the Lundgrens seemed to share her pleasure in Alex's discomfort.

"That Kate Hammond sure is a knockout," Bill contributed. "I can see why she's got so many people buffaloed, but personally, she's not my type. I'm not attracted by that sexy vulnerability that gives the teenage boys wet dreams. I like women who have it all together and have their lives under control."

. Glaring at Bill, Alex managed to eat a few mouthfuls of dinner after pushing most of his meal around his plate. Claire and the Lundgrens ate ravenously, but Alex devoted most of his attention to three vodka martinis, which he hoped would take the edge off of his pain at seeing Kate so clearly enjoying herself with Josh. Claire's expression of smug pleasure had not altered during the course of the evening, and Alex amused himself by thinking of the various embarrassing things he could do to wipe the look from her face.

Josh had finished his set and had rejoined Kate at their table when the Stamoses and Lundgrens prepared to leave just before ten o'clock. Bill found it necessary to make a snide remark about Alex being well rid of "that cockteaser", and Alex summoned all of his self-control to keep from wrapping his hands around Bill's neck. Finally, Alex managed to propel Claire through the lobby and out the door, hoping to end an extremely painful evening.

****

Just a little way down the road, Chickie brought his car to a stop in the Half-Moon Beach parking lot and turned off the engine. In the distance, the surf rumbled and swept across the sand, but the beach itself was silent and deserted as Chickie and Eve made their way toward the ocean.

"This is one of my favorite times of the year," Eve breathed. "I know a lot of people dislike autumn because things are dying, but I don't think it's a sad time at all."

"I do," Chickie replied. "My mother always hated to see the leaves fall from the trees. She used to say she knew she would die in the autumn. Now she doesn't even know what month it is."

Eve put her hand on Chickie's arm. "It really makes you sad to see your mom, doesn't it? But at least you know she's always loved you. I don't know how I feel about my mother, or whether I'd ever be able to live with her again. I guess that puts the two of us sort of in the same boat."

"Would you think I was awful if I said my mother would be better off dead? If she knew what was going on, she'd beg someone to kill her. But I certainly wouldn't have the guts to do it." Chickie picked up a piece of driftwood and hurled it toward the ocean. "I wonder what death is like. Is it just oblivion?"

"I can't tell you how many times I've thought about the same thing." Eve sat down on a big log and held her jacket together against the cool sea breeze. "Back when things were really bad at home, I used to think about killing myself, but I was afraid to leave Willie. Now he's sure he's died and gone to heaven."

Chickie lowered himself next to Eve and put his arm around her slender shoulders. "One good thing has come out of all the junk we're all going through. I've gotten to know you better, and I think you're terrific—really different from the other girls."

"You know, Chickie, I used to hate the fact that I wasn't the same as Phaedra and her crowd. I wanted to dress like they did and do all the things my parents forbade me to even think about. But now, it's not so bad, especially since you've been so nice to me." Eve glanced up at Chickie, her eyes reflecting the pale silver moonlight.

Chickie pulled Eve toward him and held her close. He could feel her heart beating rapidly as he lowered his head to brush her lips with his. Slowly, Chickie's kiss deepened and his arms tightened around her lithe body. Eve felt herself straining against him, an aching warmth spreading throughout her body as his mouth moved insistently against her lips, parting them gently. Mindlessly, Eve responded with a joyful desire she had never before experienced, not really understanding what forces were setting her on fire.

"Whoa." Chickie pulled away reluctantly, his reaction to her innocent passion still in control, but painfully apparent. "You're something else." Chickie got up and walked a little way off, surreptitiously adjusting his clothing with his back to Eve. "I better get you home, or we both might be sorry."

Unsure of herself, Eve watched in confusion as Chickie held out his hand and pulled her up from the log. "Are you angry about something?" Eve's clear gray eyes were troubled.

"Far from it," he said, gathering her against his broad chest. "For the first time in a long while, things feel just right." Above their heads, the dark blue sky was sprinkled with tiny points of light, and from the shelter of Chickie's arms, Eve looked up at the sparkling canopy.

"I'm not sure about much these days, but I don't remember being any happier than right now."

Chickie watched over Eve's head as a shooting star flashed under the moon. "Yeah, I feel that way, too. Now, if we don't leave, my legendary self-control may crumble entirely." His arm still around Eve's shoulders, Chickie took a deep breath and began to walk toward the car.

Before they had gone very far, both Eve and Chickie were startled by the sound of feet thudding on the sand behind them. A jagged cloud momentarily hid the moon, and the beach was plunged into darkness, making it difficult to see who was running toward them. Chickie drew Eve into the shadow of a scrub pine, motioning her to be quiet, as they stared at the black figures that were about fifty feet away.

"Come back here, you little bitch!" Eric Lundgren's angry tones rose above the muted roar of the wind-whipped waves. As the moon slipped out of its misty cover, Chickie and Eve could see someone skipping away from Eric, who was running clumsily, holding a bottle in one hand. "You can't get away with that stuff with me!"

"Oh, yes I can, you fucking bastard!" Phaedra Stamos stumbled as she passed by Chickie and Eve, her hair flying around her head in untidy strings, and the sleeve of her sweater torn at the shoulder. "I'll scream 'rape' so loud they'll hear it in Vermont!"

Eric swore again as he tripped over an exposed root and landed on the wet sand. "You said you wanted it, and now that you've gotten me horny as hell, you're wimping out." Eric's words were slurred as he scrambled to his feet and chased after Phaedra, who danced away from him, continuing to shout insults as she increased the distance between them.

Neither Chickie nor Eve moved until Eric and Phaedra were past them. "Do you think Phaedra will be all right?" Eve whispered. "Eric seems awfully mad."

Chickie stared after the angry couple in disgust. "Eric's totally wasted, and Phaedra is up to her old tricks. She pulls this sex-kitten number and then backs out when she gets a guy so hot he can hardly stand it. That's part of the reason I stopped going out with her. She's always playing these games. One of these days, somebody's going to get hurt."

Far up the beach, Phaedra got into Eric's car, grabbed the keys from the floor, and started the engine. Before Eric could jump over the low split-rail fence that separated the sand from the parking lot, Phaedra sped away, her left arm stretched out through the open window, middle finger extended. Eric stood at the edge of the parking lot, a bottle hanging from his hand, shouting obscenities at the car disappearing down the River Road.

"Come on, Eve. We'd better rescue the jerk before he does something really stupid." The contempt in Chickie's voice was thick as he walked up to Eric and took the beer out of his hand. "Forget that there's a game tomorrow, Lundgren? Wouldn't the coach love to see you now!"

Eric wheeled on Chickie. "Oh great, first I get shafted by Phaedra, and now his holiness is going to give me a fucking lecture. Great way to spend an evening."

Chickie grabbed Eric's arm and twisted it. "You are such a shit, Lundgren, that I'd like nothing better than to turn you in. Unfortunately, the team needs you. You know how Phaedra operates, so if you were dumb enough to fall for her little act, it's your own problem. Now shut up and get into the fucking car."

Eric mumbled something incoherent but obeyed Chickie and collapsed into the back seat. Eve hurried around to the passenger side and slipped in while Chickie was pushing Eric's legs in far enough to shut the door. "If you puke before you get home, I'll rub your face in it, I swear."

The older Lundgrens were still out when Chickie half-carried Eric, still muttering, to his front door. When Eric realized his house key was still in Phaedra's possession, Chickie rang the doorbell insistently, holding Eric up until the porch light turned on and Kelly opened the door.

"What happened to him?" Kelly stood aside as Chickie dragged Eric into the front hall before allowing him to sag to the floor. She was dressed in a filmy white nightgown that clearly outlined her body, and Chickie averted his eyes as he explained where he had found Eric.

"We better get him up to bed before my parents get home! My father doesn't care if Eric gets drunk, but my mother goes banshee. The last time she caught him, she burned his whole baseball card collection." Kelly motioned to Chickie to take one side of Eric, and she grabbed his right arm, slinging it over her shoulder as they struggled upstairs with Eric's dead weight between them.

Part way down the upstairs hall, Eric roused himself momentarily, leered at Kelly, reached over her shoulder and grabbed her right breast. "Gimme a little tittie, sister dear, and I'll go right to sleep."

Kelly shook off Eric's groping hand and ignored the shocked expression on Chickie's face. "Keep your hands to yourself, you pig. Don't worry, Chickie, he's harmless. He still thinks he's out somewhere screwing Phaedra." Kelly shoved open a bedroom door and helped Chickie to stretch Eric's limp body out on the bed. Almost immediately, Eric began to snore.

"Thanks for bringing him home, Chickie. I keep telling Eric he's becoming a booze hound, but he won't listen." Kelly stood at the top of the stairs and watched Chickie hurry down and out of the house before she slowly retraced her steps and opened Eric's bedroom door.

THE SHAPE OF DARK—Chapter Twenty-Two

When Alex opened his eyes on Saturday morning, his eyeballs felt scratchy, his mouth was dry, and his tongue seemed coated and thick. The sun streaming through the window of the bedroom hurt his pounding head, and he desperately tried to remember how he had gotten into bed.

"Good morning, darling. Did you sleep well?" The sound of Claire's voice beside him jolted Alex into complete awareness, sending waves of pain across his forehead. Turning slowly toward the middle of the bed, Alex was gripped by nausea as the cloying scent of Claire's favorite perfume, "Opium" drifted toward his nostrils from the naked body of the woman next to him. Claire let the bedcovers fall away, and she leaned toward him, idly running her hand down his bare leg.

"What the hell?" Alex realized that he, too, had no clothes on as Claire's long, pointed fingers continued their exploration of his lower body. "What am I doing in here?" Even though it was agony, Alex shook his head in a vain attempt to clear away the shadows from his memory of the night before.

Claire moved closer to Alex and allowed the sheets to drop away from her thin hips, exposing her completely to his bloodshot gaze. "Don't you remember, my love? After the Lundgrens went home last night, you and I had a delicious reunion, right here where we both belong."

Alex stared at his wife in disbelief, noticing there was no softness in Claire's angular body. "That's impossible! I don't even recall getting into bed, let along making love to you."

"Well, believe it. Oh, I'll admit all the liquor you consumed made my part of the activities a bit more demanding than usual, but the end result was divine." Claire's face was wreathed in a smug expression, and Alex struggled to keep from exploding at her.

With a groan, Alex closed his eyes and allowed his throbbing head to sink into his pillow. Dimly, he remembered coming back from the Half-Moon Inn and being annoyed that Claire had invited the Lundgrens to come in for a drink. Several brandies later, Phaedra had arrived home in Eric's car, explaining that he had been too tired to drive and that she had dropped him off.

After that, Alex's recollections became jumbled, and although he recalled saying goodnight to the Lundgrens, he remembered little else than Claire handing him another drink. "Did I pass out downstairs? How in the world did you get me up here?"

Claire tossed her head in what she obviously thought was a provocative gesture. "Phaedra helped. She was happy to see us back to normal, but she didn't have anything to do with what happened after the door was closed."

Alex felt his stomach contract, and he hastily got up and hurried into the bathroom, where he rested his head against the cool mirror and tried to control his nausea. As he stared at his red-rimmed eyes and haggard, unshaven face, he could see Claire watching him, so he quickly closed the door between his naked body and her relentless gaze.

"I don't believe it," Alex muttered to himself, splashing cold water all over his head. "I haven't been drunk for twenty years, and look what it gets me—a roll in the hay with Vampira." The thought of having sex with Claire made his stomach flip-flop. "I deserve to feel like shit."

Alex brushed his teeth and wrapped a large bath towel around his waist before he went back out into the bedroom where Claire was still lying in bed, patting the place he had vacated.

"Why don't you get back in? Now that you've sobered up, things might be a lot more interesting." Claire inhaled and allowed the sheet to fall again from her small, sharply pointed breasts.

"No thanks, I have a lot to do this morning, and I think I need some strong black coffee more than anything else." Alex struggled to keep his tone civil, but he was so repulsed by the sight of Claire's nakedness that there was an unmistakable edge of sarcasm to his words. "Why don't you get dressed now?"

Claire's eyes narrowed. "I wonder if you'd have the same reaction to an invitation from Kate Hammond. Oh, but I nearly forgot. She's probably having a little morning delight with that fascinating young musician."

Alex tried to ignore her remark as he pulled on his clothes. "I'm going into the Cumberland Country Jail to see Alf Stanton and then to the soccer game this afternoon. I don't know when I'll be home." As he turned to leave, Alex looked steadily at Claire. "If it's true we did sleep together last night, I hope you enjoyed it, because I swear I'll never touch you again as long as I live."

As Alex closed the bedroom door behind him, he heard the sound of breaking glass, and he could envision the crystal picture frame on Claire's bedside table in a thousand pieces, a thought that gave him little satisfaction. Instead, Alex trudged down the stairs to the kitchen with a sense of profound sadness.

****

At Silvertree Farm, Kate stretched luxuriously in her bed, enjoying the memory of her evening with Josh. He had brought her home around midnight, after a couple of enjoyable hours at Rossoni's, and in spite of the aching void that existed where Alex had been in her life, Josh's gallant attention made her smile contentedly in the bright morning sunlight.

"Mama! Are you still asleep?" Jessica's chirping penetrated the door between their bedrooms, and Kate sang out for her daughter to come in. As they cuddled in the middle of her big bed, Kate answered Jessica's excited questions about their day's plans while she thought back to the enjoyable evening watching Josh perform.

"Oh, stop being so silly." Kate spoke out loud without realizing it, and Jessica looked at her mother in surprise.

"I'm not being silly," she pouted, "you promised we could take Chrissy Barton to the soccer game with us."

Kate refocused her attention on her daughter. "Of course we can, ladybug. I was thinking about something else. Now let's hurry and get dressed." Kate shooed Jessica into her own room, while she dashed into a hot shower.

The front doorbell was ringing when Kate came downstairs, warmly dressed for the morning's chores and the soccer game with Northport High School. To Kate's surprise, a florist delivery boy was waiting on the front steps to present a bouquet of daisies to "My Fair Katie." The card accompanying the flowers said "To my favorite groupie."

In the kitchen, Tikka was finishing her coffee before setting off for Avesta. When Kate came into the room, grinning at the message from Josh, Tikka cocked her head and looked at her friend. "Kate

Hammond! You are positively radiant this morning, and that can mean only one thing."

Jessica, who was sitting next to Tikka, peered up at her mother, who silenced any further comment from Tikka with a fierce glare. "Your face is all red, Mama. Do you have a temperature?"

"Now see what you've done," Kate muttered at Tikka in mock anger. "Can't a person have a simple date around here?"

"Absolutely, and with all our blessings. It's about time you had some guilt-free fun. I think Josh Temple is adorable." Tikka pushed away from the table. "Big sale today at Avesta. Drop by before you go to the game. I've got a sensational jade silk blouse for you to try on."

Kate took a big bite of a crispy bagel spread lavishly with cream cheese. "I'll try. By the way, what did YOU do last night? You weren't home when I got in at midnight."

"Ed and I cooked dinner at his house. Chickie was at the movies with Eve, so there was no strain, and we sat by the fire and talked until after one. I feel so bad for Ed's situation with Sheila because he knows he can't get on with his life while she's in that condition." Tikka's normally vibrant face was drawn into lines of concern as she fumbled in her purse for her car keys. "It sounds awful to say, but it's a pity Sheila couldn't just drift peacefully away some night in her sleep."

Kate didn't say anything even though she understood how Tikka felt. As long as Sheila was alive, both Ed and Chickie were in a sort of limbo from which there was no escape, in spite of the ironic fact Sheila had no idea what was happening to her.

****

One person who was painfully aware of his condition, however, drove slowly toward Portland and the Cumberland Country Jail. Alex's hangover had not improved in spite of the advertised benefits of Alka-Seltzer, and he felt every bump and hole in the road. Gradually, he had been able to reconstruct most of the events of the previous evening, so he realized he probably deserved his agony. The one blank that still remained in his memory concerned his alleged sexual encounter with Claire, but the possibility that it could have occurred caused him as much discomfort as the effects of the alcohol.

Alf Stanton looked as wretched as Alex felt when a guard brought the prisoner into one of the small interrogation rooms. The custodian's hair was long and greasy, and his pasty complexion reflected too little sleep and too much bad food and worry. The public defender who had been appointed for Alf seemed to consider the case against his client virtually impenetrable, with the result that Alf had been strongly counseled to try to plea bargain with the prosecution prior to the trial.

"It's driving me nuts, Mr. Stamos, because this lawyer thinks I'm guilty when I know I'm not. There's got to be some way to prove somebody else attacked that girl." Alf wrung his hands as he spoke, drawing Alex's attention to the fact that his fingernails weren't any cleaner after two weeks in jail.

"Alf, I happen to agree with you. Have you every seen this before?" Alex drew the "Little Hitter" bat out of his jacket pocket and handed it across the table. Alf looked at it curiously, running his callused fingers over the gouge in the end.

"Can't say I have. It looks like some kid's first baseball bat."

"I found it buried near the hut where you're supposed to have raped Kelly. When I showed it to her she freaked, so I'm convinced that it had something to do with that night. Jim Brogan is going to help me try to figure it out, so you hang in there." Alex stood up and patted Alf on the shoulder. "See you in a couple of days."

"Thanks for everything, Mr. Stamos. If you didn't believe me, I'd have no chance at all." Alf's nearly black eyes were filled with such gratitude that Alex looked away in embarrassment.

"I'll watch the soccer game for you, buddy. It won't be long until you're there yourself." As Alf shuffled out of the room and back to his cell, Alex felt more determined than ever to discover the truth.

On the way back to Cape Mariana, Alex was surprised to find himself ignoring the access road to the Casco Bay Bridge. The old Jaguar seemed to have a mind of its own as it turned onto Peal Street and drove slowly past the line of red brick townhouses where the Euripedes Garden restaurant was located. Impulsively, Alex parked his car, and pulling on dark glasses and an old Red Sox cap, strolled casually toward number 24, stopping to examine the menu in the window of the restaurant. While he was standing there, the front door of the townhouse opened and two people came out, talking animatedly.

"I'll be damned," Alex said to himself, recognizing Susan Moore's beautiful face looking up at Adam Loring. Quickly, Alex leaned against a tree and ducked his head, while he watched Susan and Adam stroll down Peal Street toward the busy intersection of Congress Street. Just as he was about to move away from behind the tree, the door of number 24 swung wide again.

This time, Alex almost betrayed himself at the sight of the people who emerged. Claire and Phaedra came down the granite steps into the bright autumn sunlight, their heads close together as they chatted. They walked quickly to Claire's Volvo, which Alex had failed to notice, and drove away toward Cape Mariana.

All the way back to the Rocky Shore High School grounds, Alex's mind spun around and around trying to figure out some logical reason why the four people he had observed might be together in a house in the middle of Portland. The more he thought about the situation, the more confusing it became, and Alex finally arrived at the conclusion that he would have to confront Claire in some way as soon as the game was over.

The campus was swarming with spectators when Alex drew his Jaguar to a halt next to Big Ed George, who was just climbing out of his truck. As they walked toward the field, the two men chatted about the prospects for victory until Alex spotted Kate standing with Josh Temple at one end of the field.

"As much as I like him, I'm beginning to hate that guy," Alex growled as he watched Kate's hair shine in the bright sunlight. Jessica, a miniature version of her mother, stood between the two adults, holding both of their hands and looking up as Josh laughed heartily at something that Kate was saying.

Ed looked at Alex in surprise and followed his gaze. "I heard you're back with your wife. That right?"

"In a manner of speaking, I guess. It's a shitty situation because I'd like to be where Josh is right now." The regret in Alex's voice was so clear that Ed put his hand on his friend's shoulder and squeezed it sympathetically.

"I know a little bit about feeling trapped, and it ain't fun, especially if you want to do the right thing for your kid." Ed's comment was interrupted by the whooping sounds of the Rocky Shore team as they ran down the hill toward the field. "Here come the boys."

Alex said goodbye to Ed and walked slowly toward the scorers' table. To his left, he could see that Josh's arm was draped casually over Kate's shoulder, and he felt his stomach knot up again at the idea that the woman he loved was enjoying herself with someone else.

To Alex's relief, Kate and Jessica sat with Alistair Henry during the game. Chickie played extraordinarily well, even scoring a goal from his defensive position. Rocky Shore won the game easily, 6-1, with Jean Pierro accounting for four goals and Eric for one, in spite of his thundering hangover.

From his position above the field, Alex could see his daughter arrive during the second half of the game, but he was not able to observe Eric run by Phaedra and snarl while flipping an obscene gesture in her direction. Chickie, who was playing behind Eric on the same side of the field, yelled a warning to his teammate, but not before the referee rewarded Eric's rudeness with a yellow card.

At the end of the game, Alex climbed down to congratulate Carlo and his team, discovering that his headache had lessened. As the crowd streamed up the hill toward the parked cars, Alex found himself scanning the people for a glimpse of Kate and Jessica, but they were lost in the hundreds of jubilant fans celebrating the victory. At the edge of the parking lot Alex stopped to speak to Lenny, the custodian, who had begun to clean up the field.

"New fashion statement, Len?" Alex pointed to the mismatched gloves the janitor wore as he raked up some debris from around the base of the trash barrel.

"Yeah, cute, aren't they? Somebody stole one of my brand new pair a couple of days ago. They were lying right on Alf's desk in the basement. Pisses me off."

"Well, you do look a little strange with that yellow job on the other hand. Come and see me on Monday, and I'll reimburse you for the loss. Without Alf here, you're working your tail off."

"Thanks, Mr. Stamos." Lenny grinned and doubled the pace of his raking.

By the time Alex turned off the River Road into his driveway, it was almost dark with only a few rosy streaks from the setting sun visible across the marshes. Through the living room window, Alex could see Claire lighting the lamps flanking the sofa, while Phaedra was curled up in a wing chair, flipping through a magazine, looking bored and irritated.

"Hello, everybody." Alex tried to inject some enthusiasm into his voice as he opened the front door and hung his jacket in the hall closet.

"Oh, goody, Daddy's home. Now we can begin our happy family evening." Phaedra's snide tone grated on Alex's ears, but he forced himself to smile at her. Seeing that she was not going to get any reaction from her father, Phaedra turned her petulance toward her mother. "For God's sake, *Claire*, it's Saturday night. All of my friends are going to a party at Gus Cronin's barn. Are you actually going to make me stay here and play contented daughter?"

"Phaedra, we agreed when you came home that we would ALL try to put this family back together. The least you can do is spend a little time at home." Claire spoke patiently, but there was a slight edge to her voice.

****

About a mile away from the Stamos home on the River Road, Chickie turned his car into the broad driveway of Thornton Oaks and looked at the girl sitting quietly beside him. His hair was still wet from the post-game shower that he had hurried through in order to pick up Eve at Silvertree Farm. In the confusion after the game, Chickie had breathlessly asked if she would go with him while he visited his mother, and she quickly agreed, commenting only that she would have to be back in time to baby-sit for Jessica while Kate went out for dinner.

"I dread seeing my mother so helpless," Chickie explained as he and Eve walked through the dusk toward the wide front porch of Thornton Oaks. "It helps having someone else along. My dad and I used to come over together, but recently that's impossible. All he cares about is cozying up to Tikka Worthington and it drives me crazy."

297

Eve squeezed Chickie's hand before they pulled open the heavy doors and said hello to some of the people who were sitting in the living room waiting for dinner to begin. Halfway down the brightly-lit corridor, Chickie saw his father standing by the nurses' station, talking to Doc Miller. The two men were huddled in conversation, and Ed was gesturing toward his wife's room. As Chickie approached, he could hear his father's raspy voice complaining about some bed sores Sheila was developing, demanding that the doctor pay closer attention. In spite of the fact that Doc Miller calmly explained the difficulty of caring for someone in Sheila's condition, Ed became increasingly irate and finally stomped by Chickie and Eve.

"Sorry about that, Doc. Dad just gets frustrated when he comes here." Chickie followed the doctor into his mother's room and stood by awkwardly as a nurse helped to turn Sheila so Doc Miller could examine her legs. "It's not getting any better, is it?"

Doc Miller carefully pulled up the covering over Sheila and shook his head. "I wish I could tell you something positive, Chickie, but I can't. One of the reasons your father is so upset is that I just had a conversation with him about the fact that your mother is having difficulty swallowing, and we may have to decide soon whether to feed her intravenously."

Before Chickie could answer, Eve came into the room. Betty Callahan was visiting her daughter for the weekend, so the only lamp in the room was over Sheila's bed, throwing a harsh light over the bent, emaciated body curled in the center. Eve could tell immediately that it was difficult for Chickie to look at his mother.

Doc Miller moved away from the side of Sheila's bed and peered at Eve. "How are you doing, young lady? Sleeping all right?"

Eve nodded. "Thanks, Doc. I've only had to take two of those pills you gave me because it's so restful and quiet at Silvertree Farm. In fact, I think I'll throw the rest of them away when I get back tonight. It makes me sort of nervous to have medicine like that with Jessie around, although she knows not to touch anything in my room."

"Suit yourself, honey. You look fine." Doc Miller walked around Sheila's bed and made a notation on the chart the nurse held. "Chickie, tell your father we'll keep a special watch on your mom. O.K.?" Doc turned and went out into the hall, followed by the attentive nurse.

Chickie stood looking at his mother for a moment, and then switched on the tape that he had made for her. "Sleep tight," he whispered, kissing her cheek." Let's go, Eve. I know you need to get back to take care of Jessie."

At Silvertree Farm, Kate and Josh sat in the firelit library sipping drinks while Jessica had a "picnic" which Julia had prepared before she left for a special night of bingo at one of the local lodges. Tiny finger sandwiches and small pieces of fried chicken were scattered on a blanket Kate had laid on top of one of Mildred's priceless Orientals, and Jessica hummed contentedly as she poked inside the basket for the little cakes Julia had promised for dessert.

"Eve should be home any minute," Kate explained, looking at her watch. "I hope you don't mind waiting."

Josh laughed easily. "It's my pleasure. Two beautiful women at the same time. I thought Miss Hammond here was supposed to have been entertaining a friend this evening."

"Chrissy got a stomach ache." Jessica looked up at Josh and explained with a solemn expression. "Her mama made her stay home from the game and everything."

"That's why I had to shanghai Eve at the last minute." Kate knelt down beside her daughter and began to collect the leftover food, handing a miniature egg salad sandwich to Josh. "The original plan was for Chrissy to come to the soccer game with us, and then Jessie was going to sleep over at the Bartons." But Eve didn't seem to mind, and I told her she could have someone spend the evening with her. I rather imagine that her co-babysitter will be a certain good-looking soccer player."

Everyone looked up as the back door slammed shut and Eve and Chickie hurried into the library. "Sorry I'm a bit late," Eve explained breathlessly. "Chickie and I went to Thornton Oaks for a short visit."

"No problem, Eve. I just appreciate your helping me out." Kate folded up Jessica's blanket, careful to avoid dropping crumbs on the carpet. "Let me clean up here and we'll be off. Have you two eaten?"

When both Eve and Chickie shook their heads, Kate led them into the kitchen and left them devouring a plate of Julia's fried chicken before she hustled Jessica upstairs to change into her nightgown. Josh joined the teenagers at the table, chatting about the game. As he

299

watched Eve and Chickie together, Josh recognized the chemistry between them.

Soon, Kate reappeared, carrying a sleepy-looking Jessica with her blanket wound around her and Cynthia clutched in her arms. "I think that one bedtime story from now this ladybug will be fast asleep." Kate transferred her daughter to Chickie's's lap, kissing her cheek. "Thanks again, you two. We'll be home around eleven-thirty. Tikka has gone to Portsmouth, and Mildred is in Boston, so you'll have the place to yourselves. Just be sure to lock the doors behind us."

Eve followed Kate and Josh down the back stairs and turned the dead bolt, while Chickie carried Jessica into the library and settled in one corner of the couch, promising to tell his own favorite story. Eve bustled around the kitchen cleaning up the dishes, and by the time she made her way into the library, Jessica was fast asleep on Chickie's lap. He carried the little girl upstairs and laid her on her bed, while Eve covered her and switched on the night light.

"Do you mind if we stay upstairs for a little while?" Eve whispered. "This house is so big you can't hear much from downstairs, and I want to make sure that Jessie is really out for the night." At Chickie's nod, she led him next door to Kate's room, and they settled into the small seating area by the windows overlooking the pool.

Eve switched on Kate's CD player, filling the room with pleasant guitar music.

****

Down the road at Rossoni's, the dining room was nearly full when Kate and Josh were greeted by Maria and led to a quiet table in a secluded corner. Across the room, Alex glared at the new arrivals, who had been so engaged in conversation that they had not seen the Stamos family seated near the bar. Aware of Alex's displeasure, Claire swiveled in her seat and recognized Kate's glowing features, dimly illuminated by the flickering candle on the table. While she was watching them, Claire saw with satisfaction that Josh reached across to Kate and touched her face with his hand, allowing his fingers to trail slowly along her cheek.

"They make a handsome couple, don't they?" Claire ignored Alex and spoke to her daughter, who infuriated Alex by responding with the same smug smile that Claire wore. "This is the second night in a row that we've seen them together, Phaedra, and I'll bet the farm that darling Josh Temple will entrance our Mrs. Hammond with his music."

Alex contained himself with great effort, happy that they had finished their meal and would be spared having to watch Kate and Josh much longer. As he signaled to the waiter for the check, Alex heard Claire request another glass of wine, explaining that she was looking forward to the entertainment so much that she didn't want to rush. "You run along, Phaedra. I know you're anxious to join your friends, and Dad and I can walk home from here. The air will do us good."

Phaedra rose from the table and hurried out of the restaurant, ignoring both Sophia and Jean-Pierro who were helping to clear the crowded tables. Alex watched Phaedra leave and turned to Claire, who was staring at her features in a small mirror, pursing and stretching her mouth as she applied a thick layer of bright red lipstick. "Are you sure you want more wine? Why don't we just call it a night?"

"Oh, come on, Alex," Claire pouted. "You've got to get used to the idea of seeing Kate Hammond out with other men. This is a small town." Her eyes narrowed as she watched his reaction. "That woman is a real man-magnet who certainly didn't take much time to mourn the loss of your attention."

"Oh, for Christ's sake, Claire, I'm in no mood." Alex slumped in his chair and sipped the glass of wine that the waiter had just poured. "By the way, did I see you and Phaedra in Portland today? I thought I recognized your car up on Peal Street by that new Greek restaurant."

Claire looked flustered for a minute. "What were you doing up there? I thought you were going to the jail to see that rapist who works for you."

"I had an errand up near the hospital. Well?" Alex watched Claire's face. "Was it you I saw?"

"As a matter of fact, it was. Phaedra needed some new jeans from Levinsky's, and I had to drop off some papers to an old client of mine whose husband is failing to pay the amount he agreed to in their divorce several years ago. I'm going to represent her in a hearing next month."

Alex looked speculatively at his wife, sitting calmly across from him. "Oh? What's the name of this client?"

Claire shifted in her seat. "You know I can't talk about these things, Alex. Why are you so interested?"

"Oh, no particular reason. It was funny, because right before I saw you in town, I recognized our art teacher, Susan Moore and that man who owns the gallery in Boston. Even though Portland is a small city, it's kind of unusual to see so many familiar faces all at once." Alex noted with interest that the small vein above Claire's right eyebrow began to twitch, a certain indication that she was nervous.

Claire rubbed her hand across her forehead. "Well, I don't know about those other people, but you'd better get used to having me pop up in all kinds of places." The warning was clear in her voice and Claire looked defiantly at her husband. "As I said before, this IS a small town." She abruptly pushed back her chair. "Let's go. It's getting stuffy in here."

Josh recognized the tall bulk of the high school principal as Alex extricated himself from his chair at Claire's command. "There's your boss over there, Kate, and he sure doesn't look very happy."

Kate looked around and felt the familiar tightening in her stomach as she recognized Alex and Claire. "Do you suppose he's following us?" Her eyes focused on the Stamoses as Alex said a few words to Maria Rossoni at the door. "I feel really bad for him right now. His wife is very difficult, and his daughter is in a lot of emotional distress."

"I'm sorry to hear that because Alex Stamos is a very nice guy. But would you forgive me if I didn't spend a whole lot of time worrying about him?" Josh's easy grin dulled Kate's sense of sadness at seeing Alex. "Sometimes fate intervenes in these matters, you know."

Kate smiled back at her engaging companion. "You may be right about that, Josh, because I'm certainly having a good time, even before the food. I might even hang around for that talented guitarist, but I have to call home first. Julia usually gets back from Bingo about midnight, but I don't want Eve to be alone after all that's happened to her." Kate excused herself and went over to the bar where a waiter obligingly pointed out a phone. Josh watched the expression on Kate's face change as she spoke into the receiver, and when she hurried back to the table, he could see that her relaxed smile had tightened into disbelief and concern.

"I have to go home right away, Josh. Something terrible has happened."

THE SHAPE OF DARK—Chapter Twenty-Three

"Sheila George is dead." Kate quickly gathered up her purse and grabbed her coat from the back of her chair. "Thornton Oaks just called Chickie, and he rushed over to the nursing home, leaving Eve and Jessie alone, so we should get right back to Silvertree Farm. In spite of the fact that Brother Able seems to be long gone, I don't feel comfortable about Eve's safety, especially at night."

"Let's go." Josh held Kate's coat for her and then dropped several bills on the table. On the way out, he explained their hasty departure to Maria Rossoni, and within minutes, Josh's car was racing along the winding road that hugged the shoreline between Half-Moon Beach and Silvertree Farm.

"Eve said that Chickie was terribly shocked by the news, in spite of the fact that he knew his mother had no chance of recovery. When he saw her a few hours ago, there were no signs of her condition having worsened. In fact, Doc Miller just checked Sheila tonight, so something dramatic must have happened very quickly." Kate's brow was furrowed as she thought about the sudden nature of Sheila's death.

"Why didn't Thornton Oaks notify Chickie's father? Doesn't it seem reasonable that he would be the first one to hear about his wife's death?"

Kate looked puzzled. "Apparently, the line was busy at Ed's house, and after attempting to reach him for quite a while, the nurses at Thornton Oaks decided to try to find Chickie. One of them remembered hearing him say he was going to keep Eve company, so that's how they found him at Silvertree Farm. I guess Chickie was going to swing by his house to pick up his father."

"Do you think there was any foul play involved?" Josh looked over at Kate. "Or is it just my imagination working overtime?"

"I have no way of knowing, Josh, but I have this weird feeling." Kate shook her head. "And if I wonder about this, then you can bet a lot of other people will too."

Lights were blazing all over the big house when Kate and Josh swung into the driveway at the same time Tikka was climbing out of her car. A floppy hat covered her blond mane, and she struggled to lift a leather portfolio out of the back seat.

"What a long day!" Tikka moaned as Josh relieved her of the bulky case and followed the two women into the house. "Thank God that designer agreed to come to Portland with his sketches. Otherwise, I'd still be on the road from New Hampshire!"

Tikka threw her hat and coat on the bench in the back hall, her shoulders slumping with fatigue. As Kate came into the kitchen behind her, Tikka turned and looked her friend directly in the eye. "Did you know that Sheila George died tonight?"

Surprised, Kate stopped short. "Yes, I just happened to call Eve from Rossoni's. But how did you find out?"

Tikka's face turned crimson. "After I left Avesta, I drove over to Ed's house for a drink. We thought Chickie would be here for the entire evening, so we took the phone off the hook and..."

"And Chickie discovered you and his father together when he came looking for Ed." Kate finished Tikka's sentence, while Josh hovered in the background, embarrassed.

"Oh Kate, it was awful!" Tikka's eyes filled with tears, and she crumpled into a chair at the kitchen table. "We didn't even hear Chickie come into the house, and he must have thought Ed was sick or something, because he burst into the bedroom without knocking.

"Didn't he see your car?" Dan spoke up from behind Kate.

Tikka shook her head. "I guess it didn't register on him. The poor kid was so shocked at the sight of Ed and me in bed that he ran from the house and drove away towards Thornton Oaks. Ed followed him, but I haven't heard what happened."

Just as Tikka finished speaking, Eve came through the pantry door, her expression subdued and thoughtful. "Chickie called a few minutes ago, and it seems that his mother died quietly in her sleep. Doc Miller signed the death certificate, and Mr. George didn't want to have an autopsy performed, even though one of the nurses claimed Sheila was sleeping very peacefully when she checked on her earlier. Poor Chickie. He sounded terribly upset."

"I would think so. It's hard enough to lose one of your parents without anything else clouding the issue." Avoiding Tikka's eyes, Kate turned on the heat under the teakettle. "Did Chickie say how his father was holding up?"

"No, that was the strange part of our conversation. I asked about Mr. George, and Chickie mumbled something I couldn't understand and hung up the phone."

In the awkward silence that followed, Josh got up from the table and moved toward the back door. "You ladies will have to excuse me. Eve, I'll see you tomorrow at school. Hopefully, you and Sophia and I can complete the first installment of the report on Thornton Oaks." Josh disappeared down the back stairs.

Tikka stared at the ground. "Poor Ed. He must be feeling so guilty. I wish there was something I could do."

Eve looked in confusion at the two other women at the table. "I don't see why Mr. George should blame himself. He did everything he could for his wife. Chickie knows that."

Just then, the telephone rang and Kate answered, surprised to hear Big Ed's voice on the other end. "Let me speak to Tikka," he said without preamble, and Kate handed over the receiver. Tikka's answers gave no indication of the substance of their conversation, but she took a deep breath as she hung up and turned to face the others in the kitchen.

"Ed called to tell me the situation has become more complicated. Someone found an empty pill bottle in the bushes outside Sheila's window, and they're going to analyze the residue to see if there's any connection. He's asked me to meet him at the police station." Tikka shrugged into her coat and refused Kate's offer to accompany her. "Don't worry, I'll be fine. You stay here with Eve and Jessie." In spite of her apparent stoicism, Tikka's voice shook a bit, betraying her nervousness.

At police headquarters, Jim Brogan faced Big Ed George across his cluttered desk and held up a dark brown plastic vial. Most of the prescription label has been ripped off, but there was a small piece of the lower right hand corner left, and the letters "er" were still clearly visible.

"Recognize this, Ed?" Jim handed the pill container to the man across from him, knowing it had already been checked for fingerprints. Big Ed shook his head and gave it back.

"Come on, Jim. You know there must be a million of those things around. They all look alike, and that 'er' is probably the end of Doc Miller's name, since he prescribes more pills than anyone in the state of Maine." Ed sat forward in the hard wooden chair, his elbows on his knees and his feet flat on the floor. "If you're going to accuse me of killing my own wife, then get on with it. I'm telling you I had nothing to do with it, in spite of the fact that it nearly destroyed me to see her wasting away."

Jim was about to answer when Tikka came through the office door and both men stood up. "Ed, I feel terrible about Sheila!" Tikka clasped Ed's big hand in both of hers and looked at Jim. "What can I do to help?"

As much as he hated to do so, Jim began to question Tikka about her activities during the previous six hours, noting that she still held Big Ed's hand as she answered. Her affection for Ed George was very evident, but Jim's professional intuition told him that neither one of the people facing him had anything to do with Sheila's death. He decided to wait until the results of the autopsy that Ed had finally agreed to were available before he proceeded any further with the investigation. There was always the possibility the pathologist's report would make it unnecessary to inflame an already tragic situation.

Sitting outside of Jim's office, however, Chickie had a different opinion about his father and Tikka's involvement in his mother's unexpected demise. Unable to hear the words being exchanged behind the captain's opaque glass door, Chickie felt his anger rise until he was finally unable to contain himself, and he burst into Brogan's office without knocking and faced his father, still holding Tikka's hand.

"Are you two satisfied now? You got rid of the one obstacle standing in your way, but unfortunately, it was my mother!" Ed started to speak, but Chickie shouted him down. "Neither one of you could wait to hop into bed. I hope you both rot in hell!" Chickie brushed away the tears that streamed down his face, while Tikka restrained Ed from reacting to his son's accusation.

Jim stood up and took Chickie's arm, moving him out of the office into the empty corridor. "Get hold of yourself, Chickie. I'd bet my badge that your father and Tikka had absolutely nothing to do with what happened to Sheila, so don't dig yourself a hole you can't get out of. It's been a rough night for all of you, and I think it would be best if you went home."

Chickie shook away from Jim and ran out the front door of the police station, squealing the tires of his car as he tore away into the night. Ed and Tikka came out of Jim's office in time to see Chickie's headlights sweep past the front windows of the station, but Jim discouraged Ed from trying to follow his son. "It would be a foolish waste of time when you're hurting, too. Chickie's a good kid. He'll cool off and come around sooner or later. Meanwhile, why don't you go home and wait for him?"

Ed nodded, his wide shoulders sagging. "I'd forgotten how recently you lost Timmy. At least my son's alive, in spite of the fact that he hates me." Ed shook Jim's hand and moved toward the door. "Call me when you hear about the autopsy."

Outside, Tikka put her hands on Ed's shoulders, and standing on tiptoe, kissed him on the cheek. "Are you going to be all right? Do you want me to keep you company?"

"No, thanks anyway. I need to go home and be by myself while I get a hold of what's happened." Ed looked up at the clear evening sky where millions of stars were blazing. "Sheila's probably out there somewhere, and I want some time to say goodbye to her. At least she knows how much I'll always love her."

"I understand. Give me a call when you're ready for a friend." Tikka patted Ed's arm and opened her car door. "And don't worry about Chickie. I'll bet he's at my house right now, talking to Eve."

****

Unfortunately, Chickie didn't make it as far as Silvertree Farm. When he stopped at the corner of River Road and Ocean Acres, he saw the lights of Gus Cronin's barn in a broad field to the left, and he impulsively roared past the sagging weathered fence toward the crowd of teenagers clustered around a keg of beer, which was hidden by a wall of carefully stacked logs.

"Hey, Chickster, nice of you to join the common folk!" Chickie saw Eric Lundgren leaning against one of the rusting cars that cluttered Gus Cronin's barnyard, his arm draped over the shoulder of a freshman girl who was quickly gaining a reputation for heavy drinking and easy sexual favors. "Grab a keg cup and enjoy. Gus's brother provided the brew." Eric leaned down and fondled the girl by his side, causing her to sway provocatively against him.

Chickie ignored Eric and made his way inside the crowded barn, where he recognized a number of recent graduates as well as a lot of the present students. Phaedra was standing in one corner, surrounded by several of the senior boys, who were clearly appreciative of the short skirt and tight sweater she wore, having changed her clothes after leaving her parents at Rossoni's. Phaedra held a large cup of beer in one hand and twisted her silver necklace with the other, flirting openly with the goaltender of the soccer team.

As soon as she saw Chickie, however, Phaedra pushed her way through the group around her and stopped his passage across the floor. "Well, look who's here. How were you able to tear yourself away from protecting little Miss Priss? Or are you rediscovering how much fun regular girls can be?" Phaedra stood so close to Chickie he could smell the beer on her breath.

The dull ache in Chickie's entire body began to throb in time to the loud music that seemed to bounce off of the walls of the barn. As more of the people inside began to dance, the floor shook in rhythm to the pounding sound, and Chickie found himself gulping Phaedra's beer while she gyrated against him. Someone else handed him another drink, and he chugged that one down before allowing Phaedra to draw him into the circle of flashing bodies.

Before long, Chickie lost track of how much beer he had swallowed, but he was keenly aware of the fact that Phaedra was concentrating on arousing him in any way she could, much to the annoyance of Eric, who had come in from outside and was watching the dancing from against the wall. As Phaedra continued to rub herself against Chickie's numb body, Eric moved toward the middle of the floor.

"Hey, baby, don't waste your time on the Chickster. We've got a little unfinished business from last night." Eric grabbed Phaedra and swept her into his arms as the music changed to a slow dance. Relieved, Chickie backed away through the wide barn door and took a deep breath of cool night air. In spite of himself, he had begun to respond to Phaedra's blatant sexuality, and it was only by a supreme exercise of willpower that he was able to recall Eve's gentle features.

"Let go of me!" Phaedra's angry voice interrupted Chickie's concentration as she flounced out of the barn, followed by Eric, who laughed when she sought refuge behind Chickie. "When will you get it through your thick skull that the only girls who are interested in you are losers!"

Several of the people standing around the keg drew in their breath at Phaedra's insulting remark, and they watched with growing interest as Eric's face darkened. Chickie's head was clear enough to remember the previous evening and he recognized the potential danger in the situation that was emerging. Eric wasn't as drunk as he had been on the beach, and Chickie had no doubt he was capable of doing anything if sufficiently provoked.

"Come on, Phaedra. Cool it. Apologize to Eric, and I'll take you home." Chickie grinned so winningly at Phaedra that she surprised everyone by giving in immediately.

"Sorry Eric, that was a cheap shot. I really mean it."

Eric shrugged and went over to the keg, where the girl he had been with earlier was gazing at him. "Forget it. Who needs the hassle?" Eric put his arm around the freshman's waist and drew her toward the barn, where the music had become even louder.

Suddenly, Chickie felt slightly nauseated and began to walk away from the crowd toward his car, alarmed to find that his coordination was poor. "You're in no shape to drive, Chickie. Walk over to my house and I'll take you home later." Phaedra grabbed Chickie's arm and guided him away from Gus Cronin's barn toward the River Road. "My parents are probably upstairs by now, and if they're doing what I think they are, they'll never know we've come in the house."

Chickie's head was so foggy that he submitted to Phaedra's guidance along the half-mile stretch of road that was lit only by the moon and stars. Occasionally, he would stumble, but Phaedra steadied him, chuckling at his unusual state of inebriation, until they turned into the driveway where Alex's car was parked.

Inside, Claire had finally gone to bed, frustrated by Alex's firm refusal to join her, and he sat in the living room, turning the pages of a new spy novel, but not absorbing any of the complicated plot. The words gave way to images of Kate Hammond's face as she leaned toward her companion at Rossoni's. Alex found himself unable to think about anything but Kate.

On impulse, he picked up the telephone beside him and dialed the number of Silvertree Farm. When Kate answered, Alex was silent, afraid to trust himself to speak.

"Hello?" Kate repeated, sounding a bit alarmed.

"Kate, I'm sorry to call so late." Alex spoke quietly into the phone, his voice rough. "There's something important that I need to talk to you about, and I wondered if you could possibly see me tomorrow. Anytime, any place." Alex was so engrossed in his conversation that he didn't hear the slight click as Claire picked up the extension in their bedroom.

"Oh, I don't know, Alex. This whole thing is so difficult. Do you think it's a good idea?" Kate's tone was tired and troubled.

"I wouldn't ask unless I thought it was crucial, believe me. It tears me apart to see you, even across a room, and especially when you're so obviously enjoying yourself with Josh Temple." Alex instantly regretted his jealousy, but he couldn't control his feelings.

"All right. Come by tomorrow morning about eleven."

"Thanks." Alex exhaled. "Are you doing O.K.?"

"Pretty well. I guess you heard about Sheila George. We're all upset about that over here."

Alex's voice reflected his complete ignorance. "What are you talking about? What happened to Sheila?"

"She died tonight, and there seems to be some idea that it wasn't of natural causes. I'll fill you in when I see you. The worst part is that Chickie is missing, and Ed is beside himself because Chickie seems to blame his father and Tikka in some way." Kate found herself whispering into the phone even though there was no one else in the room.

"Oh my God, those poor people." Alex started to say more when he heard someone fumbling at the front door and he said goodbye quickly before startling his daughter by pulling the door open. "What the!"

Chickie practically fell into Alex's arms as he tripped over the top step and stumbled into the house. "Hullo Mishta Stamos," he croaked, "I don't feel so hot." Chickie groaned and ran to the kitchen, where he threw up in the sink. Both Alex and Phaedra followed him, but stepped back quickly as he vomited again.

Alex grabbed a kitchen towel and soaked it in cold water. "Here, Chickie, wipe your face. You'll feel better." Chickie swiped the cloth across his mouth and let Alex help him into a chair.

"What's going on here, Phaedra?" Alex turned to his daughter who was standing in the kitchen door watching Chickie with amusement.

"Chickie had a little too much to drink, so I brought him over here. I didn't think he should drive." Phaedra took the towel from Chickie and refreshed it under the tap. "I didn't think you'd be up."

Alex looked approvingly at Phaedra. "You did exactly the right thing, especially given what Chickie has been through tonight. I'll take him home and he can pick up his car tomorrow."

"What has he been through besides too much beer?" Phaedra was clearly confused by her father's statement.

"You didn't tell her, Chickie?" Alex looked at the ashen-faced boy in surprise. "Phaedra, Chickie's mother died tonight."

Phaedra was stunned into silence as she looked down at Chickie who was bent over in the kitchen chair. "Why didn't you say something? No wonder you got drunk!" Phaedra's face softened. "I'm really sorry."

Chickie mumbled something in reply and accepted Alex's help to his feet. "I'd better get home now, if you don't mind, Mr. Stamos. I was rotten to my father before."

On the way to his house about a mile and a half away, Chickie slumped in the corner of the front seat, lost in turbulent sensations of grief, anger, and disappointment in himself. Alex said a few words to him, but the unhappy boy seemed to be completely withdrawn. When Alex turned into the George's driveway, the back light was on and Big Ed ran out through the garage, his panicky expression replaced by one of relief when he saw Chickie was all right.

"My God, son, where have you been?" Ed helped Chickie out of the car and supported him when his knees buckled. The odors of beer and vomit intermingled and rose from Chickie as he stood in the enclosure of his father's burly arm. Ed ignored the stench and spoke to Alex over his son's head. "Was he at your house, Alex?"

"Eventually. Phaedra brought him home after a keg party, where he quite literally tried to drown his sorrow. I think he's going to be O.K. now, in spite of what promises to be a massive hangover tomorrow." Alex got back into his car and spoke to Ed through the open window. "I heard about Sheila, and I wish there was something to say."

"Thanks. It's been a rough night, but at least Chickie's safe. I don't think I could stand to lose both of them." The unshed tears clouded Ed's eyes as he clasped Chickie's shoulders. Slowly, Alex backed out of the driveway and watched as Ed drew Chickie into the dark cavern of the garage and turned off the back light.

The Jaguar rolled through the quiet streets until Alex was about a quarter of a mile from home, when there was a strange noise under the hood and the engine stopped abruptly, resisting Alex's attempts to restart it. Alex realized that he didn't have a flashlight in the car, so he locked the doors and decided to walk the short distance home rather than attempting to fix anything in the dark. As he approached his house, he noticed that the light was on in the master bedroom, and he could see the pacing figure of Claire as she gestured to someone else in the room.

Overcome by curiosity, Alex walked around to the back of the house and stood under his open bedroom window, straining to hear what was being said, a task made easier by the strident timbre of Claire's voice.

"I think Alex is getting suspicious. He saw us in Portland today, and he asked all kinds of questions. He also recognized Susan and Adam, but he didn't connect them with us."

Alex couldn't hear Phaedra's response, but Claire's volume increased as she moved closer to the window. Alex concealed himself in deeper shadows, holding his breath. "I think we need to move faster than we thought. In spite of what he promised, Alex has made arrangements to see the Hammond bitch tomorrow, and even with Josh Temple on the scene, I think we'll have a tough time keeping Alex and his love apart. We'd better huddle with Double A tomorrow and speed things along."

When there was no further conversation, Alex assumed that Phaedra had gone to her room, so he crept around to the front and whistled loudly as he stomped up the front steps. "Damn car," he growled, letting himself into the house.

****

313

On Sunday morning, the telephone rang early at Silvertree Farm, and Kate was surprised to hear her mother-in-law's voice on the other end. Marissa had accepted Mildred's invitation to accompany her to Boston, intending to use Saturday to drive to Ledyard Hill, where Brother Able and his congregation had lived. It was a long shot, but Marissa hoped someone in the area would remember the child who used to visit Brother Able in the summer, adding another layer of information to Marissa's relentless search for her missing daughter.

"I wish I had better news," Marissa reported. "Nobody in the area could even recall Samantha, even though nearly everyone had some kind of memory, usually bad, of Brother Able and his followers. So it looks as if this place is a dead end. Millie and I will be back in Maine this afternoon."

Kate hung up the phone and climbed out of bed, stretching as she stood by the windows overlooking the ocean and the ruined pool house. To her surprise, three human forms moved around where Kate usually expected to see white-tailed deer. It was impossible to tell who the people were or what they were doing, but Kate was fairly sure that the tallest of the three was a man, and the other two were women. They seemed to be looking for something on the ground and finally disappeared after about five minutes of careful exploration.

Kate would have been more concerned about the strangers' presence had she not been forewarned that today was to be Cape Mariana Clean-up Day. Mildred had told her that many residents of the town who would normally be too shy to approach Silvertree Farm seized the excuse of the clean-up to take a look at one of the areas' most fascinating properties. Trash bags were available at most of the local stores, and everyone was urged to travel the roads of Cape Mariana picking up debris. Kate and Jessica planned to walk around Ocean Way in the early afternoon, joining other people at the high school for a cookout sponsored by the local service organization to celebrate the clean-up effort.

After she was dressed, Kate peeked in on Jessica and found she was still sleeping, her blue bear snuggled under her chin. Downstairs, the clatter of pans and dishes in the kitchen suggested that Julia had begun the preparation of her usually spectacular Sunday breakfast, so

Kate decided to drive into town for the three newspapers they regularly devoured on Sunday morning.

There were very few cars on the road between Silvertree Farm and Dunham's, but Kate did recognize Jim Brogan as he passed her traveling in the opposite direction. Although he waved at her, Kate noticed that he had a concerned frown on his face, and she wondered where he was going. At the store, she quickly picked up the Portland paper, the *Boston Globe*, and *the New York Times*, and after exchanging a few pleasantries with the Dunham brothers, she returned home to find that Tikka had dressed Jessica. They were both already seated in the kitchen.

"That nice Mr. Temple has already picked up Eve," Julia explained. "He came by about eight o'clock and said they would be working through lunch."

Kate nodded. "I knew that was their plan. Now I can't stop thinking about Chickie. He must be terribly upset about everything that happened last night. Are you all right, Tikka?"

"As well as anybody could be, I guess. I talked to Ed last night, and Chickie was home, having gone to a keg party near Alex Stamos's house. According to Ed, Chickie got really drunk and Phaedra kept him from driving home, thank God. The worst thing was that Chickie really seemed to believe that Ed and I could have something to do with Sheila's death." Tikka's eyes were flat and sad, betraying her despondency, and Kate reached over and patted her hand.

"Anybody who knows you couldn't accept that. The tragic thing is that both Chickie and Ed have expressed the fact that Sheila might be better off at peace, so they both probably feel a bit guilty about those thoughts, now that she's actually gone. I just hope the autopsy will exonerate everybody so that you can all get on with living." Kate took the Portland paper from the pile of newspapers and opened it to the front page.

"CAPE MARIANA WOMAN DIES UNDER MYSTERIOUS CIRCUMSTANCES" "Sheila George, 42, suffering from advanced Alzheimer's disease, was found dead at the Thornton Oaks care facility last night. Preliminary investigation has revealed sufficient barbiturates in her system to cause death in a person of Mrs. George's weakened condition. No suspects have been identified, although several people have been questioned by Cape Mariana police."

Kate stared in horrified fascination at the black headline and accompanying story, featuring a photograph of an attractive, laughing Sheila before the onset of her illness. "What an awful thing for Big Ed and Chickie. Are you planning on going over there this morning?"

Tikka shook her head. "I think the farther away I stay from Ed, the better for all of us, especially Chickie. There must be some explanation for this, but right now, any contact between Ed and me will only make matters worse." Murmuring an apology to Julia, Tikka pushed away her untouched breakfast and excused herself, walking slowly through the dining room until she reached the terrace doors, where she let herself out into the brisk September sunshine.

"Why is Tikka so sad, Mama?" Jessica looked up at Kate with a concerned expression. "Did she hurt herself?"

"No, Ladybug, but one of Tikka's good friends feels really bad now, and that makes her very unhappy. We'll just have to be extra nice." Kate heard the front doorbell ring, and she left Jessica with Julia as she went to answer it.

"I think I'm early," Alex said, as he stood on the wide stone steps. "But I couldn't wait any longer to see you. I don't even care if Claire knows I'm here."

Kate found herself smiling at Alex's obvious joy at seeing her, and although she had sworn to keep their meeting formal and without physical contact, she held out her hand and drew him into the vestibule, where he enfolded her in his arms and buried his face in her fragrant, silky hair.

"I've missed you so much, and it's only been a few days. How can trying to help your child cause such pain?" Alex shuddered from the exquisite shock that he felt holding Kate's slender, rounded body against his pounding heart. When she looked up at him with brimming eyes, Alex crushed her soft lips beneath his and felt her sharp intake of breath.

After a long, sweet kiss, Kate pulled away, and Alex reluctantly released her from his embrace, conscious of the difficulty of the moment for both of them. As he followed her into the library, Alex was acutely aware of Kate's perfume, and he commanded himself to sit on the opposite end of the sofa, in spite of an almost uncontrollable desire to recapture her in his arms.

"What did you want to talk to me about?" Kate's voice was clear and calm, her nervousness betrayed only by the rapid pulse that Alex could see beating in her throat. "You sounded pretty anxious on the phone last night."

Alex was glad to have something concrete to discuss. "Things got even more complicated after our phone call, and I'm now absolutely certain my wife and daughter are mixed up in something very peculiar." Alex described his puzzling observation on Peal Street and then recounted the conversation he had overheard last night. "Who do you suppose that Double A might be, and what do they all have planned? The whole situation gives me the creeps."

Kate shook her head in bewilderment. "I agree there's something odd going on, but I haven't a clue what it all means. What are you going to do?"

"Never mind about me right now. I'm concerned that you take precautions to protect yourself, Jessie, and Eve. I think something dangerous is about to happen, and I want you to be ready." Alex's expression was extremely serious, and Kate felt a chill of fear. "As for me, I'm going to keep a very close watch on Claire, who is probably shadowing me as we speak. I only hope that Phaedra is a victim and not a player in all of this, but I'm not sure of anything anymore."

Kate looked over at the box of trash bags sitting on Mildred's desk. "I guess it would be foolish to wander out on the road today with only Jessie for protection. She'll be so disappointed, because I promised her we would help in the Clean-Up."

Alex thought for a moment. "Just skip the part between here and the school and come directly to Rocky Shore. There's plenty to do, and lots of people will be around. I'll be on hand for most of the afternoon, so I can keep an eye out without arousing Claire's suspicions." Alex stood up. "I'd better get going. I told Claire I was going to see Big Ed and Chickie, and I meant it. Even though she knows I intended to see you, I like to keep my alibis honest."

"Give them both my love and tell them I'm thinking of them." Kate took Alex's hand and squeezed it. "You take care of yourself, too."

Alex reluctantly loosened Kate's small, firm grasp and walked toward the front door. "The only thing that's keeping me sane is that Phaedra actually did something decent for someone else last night. I keep hoping that if I can hang in there with her, she'll be all right. The price is pretty high, though." Alex touched his finger to his lips and then to Kate's.

Her throat aching, Kate forced a smile as she watched Alex climb into his car and drive away. From the French doors leading to the terrace, Kate could see Tikka walking toward Morning Cove, picking her way through the long grass. Jessica was still in the kitchen, and when the telephone rang, Kate yelled to Julia that she would answer it."

"Mrs. Hammond?" A deep, faintly familiar man's voice rumbled from the phone. "I hate to bother you on Sunday. This is Adam Loring."

"No need to apologize, Mr. Loring. What can I do for you?"

"I realize this is very short notice, but I've some new interest in several of your husband's paintings, and I wondered if you'd join me for lunch to talk about that retrospective show I mentioned on the day that I scared you to death!"

Kate glanced at the clock on Mildred's desk. "I've promised my daughter that we will go to a cookout this afternoon, but I could meet you for a short time around twelve. Would you like to come out here?"

"Actually, I'm waiting for a rather important call. Do you think you could come to the place where I'm staying in Portland?" When Kate agreed, Adam gave her directions to 24 Peal Street, explaining that one of his clients had lent him her townhouse for several weeks.

After hanging up the phone, Kate looked out of the terrace door and saw that Jessica had run down the field to join Tikka near the bluff overlooking Morning Cove. Relieved that her daughter was occupied, Kate called out to Julia in the kitchen that she would be back in time to take Jessica to the barbecue at Rocky Shore. As her car turned onto Ocean Road, Kate failed to notice that another vehicle pulled out from behind a clump of trees near the entrance to Silvertree Farm and followed at a short distance, its driver gripping the steering wheel and staring at the back of Kate's car with tight-lipped malice.

THE SHAPE OF DARK—Chapter Twenty-Four

Kate sang to herself as she approached the South Portland end of the Casco Bay Bridge. The brisk September wind was stirring up whitecaps in the harbor, and the imposing bulk of the stately *Scotia Prince* dominated the pier at the International Ferry Terminal. Ahead of her, Kate saw cars begin to slow down as the yellow lights on the bridge signaled the approach of a sufficiently large ship for the drawbridge to be raised, so she flicked the radio dial until she found a station that was pleasant enough for the ten minutes she would wait while the rusting tanker was guided to the pipeline by several tugboats.

Glancing in her rearview mirror, Kate was surprised to see that the car behind her seemed to be empty. It was not unusual for motorists to shut off their engines while the bridge was raised and to get out of their cars to watch the ship pass by. Kate wondered which of the people leaning against the railing owned the vehicle she was looking at.

Before long, the efficient tugboats moved their large burden away from the bridge and traffic resumed. Kate forgot to satisfy her curiosity about the driver behind her as she worked her way up the narrow streets of the West End toward Peal Street.

"Come in, my dear." Adam Loring appeared right after Kate rang the doorbell, and she was swept into a small but charming living room that was decorated with plump, chintz-covered furniture and jewel-toned oriental rugs. Over the small fireplace was a handsome portrait of a gray-haired woman, and several Impressionist paintings were hung on the walls.

Kate stared at the face of the woman on the canvas above the mantle. "I've seen her somewhere. I'm sure of it." Moving closer to the picture, Kate recognized Max's signature in the lower right corner. "This is one of the Wentworth portraits, isn't it?"

"You have a good eye," Adam approved. "This is the first portrait your husband did of the family, and the one that caused him the most difficulty. Mrs. Wentworth had a slight drinking problem, as Max may have told you, and much of his work was done from this photograph." Adam handed Kate a picture that showed how flattering Max's rendition of Mrs. Wentworth actually was. As she studied the image, Kate had the uneasy feeling that she was looking at someone she'd met before.

"How did this happen to end up in Portland? I thought the Wentworths lived on the North Shore of Massachusetts." Kate continued to stare at the stunning portrait, impressed as always by Max's talent.

Adam busied himself at a small bar in the corner, mixing two Bloody Marys. "Actually, this place belongs to Mrs. Wentworth herself, and the picture was part of her divorce settlement. She spends a lot of her time in Bar Harbor, but she likes to have a place in Portland during the really bad weather. I often camp here when I'm in the area on business."

"Are these other paintings what they seem to be?" Kate recognized two vibrant Monets and a delicate Mary Cassatt portrait of a mother and child.

"Absolutely. Mrs. Wentworth bought them from Cyrus Lombard near the end of his life. The Portland Museum would probably try to borrow them, but nobody knows they're here. Everyone thinks these are copies."

Adam handed Kate a glass and motioned for her to sit down. As she settled on a comfortable sofa, Kate peered at the photographs that were scattered on the various tables in the room, but before she had a chance to examine the faces, Adam rose to his feet again.

"Before we sit down to talk, there's something that I'd like you to see. I think you'll be very interested." Adam moved toward the steps at the back of the narrow front hall, and Kate followed, intrigued. At the top of the stairs, he turned into what appeared to be the largest of three bedrooms, although it was hard for Kate to see the room clearly, since the draperies had been drawn.

"It's rather dark in here, isn't it?" Kate peered around her into the deep shadows, conscious of a large bed and the outline of a fireplace at one end of the room. She sipped her drink while Adam flicked a switch on the wall, illuminating the light over a large painting that occupied most of the fireplace wall.

For a moment, the picture swam before her eyes in a swirl of color and texture, but its subject sprang into sharp focus as Kate gasped aloud. "I thought this had been sold to a European collector!" As she stared at her own nude body on the wall, Kate found herself remembering the circumstances under which Max had painted the "Lady on Green."

"So did Max," Adam mused. "That's why he was surprised to find it in my possession. I fully intended to sell it to a private museum near Copenhagen, but once I had my hands on it, I couldn't bear to let it go. The subject is absolutely bewitching, is she not?"

Kate glanced at Adam, who was gazing at the luxuriant curves of the woman in the painting. It was hard to tell from his expression whether he realized she had been the model, so she purposely kept her voice even and dispassionate. "It looks to me like she could lose a few pounds."

Adam laughed, turning out the light and shutting the door to the bedroom. "There's one more you might enjoy seeing." Leading the way into a small, book-lined den. Adam pointed to another nude, smaller than the first one, whose subject faced the artist directly. Long, silvery-blond hair flowed over the girl's slender shoulders, while her lean body reclined on a chaise lounge covered with delicate peach satin.

Once again, Kate felt the breath leave her body as she recognized the woman in the painting. "That's Susan Moore," she whispered. "I didn't realize Max knew her."

"I'm afraid he wouldn't have recognized that name, but he was very well acquainted with the girl you see here. This was one of the Wentworth paintings, and the last one he did, as a matter of fact. Your husband grew very fond of his subject, as you can tell from the care with which he executed the work." Adam closed the door and led Kate down into the living room.

As she reached the bottom of the stairs, Kate was conscious of a ringing in her ears and a lightheaded sensation. She put her glass down on an end table and sat heavily on a small slipper chair, aware that her legs were rubbery and her tongue felt thick. "I must be more tired than I realized. That Bloody Mary has gone straight to my head."

Adam refreshed his own drink and studied Kate. "Nonsense, it had very little vodka in it. You're just not used to alcohol in the middle of the day." As he spoke, Adam's voice became fainter and hollower, while his face grew fuzzy and dim. Kate struggled to focus, but she was unable to keep her eyes from closing.

"Maybe I'll just sit here for a moment," she slurred, allowing her head to fall back on the chair before she slipped from consciousness.

"Nicely done, Adam. She never knew what hit her." Claire Stamos strode into the room and raised Kate's heavy eyelid with a pointed red-tipped finger. "Let's get her upstairs."

Adam lifted Kate into his arms, and although her body was dead weight, he easily carried her up to the bedroom where her portrait hung on the wall. "She should sleep for hours, so we should have plenty of time to get the others."

Two other people came to the door of the room where Kate lay sprawled in the middle of a heavy four-poster bed. Alice Wentworth looked down at the drugged woman whose features were still beautiful although very pale. "No wonder Max was so torn. He would have done anything to keep her from finding out about Susan, but once their affair started, it was like Max was possessed. He went crazy when he found out the truth. We should have told him before it was too late."

Adam's eyes hardened as he watched Kate stir. "It wasn't my idea to have Max do a nude of Susan, and by the time we discovered they were lovers, nothing could be done about it. I just couldn't pass up the opportunity to control Max's work, especially when we discovered what a skilled forger he was."

"What are you going to do with her once you get the others?" Phaedra peered around her mother at Adam, who seemed unable to take his eyes off the "Lady on Green".

A slight sheen of sweat began to form on Adam's forehead, and he ran his tongue around his dry lips. "Who knows? Maybe life will imitate art. But for now, keep an eye on her."

When Adam disappeared down the stairs, Claire fumed at her daughter, who started to follow him. "Wait a minute. Did you hear what he just said? Don't tell me that Adam has fallen for Kate Hammond, too! I won't stand for it."

Phaedra put her hand on Claire's shoulder. "Relax. Looking at that damn portrait is like reading *Playboy*. It's only temporary. Besides, before Kate realizes what's happening, she'll no longer be a pretty sight. Now I have to go do my thing. Are you all set here?"

Alice Wentworth came out of the study carrying a small flask. "Have a bit of this, Claire. It will calm your nerves." Before handing the liquor to Claire, Alice took a long gulp and sighed.

Claire shook off the offer. "Watch it with that stuff. You know how angry Adam will be if things don't go as planned." Alice petulantly capped the flask and put it in her jacket pocket, while Phaedra slipped down the stairs to the back of the house where her car was parked.

Adam was waiting by the kitchen door. Taking Phaedra's arm, he handed her a brown paper bag. "Everything's in here. Just take your time." As Phaedra's car backed out of the narrow space behind the townhouse, Adam retraced his steps through the kitchen and picked up the telephone.

At Silvertree Farm, Julia was about to feed Jessica her lunch, when the sharp ringing of the phone startled them both. Tikka had left for an errand at Avesta, and Jessica was tired after spending much of the morning on the beach, so Julia hoped that a sandwich and a nap would be good for the little girl before the afternoon's festivities at the school.

"I see," Julia spoke quietly into the phone. "Jessie will be ready to go in about fifteen minutes. Tell Kate to stay off her ankle and soak it in hot and cold alternately."

"What's wrong with Mama's ankle?" Jessica's bright green eyes looked at Julia anxiously. "Aren't we going to the barbecue?"

"Don't worry, darling. That was the man your mother went to visit in Portland. He's going to drive her over to the school and then pick you up so you can meet her there. I guess she twisted her ankle on his front steps."

"Oh." Jessica seemed perfectly satisfied with Julia's explanation and went back to munching on her sandwich.

In a short time, Adam Loring drove up to Silvertree Farm and placed Jessica in the back seat of his Mercedes, carefully buckling the little girl in for the short ride to Rocky Shore. As Julia waved goodbye, she felt a peculiar tremor of uncertainty, but since Kate had spoken of Adam several times, she dismissed her doubts.

When Adam's car passed the entrance to the high school, Jessica twisted in her seat belt and spoke to the silver hair on the back of Adam's head. "Isn't my mama waiting for me at her school?"

Adam glanced back at Jessica. "Her ankle hurt so much she decided to rest at my house until after I picked you up. We'll be there in a minute. Just sit back and relax."

"Did you know your voice sounds just like my Daddy's?" Jessica piped up as Adam threaded his way across the bridge to Portland. "I told my mama you looked like him, too, only much older." Looking up at Adam's reflection in the rear view mirror, Jessica could see Adam's clear blue eyes watching her, and she continued to talk at him until the car pulled in behind the townhouses on Peal Street.

"Here we are!" Adam boomed, walking around to help Jessica out of her seatbelt. "Everybody out." In her excitement at seeing her mother, Jessica allowed herself to be picked up and carried into the house, never noticing the slight prick in her tiny bottom.

Upstairs, Claire looked at Kate, still soundly asleep in the darkened room. Hearing the back door open, Claire slipped downstairs and watched Adam lay an unconscious Jessica on the living room sofa. "Have you got everything ready?" Adam inquired. "I'm not sure how long this stuff lasts, because I was afraid to give her too much."

"All set. Bring her up." Adam lifted Jessica and followed Claire to the third floor, where she unlocked a room containing a single bed and a large crib with a covering over the top. Placing the body of the child in the enclosure, Adam checked the reliability of the clasp that secured the top. "Be sure to look in on her every fifteen minutes. The last thing I want her to do is start howling."

On the second floor, Kate forced her eyes open and looked around her, unable to figure out where she was or how she had gotten there. Gradually, as her eyes became accustomed to the dim light, she saw the painting over the fireplace, and her recent experience with Adam Loring swam into her memory. Instinct told her not to move, however, and when the door from the hall opened, she closed her eyes and feigned unconsciousness. She was aware of at least two people standing beside the bed, and she willed herself to breathe slowly and evenly.

"Still out." Kate recognized Adam's deep voice, but the woman who answered him caused her to exert enormous control to prevent reaction.

"You must have really loaded that drink!" Claire's metallic tones were unmistakable. "We can leave her alone for a while. She's not going anywhere."

"I think you're right. Phaedra should be back soon, and we'll have more than our hands full."

When the door closed behind Adam and Claire, Kate struggled to clear her head. She heard footsteps climbing to the third floor, and she gritted her teeth as she forced herself to sit up and swing her legs down, wincing as the blood rushed to her feet. As quietly as she could, Kate moved to the door and opened it a crack. The hall was empty, but she could hear voices above her.

Holding her breath, Kate eased out of the bedroom, down the narrow hall, and onto the stairs leading to the first floor. Her stocking feet made no sound as she inched her way down, praying that the carpeting in the center of the steps would prevent any accidental creaking. A big grandfather clocked ticked in the hallway, but nobody was in the living room. Kate grabbed the purse she had left on the demi-lune table in the foyer and let herself out the front door. She heard footsteps inside the house as she ran toward her car, but she only glimpsed the contorted faces of Adam and Claire in the open doorway as she raced down Peal Street.

In her haste to get back to Cape Mariana, Kate didn't notice Eve's worried face in the small car that passed her on Commercial Street. "Are you sure Jessie's all right?" Eve twisted anxiously in the seat of the car that was speeding toward the hospital.

"I think so. The cook just said the little girl had fallen down those big stone steps leading to the pool and had several really bad cuts on her leg and one on her face. I guess Mrs. Hammond didn't want to take any chances, so she took Jessica right into Maine Medical Center. The cook told my father she'd tried to reach you at school to see if you could go in and give them some moral support, but evidently there was something wrong with the phones. So, I volunteered to find you and drive you in, since I have an appointment in town."

Eve relaxed a bit. "I really appreciate this. Jessie seems like my little sister, and I know how Mrs. Hammond worries about her. You said you told Mr. Temple where I was going?"

"Yes. While you were getting your things, I found him and Sophia in the library, and he said to stay as long as you needed to."

About a quarter of a mile past the International Ferry Terminal, the car slowed down and turned into a narrow alley which ran between two ancient buildings, one with a rusty sign announcing the Casco Fish Company, and the other grimly anonymous except for a peeling bumper sticker plastered on the door that tersely stated "Life sucks and then you die."

"Why are we stopping here?" Eve looked around and saw a battered car across the street displaying dirty white plastic buckets of carnations and a hand-lettered sign promising "Roses."

"Sorry, we'll be just a minute. There's something wrong with my contact and I can't see very well. I've got some wetting solution in the glove compartment."

Eve felt a sharp sting in her thigh as her companion's hand reached across her lap. Within seconds, the familiar face next to her had begun to blur, and Eve's ears were ringing so loudly that she could barely hear her own voice. "What's happening to me?" Then everything went black.

Josh Temple was waiting at Silvertree Farm when Kate's car screeched into the driveway. One look at her terrified face confirmed Josh's suspicions that something ominous was going on, but he tried to control his concern as he helped her from her car. Kate's legs wobbled as she stood up, and she grabbed Josh's arm for support.

"For God's sake, what happened to you?" Josh noticed Kate's makeup was smudged, her clothes were badly wrinkled, and her shoes were missing. "Where have you been?"

"It's a long story, and I'm not sure I've figured out all the details. But why are you here? I thought you'd be working on that report with the kids."

Josh put his arm around Kate's waist and moved her toward the back door. "I was, but then Eve disappeared. I thought she might have walked home for some reason."

The feeling of foreboding that had followed Kate from Portland grew in intensity. "Let's go in and see if Julia knows anything."

The old cook was waiting at the top of the back stairs. "Is your ankle all right? You don't seem to be limping." Julia peered behind Kate and Josh. "Where's Jessica?"

Kate felt as if her skull were squeezing her brain as she collapsed onto a kitchen chair. "Jessica should be here with you. You knew I was going to be in Portland for a short time."

Julia was alarmed at the way that the color drained from Kate's face. "That man you were visiting came and picked Jessie up about an hour ago. He said you had hurt your ankle and wanted him to bring her to meet you at the barbecue."

An image of Adam Loring's face flashed across Kate's mind, sending chills throughout her body as she remembered the bizarre circumstances of her visit to Peal Street. As if she were watching a jigsaw puzzle being completed, Kate felt the terrifying pieces fall into place, and in spite of herself, she slipped from consciousness as Julia and Josh watched helplessly.

****

Back at school, Sophia followed Josh's instructions to look for Eve. When she had been missing for a half an hour, Josh had efficiently organized some students who were there for the clean-up effort into teams, while he sped off toward Silvertree Farm. Kyle Monkton and another boy set out to look through the building, while Eric and Sophia were responsible for the grounds.

As she walked slowly around the circular driveway surrounding the flagpole, Sophia's eyes were focused on the tire marks on the gray pavement. "It looks like a car pulled up right in front of the building, but we all parked in the student lot."

"I think you're right," Eric agreed, scuffing his feet through the piles of leaves that had blown across the driveway. "I have a really bad feeling about this."

The strained note in Eric's voice caused Sophia to look. His expression was so troubled that she stopped and placed a delaying hand on his arm. "What's up, Eric? Are you this bummed over Eve's situation?"

"Not completely. I need some advice real bad, but you need to promise you won't say anything to anyone. This is my problem, and I need to solve it the best way I can without hurting more people than I have to."

Sophia was alarmed by the implication of Eric's words, but she signaled her agreement and sat down next to him on one of the stone lions in front of the school. "So? What's the story?"

Eric kicked the ground with his foot. "Remember the night Kelly was raped?"

"Sure, who could forget? Especially when the attacker had been under this roof, emptying the wastebaskets."

"That's just the problem. I don't think Alf was the person who was responsible for what happened to Kelly. In fact, I know he wasn't." Eric looked miserable.

"How can you be so sure?"

"I can't really say, but ever since that day we talked on the beach, I've been looking at things a little differently. I hate for an innocent man to go to jail."

Sophia glanced up at Eric and was surprised to see that his usual sneer had been replaced by an expression of genuine concern. "Listen Eric, I don't know what's up with you, but you really helped me on the day that I was so upset about my mother, so I'd like to return the favor, if I could."

Eric smiled sadly. "Thanks, Sophia. That means a lot to me. I've got to think about it for a while."

"Sophia! Eric!" Kyle's high-pitched voice cut through their concentration as he yelled from the door of the school. "Mr. Temple just called to tell us all to stop looking. I guess he found out what happened to Eve."

****

Josh replaced the telephone after talking to Kyle and sat down next to Kate, who was lying on the library sofa with a cold cloth draped across her forehead. Waves of nausea assaulted her body, but Kate willed herself to ignore them and focus on the two men who were looking distressed at her greenish-white pallor. "Are you sure you don't want me to call the doctor? You may have been poisoned by whatever Adam Loring put into that drink." Josh gripped Kate's cold, damp hand while Jim Brogan perched on the edge of a chair.

"No. Tell me again what the phone call said, Jim." Two bright spots of crimson had appeared on Kate's cheeks, emphasizing the ashen cast of her skin. "Are you sure they have both Eve and Jessie?"

Jim shifted uneasily, hating to meet Kate's frightened eyes. "The caller, who didn't identify himself except to say he was a follower of Brother Able, announced they would punish both Eve and Jessica unless we deliver the real sinners into their hands."

"The REAL sinners?" Kate looked at Jim in bewilderment. "Did he say who they are?"

"Yes, he did. The people Brother Able really wants are you and Willie Calvert. He's got this crazy notion of 'an eye for an eye', and I guess your role in the death of your husband qualifies you for this vigilante justice thing. I'm just concerned about what that idiot will do to Eve and Jessica if we don't follow his instructions."

Kate closed her eyes at Jim's words, feeling tears sear her cheeks as they flowed unchecked. "No matter what I have to do, I won't let that monster hurt my baby or Eve. If only we knew where they were keeping them!"

"All we can do is wait for further instructions. Meanwhile, the last thing this man said puzzled me. He warned me that if we made any attempt to locate Jessica, he would make sure her last meal made her very happy. Something about chocolate chip cookies with walnuts..."

THE SHAPE OF DARK—Chapter Twenty-Five

It was hard for Eve to tell whether it was day or night when she opened her eyes. Her head throbbed, and it was so dark in the room where she lay that she could only see the dim outlines of pieces of furniture. She was lying on a narrow bed covered with a rough chenille spread, its bumps and ridges pressing against her back and legs, which were tied together securely and fastened to the footboard. Similarly, her hands had been stretched over her head and were bound by a rope to the top of the bed. A boxy shape was pushed up against one wall, and Eve thought she heard steady but light breathing.

"Has she come to yet?" Eve heard a man's voice outside the door, and she quickly closed her eyes and pretended to be unconscious. Someone came into the room and stood beside the bed. Then the door closed again, and Eve heard a woman speak.

"She's still out. That was a very powerful drug, so it may be awhile. Did you call the police again?"

Eve couldn't hear the man's reply, but she could make out other voices, all female, mingling with his deeper tones. There was something familiar about the way he sounded, although Eve couldn't associate it with a particular face.

As her vision sharpened, Eve surveyed her prison. Heavy pieces of furniture were placed around the walls, which seemed to be covered with paper in an ornate floral design. The windows had lacy curtains and heavy black shades, around which glowed a tiny box of light, just enough for Eve to recognize the slatted outline of a crib across the room.

Downstairs, the chimes of a grandfather clock struck three times. It had been a little less than four hours since Eve had voluntarily left Cape Mariana, and her mind raced as she tried to reconstruct the events that led to her being here. Normally, she would have thought it strange for Phaedra Stamos to have done anything nice for Kate Hammond, but Phaedra had seemed so concerned about Jessica, that Eve never gave a second thought to getting into her car. But what did Phaedra have to do with the people who were holding her?

The door opened again and Eve was aware of two people standing next to her. The distinctive aroma of "Opium" perfume wafted into

Eve's nostrils, and she felt the urge to sneeze, but she was able to control herself and lie still. "Is she alive?"

"Of course she is. You can see her breathing." Eve recognized Phaedra's voice, and she knew she had heard the clipped tones of the other woman before, but she couldn't place them. "She's just more out of it than usual!" Phaedra giggled at her own joke. "I certainly can't figure out what Chickie sees in this loser."

"Really, Phaedra, can't you keep your mind on more important things? We've got a job to do here, and Eve Calvert is only a means to an end."

"Yeah, well, as soon as Chickie hears she's in trouble, he'll come galloping across the bridge on his white charger, but he'll look kind of dumb careening around Portland looking for his damsel in distress." Phaedra's sarcasm had a wistful edge to it.

"Don't spend your time worrying about Chickie George. After his mother's death last night, I'm sure he'll have other things on his mind than chasing around after Miss Pure and Simple here. Who knows, after your rescue of him at the party, he may see you in a whole new light with Eve out of the way." Eve almost gasped as she finally recognized the brittle voice of Claire Stamos.

****

Outside, in the bright afternoon sun, Alex was becoming very frustrated. He had arrived in Portland around twelve-thirty, hoping to catch sight of something unusual on Peal Street, and he had been initially rewarded by the arrival of his wife shortly after he had stationed himself behind a dumpster in an alley across from Number 24. A gray-haired woman he didn't know had opened the door for Claire, and Alex could spot several other people in the dim recesses of the front hall, but he was unable to identify anyone.

Of slight interest to Alex as he inspected the exterior of the house was the fact that heavy black shades had been drawn in one of the rooms on the third floor. Most of the other windows were lightly covered in filmy sheer curtains that softened but did not completely hide movement within.

After watching without result for another hour, Alex decided to head back to Cape Mariana where he was expected to coordinate the clean-up effort at the high school. He looked forward to seeing Kate again, but he also regretted leaving Peal Street without more satisfactory results from his surveillance. As he walked around the block to where he had parked his car, Alex glanced at the back of the red brick building and ducked quickly behind a fence as the rear door of Number 24 opened and his daughter came out and got into her car, which was parked in the alley behind the townhouses.

While he looked on, Phaedra turned on the engine and then got out of the car again, carrying a brown paper bag, which she tossed in one of the trashcans lining the fence behind which he was squatting. She then backed her car out of the alley and turned in the direction of the Casco Bay Bridge.

Alex moved around the weathered gray fence and reached into the trashcan, extracting the bag Phaedra had discarded. Without looking at the contents, he hurried to his well-concealed car and drove several blocks away before pulling over and opening the bag. Inside was a used syringe, and a small silk scarf, whose delicate paisley designed was marred by several large bloodstains.

At the school, hundreds of people had gathered for the culmination of the town's Clean-Up Day. Town trucks were heaped with plastic bags of trash and the local Lions Club had set up barbecues from which issued the delicious aromas of hamburgers, hot dogs, and onions. The custodian, Lenny, still wearing his mismatched gloves, directed people to various locations on the campus that still needed work, and he waved proudly to Alex, thoroughly enjoying his moment of power.

"Everything going all right, Len?" In spite of his concern with the events in Portland, Alex smiled at his employee's enthusiasm. "Quite a turnout." Alex scanned the crowd for a glimpse of Kate and Jessica, but was disappointed. "Have you by any chance seen Mrs. Hammond this afternoon?"

"No sir, but she's probably very upset. I don't know if I'm supposed to say anything, but I was here this morning to open the building for that Josh Temple fellow and two of the kids, including Eve Calvert. Some time before noon, Eve disappeared, and Mr. Temple called the police. Captain Brogan came and made everyone search the building, but there was no sign of the Calvert girl."

Lenny's narrative was interrupted by the arrival of several carloads of teenagers.

"Listen, Len. Can you hold the fort here for a little while? I've got an important errand to do."

"Sure, Mr. Stamos. No problem. Take your time." Alex sprinted toward his car, which covered the distance between the school and Silvertree Farm in only a few minutes. Several cars were parked around the circular driveway, including a police cruiser, and Alex grabbed the bag he had found and ran to the front door.

When Kate answered the insistent ringing of the bell, she was surprised to see Alex pacing back and forth across the wide stone steps, his face carved into lines of grim determination. "Have you found Eve?" Alex's voice was harsh while he searched Kate's face for some hint the girl was safe.

"No, and we're terrified for her. Brother Able has taken her and Jessie somewhere and he threatens to harm them both unless Willie and I give ourselves up to him for some kind of divine retribution. The police tried to trace the last call that came in from that horrible man, but he's too smart and hung up before they had time." Kate beckoned Alex into the library where Tikka and Jim Brogan were waiting.

"Are you absolutely certain it's Brother Able who is holding Eve?" Alex asked Jim. "Because I have a terrible feeling I know where she is."

All three people in the room stared at Alex, who opened the bag he was carrying and took out the bloodstained scarf. "Haven't I seen Eve wearing this?"

Kate gasped and examined the square of silk, running her fingers over the ugly splotches of red that marred the soft peach and green pattern. "This is mine. I've lent it to Eve on several occasions. In fact, I was going to give it to her. Where did you find it?"

"That's not as important as finding out if she had it on today. Did you see her this morning before she went off with Josh?" Alex didn't want to alarm Kate by showing her the syringe unless they could be sure that Eve was wearing the scarf.

"I wasn't up when Eve left, but Julia saw her." Kate hurried into the kitchen and came back immediately, followed by the old cook.

"Was Eve wearing this today?" Kate held up the scarf, but hid the bloodstains from sight.

"Yes, she was. I remember specifically because she was worried about borrowing it without your permission, and I told her I would take the responsibility." Julia's deeply lined face showed her concern.

"Then I guess you need to see this, too." Alex took the syringe from the bag and held it up so the sharp metal point caught the late afternoon sun. "I found it with the scarf."

Jim squinted at the object. "Hopefully there's enough material left in the barrel so we can analyze what kind of injection was given. O.K., Alex, give us the details."

Reluctantly, Alex recounted the strange behavior of his wife and daughter over the past few days, culminating in Phaedra's disposal of the scarf and syringe. He felt uneasy as he implicated Claire and Phaedra in Eve's disappearance, but he pushed those feelings aside when Kate described what had happened to her earlier in the afternoon. "What in the hell does Adam Loring have to do with this whole thing, and why would Claire have been with him? I feel as if a vital part of this picture is missing."

"I agree with you, Alex, but the most important thing is to protect Eve and Jessie." Jim described the vicious tone in Brother Able's voice as he placed his demand with the police. "There's no question he meant business about taking his revenge on them if Kate and Willie don't do what he says."

"Suppose both Eve and Jessie are still in that house on Peal Street. What's the next step? With a sicko like Brother Able involved, there's no telling what would happen if he were threatened." Alex voiced all of their concern, and Jim ran his hand over his forehead.

"As much as I hate to say it, folks, we're going to have to go very slowly on this thing. It would be foolish to put Brother Able into a panic. We can put the house under surveillance, but we've got to be careful, and we can also try to keep tabs on Claire and Phaedra. Alex, that's your job." Jim spoke calmly and carefully.

"Is there anything else we can do? My baby must be terrified. And she was just beginning to come out of the shell she built up after Max…" Kate felt sick to her stomach at the thought of Jessica's small body and soul at the mercy of a demented fiend like Brother Able.

"Just sit tight and keep an eye peeled. If he's this determined to get revenge, I wouldn't put anything past him. Scott Dean will be outside, and I suggest you take every precaution." Jim walked toward the back door. "I'll be in touch if anything develops."

Alex followed Jim out and drove to his own house after checking on the activities at the high school. Phaedra's car was in the driveway, but Claire's was missing. There was a note on the kitchen table announcing that she and Phaedra had gone to Boston overnight, since the next day was a holiday for Phaedra. They would call later in the afternoon.

Suddenly exhausted, Alex flung himself down on the sofa and squinted at his wife's bold, angular handwriting before he went to the phone and called the police station, informing Jim about his family's abrupt departure from Cape Mariana.

Jim was not surprised by the news. "I've got two of my best men watching the house on Peal Street, so we should begin to gather information about the people inside. Those black shades you mentioned are still drawn, but the lights are on in the rest of the rooms, and my men tell me they can see in fairly well. No sign of Eve or Jessica."

Alex hung up and got himself a beer, trying to sort out the issues which were boiling in his mind, when a grumble from his stomach reminded him that he hadn't eaten recently. After searching the empty refrigerator for something edible, he jumped into his car and drove the short distance to Rossoni's.

The restaurant was just beginning to fill up when Alex arrived, and Sophia, who was helping her parents for the evening, showed him to a table. "Any news about Eve, Mr. Stamos?" Sophia's dark brown eyes were troubled as she handed him a menu.

"Afraid not. The police are working on it, so we're all hoping she'll be all right until they find her. Hold good thoughts for her."

"I will." Sophia moved toward the front of the restaurant, where the door was opening to admit another party. When she caught a glimpse of the four people waiting to be seated, Sophia found herself smiling at Eric.

"Good evening Mr. and Mrs. Lundgren. Hi, Kelly. Eric. Right this way please." Sophia led the Lundgrens to a round table by the bar and passed out menus while reciting the specials that were being offered. Eric looked up at Sophia, whose face was flushed, and casually patted her rear end, surprising Sophia and causing her to jerk away from him.

"Behave yourself, Eric," Bill Lundgren laughed indulgently. "Miss Rossoni might be offended."

Sophia glared at Eric, finding it difficult to remember how nice he had been earlier in the day and signaled the busboy to pour water for the table. "Your waiter will be right with you," she declared icily and moved away from the table as fast as she could, haunted by the memory of Eric's comments about Alf. As she watched the family from across the room, Sophia realized that the idea of an innocent man suffering because of someone else's action and lies made her feel sick.

Then, Alex Stamos came into focus at his table in the corner, and Sophia knew what she had to do. When Alex finished his meal and paid the waiter, he was handed his change and a note, which he opened and scanned. Sophia saw him look around the room, pausing at the Lundgren's table and then continuing until he met Sophia's eyes. Alex put the note in his coat pocket and made his way between the crowded tables to the door.

"Message received," Alex nodded to Sophia as he passed her at the cash register.

****

In Portland, one of the police officers staked out on Peal Street straightened up. "It looks like someone turned on the light in that room on the third floor. What do you think?"

Officer Peters looked up at the house and saw a faint strip of light around the edges of the dark shades. "Yeah, you're right, although I'm not sure how that helps us."

Having feigned unconsciousness for nearly six hours, Eve finally decided she would open her eyes the next time someone came into the room, especially since she was concerned about the person lying absolutely quiet in the nearby crib. Her heart pounded at the sound of the creaking door hinges, but Eve forced herself to moan and slowly lift her eyelids in what she hoped was an accurate portrayal of someone emerging from a drugged state.

"She's coming to." The light in the room went on, and Eve closed her eyes again as a sharp twinge shot through her head. A woman, smelling faintly of alcohol, bent over Eve and took her pulse, while several people hovered in the hallway beyond Eve's line of vision. Eve mumbled that her wrists hurt, and after looking in back of her for permission, the woman untied Eve's hands, which tingled as the circulation returned.

"Where am I?" Eve looked around her groggily. "Who are you?"

The woman remained silent, but a tall figure stepped around her. "You're where you should have been all this time, Eve."

"Brother Able!" Eve stared up at the looming presence of the man she feared and hated most in the world. Long, oily hair escaped from beneath his large black hat, and his heavy, dark eyebrows bristled above eyes that were like pieces of faceted jet. "Why are you doing this to me?"

"Because it was your evil that caused the death of your father and the wounding of your mother. You and your brother need to be punished severely to atone for those sins, as will the people who tried to keep you from me." Brother Able's hoarse voice grated on Eve's raw nerves, making her shudder. "I swore before God I would deliver His justice, and you saw what happened to the young man who helped your brother escape from my disciples. His death is positive proof God believes my cause is just."

Eve was frightened by the fervent gleam in his eyes and in spite of the fact that her hands were free, Eve felt frozen in her position on the bed, gripped by her fear of the man who towered over her.

Brother Able motioned to the woman at his side to retie Eve's hands, but he didn't object when she fastened them together in front, rather than over her head. Brother Able stepped aside, and something was injected into Eve's hip before she could inquire about the person in the crib. Within minutes, Eve's head was spinning dizzily, sending her into a deep, woolly sleep, while the policemen watching from outside saw the box of light disappear from the third floor window.

THE SHAPE OF DARK—Chapter Twenty-Six

It was bleak and raining when Alex arrived at school on Monday morning, glad that about half the student body would be staying home, while the others kept individual appointments with their teachers. Next month, the process would be reversed, with the result that by the end of the year, all of the students would be able to confer with their teachers several times.

The lobby was virtually deserted, but Alex saw Kelly Lundgren standing by the big easel on which were listed student appointments for the day, and he hurried over to catch her before she went upstairs. "Kelly, I'd like to see you in my office this morning. Do you have any free time?"

Kelly looked surprised but not alarmed and studied her schedule. "It looks like I could come in at 9:00, right after I talk to my history teacher. What's this about, Mr. Stamos?"

"Oh, just a few details I'd like to clear up. No big deal. I'll see you later. Alex watched relief flood over Kelly's face as she turned back to her friends who had begun to move toward the stairs. Out of the corner of his eye, Alex saw Eric strutting into the dining hall with a couple of members of the soccer team.

"Eric!" Alex called across the echoing lobby. "Come here a second, will you?" Reluctantly, Eric left his companions and came over to where the principal was standing. "Are you scheduled for an appointment right now?" Eric muttered something about needing a cup of coffee before he faced his teachers.

"Thank God I'm done at ten o'clock so I can go home and sleep before practice."" Eric's eyes were bloodshot and Alex detected a faint odor of alcohol, but he decided to ignore Eric's condition for the moment.

"Will you stop and see me before you leave? There's something I need to check out with you." Alex's voice was casual and friendly, and Eric said that he would be in soon.

When Kelly appeared in the doorway of Alex's office an hour later, she was irritated from the scolding she had received from Chief Wallace about failing to put together her community service project. In spite of her claims that either she or her partner, Phaedra, had been absent for much of the school year, her teacher had informed her that a warning would be sent home.

"Do you think he's being fair, Mr. Stamos?" Kelly pouted as she sat down opposite Alex. "You know how upset Phaedra has been, and my life hasn't been exactly fun recently."

"That's just what I wanted to talk to you about, Kelly. I hope the horrible experience you had hasn't put so much stress on you that other aspects of your life will be affected." Alex made his tone sympathetic and warm, noting that Kelly immediately assumed an expression of innocent vulnerability.

"Well, I wish other people around here understood me as well as you do! All of my teachers want me to make up the work I missed like, yesterday. One of the worst is that Kate Hammond, who hates me." Kelly's petulance was growing by the minute and Alex spoke soothingly to her.

"I can't imagine that anyone would dislike you, Kelly. But it's interesting you should bring it up. Someone IS spreading vicious stories about you, and I want to get to the bottom of it." Alex casually opened his safe and took out the "Little Hitter" bat, turning it over and over in his hands.

Kelly sat up straight and looked at Alex suspiciously. "What kinds of things have you been hearing?" She couldn't take her eyes off of the bat, and Alex turned it so the deeply gouged end with its rusty stains was pointed toward the girl.

Alex took a deep breath. "Are you ready for this? Your brother evidently told one of his friends you were lying about Alf."

Kelly's face lost all of its color, and Alex was afraid for a moment she might faint. Slowly, however, she regained control of herself as anger overcame the shock of Alex's statement. "Eric wouldn't say anything like that because it isn't true. For once and for all, Alf Stanton raped me!"

Alex looked at the bat in his hand. "Did Alf use this to hurt you?"

"YES!" Kelly cringed at the sight of the weapon. "He stuck that inside me when he couldn't make his own thing work."

"Then why did you deny having ever seen this when I showed it to you a while ago?" Alex stared at Kelly, whose eyes darted around the room, as if looking for help.

339

"I don't know, I didn't like to think about it." Kelly stuck out her bottom lip and glared at Alex. "Why are you asking me all of these questions now?"

"Because there's more to the rumors that are going around, and I'm not sure who has started them."

Kelly buried her face in her hands. "I don't believe that anyone could say such awful things," she sobbed. "Wait until my parents hear about this!"

"Now Kelly, just calm down." Alex pulled open his desk drawer and handed her a box of tissues, surreptitiously switching on the small tape recorder he kept for dictating memos and reports. "Let me go out and get you a glass of water while you pull yourself together."

Alex patted Kelly's shoulder as he left the office and found Eric sitting by Marta Stone's empty desk. "Eric why don't you go in and see if you can talk to Kelly. She's very upset and would appreciate some brotherly support, I'm sure. I have to go over to the teachers' lounge for a minute, but I'll be right back, and we can all talk about the situation."

Eric looked puzzled, but he walked into the principal's office and shut the door. When Alex returned five minutes later, Kelly and Eric were sitting on two wooden chairs in stony silence, with Kelly sniffling and Eric glowering at her.

"Did Kelly tell you about these nasty stories that are circulating?" Once again, Alex kept his tone light and conversational as he casually opened his desk drawer, to see the tape still turning.

"Yes she did, and I think it's a bunch of fucking garbage! I'll bet you made up that rumor to take the heat off that pervert who raped my sister." Eric's face was contorted in anger, but he didn't look at Kelly. "She's positively identified Alf, and there's no other evidence to the contrary."

"You're probably right, Eric." Alex lifted the tape recorder out of his drawer and placed it on the desk in full view. "Gosh, look at this. I must have forgotten to turn this thing off after I finished dictating. It's been running all of this time."

Eric leapt out of his chair and tried to grab the tape machine, but Alex snatched it away and replaced it in his desk drawer, pressing "record". "Now, before we listen to whatever is on that tape, do either of you have anything to tell me."

"He made me do it!" Kelly screamed, pointing to her brother. "It was all his fault."

Eric raised his arm as if to slap Kelly, then lowered it as Alex sprang to his feet. "If you believe that, Mr. Stamos, you're crazy. This little tramp has been coming onto me for years, ever since we used to play doctor. Only now the instruments are a little different, aren't they, Sis?"

Alex watched the interchange between Kelly and Eric with growing distaste. He was certain the tape would reveal that there was equal blame, but the immediate problem was how to deal with the situation. "What are your parents going to have to say about this?"

Kelly looked panicky at Alex's question, but Eric stuck out his chin arrogantly. "At least one of them won't be very surprised, Mr. Stamos. We've always had complete freedom in our house, like about nudity and everything. My father thinks it's cool to be sexually active, and he's always asking me what I do with girls."

"Do you mean to tell me your parents knew you two were involved?" Alex couldn't believe what he was hearing.

"Not exactly." Eric studied his hands. "My father thinks he's a stud, but my mother is a real cold fish. When he gets drinking, my dad tells me all this stuff about his sexual conquests in Portland, and he really gets off on the idea of young girls. He's always grilling me about what Kelly is doing and sometimes he tells me how hot he thinks Kelly has become."

Kelly watched Alex's face twist in disgust and she began to cry again, causing Eric to glare at her. "Stop sniveling, for God's sake. You knew what you were doing."

Alex picked up the bat again and ran his fingers over the deep cut in the end. "Whose idea was this?"

"Mine." Eric's eyes were locked on the object and he refused to meet Alex's gaze. "It seemed to be about the right size and shape."

"Well, you were right about that." Alex reached for the telephone.

"Who are you calling?" Eric shot out of his chair and stood in front of the desk, breathing hard.

"Your parents and then the police. You two have done a terrible thing to an innocent man, but you've done worse harm to yourselves all these years, and we need to get some help for your whole family."

341

Alex waved Eric back into his seat as he dialed the number of the Lundgren Realty office and left a message for them to come to the high school as soon as the secretary could make contact.

An hour later, Mona and Bill Lundgren arrived in Alex's office, alarmed to see both of their children sitting pale and shaken in the waiting area. "What the hell is going on here?" Bill snapped at Alex. "I'm a busy man, you know."

Mona glanced back anxiously at Kelly and Eric as the door closed them from view. "Yes, Alex, do be kind enough to let us know why you dragged us away from an important closing. Our clients are fit to be tied." Mona slid onto a chair and crossed her silk-clad legs, swinging her foot.

"There's something you need to hear." Alex brought out the tape recorder he had left running during his conversation with Kelly and Eric. Rewinding the tape to the beginning, Alex explained he had received information that had led him to question Kelly about the events on the night she was supposedly attacked.

"What do you mean 'supposedly'?" Bill bristled as Alex pushed the "PLAY" button and Kelly's and Eric's furious whispers filled the room, exchanging accusations and vindictive threats. When the sound of a door opening was heard and Kelly and Eric were suddenly silent, Alex shut off the tape and faced the Lundgrens, both of whom looked frightened and guilty.

"You both knew about this, didn't you? Alex's steely gaze ripped across the two people facing him. "You let this all happen."

Bill Lundgren looked at his wife before he answered Alex. "There is no way you can prove any of this, Stamos. That tape would be thrown out of a courtroom, and you know it. Kelly and Eric must have been temporarily insane to say what they did, and I for one am not going to let you play mind games with them."

Alex was astonished by the cold, calculating expression on Bill Lundgren's face, and watched incredulously as Mona's initial fear changed to hostility and defiance. Before he could play the last part of the tape for them, the Lundgrens stormed out of the office to where Kelly and Eric sat waiting.

"Come on, you two. I'm not going to allow this man to accuse you of actions you're not capable of, just because he wants to spring his precious criminal. He's trying to nail two innocent children, and he's not going to get away with it!" Bill's voice was shrill as he grabbed Kelly's arm. Mona followed more slowly, trailed by Eric, leaving Alex to watch in stunned silence as the big front door slammed behind them.

****

"Those people are really sick!" Jim Brogan listened to the entire tape about a half-hour later, having responded immediately to Alex's urgent call. "But Lundgren is probably right about one thing. That tape, although a very effective way to coerce the kids would probably be considered entrapment of some kind. The Lundgrens could stonewall this thing, in spite of the fact that Kelly and Eric were so honest with you."

"What about Alf? He's been indicted and is sitting in that jail as innocent as you or I." Alex's concern was clear as he leaned across the desk toward Jim. "Isn't there something you can do?"

"Not that I can think of, unless Kelly and Eric will come in voluntarily and sign a statement." Jim shook his head in frustration. "I'll go back out there to that shack. Maybe there's something concrete we overlooked before we knew the whole story."

"Jesus, Jim. Your plate is really full. What about the situation with Brother Able? Any further developments there?"

Jim looked discouraged. "Nothing. We're waiting to hear from him, and Kate insists she will be exchanged for Eve and Jessica, but we need to come up with a plan to protect them all."

"What about Willie? Isn't Brother Able trying to get his hands on him, too?"

"Yes, but Dr. Ephron is afraid even the sight of Brother Able would drive Willie even farther away from reality, and he doesn't want to subject the boy to any more stress. We're investigating using someone to impersonate Willie if we can put together a scheme where we're in control." Jim's expression was deadly serious. "Our only hope is that Brother Able is so obsessed he'll make some mistakes. Right now, all we can do is wait and hope Eve and Jessica aren't being harmed."

In fact, Eve had been in and out of consciousness for the last twenty hours, having been injected at three-hour intervals. When she awoke briefly between shots, her hands were untied and she was given water to drink and was taken to the bathroom by the woman who continued to administer the sedative. The crib in the room was empty now, and occasionally Eve heard a child crying for her mother from a nearby room.

Claire and Phaedra Stamos did not reappear at Eve's bedside, once it was clear she had regained consciousness, but she heard their voices occasionally and was completely confused as to their relationship to Brother Able and the other people in the house. Although she tried to figure out the elements of the situation she was in, Eve found her mind so clouded with the drug that she couldn't concentrate and instead drifted off to sleep, in spite of her efforts to stay awake.

Outside the house on Peal Street, the watching police waited for some kind of activity. All they could observe, however, was the opening of the front door and the brief appearance of a gray-haired man who withdrew quickly after plucking the newspaper from the front steps.

"There's absolutely nothing going on here, Captain Brogan. The windows on the third floor are still shaded and we can see people moving inside, but it's impossible to make any positive identifications. Have you heard from Brother Able again?"

"Yes, he just called." Jim sounded weary and discouraged. "He insists both Kate and Willie go to Morning Cove tomorrow before dawn, and he said that unless he's sure they're alone, he will kill Eve and Jessica. He wants Kate and Willie to come at low tide and walk out to Angel Rock, where he'll make the swap."

When Jim Brogan called and told her of Brother Able's latest directive, Kate went to the dining room windows and looked out at Angel Rock, jutting up alone in the middle of Morning Cove. Right now, seagulls gathered in bunches, and Kate could see the wind-whipped breakers crashing over the algae-covered slopes leading up to the two points at the top that faintly resembled the wings of an angel. The cove itself was deserted and nearly treeless, affording very little opportunity for concealment.

Strangely, Kate felt very calm and unafraid of the prospect of facing Max's father in his quest for retribution. She was so worried about her daughter and Eve that she couldn't think of anything else, and she hoped that Jim would be successful in finding someone who looked enough like Willie to fool Brother Able. Jim had cautioned Kate not to tell anyone about the proposed exchange, since secrecy was the key to avoiding interference that might cause accidental tragedy, and he promised her he would be able to protect her and Willie, in spite of the apparent difficulties presented by Morning Cove.

Kate shook herself out of her reverie to go through the vast living room lighting the lamps which turned the space from shadowy dimness to warm, inviting clusters of sofas and chairs. On impulse, Kate lit the fire that had been laid in the living room and settled down in the corner of an oversized wing chair to watch the flames. So much had gone on in a very short time that Kate found herself seizing a quiet moment to try to sort out her feelings.

The insistent ringing of the front doorbell interrupted Kate's jumbled thoughts, and as she pulled open the heavy door, she recognized the broad outline of Alex's body, his shoulders and head covered with the misty rain that had fallen throughout the day. Half-expecting to see Josh Temple, Kate was surprised at her visitor, but she was pleased, and took him in by the fire, where he rubbed his chilled hands together before turning to Kate.

"I probably shouldn't be here, and I certainly shouldn't tell you about what happened to me this morning, but I've got a hell of a situation." Alex summarized his experiences with the Lundgrens, including the contents of the tape and the elder Lundgrens' subsequent rejection of the truth. "By this time, Mona and Bill have probably convinced their kids I brainwashed them, and they've come up with a story to cover themselves. The only thing they don't know is that Kelly and Eric implicated their father in this whole sordid mess."

Kate shuddered. "What a horrible thought."

"Well, it may come down to their word against mine, so it's nice to share the burden with someone else, in spite of the fact you've got more than enough to worry about." Alex frowned at the sadness in Kate's eyes. "Things are going to work out, you know." He took her hands in his big grasp and gently brushed her lips with his before grabbing his wet raincoat and disappearing into the stormy twilight.

Alex went directly from Silvertree Farm to the police station, where he was surprised to find Kyle Monkton sitting in Jim's office. "Come on in, Alex," Jim called, covering the telephone receiver. "I'll be right with you."

"Hey, Kyle, what's up?" Alex sank into a chair next to the diminutive teenager. "Making plans for college yet?" Alex and Kyle carried on a superficial conversation until Jim hung up the phone and stood up.

"Alex Stamos, meet Willie Calvert." Jim chuckled at the look of surprise on Alex's face. "Don't you see the resemblance?"

"Actually, I do," Alex admitted. "Kyle's bigger than Willie, but from a distance, they would look a lot alike."

"I've been wracking my brain to think of someone who would look young enough to fool Brother Able, but who would have sufficient maturity to handle the instructions and responsibilities of a situation like this. Then I remembered Kyle told me right after Timmy died he would do anything he could to help us find the man responsible."

"And Sandy is willing to go along with this?" Alex was astounded that Kyle's mother would permit him to be part of something that was so potentially dangerous.

"Well, she doesn't know about it yet, but she's on her way down here now." Kyle's eyes were determined behind his glasses. "This is a chance for me to do something to prove I'm not the nerd geek Eric Lundgren always tells me I am. I'll make sure my mom lets me do this."

Alex reached over and shook Kyle's hand. "Trust me, buddy. You're one hundred times the man Eric is. This is a terrific thing you're willing to do. Now, Jim, how can I help?"

An hour later, Alex parked his car in his driveway and was surprised to see the unmistakably battered Jeep that Eric Lundgren owned waiting in front of the house. Alex could see that there were two figures in the darkened vehicle, and he waited by his front door to see what they would do, tensing himself for what he was afraid would be a nasty confrontation. Slowly, the car doors opened, and Kelly and her mother made their way up the front walk to where Alex was standing.

"Can we talk to you for a minute, Mr. Stamos?" There was an ugly bruise on Kelly's cheek as well as swelling over one of her eyes. Mona Lundgren's lip was cut and it was obvious she had been crying.

"Sure, come on in." Alex flipped on the hall lights and led the two women into the house. "Are you both all right? Do you need ice or anything?"

Mona shook her head and took her daughter's hand, leading her to the couch. "Kelly got the worst of it, I'm afraid. Bill is home drinking himself silly, and Eric ran out of the house after he beat up Kelly, so we have no idea where he is now."

Alex was puzzled. "Why did this happen? I thought you and Bill were going to fight me on letting the truth out about what happened to Kelly."

"We were. But when we all got home, Kelly and I talked and began to realize how badly we all needed help. You don't know this, Alex, but we had to leave Connecticut and move here because our neighbors accused Bill of doing some pretty awful things with their teenage daughter. They threatened to go to the police if we didn't move away. In hindsight, we should have faced our problems then, but it didn't seem so bad when the children were younger. Now, the more I think about what's been going on, the sicker I feel." Mona held Kelly's hand as she spoke, wiping her tears at the same time.

Alex turned to Kelly. "Are you ready to make a statement about Alf's innocence? If you clear him of the charges, I'm sure something can be worked out to help you and your mom deal with the family issues."

Kelly nodded mutely and collapsed into her mother's arms. Mona patted her daughter's back, and was murmuring to her softly when she let out a scream at the sight of her husband's face framed by the living room window. Alex whirled and only had a moment to recognize Bill before there was the loud clatter of glass breaking and the deafening boom of a gunshot.

Throwing himself on the floor, Alex grabbed a heavy brass vase and hurled it at the window, hoping to keep Bill from taking aim again. Mona pushed Kelly to the side and half rose to say something to her husband when the gun fired again, and she sank to her knees, blood gushing from a gaping wound in her chest.

"MOM!" Kelly began to crawl toward Mona when Alex grabbed her arm and pulled her out of sight of the window where Bill stood, still pointing the gun into the room. There was a moment of silence, broken only by gurgling gasps from Mona, and then another shot reverberated from outside the house.

In the quiet that followed, Alex crawled over to the window and looked out. Bill Lundgren lay sprawled under the lamppost, the top of his head blown away into the darkness while streams of blood mixed with the driving rain. A rifle made a black slash across Bill's light shirt, which was turning red.

"Mr. Stamos! Quick! You've got to help my mother!" Kelly was bent over Mona, frantically pushing a sofa pillow against the pulsing wound. Mona was unconscious but still breathing as Alex raced to the telephone and called the Cape Mariana Rescue before he returned to Kelly's side and helped her apply pressure to her mother's chest.

It was not long before a police car roared up, its blue lights punctuating the rainy darkness. One of the two officers ran into the house carrying oxygen, while the other knelt beside Bill on the ground outside. Within less than ten minutes, the ambulance screamed up beside the several police cruisers that had gathered, and Ed George led five other volunteers into Alex's house, where Mona's life was slowly oozing away.

"Jesus!" Ed breathed as he began to take Mona's vital signs. "She's in tough shape. Call the hospital and tell them we're on our way." As the rescue members loaded Mona onto a stretcher, Doc Miller lumbered through the front door, having heard about the shooting on his police scanner.

"Let me have a look, Ed. There may be something we can do here." Doc quickly examined Mona and shook his head. "It'll be a miracle if she makes it, but I'll go with you and see if I can help." Ed nodded and Doc climbed into the back of the ambulance, which hurtled out of Alex's driveway and onto the long, black River Road.

Kelly huddled in a corner of the sofa, sobbing hysterically. She had glimpsed her father's body through the window, but had not seen the extent of the damage he had done when he put the gun in his mouth and fired. Before Alex came back into the living room, he saw two policemen covering Bill's corpse with a blanket, so he felt able to lead Kelly out to his car for the trip to the hospital. On the other side of the road, hidden from view, Eric watched the principal place his sister carefully into the front seat of his Jaguar. After the lights of Alex's car faded into the darkness, Eric walked across the street and got quietly into his Jeep, unnoticed by the policemen who were standing by Bill's body.

When the Jeep's loud motor turned over, the officers shouted at the driver, but he sped away, followed shortly by one of the cruisers. At the intersection of the River Road and the causeway through the marshes, Eric felt a sudden sense of peace flow through his body, and he jammed the accelerator to the floor, laughing wildly as the car floated from side to side on the narrow road. Had there been a moon, Eric might have seen the stand of pine trees that guarded the only sharp curve on the causeway, but in the dark rain, their tall shapes appeared only when his headlights raked across their shaggy foliage.

Later, the policeman following Eric said that his brake lights never illuminated as he plunged through the trees into the deep water of the marsh at high tide. The car disappeared almost immediately, and everything was black and still as the officer radioed for help.

At Maine Medical Center, Mona Lundgren was rushed into one of the two trauma units, where a team of doctors, nurses, and technicians fought to save her life, pumping blood into her shattered body. The rescue team began to restore order to the ambulance for its return to Cape Mariana, but both Big Ed and Doc Miller hovered near the trauma unit for news about the woman they had tried so hard to keep alive.

"This life and death thing is hard to figure, isn't it, Doc?" Ed said, shifting from one foot to another.

Doc looked at Ed sympathetically. "I'm real sorry about the mess with Sheila, because I know you had nothing to do with her death. If that damned pill bottle hadn't been found, I could have signed the death certificate, and there wouldn't have been any trouble. Now that they've done the autopsy and discovered barbiturates in her system, I've got no choice but to tell the truth, even though it will be the end of my medical career, such as it is."

"What the hell are you talking about?" Ed wheeled on Doc and grabbed his arm.

"Take it easy, Ed. I was on my way to see Jim Brogan when the police call came through about the Lundgrens. It was a tragic accident, and I certainly didn't intend to kill Sheila, but she must have been in weaker condition than I thought." Doc sat on one of the plastic chairs outside the trauma unit and motioned for Ed to sit on the other.

"When I went into Thornton Oaks on Saturday night, you had just left and Sheila was very agitated for some reason. I don't know what went on between you, if anything, but she was writhing around on the bed and had to be restrained. I couldn't stand watching her like that, so I asked the nurse to prepare a shot of Thorazine to calm her down. Even that didn't work, so I took some Seconal from my bag, crushed it up in a little water, and fed it to Sheila. She quieted down almost immediately, and after I turned on that tape that Chickie made for her, she seemed to go to sleep very peacefully."

"The trouble is, Doc, I can't even get mad at you, because I blame myself for upsetting Sheila." Ed's face was grief-stricken as he looked at the doctor. "I had this foolish idea I needed to be truthful about my feelings for Tikka Worthington, so I blurted the whole thing out, thinking Sheila wouldn't understand anything I said. I guess I was wrong."

"We were both mistaken, Ed. I've always had this idea that I knew what was best for my patients. I guess it's about time I realized the truth about myself as a doctor." Doc put his hands on his knees and pushed himself up slowly. "I better get back to the Cape as soon as I can and have that talk with Jim."

The curtains over the door in the trauma unit parted and a short, bearded doctor came out, his face grim and his surgical garments splattered with blood. When Ed and Doc looked up expectantly, the surgeon spoke quietly just as Kelly and Alex hurried around the corner from the entrance to the Emergency Room.

"Are you her daughter?" The doctor turned to Kelly, who nodded, her eyes round and frightened. "It'll be touch and go for a while. She's lost a lot of blood, and we're replacing it as fast as we can. All we can do is hope the next twenty-four hours go well." The doctor peered at the darkening bruises on Kelly's face. "I think you need some attention, too. Nurse!"

The men watched as Kelly was led away into another cubicle by a motherly, plump woman, who put her bulky arm around Kelly. "There's someone who is going to require a lot of help," Alex observed. "And I'm not sure what can be done for Eric, but we'll have to try."

One of the women on the Cape Mariana Rescue Unit came up and informed Ed that the ambulance was ready to return. "Would you like me to stay here with Kelly? We're neighbors of the Lundgrens, and although nobody knew them very well, I'd be happy to keep Kelly company while Mona is in danger."

"Thanks, Joan. I think we'd all appreciate that, because the rest of us have unfinished business at home." Ed smiled at his colleague, who shrugged out of her heavy black coat and sat in the seat Doc vacated.

As the ambulance made its way across the Casco Bay Bridge, the radio crackled with the news that Eric Lundgren's car had gone off the causeway in the marshes and police were at the scene. Ed and Doc Miller looked at each other in disbelief. "There was always something funny about that family," Doc observed, "and I never believed Kelly's story about the rape, especially since she had come to me several months before and asked for birth control pills."

"Doc, if there's one thing I've learned recently, it's that nothing is ever as it appears to be." Ed sat in the swaying ambulance and watched the doctor's troubled expression. "If there is a God, then He's the only one who knows why these crazy things happen. All we mere mortals can do is to be kind to each other and get through the night."

THE SHAPE OF DARK—Chapter Twenty-Seven

The sea was flat and glassy under ashy dawn skies when Kate rose from her bed, fully dressed as she had been all through the sleepless night. The rain had stopped, but a thick layer of fog hovered near the ground, obscuring Kate's view of Morning Cove as she hurried soundlessly down the hall to the stairs. At the same moment, Tikka opened her bedroom door and came toward Kate, her face lined with concern. "Downstairs," Kate whispered before the two women moved quietly through the dark rooms to the kitchen.

At exactly 5:30 a.m., Jim Brogan drove up with Kyle Monkton by his side. Kyle wore a faded plaid flannel shirt, blue jeans, and a tan windbreaker, clothing very similar to what Willie had on the day Timmy was killed. An oversized baseball cap made Kyle look small and vulnerable, and when Kate let him in the back door, she was stunned at how young he appeared to be.

Over his shoulder, Jim carried a heavy canvas bag, which he heaved onto the kitchen table and began to unload, handing Kate a dark-gray bulletproof vest to put on under her bulky sweater. Next, he wired both Kate and Kyle for sound, concealing the microphones carefully inside their jackets.

"In my last conversation with Brother Able, he seemed almost reasonable. He claimed that he didn't want to hurt anyone, but that he was on a mission from God to show sinners the light. He promised that in return for a chance to talk to you two and try to point out the error of your ways, he would give up Eve and Jessica, provided we assure him the opportunity to reach international waters without interference." Jim's skeptical expression indicated his true assessment of Brother Able's credibility. "I had to promise that there'd be no one else on the beach and the Coast Guard and police boats would stay in Portland Harbor."

"Were you able to hide people in the woods?" Kate's stomach was beginning to tighten with nervousness, and she looked at Jim for some reassurance.

"Yes, there are several sharpshooters who climbed up into the oak trees last night. Luckily, the leaves haven't fallen completely, so they have some cover. However, it's a long distance from the woods to Angel Rock, so we have to depend on some other things."

Kate looked out at the ocean, now almost at dead low tide. "What else is there? I only see those two lobster boats that are always moored in Morning Cove, and they'll probably be gone by the time we get there."

"Relax," Jim counseled. "Unless Brother Able has a trick up his sleeve we haven't anticipated, I think we have things covered. Are you two all set?"

Kate and Kyle looked at each other. Tikka got up from the kitchen table and put her arms around Kate. "Be brave out there. I'll pray all of the time." Tikka had tears in her eyes, but she tried to smile.

Unable to reply, Kate led Jim and Kyle to the terrace doors, and the three of them walked down the wide slate steps toward the pool. In the distance, Angel Rock lay almost completely exposed by the dead low tide, inviting seagulls to perch at various levels of its craggy incline. Kate took Kyle's hand and found it warm and almost as small as hers. "Are you scared?" Kate asked, impressed by the young boy's composure.

"I think the appropriate term is "shitless," but of course, I don't use words like that." Kyle squeezed Kate's hand. "We'll be all right. Remember that line from *Julius Caesar* we were talking about in class. The one about cowards dying many times before their deaths?"

"The valiant never taste of death but once./ Of all the wonders that I yet have heard,/ it seems to me most strange that men should fear;/ Seeing that death, a necessary end,/ Will come when it will come." Kate recited the familiar words quietly, as if to herself. "Do you really believe that, Kyle?"

Jim, who had been listening, put his arm around Kyle's thin shoulders. "I know he does, Kate, and so does his mother. The strange thing is that Timmy and I talked about that same thing just a couple of days before he was shot. My son had absolutely no fear of death, and his certainty gave me a lot of courage."

Kate looked into Jim's steady gray eyes and saw a reflection of the vitality and strength that had been so magnetic in Timmy. The black knot of terror that gripped Kate began to loosen, and she took a deep breath as they neared the edge of the beach. Looking back, Kate could see the long stretch of field they had just crossed, while ahead was a steep bluff on which were tall grasses and a dried curtain of Queen Anne's Lace.

"This is where you have to go on your own." Jim's deep voice startled Kate as he stopped and gestured toward Angel Rock. "I had to promise to stay at least a quarter of a mile away, but I can hear everything you're saying, and I'll be down there immediately if you call for me." Jim put his hands on Kate's shoulders and kissed her lightly on the cheek. "Not very professional of me, I'm afraid. But good luck." He shook Kyle's hand and watched intently as the two figures began to move away.

Kate held Kyle's hand as they picked their way across the uneven ground toward the sandy incline that led down onto the beach itself. Large rotting timbers had washed up here and there, along with the remains of storm-tossed lobster traps, a yellow and red Styrofoam buoy, and the tattered remains of a child's sock. The blue-black mussel shells scrunched beneath their feet, and before Kate and Kyle approached Angel Rock, they stopped and looked around cautiously.

"Nobody's here," Kyle whispered. "Maybe he's not going to go through with it."

Kate squinted into the misty fog, which cloaked the open ocean from sight. "I have a feeling he's right out there, waiting for us to become more exposed and isolated from the beach. Once the tide starts to come in, we'll be stuck on Angel Rock, and I'm sure he's counting on our caring enough about Eve and Jessie to do what he says."

Reluctantly, Kyle agreed, and they began their slow ascent of the slippery surface of Angel Rock, helping each other over the gooey seaweed at the base and the steeper parts at the top. Finally, Kate reached the small, flat area that was between the two "wings" and stood up on shaky legs. Kyle scrambled up next to her, but quickly lowered himself to his knees so he would look smaller next to Kate. A confused seagull squawked at the invaders of his territory, diving around their heads and then soaring off to plummet into the ocean after an unlucky fish.

The two lobster boats that were such a familiar sight in Morning Cove were deserted and silent, riding up and down rhythmically on the gentle swells that marked the incoming tide. On the back of each boat, stacks of lobster traps waited to be transported out to the deep water where the lobstermen found their best harvest in the winter months.

"What's that?" Kyle grabbed Kate's arm and pointed into the fog, which was gradually lifting. The shadowy form of a large sailboat was sliding quietly toward them, propelled by a small motor, since there was little wind. Two tall masts loomed above the mist, and Kate could see several black-clad figures moving on the deck. As the boat drew closer, the silence of the early morning was shattered by a scream, causing both Kate and Kyle to jump in surprise and clutch each other for support on the slippery rock.

"Oh my God, look at this." Horrified, Kate described the scene on the boat because she knew that Jim's view would be obscured by the bulk of Angel Rock. "They're dragging Eve out on deck and tying her to the forward mast. She looks doped because she can't hold her head up. There are four people around her, and I can't tell if they're men or women because they have caps on their heads. Wait—here comes a man with a big black hat."

By now, the tide had risen enough so that the base of Angel Rock was under water and the sailboat was able to come close enough so that the fog no longer shrouded it. "That must be Brother Able!" Kyle breathed to Kate as the large man on deck picked up a bullhorn and spoke in a rough, cruel tone.

"Listen carefully, you murderers who await God's justice. If you want this girl to escape a horrible death, you must follow my instructions exactly. She will be sacrificed immediately if you or anyone else fails to comply with my orders." Brother Able put down the bullhorn and picked up a red can of gasoline, which he carefully poured over the lower part of Eve's body, partially soaking the white robe that she was dressed in. Signaling to one of the other people standing nearby, Brother Able held up a box of kitchen matches.

Kate shuddered as she thought about what would happen if Brother Able were to light a flame near Eve. The boat was close enough to Angel Rock so that the fumes from the gasoline assaulted Kate's nostrils, and she watched helplessly as Eve coughed at the strong smell and swayed against her bonds.

While her attention was focused on Eve, Kate failed to recognize the blond woman who came out of the sailboat's cabin. Carefully, and almost tenderly, Susan Moore put a whimpering child down next to Eve and wrapped a rope around the little girl's waist, attaching her to Eve's legs. As her ability to move decreased, Jessica began to wail, sending chills of terror through Kate.

"What do you want us to do, Brother Able?" Kate called, cupping her hands around her mouth to amplify her voice. "You promised you would release both girls if Willie and I agreed to meet with you." As she spoke, Kate became aware of dark shadows slipping over the far sides of the two lobster boats, and she knew that it was only her lofty vantage point that allowed her to observe their stealthy movement. She knew that she had to engage Brother Able's attention on her and Kyle, so she whispered instructions to the boy at her side.

"You must make your way into my presence," Brother Able boomed, his hoarse voice reverberating in the misty air. "Start down slowly and make sure you stay on this side of the rock."

Suddenly, Kyle threw his arms around one of the wings of Angel Rock and began to sob loudly. "I can't get down, Mrs. Hammond. I'm scared." Shaking and whimpering, Kyle clutched his stony support, while Brother Able stared at him, trying to understand what he was saying.

"What's wrong with him?" Brother Able paced around on the deck, while Kate pretended to try to drag "Willie" away from his death grip on Angel Rock. "Make him come down right now!"

Kate grunted as she struggled with Kyle. "I can't. He won't let go. It's as if his hands are glued here." While Brother Able fumed beneath them, Kate managed to tug at Kyle without sending them both into the swirling waves.

Brother Able waved the box of matches in the air. "Tell him I'll set his sister on fire if he doesn't do what I say!" Kate cringed as she watched Brother Able swing dangerously close to Eve's highly flammable body, and she hissed at Kyle, "Now faint!"

Kyle released his grasp on the rock and fell down at Kate's feet, knocking her backward so that she had to grab hold of the other wing to keep from slipping down the side. "Nicely done," she muttered as she struggled to her feet. "He's passed out!" Kate yelled to Brother Able, whose black eyes narrowed as he stared up at the two people above him. "Do you want me to come down alone?"

"NO!" Brother Able exploded. "It's both of you, or I will make sure the fires of hell burn brightly. Now try to revive him, quickly."

Kate pretended to slap Kyle, and then she shook him vigorously, but he remained limp and unresponsive. Brother Able watched Kate's apparently violent treatment of the boy with increasing frustration, and he finally handed the matches he was holding to the person next to him. "Here, take these and light them if I tell you to!" Brother Able motioned to Susan Moore to launch the small dinghy that was attached to the side of the yacht, and they both climbed in with Susan rowing the short distance to the base of Angel Rock.

"I'll show that kid something he'll never forget!" Brother Able shouted as he leapt awkwardly from the bobbing boat to the slippery base of the rock. The ocean side of Angel Rock was very steep, causing Brother Able to make slow progress as he worked his way toward where Kate stood over Kyle's prone body.

In her peripheral vision, Kate was aware of movement behind her, but she didn't dare look around, afraid she might attract the attention of Susan, who was rowing around in small circles, while watching Brother Able climb laboriously, hauling himself up hand over hand. As she peered down at the black-hatted figure moving toward her, Kate was thankful for the height and pitch of Angel Rock, which gave her time to think.

On the yacht, Eve struggled to remain conscious. Tied to the mast, her body was encased in scratchy ropes, while her head spun from the drugs she had been given and the acrid fumes of the gasoline. Jessica, whom Eve had seen for the first time early this morning, huddled miserably at Eve's feet, her thumb stuck in her mouth, and her eyes glazed over in uncomprehending fear.

Nearby, Claire Stamos stood holding the box of matches, a maniacal gleam in her cold, bitter eyes. On Eve's other side, Phaedra leaned over the rail of the yacht and watched as Brother Able worked his way up the craggy face of the rock.

"It won't be long now, Eve. You and your brother and the Hammond bitch will pay for all the harm you have done to our family."

Eve was thoroughly confused by Claire's snarling words, having no idea what she or Willie could have done to hurt the Stamos family, but she didn't say anything, afraid Claire would become angrier and careless with the matches.

Above them, Brother Able had almost reached the top of Angel Rock, when Susan called out a warning. "Stay down! I think I see something moving on that lobster boat over there." As Brother Able clung to a crevice just below Kate's feet, all eyes swung toward the bow of the *Special K* where a white-robed figure appeared on the forward deck. As the apparition raised its arms, and the boat began to move slowly and silently toward Angel Rock, a glowing light increased in intensity around the ethereal figure, whose long, golden brown hair framed a strong, classically beautiful face.

Crouched over Kyle's still body, Kate stared at the lobster boat, which was sliding smoothly without any visible means of propulsion. The strange, shimmering aura around the figure in the bow continued to shine more brightly as the vessel approached Angel Rock, and then Kate heard the sound of her own voice screaming.

"OH MY GOD!"

Kyle's head shot up at Kate's words, and he gaped at the sight below him when he recognized the identity of the glowing entity. "It's Timmy!"

Brother Able gasped aloud and lost his grip for a minute, sliding down to a protruding piece of ledge that stopped his fall. "Who are you?" He rasped. "What do you want?"

The ghostly figure remained silent and shook his head at Brother Able, whose hands were shaking visibly as they clung to the wet rock. Kate was so transfixed by the spectacle below her that she wasn't aware of anyone else on the beach side of the rock, until a rubber-covered hand touched her ankle. Glancing back, she saw three muscular men in wetsuits plastered against the slope of the rock, and one gestured to her and Kyle to begin inching away from their narrow platform between the rocky wings.

"Why are you doing this to me?" Brother Able whimpered at the brightly glowing figure of Timmy Brogan. "All I want to do is bring these sinners to justice."

"Vengeance is mine, saith the Lord." The angel raised one arm and pointed it at Brother Able, who was now quivering with fear. "YOU are the sinner, and God will be avenged!" At his words, swirling clouds of smoke surrounded the angel, and when it cleared, the bow of the lobster boat was completely empty.

Looking up from the yacht, Claire watched Brother Able lose his grip on the slippery stone, his face contorting in pain. As she started forward in alarm, a strong grip paralyzed her right arm, and while she struggled with the rubber-suited man who held her immobile against the bulkhead, the box of matches went flying into the sea.

When Phaedra saw Brother Able slump against the rocks and begin to slide toward the waves, she called out to the oarsman in the dinghy to come back and get her. She barely had time to yell "SUSAN!" before she, too, was under the control of one of the four scuba divers who had climbed silently on board while all attention was focused on the heavenly apparition on the *Special K*.

Speechless, Kate watched the action on the deck of the yacht and was relieved to see one of the divers untie Eve, who collapsed into his arms and wept uncontrollably, while another of the rescuers scooped Jessica from the deck and held her tightly. Then, Kate saw the wheelhouse door of the *Special K* open and a blue-jeaned Timmy Brogan stepped onto the deck, his flowing robes discarded for a plaid wool shirt.

"Mrs. Hammond!" One of the men positioned behind her motioned for Kate and Kyle to get off of Angel Rock as quickly as possible, and as they scrambled down the slimy surface, the three men in wetsuits took their positions above Brother Able, who was clutching his chest and screaming obscenities at the divers on the yacht.

"SHOOT THE FUCKING BASTARDS!" Brother Able's shriek echoed across to the dinghy, where Susan pulled a revolver from inside her jacket. She aimed at the top of Angel Rock, only to scream in pain as a bait iron came flying off the *Special K* and knocked her out of the boat, her long, blond hair swirling around her head. Sputtering, Susan clung to the side of the dinghy while above, on Angel Rock, her father lost consciousness as a massive heart attack exploded in his chest.

"Help him!" Susan screamed to Timmy, who had just switched on his boat's powerful diesel engine. Timmy put the *Special K* in neutral and pointed to the top of Angel Rock where three men in black wetsuits were climbing down to Brother Able's precarious position on the steep face.

"One of those guys is a paramedic. He'll know what to do." Timmy threw a circular life preserver toward Susan who was shivering violently in the cold autumn ocean. "Hang on, and I'll pull you over."

With stiff fingers, Susan gripped the Styrofoam ring and allowed herself to be dragged to the *Special K*. Timmy lowered a ladder and hauled the severely chilled young woman to the deck of his boat, checking to see if she were armed.

"That was a horrible trick you played on my father," Susan spit out bitterly through chattering teeth. "And if he dies because of it, you'll burn in hell!" The stunning woman's eyes were filled with hatred even as she accepted the wool blanket Timmy draped around her shoulders. "Everybody thought you were dead!"

"That was the point," Timmy snapped back. "As long as Brother Able thought he had killed me, he felt justified in carrying on this holy war of retribution. Shocking him like that was the only way we had to beat him at his own game." He looked out of the *Special K's* cabin and saw that the men on the rock were administering CPR to Brother Able, whose face was a blue-white mask against the glistening gray stone. Susan watched the procedure anxiously, cringing as the paramedics struggled to keep Brother Able alive.

Almost immediately, several police cruisers and an ambulance arrived at the edge of Morning Cove, having been summoned as soon as Jim Brogan saw Kate and Kyle begin their descent from Angel Rock. At the same time, a Coast Guard cutter steamed into position next to the yacht, where Claire and Phaedra were securely tied up. Eve, her gasoline-soaked robe exchanged for an oversized yellow rainsuit was resting in the cabin of the yacht, still groggy from the drugs she had received, with Jessica snuggled securely in her arms.

Aboard the cutter, Alex Stamos looked on in a mixture of despair and disgust as his wife and daughter were brought over from the yacht, both dressed from head to toe in black coveralls and concealing caps. Claire's chin was lifted in a haughty expression, and she looked strangely triumphant when she saw her husband standing beside the commanding officer.

"Surprised, my darling?" Claire stumbled as she came aboard the cutter, but she angrily shook off the hand of the enlisted man who tried to help her. "I'll bet you had no idea of the exciting life your wife and daughter were leading!"

"Don't try to glamorize this sickness, Claire. It nauseates me to see what you've done to Phaedra by getting her mixed up in all of this. What in hell do you have to do with an insane man like Brother Able?" As Alex spoke, he saw Phaedra climbing onto the cutter, her face pale and devoid of expression. "And why is our daughter involved?"

"I'm afraid I have some bad news for you, my love," Claire snarled. "Phaedra's real father is over there." Claire pointed proudly toward Angel Rock where paramedics were struggling to lower Brother Able down the beachside slope toward the waiting ambulance. The oversized black hat had fallen onto the rocks, along with the straggly black wig that was attached. Even from a distance, Alex could recognize the patrician features and gray hair of Adam Loring.

Alex felt a stab of horror as he looked at the ashen face of the girl he had raised for seventeen years. "That can't be!" he stammered. "You swore to me Phaedra was my child and that we had to get married immediately."

"That's what you wanted to believe, but Adam was in my life at the same time. Don't flatter yourself by thinking you were ever man enough for me." Alex shivered at the hostility in Claire's eyes. "However, I was content to let your mother raise Phaedra for a while, especially while I was in law school."

Alex looked over at Phaedra, who stared vacantly out to sea. "Why didn't you marry Adam? Given your recent behavior, you must have preferred him to me."

"Adam already had a daughter, and he made it clear to me he didn't want any more children. I was afraid he would be so angry if he found out I was carrying his child, he would refuse to see me again. And I couldn't bear that." Claire had a fanatic gleam in her eyes, and Alex found it hard to understand how someone like Adam Loring could inspire such adoration.

"So you trapped me and went on seeing him? What exactly was the big attraction? Most of the time he acts like an abusive lunatic." Alex's words were filled with contempt, stinging Claire into an immediate defense.

"You may think that, but those of us who truly believe in the man understand everything he does is for our own good. When Willie Calvert failed to appreciate that and killed his father, Adam knew it was his responsibility to avenge the death, as well as that of his son at the hands of your Kate Hammond." Claire's voice had taken on a strange quality that reminded Alex of children reciting a nursery rhyme without really understanding the words. "Someone like you wouldn't understand a complicated personality like Adam's."

"Mr. Stamos, sir, we're heading back into Portland now. Do you want to come with us, or would you prefer to go ashore here?" The lieutenant in charge of the cutter gestured to the *Special K*, which had swung alongside to deliver Susan Moore into the hands of the authorities.

Alex looked over at Timmy, balancing himself easily on the swaying deck of his lobster boat, while several of the scuba divers climbed aboard. "I think I'll go ashore here and find out the rest of the story, because right now nothing is making much sense."

The lieutenant motioned for one of his crew to assist Alex aboard the *Special K*. "No problem. We'll take these ladies into town, where they have a lot of explaining to do. Apparently, the police have picked up the owner of the house on Peal Street, an Alice Wentworth."

As he passed by Phaedra on his way to the rail, Alex put his hand on her shoulder and spoke softly to the girl he had raised as his daughter. "Are you going to be all right?"

Phaedra looked up with dull eyes, not seeming to recognize Alex. "I've never really known who I was until I found out that Adam Loring was my father. I'm not sorry for the things that I did to help him." She turned away, her back stiff and angry, while Alex made his way down the cutter's ladder and onto the deck of the *Special K* while Timmy swung his boat over to the side of the yacht.

"Here are two more passengers for you!" A CoastGuardsman led Eve and Jessica over to the rail. "I'm sure this young lady's mother can't wait to get her on dry land!" Timmy reached up and lifted Jessica in his strong arms, while Alex carefully helped Eve onto the deck of the lobster boat.

Timmy revved up the motor and headed toward the dock at the far end of Morning Cove. "Strange group, aren't they, Mr. Stamos?

Who'd have thought that beautiful Susan Moore could be the daughter of someone so ugly and evil? And you must be blown away to learn about Phaedra!" Timmy's warm hazel eyes were sympathetic as he came alongside the dock and idled the motor.

"Well, nothing has surprised me more than last night when your father told me you were alive and were planning an appearance as the avenging angel! How in heaven's name, if you'll pardon the pun, did you come up with that idea?"

Timmy laughed. "Actually, it was my father's scheme. I was wounded trying to get Willie away, but when Brother Able threatened to kill anyone who interfered with his revenge plans, Dad decided I should pretend to have died so I could watch over Willie in Merton House. The gamble seems to have paid off! You didn't see Brother Able's face when he saw me all lit up like a Christmas tree. He nearly shit his pants!"

"How could they keep your real condition a secret for so long?" Alex frowned, trying to keep all of the pieces of the puzzle straight.

"I was taken out of Maine Med in a hearse and then hidden in Merton House under an assumed name. Only Dr. Ephron knew who I was, and Willie Calvert."

Alex stared at Timmy. "Then Willie wasn't hallucinating! He really did see you all of the time that we thought he had lost touch with reality."

"Right you are. We told Willie we were playing a game, and he went along with the whole thing. Everybody thought he had lost his mind." Timmy looked up as his father made his way along the creaking pier, followed by Kate and Kyle, whose grin split his face from ear to ear. "Dad, the reports of your son's death are greatly exaggerated!"

Kate ran to Timmy and grabbed Jessica from his brawny arms, hugging her fiercely for several minutes before turning to Timmy. "I've never seen anything like that performance. You've made a born-again Christian out of both me and Kyle. It was the cloud of smoke that really did it."

Timmy chuckled and looked at Kyle, who was standing alongside Jim Brogan. "Hey little buddy, you are some brave dude!" Timmy enveloped Kyle in an enthusiastic bear hug that left the smaller boy gasping but obviously pleased. "When Dad told me you had offered to take Willie's place, I assured him that I knew you had the right stuff all the time, even when you were upended in a garbage can!"

Kyle toed the ground, clearly embarrassed. "Thanks, Timmy. I'm just glad you're alive!"

"Me too, pal. Me too." Timmy stepped around Kyle and went over to his father who was standing beside the *Special K*. "What do you think, Dad? Mission accomplished?"

"Except for a few loose ends, everything went exactly as planned. Brother Able was even more superstitious than we'd thought, because no one expected him to have a heart attack at the sight of you. Your mother will be delighted to be able to tell her friends that her son was miraculously resurrected."

"Yeah," Timmy grinned. "Mom isn't exactly famous for being able to keep secrets."

A few feet away, Alex wrapped his arms around Kate and Jessica and held them close. "Don't ever do anything like that again, or so help me, I'll fire you. Can you believe that I had to hire a substitute teacher so you could try to get yourself killed?" Alex's tone was gruff, in spite of his efforts to keep his voice light.

"It's a promise. After today, the duller my life is, the better I'll like it." Kate snuggled into the warmth of Alex's embrace, while Jessica clung to her mother.

"EVE!" Chickie came running down the field followed by his father and Tikka. "Are you hurt? What did they do to you?" Chickie grabbed Eve's shoulders, and supported her as she sagged against him.

"They kept both Jessie and me fairly well drugged, but I think we're O.K. Jessie cried a lot, but Brother Able wasn't angry at her. I heard him tell Mrs. Stamos this was his only grandchild."

"Thank God for some vestige of humanity in the man." Kate allowed Tikka to take Jessica for a minute and collapsed on the bench at the end of the pier. "I guess we won't know the whole story until he decides to tell us, IF he makes it. At least we know Susan Moore is Marissa's lost Samantha, but I wonder how Marissa will feel when she finds out that her little girl was Brother Able's accomplice in all of this evil!'

"Well, at least all of the vandalism and graffiti at school is beginning to make a little sense. Susan must have used that hidden stairway to get to your room, and I'll bet that Phaedra helped her. All of this time, those two were half-sisters, each with a separate vendetta against Kate." Alex shook his head. "They must have had their plans in place from the time Kate moved to Maine. Eve and Willie just complicated the situation."

"And our feelings for each other surely tossed kerosene on the hatred they already felt for me. Claire must have been going crazy trying to keep us apart while helping Adam or Brother Able, or whatever you want to call him, got his pound of flesh." Kate gripped Alex's hand. "Adam said something when he was showing me Max's nude painting of Susan that led me to believe my husband had an affair with his own sister. Maybe there's more to this than we know, perhaps even the answer to Max's strange behavior before he died."

Jim Brogan followed his son along the pier to where the rest of the group was assembled. "I'm going to take Eve back to Merton House so she can tell Willie what happened. Kate, do you want Jessie checked out at the same time?"

Kate looked closely at her daughter, nearly asleep in Tikka's arms. "I think all she needs is a little rest. You go ahead, and if Dr. Ephron is willing, why don't you bring Willie back to Silvertree Farm? It's time he started living a normal life."

"I'll come with you, Dad." Timmy strode after his father, followed by Eve and Chickie. "I want to tell Willie that he really is safe." Timmy dropped back and took Eve's other arm. "If you'll let me, I'd like to spend some time with Willie."

Eve smiled up at Timmy's broad, handsome face. "That would mean a lot to him. You know he's sure you're an angel!"

Timmy chuckled. "That kid is a great judge of character."

Alex lifted Jessica into his arms and began to move toward the house with Kate, Tikka, and Big Ed. "Now that the fireworks are over, there's another issue we have to solve."

Kate peered up at Alex. "And what might that be?"

Alex shifted uneasily. "Well, there's this ex-rock star who has been lusting after you. I'd like to kill him."

"Relax," Kate replied calmly. "There's been quite enough violence for one day, and in spite of how nice Josh has been to all of us, he isn't quite my type." Kate moved closer to Alex so only he could hear her next words. "From where I stand, those young, good-looking types come and go. Give me the guy next door, and I'm happy."

As she looked up from Morning Cove toward the house, Kate could see that a cool sun had broken through the last wisps of fog and was glinting on the graceful windows along the terrace. Behind them, gentle waves lapped the beach, stirred up by a lobster boat motoring slowly toward open sea. Taking Alex's hand, Kate turned and inhaled the sharp salt breeze before heading up the field. She was home.

THE SHAPE OF DARK—Epilogue

Large flakes of snow swirled into the warm interior of Rossoni's as Kate and Alex came through the door, followed by Mildred. Jessica, riding on Alex's shoulders, clapped her mittened hands in delight as she saw the room full of people, most of whom she knew. In spite of a fierce northeast storm that had a freezing grip on the Maine coast, nearly all the people associated with the Rocky Shore State Championship soccer team had made their way to the restaurant.

"It's almost time." Maria Rossoni, looking healthier than she had for months, bustled up and ushered her newly arrived guests to a table near one of the large-screen televisions that had been set up. At the far end of the room was a long buffet table on which a lavish supper would be spread after the screening of the game film, and a wide banner over the bar proclaimed "Congratulations State Champs."

Kate looked around the room and was pleased to see Tikka sitting with Big Ed, Chickie, Eve, Willie and their grandmother. The sweet-faced woman had arrived shortly after Halloween to care for her daughter and grandchildren after Jim Brogan had conducted an exhaustive search to locate her. Ruth Calvert was still bedridden and partially paralyzed, but Eve and Willie had blossomed in the new warmth of their home and seemed to be able to put the hideous memories of their suffering behind them.

"It looks like the whole town is here," Alex muttered as the lights dimmed and the four televisions simultaneously displayed the action of the hard-fought game that had taken place early in November. After Eric's death, Chickie had moved back to his position in the front line, and the synchronicity with which he and Jean Pierro handled the ball was electrifying. Although their opponents struggled valiantly and managed to keep the game tied until the last period, a dazzling display by Chickie and Jean Pierro resulted in a final score of 5-3.

"That was incredible." Alex shook his head in disbelief. "I knew that Jean Pierro was good, but the way he supported the other members of the team and worked so smoothly with Chickie is a pleasure to behold."

"Did you know that both boys have received a tremendous amount of attention from the college scouts? Tikka told me that Chickie's being wooed by four different schools, including Bowdoin, which is where he really wants to go." Kate looked over at the table where Big Ed beamed in obvious delighted pride.

"Couldn't happen to a nicer kid. I imagine that the fact that Eve is also interested in Bowdoin might be a factor." Alex's praise was interrupted by the arrival of Timmy Brogan, who straddled a chair next to Jessica and solemnly shook her hand.

"Good evening, Miss Hammond. You're looking lovely tonight." Timmy's mock formality reduced Jessica to helpless giggles. "Watching that game reminded me of my youth." The wistful expression on Timmy's face made both Kate and Alex hoot with laughter.

Timmy's eyes became serious as he turned to Alex. "I want to thank you, Mr. Stamos for all those nice things at that memorial service you had for me. It's great for the ego. And Mom and Dad needed to hear some good things about my high school years after the way I kept them hopping." Timmy gestured toward Jim and Ellen Brogan, who were seated across the room.

"Well, the stuff that people had to say about you was pretty impressive. There's as much drama in truth as there is in fiction." Alex clapped Timmy on the shoulder as the young man stood up to join his parents at the buffet table.

"I wonder what Phaedra's doing tonight." Alex's face darkened at the thought of the troubled girl who had spent the last few months in a psychiatric hospital in Boston. Both Claire and Susan had gone to jail for their roles in the kidnapping of Eve and Jessie, but the District Attorney had agreed with Alex and his lawyer that Phaedra had not been responsible for her actions. In spite of his efforts on her behalf, on the few occasions Alex had visited Phaedra, she had been hostile and withdrawn, continuing to hold him and Kate responsible for her biological father's death.

Recognizing the reason for Alex's sudden silence, Kate took his hand in hers. "There was nothing you could have done differently, darling. Don't beat yourself up. Some day Phaedra will come around."

Jessica peered up at Alex, sensing his pain. "Don't be sad. You still have me." Kate swallowed hard as her daughter placed her tiny hand on Alex's arm. "Mama and I love you."

A burst of hearty laughter from the table behind them signaled the return of Timmy Brogan, his plate piled high with Arthur Rossoni's specialties. Distracted, Jessica watched the big fisherman devour his plate, while Alex looked hard at Kate. "If Jessie's right," Alex said in a low voice, "nothing else matters."

Kate turned to watch the wind-whipped snow frost the corners of the dark windows before she spoke again. "My daughter always tells the truth."

ABOUT THE AUTHOR

Sally Martin is a former high school English teacher who lives on the coast of Maine with her husband near their three grown children. *The Shape of Dark* is Mrs. Martin's first novel but she has written extensive non-fiction and has provided editorial services for other authors. Drawing on her many years in the classroom, Mrs. Martin is in the process of writing a second novel in the Cape Mariana series and plans to complete the trilogy in 2004.